75

FSG

THE RECENT EAST

THE RECENT EAST

THOMAS GRATTAN

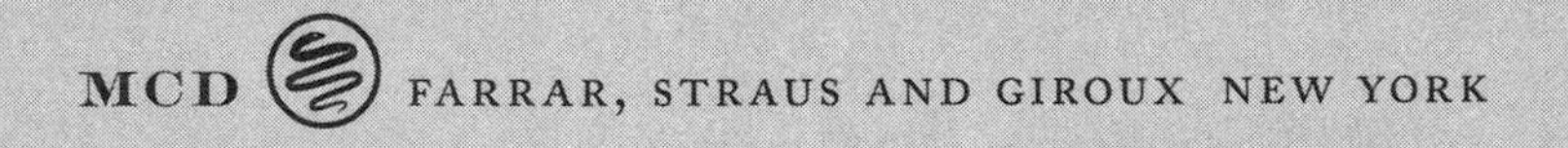
MCD FARRAR, STRAUS AND GIROUX NEW YORK

MCD
Farrar, Straus and Giroux
120 Broadway, New York 10271

Printed in the United States of America
First edition, 2021

Library of Congress Cataloging-in-Publication Data
Names: Grattan, Thomas, 1974– author.
Title: The recent east / Thomas Grattan.
Description: First edition. | New York : MCD / Farrar, Straus and Giroux, 2021.
Identifiers: LCCN 2020028190 | ISBN 9780374247935 (hardcover)
Classification: LCC PS3607.R3774 R43 2021 | DDC 813/.6—dc23
LC record available at https://lccn.loc.gov/2020028190

Designed by Abby Kagan

1 3 5 7 9 10 8 6 4 2

For my mother

It was as if a curtain had fallen, hiding everything I had ever known. It was almost like being born again. The colours were different, the smells different, the feeling things gave you right down inside yourself was different. Not just the difference between heat, cold; light, darkness; purple, grey. But a difference in the way I was frightened and the way I was happy.

—Jean Rhys, *Voyage in the Dark*

PART ONE

1968

1

Everyone talked about the West as if it were a secret. They leaned in to share stories of its grocery stores that carried fresh oranges, its cars with built-in radios. Covered their mouths to mention a Düsseldorf boulevard that catered to movie stars and dictators, whole Eastern month's salaries spent on face cream. There were entire, whispered conversations about its large houses and overstuffed stores, its borders crossed with a smile and a flick of one's passport. Some talked about it as if it were the most boring thing. Others like it was an uppity friend. But everyone talked about it, also pretended it never crossed their minds. Whenever Beate heard these stories, she felt frightened. Because its freedoms seemed vast, because each story said something different. The West a puzzle she couldn't begin to solve. Now Beate's mother stood in her doorway—coat on, pulled-back hair turning her face peevish and alert, like a nun's—and told her they were going there.

"West West?" Beate asked.

"Saying it once will do," Mutti answered.

Beate tried to decide if this was information or a joke, though her mother rarely joked. She finally settled on, "We never go anywhere."

A sigh lifted her mother's chest. *You're just an old woman*, Beate thought. At twelve Beate was already taller than her, close to the height of her father, who when she stood next to him often said, "I used to be tall, too," as if height were something—like keys—to lose track of.

Mutti fussed with her coat's buttons.

"I should pack something," Beate said.

"I've packed for you already," her mother answered. "We're leaving in five minutes. Wear something warm."

On their one trip to Berlin, Beate had glimpsed the wall guarded by soldiers and barbed wire. At home in Kritzhagen, radio stations sometimes came in from Lübeck, talking about the same weather but advertising brands she'd never heard of. She rifled through her closet. "Three minutes," Mutti called, then, "One." Beate's stomach ached. She put on her favorite shoes, though they were a size too small.

In the bus to the station, Beate sat wedged between her parents. She felt sick from its diesel smell and from the cobbles jostling her body. As their city smeared past, as her nausea rose and receded, Beate conjured the West—streets with identically shaped trees, wares shimmering in shops. Its alleys boys at school talked about, filled with blow jobs and people so drunk they had no pupils. Beate wore a hand-me-down jacket, a fake broach for its top button. She lifted the broach to her mouth; it tasted bitter. Neither of her parents noticed what she was doing.

Soldiers gathered in the train station where Beate and her parents sat. A pigeon strutted across the floor, pecking at crumbs and garbage. Beate's father looked even older that day, his thinning hair a dazzle of pomade, his stomach a spongy ornament. Her parents were professors, always dressed as if they were off to teach a class. That day Vati wore a tie and cardigan, Mutti a mud-colored dress that seemed both disappointing and right.

"I will sit with the luggage," Vati said.

"I'll take the girl to the toilet," Mutti answered.

"I don't need to use the toilet," Beate said.

She moved her hands through her hair, making sure her ears were covered. Beate had ears like the leaves of a houseplant, thin and large and loath to hide from the sun.

"The toilets on the train will be terrible," Mutti said, and slid a hand under Beate's arm.

Inside the bathroom, Mutti crouched to look under the stalls. Her tights bunched at her ankles.

"Mutti," Beate said.

"You need to learn to be quiet," her mother answered.

Water plinked into a sink's basin.

Taking Beate's arm again, her mother brought her into the last stall. Its toilet was old. A tank crowded the wall behind it. Beate stared at the pores on Mutti's neck, the lipstick clumped at her mouth's corners. Her mother lifted something from her pocket and handed it over, then pulled on the toilet's chain. It was a passport. The tank burst into action.

"We live in Cologne, thirty-four Wevelinghovenerstraße," she whispered. "You attend the Ursulinenschule. We were here visiting a cousin who is sick."

"We don't have any sick cousins," Beate answered.

"Whisper."

"We don't have any sick cousins," she whispered.

Mutti answered that she did, that his name was Peter Bergmann.

"Is he young or old?" Beate asked.

Her mother flushed again. "Of course he's old. We're visiting an old cousin. Your father's."

"Is it because Vati's old?"

"Your father isn't that old."

"But Mutti—"

"Child. When they ask, your father and I will talk. Unless they ask you in particular."

Beate had no memory of the passport's picture being taken, the name on it so fake-sounding they'd surely see through its disguise and arrest them. Arrest was everywhere in Kritzhagen, like traffic or rain. Mutti pushed her lips together and Beate felt a sadness for her that she couldn't explain. The two of them were rarely this close, though they'd been very close once. Beate had just learned about reproduction in science class and felt embarrassed for her former tenancy inside Mutti, like a kidney.

"We live in Cologne. Thirty-four Wevelinghovenerstraße," her mother repeated. "You attend the Ursulinenschule. We were visiting a sick cousin. Please repeat."

"We live in Cologne."

"Whisper."

"We live in Cologne, thirty-four Wevel—"

"Wevelinghovenerstraße."

"Wevelinghovenerstraße. I attend Ursulinenschule and I love art."

"Don't add," Mutti said. "You don't even love art."

The bathroom door opened and Mutti grabbed her daughter's cheeks. Beate wanted to laugh but did not. Though not a relic like her father, her mother was old, too. People regularly mistook her for a grandmother or spinster aunt, in part because of the stiff discomfort that spread across Mutti's face when Beate cried in public or made up dumb songs. Or when Beate adjusted her skirt and Mutti growled that she looked like she was fiddling with her private places.

"Open the door," her mother said, flushing for a third time.

The woman who'd come in reminded Beate of a painting she'd seen once, one in a room of long-faced portraits. It had been warm that day and the museum had opened its windows. Stray leaves crackled over the floor that Mutti had stopped to pick up over and over.

"She gets nervous with traveling," Mutti said to the woman. "Beate, wash your hands."

Beate turned the water on. It was freezing. She wanted the woman to say something about how nice it was for a grandmother and granddaughter to travel together, though she did not.

"I'm not nervous," Beate mumbled. "I didn't even have to go to the bathroom."

The women exchanged looks, as if they knew everything and she knew nothing, though the opposite felt true. Beate could tell the station's soldiers that she and her family lived in Kritzhagen, that these passports were fake, West not home but a mystery. There was no cousin or street she couldn't remember; she liked art despite what Mutti had decided was true. Her mother turned off the faucet and ushered Beate outside, where her father sagged next to the luggage.

"They called our train," he said.

"Wevelinghovenerstraße," Beate whispered, and picked up the suitcase her mother had packed for her.

Her father shuffled more than usual. Perhaps this—along with the new, reedy quality in his voice—was part of their scheme. It hit Beate then that this was dangerous, that they hadn't told her about the trip or the passports as a protection. Love for her parents rose with the surprise of a sneeze. Beate walked close to them. She talked loudly about going home, in case anyone was listening.

When soldiers examined and reexamined their passports, when at the border crossing outside Lübeck they were taken into a room and asked questions, all of them directed at her father, Beate itched. She wondered what the GDR would steal from her suitcase. Felt sure her mother had packed sweaters Beate no longer fit into and left behind the pants she'd had to finagle for five months to get. Beate's hands itched, also her arms. Vati touched her shoulder. This display felt as fake as the opera they'd once gone to, where everyone sang with faces of extreme constipation. They weren't going back home, Beate realized. Both soldiers had acne.

"Your cousin," the first soldier said, his chin a suggestion. "Quite sick, you say."

"I almost didn't recognize him," Vati answered.

"Close?"

"I'm sorry?"

"So close you all came to see him?"

"I wanted him to meet our girl," he said, squeezing Beate's shoulder. Beate smiled. She touched the back of her teeth with her tongue and worked to blink slowly.

"And she was happy to meet him?" the soldier asked.

"I believe she was," her father answered.

Beate's itching grew, as it did after coming in from the cold.

The room had no windows. In Kritzhagen, Beate's cousin Liesl had talked about her fear of small spaces so exuberantly that Beate assumed she was making it up. She understood it now. The walls leaned. Smells of coffee and ashtrays left little room for the rest of them.

"But seeing someone so close to death? Was that not hard for her?"

"Life is sometimes hard," her father answered.

Beate had never heard anyone question him, let alone someone the age of his students. Though her father didn't yell, though he was hunched and slow, he was always in charge. A cluster of stubble sat below his ear. He held letters filled with their fake last name, which had something to do with the sea. The itching spread to Beate's knees.

Beate wanted nothing more than to run outside and rub against something as a cat might.

"But it was important," her father went on. "To see him."

Beate moved her hands to the back of her knees, but Mutti stilled her. Her fingers were so close. Her mother's cruelty felt exceptional. She tried to grab on to anything outside of her body—the stink from nearby traffic, the soldier's blackened thumbnail—unsure if she wanted to go West at all. The officer closed their passports, which perhaps meant they'd been caught or were cleared to go. Beate placed one foot on top of the other, slid it back and forth and back again. She needed to get out of this room, which was warm and smelled of old sandwiches.

"I was happy," Beate blurted. "To meet my cousin. Though he was dying, I was happy to know him."

The soldier wrote down: *She was happy*. Beate thought to say more, but the room's size, the plague of itching, turned thinking into a steep mountain. A soldier's foot shifted, touching hers. Perhaps he'd mistaken it for a table leg; perhaps he and the other soldier communicated in a language of taps and pressures. Beate pressed back and watched the soldier write something down and couldn't remember if she'd brushed her teeth that morning. When he told them they could go, Beate felt as she imagined her friend Astrid Münster did when she'd come to sudden, happy conclusions about Jesus.

Beate and her parents stood in a hallway in Lübeck's train station, its walls lined with ads for items she'd never seen. People parted and came together around them, as if they were a rock in a river.

"Do we really live on that street?" Beate asked.

"That was just for getting out," her father said. "You are Beate now. Again."

"We're not going back," she said.

Her parents smiled, as if minutes before their true, useless selves hadn't shone through, her father gripping fake papers, Mutti saying nothing at all. Beate scratched her neck and collarbone. "Don't," her mother hissed. Beate wished she'd stayed quiet as they'd been questioned, that she hadn't announced a happiness she hadn't felt for a person that hadn't existed. She scratched the back of one leg with a foot, trying to imagine that buildings and the smells of winter would be different in the West, better.

⟡

The apartment they were staying in, in Cologne, was tiny. It belonged to the mother of one of Vati's many faceless friends, an old woman who'd recently, suddenly died. This should've frightened Beate, but the place was too small for ghosts.

Vati got the twin bed in its bedroom, Mutti a row of cushions on its floor. Beate was given the living room couch, its pillows patterned in buttons.

"How long is this ours?" Beate asked.

She'd only slept in houses before, with bedrooms on a different floor, and long, large rooms. Here was a room that wasn't a bedroom. Traffic rumbled down the street outside.

"Vati is teaching at the university this semester. Then we'll make other arrangements."

"So this apartment isn't ours?"

"We're making arrangements," Mutti repeated.

Vati was asleep already. Mutti soon followed suit. Beate

stared out the window, which showed little apart from the narrow street, windows warm behind curtains. People passed. A man in a green hat talked to his dog. The highlight came when a car tried to wedge into a tiny spot. "You'll never fit," Beate whispered, though it did, and in this little living room—closet of a kitchen on one side, the bed and bathroom on the other—she admired the driver's skill. The driver turned out to be a woman in a loose sweater. There was something beautiful in the way she lifted one foot off the ground as she double-checked the locks, the swish as her purse rocked against her hip. Beate wanted to go with her to her apartment, to be in a place where someone actually lived. To ask this woman about Cologne and her car and the comedy programs on television.

⟡

The next morning, Mutti out for groceries, her father at a meeting, Beate explored the apartment. A box full of jewelry sat on the dead woman's dresser. Beate clipped earrings on. She opened drawers in hopes to find a picture of this woman, Frau Eggers, though the only ones she discovered showed dour children on bicycles and in a pool. It felt strange to look through this woman's clothes, to smell her coats and use her dishes while not knowing if she'd been a toothless old person or a regal one, whether her hair had been white or dyed, short or long.

The knock startled Beate; she opened the door without thinking. The man outside it wore matching shirt and pants. Pencils rested behind each of his ears.

"I'm here for the furniture," he said.

"You're taking the furniture?" Beate asked.

"Measuring. Herr Flegmann was meant to call." The pencils bobbed as he spoke.

"I'm here by myself," she answered.

"It'll only take a minute," he said.

Letting the man in felt right, also not, Beate unsure if the fearful reluctance she'd learned in Kritzhagen was universal or specific, or if trust was an easy thing to wear in Cologne, some cotton sweater.

"My boss told me there were people staying here, that your last name is Haas. It'll only take a minute. Though I've said that already."

Beate let this man in. His measuring tape clanked open.

"We defected, you know," she said. "Yesterday, I lived in Kritzhagen."

The man wrote down the size of the dresser and bed, the end tables.

"We had fake passports," Beate went on. "I had some other name."

He measured the sofa that was Beate's bed. The tip of his pencil broke and he pulled out the other. The dead woman's earrings ached against Beate's lobes.

"Why are you measuring all of this?"

"We'll buy it. Then sell it."

"Did you know Frau Eggers?"

"This is just my job," he answered.

While he measured the icebox, she went into the bedroom. Her parents' suitcase was formidably neat. If the passports were there, she couldn't imagine the unearthing it would take to find them. Her parents had no patience for Beate looking through their things. In their house, when they'd caught her hiding in their closet, they removed her by the elbow and wouldn't talk to her for a day, apart from declarations about what was hers, theirs. Thinking of that closet, with its shoes in rows, its air cool even on Kritzhagen's hot days, Beate realized that, like someone living, then dead, that house had moved from place to memory.

Beate replaced the earrings with a different pair.

After a week at school in Cologne, which was both easy and hard, where girls reminded her of dogs from a book she'd had with pages of collies and shepherds alertly fluffy, Beate came home to the relief of an empty apartment. She wore a cheap skirt and blouse. Frau Eggers had a closet of gray and brown dresses. Bolts of the same fabric sat behind them, next to a sewing machine. Beate took the fabric and machine from the closet.

"Make my clothes with these," she said when Mutti returned, not with groceries, or anything at all.

"I've taught you to sew," her mother answered, and took the opportunity of Vati's absence to nap on the bed with her shoes on. After lying on the fabric to take crude measurements, Beate sewed herself a brown sack dress that smelled like Frau Eggers, whom Beate had started calling by her first name: Adela.

The next day, girls at school commented on it. "Are you Russian?" one asked. Another did a dance that had something to do with gypsies. They were in math. A girl with a pig nose leaned in to Beate and sniffed. Another asked if she'd ever met Brezhnev.

"The little Soviet," classmates started to say.

Though Beate knew it was an insult, the truth of it felt good. After girls called her this name, Beate stared at them with the unblinking frown of the soldiers who'd questioned them until those girls blushed into their laps. When a boy from a neighboring school followed her home one afternoon and said, "You like fucking, little Soviet," Beate stared the same way and answered, "I'm taller than you." A swallow stuttered down his throat, and the unreal feeling of Cologne slipped away. The next day, the girl with the pig nose walked past and didn't say anything. Beate stared. "What?" the girl asked. "Adela Eggers," Beate answered. She walked into literature class and sat at an empty table. Students saw her there, then squeezed into tables that were already full.

She kept wearing the dress, blotting its stains each night and spraying its armpits with Frau Eggers's lavender water. And after weeks of wearing it, as the credenza and television were taken to be sold, her father finally noticed. They sat at the kitchen table that would be gone in a week. A crooning from the apartment below may have been Elvis.

"That dress," he said. "You look like a Bolshevik."

"It's just a dress," Beate answered.

"I think she made it," Mutti said.

For the rest of dinner Vati called her "the girl," as if she were something that had come with the apartment and would also soon be sold.

The next morning, changing in the bathroom as was her custom, Beate put the dress on, took it off, and settled on a cheap blouse and skirt that Mutti had gotten her. At school she turned invisible again. She missed the confused fear of other girls when she stared or finished her math minutes before the rest of them and announced to the room: "I learned this already."

She took the dress out each morning and tried it on, put on her Moscow face, worked on her Leningrad walk. After she hadn't worn it outside of the bathroom for a week, her father spoke to her normally again. One night he asked: "Child. How *is* school?"

As she stared at her soft-boiled dinner, Beate realized that the perplexed looks from classmates mattered to her more than Vati's talking or not talking to her. She wanted students to whisper, *Soviet*, then say, when she stared, *It wasn't me!* As she told Vati about the algebra she was learning—not mentioning that she'd mastered it the year before—she decided to wear the dress again the next day.

When she snuck out of the apartment in the morning, she thought of girls in her class punished for wearing short skirts. Her sneaking a different subversion. Walking into school, she held down a smile at the looks that at any moment might come.

She walked up to the girl with the nostrils and said, "Notice anything?"

Alarmed, the girl answered, "Are you making fun of me?"

"My dress!" Beate answered.

The girl found a classroom and slid inside.

By week's end, the Soviet comments petered out. When Beate stared at a girl one day, that girl handed her a pencil, then said, "Pencil," slowly, and people smirked. When another student looked at Beate, then asked a friend, "What's wrong with her?" the friend answered, "That's just what she does."

At home, Vati went on about his terrible students. Being in a free country, according to him, meant it was their right not to know things. She tugged at the dress as she sat down to dinner, a muddy soup with fists of floating potato. She tried to get each swallow down before its taste registered. Vati complained about a student who'd confused Plato with a self-help book. Beate closed her eyes so as not to look at what she was eating. It had a fetid, toilet quality, and she was sure it would reverse course and pummel her tongue and nose. Beate lifted her spoon. As it veered toward her chin, soup slipped onto her lap. And her parents laughed. Beate dreamed of soup spilling on them instead. Imagined the soldiers arresting them rather than letting them cross to Germany's democratic side, her parents in jail, Beate living with her aunt and her cousin Liesl, who taunted Beate but also made her laugh, Liesl, who knew when she needed an extra blanket or to be told to stop talking. "It's nothing," Beate said, and her parents tried to hold in their laughter, which turned their faces grotesque. She could tell them she hated this place, but they'd answer with pity. Could throw her bowl against the wall, but that would turn her into a culprit. Also, the bowls were being sold. As Beate went to the bathroom to rinse the dress in the sink, she thought of the other dresses she'd make in the week and a half they had left in Adela Eggers's apartment. Mutti had found them a new place to live. Beate would have her own room, though it would take her an hour to get to school. As she scrubbed, more dresses became her singular remedy. Brown and gray and sweetly scented in Adela Eggers's perfume. Sacks so shapeless that her classmates would have to react to them.

People outside bellowed as they left a bar. Vati snored in the other room. Beate lay on the sofa and tried to remember her bedroom in Kritzhagen, alarmed as parts of it already started to fuzz over. She would forget this place, too. The dresses she made would stick with her longer than anything about Frau Eggers, whose picture Beate still hadn't seen, whose furniture was being plucked from the apartment each day, like ripened vegetables. Beate tried to memorize the ceiling she stared at each night as sleep hovered but refused to land.

The bedroom door opened. Mutti tiptoed to the living room window. Her hair, usually up, tumbled past her shoulders in a way that felt girlish and strange. Streetlamps deepened her wrinkles.

"Hi, Mutti," Beate said.

"You're awake," Mutti answered. Her shadow crowded the ceiling. Adela Eggers must have stared at this ceiling, too, must have fallen asleep on this sofa while reading or watching television. Maybe she'd died there.

"My bed is not a real bed," Beate said.

"I sleep on some cushions," Mutti answered. Perhaps she came out here most nights and stood next to Beate, moving hair from her sleeping daughter's face. Or she stared out the window, trying to make sense of this city's crowded streets and loud people.

"I was here once years before," Mutti said.

"This apartment?" Beate asked.

Her mother's consternation was, in its familiarity, relieving.

"I was close to your age and we were in Cologne, though I don't remember why. We spent some time near the river."

"Did you like it?" Beate asked. Mutti didn't answer.

In those moments of near-sleep Beate sometimes imagined Adela Eggers walking into the room, seeing Beate there. *Stop using my fabric*, imaginary Adela would say. *You're dead*, Beate would answer, waiting to see if the woman would turn angry or stare out the window as Mutti did, talking to Beate without looking at her.

"Why did we leave Kritzhagen?" Beate asked.

Outside, a car door closed. Beate hoped it was the woman she'd watched parking weeks before.

"You know your father," Mutti said.

"Vati made the decision?" Beate asked.

"Not only Vati."

"Did he say? Why?"

"It was more than your father," she repeated, though perhaps he'd declared one day that it was time—declarations his favorite form of talking—Mutti too afraid to challenge him.

"Sleep, child," her mother said.

"I want to know," Beate answered.

Her mother's shrug told her to sleep anyway.

That day, Mutti had worn the same brown dress she'd had on when they'd defected. So Eastern-looking Beate couldn't imagine their luck in getting to the other side. Unless Mutti hadn't wanted luck, her mother won over by stories of the West as a dangerous animal. Her annoyance at Beate in the train station not about the fake street her daughter forgot, but about decisions others made. Maybe Mutti had worn that dress in hopes of being found out. Perhaps she tried and failed to find a way to stay. Maybe Mutti had gone into Beate's room the day before they'd left and packed useless things for her daughter, certain they'd never make it across the border.

1990

2

Michael and Adela got home to find their father gone. His books swept off shelves. Closet empty apart from a button-down and a pair of fancy shoes, remnants of the teaching job from which he'd been fired. Dust lined the closet floor.

"*Ein Wunder*," Michael said. A miracle. Because after years of Dad's sulky pronouncements, after fights with their mother where he howled that he was leaving but never did, he finally took action. Michael grinned. He grabbed Dad's shirt, pointed to the shoes with his chin. Adela picked them up and followed.

"Where are we going?" she asked, annoyed, as she usually had a say on their wheres and whys.

"Can't it be a surprise?" Michael asked back.

They walked to the lot behind the Grand Union. The rumor for as long as they could remember was that it was going to be turned into a park. But no park appeared, only collages of bottle caps and cigarette butts, and a car left there so long squirrels now lived in its engine. Michael—thirteen, Adela underneath him by a year and change—moved past all this. Stopping at a patch of dirt, he tried to dig a hole.

"Isn't the ground a block of ice?" Adela asked.

"Don't they bury dead people in winter, too?" Michael answered.

A game of theirs was to speak only in questions. Their record was thirty-eight.

When hacking at the ground did nothing, Michael covered Dad's shirt and shoes with swathes of leaves, reminding Adela of the story they'd been obsessed with a year before about a dental hygienist who'd left her office late one night and disappeared. It had become a staple on the evening news. Search parties scouring forests. A befuddled sheriff who leaned too close to any microphone he talked into. When the woman's body was found, in a spot like the one they stood in now, she was covered in what Michael had called a bikini of leaves.

"Janet DeMarco," he said, invoking her name. For a minute, Adela worried he could read her mind.

They left the vacant lot and Michael turned quiet. Passing the convenience store where their mother sometimes worked, he blew into his fists. Two blocks more, and his ears brightened to bologna-pink. Michael stopped. He pulled on Adela's sleeve.

"He's not coming back?" he asked.

Dad's most muscular annoyance was reserved for Michael, whom he saw as too girlie and afraid, too confused by what should have been easy.

"Why didn't you wear gloves?" Adela said.

"Maybe Dad took those, too?" he answered.

When she asked Michael if he wanted to head home, he shook his head. He was short and scrawny, with large eyes that were often tearing up, or bugged out for comic effect. Wild hair that the various gels failed to tame.

"Come," Adela said.

They moved out of town, into the woods where they'd taught themselves to climb trees and once were certain they'd spotted a bear. Branches scraped their shoulders.

Michael lifted himself into a towering pine, moving up the tree with the ease of climbing a ladder. Adela kept track of him via the whites of his sneakers, his hands stung with sun. Then he was gone. Branches he'd stepped on shivered. No other sign of him existed. After saying Michael's name twice without an answer, Adela hoisted herself into the tree, kept going until she could see sky. She imagined him gone, not as Dad was—sleeping on his friend Raymond's pull-out—but like Janet DeMarco or their recently dead grandfather in the open casket Dad had forced them to linger in front of at the wake, telling them over and over, "Wish him a proper goodbye."

"Michael," Adela repeated.

She pushed a bough from her face, her stomach hot and knotted. From her perch Adela saw roofs, the frozen river.

"Janet DeMarco," she said.

"Again?" a voice whispered.

"Janet," she said again. "DeMarco."

"Polo," the voice answered.

"What?"

"DeMarco Polo," Michael said, and she heard him laugh, saw him folded into a crook of the tree like another of its branches. Sap stuck to Adela's gloves.

"You're an asshole." Her brother nodded, his laughter so loud it echoed.

As Michael moved to stand, his feet slipped and he began to fall, pinballing past branches he'd just climbed. His feet kicked, arms flailed. Boughs hissed as he flew past them. Adela stared at the ground, waiting for him to slam against it, her brother dead or paralyzed, either state her doing.

But then his hand caught a branch, stopping him as abruptly as he'd begun. His feet swung back and forth. The ground that might have ended him only a few feet away.

"Fuck a duck." Michael smiled, coughing and grinning and scratching his nose.

Her brother was afraid of the wrong things. A perceived slight left him uneasy for days, though he treated near-injury as a joke. As his laughter rose to a whinny, as he swung back and forth and clicked his heels, Adela worried he'd turn dumber now that Dad had left them. She climbed down the tree, darted out of the woods and onto the frozen Hudson. She slid across its ice until frigid wind erased any thought of Michael dead or stupid.

As Adela glided under a railroad bridge, Michael caught up with her. She tried to move faster, but he stayed in the periphery. He pointed a leg behind him, grabbed her scarf to steer her to a stop. After a comically bad spin, Michael lay supine on the ice. He folded his hands behind his head as if it were the most pleasant experience.

"Aren't you going to join me?" Michael asked.

Though he presented himself as a joke, there was worry he tried to cover. Maybe it hit him that he'd come close to real injury. Michael afraid that he hadn't been afraid. His brow tilted toward her.

"Isn't your ass freezing?" Adela asked.

Michael listed other frozen body parts. Adela lay down next to him.

Michael scooched until their shoulders touched. And Adela understood then that he knew he'd been stupid, that he was asking her to forgive him. She pushed her shoulder into his until he pushed back and leaning against each other turned into a game.

They got home to the German Lady making dinner. They called their mother that behind her back, or when she wasn't paying attention.

"Thought you were working tonight," Adela said.

"You can't just scare a person," the German Lady answered. She leaned in to the stove, which took up much of their tiny, grease-marred kitchen.

The German Lady was tall and meatless, a mirror to Adela except for the straightness, the blondness of her hair. Steam dampened her face. She looked younger than her thirty-four years.

Sitting down, their mother moved food around her plate in lieu of eating. She asked questions about school, only to interrupt with a story about Dad's cousin she'd seen at the supermarket who'd asked about their father as if he still lived with them. Michael asked how she'd answered. Their mother moved to the window, lit a cigarette, and said, "Is it Wednesday?"

They finished eating, and the German Lady sent them to bed. It was 7:15.

"You can't just scare a person," Michael whispered through the vent connecting his room to Adela's. It glowed on her wall like a tiny hearth.

"He's not coming back," Michael added, and Adela could tell he was happy.

She thought of Dad teaching her complicated words, or asleep in his friend's living room. Also of Michael, had he not found a branch to stop his fall. But as her brother kept talking, Adela remembered his excitement when he'd buried Dad's clothes and lay on the ice listing parts of him that were certainly frostbit. Adela tried to put that feeling on, as if it were a sweater to borrow.

In that same week—along with Dad's retreat and an ice storm that reduced Glens Falls to a skating rink—came the next miracle. A registered letter telling the German Lady that the house she and her parents had left decades before was hers again. She spent days scouring that letter. Read parts of it out loud. Sometimes she talked to it, saying, "Yes" or "No" or "I don't know what you're telling me."

Ice thickened until they couldn't see through their windows; branches shattered on the sidewalk. And in those handful of days when they ate everything in their pantry, when the German Lady reread the letter's most complicated sentences a dozen times, Adela and Michael learned a whole set of words they hadn't known in either English or German: Notary and collateral. Indefeasible.

Weeks passed. Ice lost out to a thin sunshine. The German Lady went to her jobs at the Laundromat and as a crossing guard with the letter in her pocket, folding and unfolding it so often its creases softened to fabric. She taped pictures of the house from when she was young onto their refrigerator. When Adela asked what she planned to do with it, the German Lady answered, "I'm still thinking."

Michael stopped in front of the photos, to point out some detail he noticed or invented.

"I think that's the shadow of our grandmother in that window," he said one night as they ate cereal for dinner.

"I think that's the shadow of your ass," Adela answered, and Michael laughed in the girlish way she'd expected their year and a half of junior high to have strangled. (Years before, Adela had bypassed an academic year to join Michael's grade.)

"A beautiful shadow, then," he said, and poured flakes into a bowl.

Other nights, through the vent, he'd whisper, "*Miracolo*" or "*Himalang*."

"How do you know that word in so many languages?" Adela asked.

"You want to hear it in Russian?" Michael asked back.

Though he treated the house as a joke, it did feel like a miracle. Just like Dad's departure and the end of the Berlin Wall they'd watched on television, some sections crowded with people, other parts keeling over like rotten trees. The stories that suddenly spilled from their mother about her seaside city were a miracle of a different sort. Because as she talked, she turned happy. And her stories reminded them that their mother had had an entire, illustrious life before the one they lived now in freezing, aluminum-sided upstate New York.

"What if I *did* want to hear it in Russian?" Adela said.

"What if I'm not a Communist?" Michael answered. "What if Dad's actually a Communist? Maybe that's why he's such an asshole."

As Adela imagined their father in Red Square, in line to wait on bread or other rations, what struck her was how little she actually knew him. He was a presence, a few emotions she either appreciated or avoided. But if someone had asked what his favorite color was, she'd have no idea. If they'd wanted to know what made her father happy, she'd have to guess. If someone wondered if he was as mean as the stories Michael told, she would have answered, *Sometimes. But he's other things, too.*

For as long as Adela could remember, she and Michael had been treated as a single entity. Their parents called them "the children." Said their names so quickly that they sounded like one word. When people asked if they were twins, Michael always answered, "Yes." On nights their parents fought, Michael slipped into her room and asked Adela to read to him. Soon he'd be asleep and she'd keep reading, stopping only to answer questions he mumbled in his sleep. On days Dad bristled at Michael, Adela reminded him of their father's asshole qualities. When boys at school called him out for the way he threw or walked or chewed, Adela defended him with her growing repertoire of filth. *Cunt bag* and *dick sweat. Breath that smells like your mother's asshole.*

Michael paid her back with invention. In summer, when they spent hours at the library for its order and air-conditioning, she'd recite passages from romance books for him to act out, Michael shifting from farmhand to mistress with an adjustment of posture or expression. She'd wander down an aisle to find book spines he'd rearranged, their titles turned into strange sentences. *Where the Wild Things Are Housekeeping. A Clockwork Orange Juice Lover's Best Recipes.* At home he snuck notes into the books and magazines Adela couldn't do without. He wrote single words, or question marks. Scribed fortunes from when they ordered Chinese. "Ordering Chinese" became a joke they shared. When their father was in a mood, they'd talk about its scope and size with code about a sweater. With each joke, each night one stayed up when the other couldn't sleep, each fight between their parents that they listened to, then treated as entertainment, they didn't turn into the twins people pegged them as, but rather a system. Her protection for his amusement. Her understanding of the world for his boundless imagination. His jokes about the miracle of their father's departure in moments Adela worried that she missed him.

A whisper woke Adela up. At first she assumed it was Michael. But as she heard it again, she shifted from asleep to awake and saw the German Lady standing at her door. Her mother slouched. She did that more now that Dad—and his beliefs about good posture—had left them. Adela turned on the light. Something in the color of the German Lady's face made Adela worry she was ill. When their mother knocked on Michael's door, Adela said,

"He sleeps like a dead person," went into his room, and flipped on his lights. Michael didn't have a shirt on. On his chest, a sudden garden of hair. Adela shoved his shoulder.

"Fuck a duck," Michael said.

His face was lined from sleep. With the lilt of his eyes and his chin's sharp conclusion, she saw the beginnings of handsomeness. Adela picked a shirt off the floor and threw it at him.

As the German Lady stared at them, Adela wondered if Dad had found someone new or if she'd been fired from one of her jobs. She imagined the three of them sharing a single can of soup, the one bath they'd run and take turns using, as if they were pioneers. Adela flicked through other tragedies. There were no grandparents left to die. Their only aunt lived in California, and they hardly knew her. Adela's former fear of nuclear war had vanished several years before, after America and Russia had chosen to play nice. She felt dumb as to what might be happening.

"What time is it?" Michael asked.

"Late," Adela said.

"That wasn't a question," he answered.

"I want to say," their mother said, then stopped.

Adela grew frightened for the second time in a week and worried that fear—like her brother's chest hair—was a sudden, certain part of her.

"We should go there," the German Lady said finally.

She pulled the letter from her pocket, its text framed in her handwritten notes.

"A house with so many rooms," Michael said. The German Lady cupped her elbows.

Michael marched into the kitchen, where pictures of the house hung. He pointed to a window, asked the German Lady what lived beyond its shimmer.

"That was an office, I think," she said.

When he pointed to another, Mutti answered, "That's one of the guest rooms."

"*One* of the guest rooms?" Michael balked. "So many rooms, yes, Dela?"

She nodded, thinking of the German the three of them spoke to complain about prices at the grocery store or when Dad wasn't home. As the worry in the German Lady's face began to fade, she kissed Michael's forehead and went for her daughter next, though that sort of affection didn't bring Adela comfort but felt as if someone had walked into the bathroom with her to see what she might do there. But as Adela let her, she wondered what it would be like to give and get hugs easily, to feel a hand on her shoulder and know she'd gotten something good.

Adela liked to think later that she was wooed by Michael's newfound excitement, so overblown that, the next time their neighbor Darren Cross called him a sissy faggot as he often did, Michael didn't run or look at the ground but smiled until Darren said, "What?" over and over. Without Dad to contend with, the three of them switched exclusively to German. Their mother filled their walls with lists of words they didn't know. Michael studied them as if in a museum. "*Ich empfange, du emfängst, er emfängt,*" he mumbled. "*Er log, wir logen,*" he repeated as they walked to school. Letters came each week about the house and the savings account that would be returned to her, about how to get their water turned on. The German Lady read those out loud, too. German turned so natural that one afternoon in history class—the only one they shared—Michael raised his hand and answered a question in a long German sentence. Even the sleepiest members of the class perked up with interested confusion.

"We're not reading *Mein Kampf*," Mr. Hart said.

Michael reddened. But the tears this might have led to in the past didn't come. Instead, the red that filled his cheeks and ears vanished, and Michael stared at Mr. Hart until their teacher turned uncomfortable and gave the class notes to write down.

There were days when the German Lady's certainty was the biggest thing in the room, and she'd talked about the house's extra rooms and the friends from elementary school she'd find phone numbers for. Other times, she mumbled about the move as if they'd been forced into it, and she enrolled them in school in the States for the following year. When Adela asked about the enrollment, Mutti answered, "Just in case."

"Just in case what?" Michael asked.

"You never know," Mutti said, Adela answering back, "That's just another way to say just in case."

Even then, Michael smiled at his sister with an unworried prescience, and Adela wondered if he knew something she didn't, if he finally decided to embrace his role as a knowing older brother.

But really, Adela wanted to believe that Germany would be different for them. She listened to stories Michael invented about the house's dozen rooms, the sea they'd swim in until their stomachs were corseted in muscle. And she chose to believe him. Perhaps that was the beginning of it, that she pretended she could know things as good or terrible without seeing or hearing or touching them.

⟡

Landing in Germany on a mid-June morning, eyes burning from the sleep they hadn't gotten, the three of them boarded a bus. German summer was foggy and cool. They passed squares of farmland; village structures clustered together like gossips. The bus crossed into what had recently been East. Buildings were skirted in graffiti. People there squinted at the bus with resigned annoyance, communism a disease they might never recover from.

When they got to the house, its bricks weren't bright, as they'd been in the photos, but the crumbling pink of a scab. Its long lawn slapped their knees. Adela walked into one room where mouse shit crowded its corners like blown snow. Discovered a pigeon flapping through another one and rushed to open a window. The bird flew out. Michael came in and said, "That bird's a lucky fuck," before he called the house a mansion and disappeared. There was none of the ornate wallpaper he'd whispered to her about, no friends from the German Lady's childhood waiting to greet them. There wasn't even electricity. The rotten smells of this half-emptied city, its cars small and old, left Adela feeling as if the plane had flown them into an earlier decade.

At the first signs of evening, the German Lady, without saying good night, slipped into a bedroom and fell asleep on its floor. Michael kept exploring, kept calling Adela's name. He found a second staircase and let out a pleased yelp, showed Adela which room he'd picked with a glee that left her feeling underwater.

Adela went to sleep using a towel for a blanket, a balled-up sweater as her pillow. Mice skittered close to her. She took out the flashlight she'd brought, the books on Germany she'd taken from the Glens Falls library. She opened one about Goebbels. It included pictures of him at his high school graduation. More of his children that he'd killed. As she stared at his eyes and batwing ears, wondering if she could see kernels of murder in his features, Adela imagined now was then, this country in the midst of the campaign that became its undoing. She and

Michael, with their father's darker features, might have been mistaken for Jews, taken from the German Lady no matter how hysterically she'd fought for them. Adela felt a sluicing in her gut and moved her flashlight toward a noise. A mouse froze in its beam. Its eyes were black, its tail a fleshy pink.

"Fuck this," Adela said.

She slipped past the room where the German Lady had been asleep for hours, toward the one Michael had chosen. Adela hoped he was awake, that the pitch-black strangeness of this place left him too terrified to move from where he lay on the floor. Hoped to take on the burden of having to comfort him.

But as she knocked and walked in, when she tiptoed through the room until she found his shoulder, it was clear he was asleep. She pushed her toes into his arm, harder when he didn't stir.

"You awake?" she asked, and shone her flashlight at him. Michael was shirtless again. He squinted, then smiled, not knowing a smile was the last thing she wanted from him. He slept with a towel over his middle. Adela worried he might be naked underneath. He seemed disgusting then, with his sprouting hair and guileless smile and the towel that, with the smallest shift, would have shown her everything.

"Flashlight," Michael said, as if it were another gift the house had given them.

"Remember when we sort of buried Dad's clothes?" he asked.

Michael propped himself on an elbow. His biceps flexed with the weight it held. Adela thought of Janet DeMarco in her killer's trunk, the rocks and roots pushing into her back as he strangled her.

"That was like five minutes ago," Adela said.

Michael's smile grew and Adela understood he could not help her. She went back to her room, pulled another book from her luggage, and began to read about Elie Wiesel's arrival in

Auschwitz. She read as mice moved through the walls. She read and imagined the ache of hunger and cold and fear Wiesel felt as he was pushed from one place to the next, all the while smelling burning bodies. She read and thought of Dad, who'd decided to move to his sister's in California, traveling without a change in language or currency. Burying Dad's things felt stupid then. Perhaps he'd just forgotten them and wondered where they were.

Adela stayed up reading until the sun rose. She heard water slide through their pipes, the chatty back-and-forth of birds. Listened to their stairs crack as someone walked down them. From her window, she saw Michael move out of their house and into the street. He stared left and right as if making some large decision. He chose left. Adela watched as he moved past the lot next door that must have once been a house, though now it was rubble, home to a dozen stray cats, also shrubs growing out of what used to be a wall.

3

In that first German week, Michael experienced more new things than he could keep track of, though vandalism and drinking until his center of gravity shifted topped the list. He leaned against a wall at a party held in a barracks that a year before had required security clearance. A place that had housed the Soviet troops that no longer existed, in a country that no longer existed, either. A dozen of his new friends moved through its halls, decorating every clean surface with spray paint. Michael was in the midst of a message about George Bush when Lena turned to ask if he was *schwul.*

He'd known Lena for four days. Already, she felt as essential as a kidney.

"*Schwul* is gay?" Michael asked.

Lena was his first cool friend. His friends back in the States loved novels about the prairie; they joined clubs about government and French. Lena nodded. Behind them, someone filled a wall with a message about the fascist who worked at the grocery store.

"Yes," Michael answered. Lena put a hand on his arm and squeezed.

He asked Lena how to say kidney in German, and they both started laughing, Michael so stoned his cheeks felt numb. Lena was striking, mean-looking. She wore large shirts that failed to hide the fact that she had an enormous chest. Michael spray-painted a kidney on the wall and her face returned to the flat expression Michael most associated with communism, along with the cheap cabinets he found in the empty houses he went into, the shapes of people's glasses.

In the next week, each of them would spray-paint kidneys on buildings for the other to find. When Michael passed one on his way to the store or the sea, breath thrummed against his ribs like the beating of wings.

Lena found a room that was once a bathroom—toilets pulled from it like rotten teeth, only holes left. She crouched over one of those holes and peed.

"Still *schwul*," Michael said, when she returned.

They wandered into a room bisected by candles. It carried the same musty coolness Michael used to associate with basements, though now it brought to mind the house the German Lady had inherited where she was hibernating at that very moment, where Adela read by flashlight.

Someone brought a boom box. With the antenna angled just so, a university station from Lübeck came through. A song started. People tried and failed to sing along. Michael found this funny. His sister often accused him of finding too many things funny, as if it were something to monitor, like binge-eating or a tropical storm.

"Now that you're *schwul*, we can mess with them," Lena said, eyeing a crew of young men standing against the opposite wall. Lena leaned on his shoulder, combed her fingers through his hair. Being touched felt amazing and Michael worried that he wasn't *schwul* after all but just needed to be touched a certain way. But then he thought of Darren Cross, their neighbor back in Glens Falls, the cutoff shorts he always wore loose across his hips. Michael stopped that train of thought when he started to get hard.

"Kidney," Lena whispered.

"Still *schwul*," Michael said.

His Glens Falls version would have thrown up had someone asked if he were gay, would have been too afraid of these barracks to have slipped inside. Michael tried to consider what had changed, grew bored with considering, and asked the room for a cigarette. One of the young men who'd been watching them was happy to oblige.

Michael walked home from the party with a teenager nicknamed Maxi Pad, who looked dubious when Michael told him what his English nickname meant. Maxi was tall, skeletal. He asked questions about places in New York Michael had never heard of. In the driveway, when Michael went to say goodbye, Maxi kissed him. His jaw unhinged. His tongue moved over and under Michael's. The shock of what was happening was quickly replaced with a scraped-out feeling in Michael's stomach. Maxi grabbed his hair. Michael pulled on Maxi's earlobes.

Then Maxi stepped back. He let out a single, hacking laugh. Michael wondered if he was being laughed at, realized he didn't care. He kissed Maxi again. Some part of Michael thought of his father, though he wasn't sure why. Probably because Dad would have found this kiss disgusting, or because he was too far away to know about Michael and the houses and the party he'd gone to. Or about the boy he'd just kissed, whose Adam's apple was identical to his nose.

Walking inside, Michael was blinded by a flashlight's beam. For a moment he was certain he was being robbed. But then he remembered Adela's newly hermetic existence and asked her, "What did you see?"

"I'm not playing," Adela answered.

"An actual question," he said, part of him hoping she'd seen that kiss, that she found him disgusting or unrecognizable.

With the flashlight scorching his eyes, Michael couldn't see her or the room they stood in. He wiggled his fingers through the beam.

"Aren't you going to ask what I'm doing?" he asked. When Adela didn't answer, he pushed his fingers into a beak and said: "Shadow puppets." Michael hoped she'd laugh or tell him he was an idiot. But the only answer came from a skittering mouse and an overgrown shrub that tapped one of their windows.

Adela turned the flashlight off and Michael became differently blind, thinking of the short story she'd once read to him in which a dead man felt everything as he lay in his coffin—water dripping on his forehead, the snail's-pace growth of his fingernails. But, as had happened to Michael a dozen times in this new city, when fear came to claim him, something stood in its way.

"It was an actual question," Michael said.

He stepped out of the living room and, with hands for eyes, walked upstairs.

He found his room with surprising ease. Lit the candles he'd melted onto his windowsill until the whole place glowed. Lying on his sleeping bag, Michael thought of Maxi's mouth, Maxi's hand on his chin. Also how American Adela would have kept the flashlight on his face as she explained to him exactly how he was being an asshole.

The looting had begun five days before the party, their mother asleep, Adela reading on the dust-grayed floor with no interest to see what lay outside. Michael was hungry, so he left in search of a store. Coming back from the grocery store, he found one house after another left behind. The first was a gallery of broken windows. Another had mail crowding its stoop. And the lawns, like their own, were long. Crickets clicked through them. Wind pushed and pulled and parted their blades. Though Adela had told him about this place before they'd moved here, Michael had doubted her when she'd insisted that, with the fall of the wall, Kritzhagen had gone from prom queen to old maid in a single season. But she'd been right. This shouldn't have surprised him.

The next house had furniture crowding its lawn. Michael moved across it, tiptoeing past a pile of rain-swollen cookbooks. Also a table, large enough for Michael and Adela and the German Lady. His jeans turned heavy with dew. Garbage flitted across the lawn like birds on water.

Michael moved toward the house, with curtains in its windows they could use. As he opened its door, his fear lifted to a symphony. He stepped inside.

Michael moved through the kitchen, where an unplugged refrigerator stood like a sentry. "Empty," he said as he opened drawers. "Empty," he repeated as he explored a closet. In one room he found a black-and-white magazine, communism's toothless equivalent of a tabloid, and read in it about a novelist who'd dedicated his work to a state that no longer existed.

In a bedroom he discovered a mirror. He removed his pants and underwear to gaze at the hedge of hair that had recently thickened above his dick. Michael turned hard. His dick of late had provided him with a new kind of helplessness, turning hard for small reasons or no reason at all. It also felt like some great invention, rescuing him from bouts of worry and boredom and shame. He masturbated fast and twice, barking out names of men he'd loved from a careful distance. Michael went into another empty house. Its owners had packed with less care. They left plates and pillows that he took, along with bags to transport his booty.

When he returned home, weighed down with dishes and bedding and groceries, Adela said nothing about the pillows he'd brought with him. And the German Lady, when she finally got up, drank from a stolen water glass as if it had always been there. It was only later that day, Adela walking past a lamp he'd gotten, that she stopped, the dopiness she'd taken on since they'd landed in Germany gone for a moment, her familiar version such a welcome sight that he started to tear up as he did at commercials and award shows and when he watched a dog strain to shit in front of its owner's audience. He dug his fingers into his pockets, pinched his balls until pain was his only horizon.

"Why'd you get a lamp?" Adela asked.

"To light things?" Michael answered.

She blinked with slow confusion. His sister rarely did things slowly, was confused even less. But as they'd landed in Germany they'd had to wait for minutes while she located her passport. As they got to the house and Michael told her about its bedrooms, she acted as if the word bedroom were a foreign, strong-smelling food. What's more, on their arrival in this place, Adela abdicated the responsibility that before she'd claimed so certainly it hadn't seemed like a choice. She'd spent their first morning sitting on the floor, staring at Michael as if he were a window to look through. It left him annoyed or sad or some combination of the two.

"We don't have electricity," Adela finally answered.

"We will someday," Michael said, and left.

On the flight over, while Mutti kept getting up to use the bathroom, Adela had read to Michael from her scrapbook of articles about their new city. One showed pictures of the Volksmarine shining on its shore. Another talked about the lengths its now-defunct government had gone to, to keep people from defecting. The one Michael remembered most explained that, with the falling of the wall, people who'd been kept in for decades began to leave. But it was the city's emptiness that Michael now loved, streets he could walk down without a single car parked on them, houses as breathless as graves; the clerks at this or that store who greeted him with an overeager hello, this city a shelter dog ready to roll over and follow you forever if you approached with a soft voice and gentle hand.

On his second day of looting, Michael found a flat, rolling dolly. He rested a pair of chairs on it, also mixing bowls. At another house, he added a poster for a movie called *Disco Story* as well as a desk for Adela, who in their time in Kritzhagen still hadn't left the house. He rolled the dolly down the street. A woman passed, walking her dog. When the dog sniffed the dolly's contents, the woman apologized.

"My things can handle a sniff," he said, and she answered with a Samaritan smile that Michael added to his love for this city along with its rinky-dink cars and empty houses and old people always weeding their gardens.

And the day after that, he slipped into a house and smelled spray paint's sharp bouquet. A young woman, who turned out to be Lena, defiled a wall.

"That word is crooked," Michael said.

She turned, with the slow resignation that she'd been caught.

"You a cop?" she asked.

"You an artist?" Michael answered.

Lena lit a cigarette. Paint darkened her fingers.

"What's that accent?" she asked.

"I'm from America," he said.

"I'm from Africa," she answered.

"I figured."

Amusement slipped across her face before she righted it. Michael repeated that the word was crooked. Lena told him to fix it. As he did, she talked about how she'd lived in Kritzhagen since birth, the biggest change in her life being when her family moved to an apartment three stories higher. Paint fumes burned Michael's throat.

They left the house and walked to the beach. Like everything in this city, it sat uninhabited. Its sand was pale, dunes walled by wind-sculpted trees. When Lena suggested a swim, she took off all her clothes. Mimicking her indifference, Michael undressed, too. They marched into the freezing water, negotiating jellyfish and food wrappers. They got out and toweled off with their T-shirts, went to a park where they smoked cigarettes and split a large can of beer.

"My sister has that disorder when you stay inside all the time," Michael said as they climbed onto side-by-side swings. "It's not claustrophobia."

"The opposite of claustrophobia," Lena answered.

As their swings met, she handed him her cigarette, which Michael somehow grabbed, though when he tried to hand it back, it flitted to the ground. They moved onto their hands and knees until they found it, lying in the grass and lighting it again. Smoking felt like something Michael had always done, as had exploring houses. When Lena invited him to a party, that, too, felt part of Michael's most trusted routine.

In a house on Osloer Straße, Michael found andirons. The one on Rosenhof, a rack to dry dishes. There was the trio of houses that held a bounty of trashy magazines, also trash bags and a garden hose. The Werftallee place had nothing but carpet so sun-kissed that he went there several mornings in a row for naps and masturbation. *Mine*, Michael thought as he touched the walls of the Sonnenweg house. "Mine," he said as he found a place that still had electricity.

In another, Michael discovered an unused notebook. He wrote *Kritzhagen* on its cover. On its first page he mapped their street, marking the houses he'd gone to, what he'd gotten there. Each day he added more, peppering its margins with comments about bakeries or his favorite scraps of graffiti: *Honecker is Your Boyfriend . . . This City is on Deep Discount*. He piled his dolly with furniture, learned how to pack it so that it was aerodynamic and balanced. He brought home two wingback chairs and angled them in front of their fireplace, turning the living room from some anonymous room to his own. After days of sleeping on the floor (in her one venture out of the house, the German Lady hadn't returned with beds or someone to turn on the electricity, but with sleeping bags), the chair's cushions felt like what he imagined a massage might be. Fingers digging into his back, the smells of different lotions. Michael climbed up to his room and closed the door.

As he got home one afternoon, Michael found the desk he'd gotten Adela had been moved instead into his room. He stepped to her doorway. As usual, Adela sat on the floor, reading.

"Good book?" Michael asked. His sister turned a page.

A mouse moved into the room with a police officer's impunity. Michael lobbed a pillow at it, watched it scamper away.

"Don't," Adela said.

It felt good to scare the mouse. Michael listened to their traffic through the walls at night, felt them crackle around his sleeping bag.

"Are you a lover of mice now?" Michael asked.

"Why'd you throw a pillow at it?"

"Isn't it a problem that they aren't afraid of us?"

"Afraid of us," Adela repeated.

"That was only three questions," Michael said, and stepped toward his sister.

He yanked the book from her hands. Slid the author's photo to his crotch, cooing out the man's name. Adela's eyes—which had always seemed foxlike—reverted to round. "Elie," Michael moaned. Adela put her hand out. "Elie," he hissed, shoving the book toward his zipper.

Prying the book away from him, Adela spun through a series of ugly faces to keep from crying. She began listing the family members Elie lost in the camps, along with the awful ways each of them died. Michael reddened at the details of a father's slow starving, more as she told him about the gas chamber that ended his mother and sister.

"I get it," Michael said. Adela kept going.

"Fuck a duck!" he added. She read passages out loud.

Michael spun out of her room. He stomped down the stairs, landing in their vestibule with such force that the mousetraps he'd set there snapped. Upstairs, Adela's voice kept droning.

Michael ran outside, grabbed his dolly, and rolled it to one of the city's more substantial hills. He lay across its wood, pushing against the ground until he picked up speed. Houses flew past. Wind cheered in his ears. Michael felt each bump in his hips, remembered Adela's face as she talked about a woman Wiesel had seen shot by Nazis for walking too slowly. The dolly veered to one side. Michael shifted his weight to right it. Wiesel had witnessed infants hurled into furnaces, more thrown in the air for target practice. Michael's face was inches from the pavement. "It's centimeters now," he mumbled just as a wheel caught in a gap left from a missing cobble. The dolly stopped, but Michael skidded across the pavement. Blood darkened his knees.

"Fucking ass Elie!" he shouted. The dolly stopped in a gutter.

As Michael lay on the pavement trying to catch his breath, the pain hit him. His left wrist burned. Flexing his fingers brought agony. In a nearby house, he found a bandanna to use as a bandage. As he used his good hand to bind the injured one, the ache rose to his elbow.

Michael winced, trying to move his hand from side to side.

At the grocery store, the clerk saw Michael and said what he always did: "How is my favorite customer?"

Michael unwrapped the bandanna, showing off his wrist's bracelet of bruises.

"That's something," the man said.

"It is," Michael answered, a croak in his voice he couldn't stave off. "And it needs some ice."

The man left, returned with a cup of ice. Michael spread it across the unwound bandanna, placed his wrist in the center of it, and tied it up again. He thought of the years when the German Lady took them to the ER with every fever, the taxis she paid for in quarters. Part of him wanted to find a hospital, its waiting rooms unoccupied, doctors doing crosswords as they dreamed of patients. But the ice, the bandanna, felt like enough. This city tugged self-sufficiency out of Michael, like a magician pulling an endless scarf from his mouth.

Later that night, after another party with Lena, Michael lay on their front lawn deciding whether or not to go inside. The flashlight glow of Adela's window meant she was reading still, probably about Elie Wiesel. Perhaps, after he'd left, she'd allowed herself to cry, his sister who held certain emotions in as if that were the same as not feeling them; who read about their new city rather than walking outside to see and feel and smell the place.

He finished a cigarette. Grass swayed past his chin. And as Michael contemplated standing, which in his stoned state was a marathon he hadn't trained for, he heard the shush of footsteps. Under a nearby streetlamp, the German Lady appeared. She moved through its light and into their driveway. Since their arrival in Germany her uniform had been the same sweater, a mascara of crud. Mutti looked back to the street.

"Not far," a man's voice said to her.

The German Lady waved, then walked down the path Michael had cut through their yard. His mother had been out with a man.

The drinks Michael had guzzled with Lena suddenly turned a corner, and he grew certain he'd throw up. As he lay there, stomach spinning, he thought of Adela's hand on his back when he'd been sick before. His nausea thickened. Michael had humped her book. Adela had answered with a terrified expression, as if her new, strange self were something he'd done to her.

Michael slid behind a shrub and quietly threw up. He pulled out a sheaf of grass, chewing on it in hopes of getting sick's vinegary burn from his throat. It only made it worse.

After standing outside their front door for close to a minute, the German Lady slipped inside. And as the house swallowed her, the sick in his stomach again gathering steam, Michael realized that this was the first time he'd seen his mother in days.

4

Adela stood in their vestibule. She wore ill-fitting jeans and a T-shirt from a race Dad had run. She smiled, and Michael veered between fear and excitement. Since he'd assaulted her book three days before, she hadn't talked to him.

"Where are you going?" she asked.

"Can't a guy buy groceries?" Michael answered.

"Can't his sister keep him company?"

On their walk to the store they passed the house where Michael had gotten their kitchen table, another where he'd found all their cutlery.

"This is it?" Adela asked, when Michael stopped outside the local grocery store.

"You were expecting the Shangri-la?" Michael said.

"You don't even know what that is," she answered.

As they walked into the store, whose insides carried the muggy confinement of an attic, passing a box fan that flung detritus across the floor, Adela seemed to return to him.

"What the fuck is *this* dung?" she said, picking up a dark brick of bread.

"What the fuck is *this* feces?" Michael held up a jar of pickled fish.

"This excrement?" Adela asked and translated ingredients. "Number one: goose giblets. Number four: blood."

They whispered in English. When Adela wanted his attention, she touched Michael's sleeve. He wanted to welcome her back, but felt afraid that, like watching some wild animal, her former self might notice him noticing and dart away.

On the walk back home, her quiet returned. He pointed out the department store where everything was practically free. Adela answered by telling him about Elie marching barefoot through a blizzard, this story more real to her than the church they passed, graffiti rising to its steeple.

At home, they found a large teenage boy lying on their lawn. He was white-blond and white-skinned, with a small, pink mouth. A bike lay on the grass beside him.

"Is he dead?" Michael asked.

"Not dead," the boy answered. His mitt of a hand gave a thumbs-up. "A lot of cats here," he said, eyeing the gaggle that lay in their sun-streaked garden.

"Mengele loved cats," Michael made up. He hoped Adela would correct him.

The boy stood, yanked a plum from a branch, and ate it in a few bites. "My mother asked me to come."

"Who's your mother?" Michael asked.

"Your aunt Liesl."

"We don't have an aunt. Not here, at any rate."

This large boy-man reminded Michael of the Stasi minions Adela had talked about, strong and quiet and open to murder.

"She's not, technically," the boy went on. "But related. Me, too. Udo Behm. Your cousin."

"We don't have any cousins."

He answered that he was there to get them bikes and be their tour guide.

"You like to run?" he asked Michael.

"Don't know," Michael answered.

Udo pointed to the seat of his bike. As if given explicit instruction, Adela hopped on. Udo stood on its pedals, told Michael to follow on foot, which he did.

They moved through ornate, crumbling neighborhoods, past small-windowed apartment buildings that lifted to ten stories. Udo pointed out the post office, the spot where a Western bank was rumored to soon open. An old man crossed in front of them, pushing trash out of his way with his cane. Seagulls floated in a nearby puddle.

The three of them crossed into a neighborhood of warehouses and gas stations. The ache of running gnawed at Michael's still-injured wrist. Each time he stopped to catch his breath, Udo and Adela waited for him.

Getting to a garage, Udo fished out a pair of bicycles. Michael asked what this place was; Udo mumbled something about confiscations. Adela's bike was blue, Michael's green. A rusting basket sat above its back tire.

Udo biked them to a place for *currywurst*. Showed them the store that always had bananas and lemons.

"Yellow," Michael said. No one answered him.

Udo pedaled them past the school for smart people, another for everyone else. A wad of gum flipped across his tongue, Udo's chewing reminding Michael of a cow from a picture book he'd once loved.

In the city's main square, people at an outdoor café held their napkins against the wind. On one side of the café sat a church. On the other, a row of buildings, intricately decorated but weather-beaten, like moldy confectionaries. Adela stopped. She squeezed her bike's handlebars.

"Why haven't you visited us until now?" she asked, her underused voice a rusted hinge.

Udo leaned close. His eyes were small. His neck as thick as a Doric column.

"Vacation," he answered, and explained that his mother had insisted that they go to the West for their trip, now that the West was an option. They'd gone camping in France.

"How was it?" Michael asked.

"Don't speak French," Udo answered.

Michael smiled. Because Udo seemed ridiculous. Because he got them bicycles and got Adela to leave their neighborhood.

When Udo offered to take them to the beach, Michael answered that he'd been already.

"I haven't," Adela said.

"Let's go, then, good cousin," Udo answered, and pedaled down a tiny street. Adela—who'd ignored the furniture Michael had gotten, who'd answered her brother's questions about why she sat on the floor with something about glasnost, or a blank stare—followed him.

After that, Udo was everywhere. Michael came home that afternoon to discover him with Adela in their yard, plums they'd harvested cradled in their T-shirts. Biking to meet Lena a few days later, he encountered them riding back from the beach. Adela's hair was kinky from the salt water. Her hands waved as she talked. Seeing Michael, Adela stopped talking, stopped pedaling, too. Udo wore only his bathing suit. His chest was giant, muscled and soft-looking at the same time. Curls of peeling sunburn sat on his shoulders.

"Good cousin," Udo said, "where are you going?"

"To meet someone," Michael answered.

Adela brushed sand off her legs, mumbling to Udo that they were late. Their bicycle spokes clicked as they rode away. When Michael turned around, he saw that Adela had resumed whatever story she was telling, hands in the air, as if in praise. Michael had never seen her bike without gripping the handlebars, without a crouching grimace that made her look elderly.

Out with Lena and company that night, Michael told them that he'd discovered a cousin named Udo Behm. After the initial shock of it ("But he's giant and you're not giant," one friend kept saying), people shared stories of the stray dog that had followed Udo everywhere until one day it was gone and people joked that poverty forced him to eat it. Another about Udo getting so wasted at a party that he passed out at a bus stop. Someone else said he was a math genius.

"Udo's mother is my mother's cousin," Michael added.

For the rest of the night, people argued about whether Udo was his second cousin or a first one, once removed.

Maxi Pad was everywhere, too, though he pretended not to know who Michael was. One time, Michael and Adela in their front yard, he biked past them.

"Hi," Michael called. Maxi kept going. He was so thin Michael could see his spine through his shirt.

"Who was that?" Adela asked.

With her dark, tight ponytail, she looked like the Russian figure skater they'd watched in the Olympics, the two of them joking that a gold medal meant she'd get an extra ration of potatoes.

Michael continued to wave. Maxi didn't wave back. He felt embarrassed, annoyed at his embarrassment, as if it were something Adela had done to him. His sister was reading a book about Mielke. Michael pretended not to know who that was.

"I guess he didn't see me," Michael answered.

Udo arrived, carrying two folding chairs. Adela placed them in the kitchen.

"I got us chairs already," Michael said, following them inside.

"You're speaking English," Adela answered.

Udo ate a plum. His rubber-pink lips encased the entire, unwitting piece of fruit. Michael was shocked by the disgust he felt, relieved, too, that he had limits, when on most days he eyed every man he saw, hoping to spy a dick's outline through his pants. He'd recently told Lena how he could find even the plainest men attractive. "Democracy," she'd answered, then gave him an acetaminophen coated with codeine as they snuck onto a bus without paying.

Udo whirred the plum pit out the open window.

"I got nicer chairs," Michael added.

"I prefer these," Adela said, and offered Michael a plum. He took it, though he wasn't a particular fan, any kindness from his sister a reminder of the kindness they used to pass back and forth. He bit into the plum and complimented her on it, which he understood was strange as soon as he did it. Adela picked up a newspaper and asked Udo what a word meant. Udo tried explaining it with other German words. Michael's wish then was to know its meaning, to say it in English as if it were nothing special. Adela seemed to get the gist of Udo's mumbling and moved on. A minute later, another unknown word emerged.

"It means fuck a duck," Michael interrupted.

Udo lifted up a different section of the paper, with photos of stateside places Michael had never been to—the Statue of Liberty silhouetted in fireworks, some small-town street lined with flags.

"Happy Independence Day," Udo said, in halting English.

Michael thought of his former country's calendar, no more relevant to him now than the books Adela buried herself in.

"Not here," Michael told Udo, and went outside. He wondered if he was being stupid, if with the desk Adela returned there was a warning he should heed. If her blank stares meant to show him what he didn't want to see: that his newfound bravery would come and go, that in time he'd need her and feel stupid for thinking he wouldn't. He and his sister as they'd been before rolled over him in a wave—the two of them hiding in a bedroom closet to see how long it would take their parents to notice, Adela running toward Michael in the cafeteria when boys called him a faggot or an idiot or some combination of the two. "Look who's here to save you," the boys would say. And though he knew he was meant to feel ashamed, listening to Adela cut these boys off at the knees with a few aptly obscene insults, Michael was always flooded with relief.

He stood in the driveway, listened through the walls as Adela laughed at something Udo said. He wanted to walk back inside and tell her he'd take the furniture back, that he wouldn't go out with Lena that night or the night after, either. But as he tried to make out their words through walls and windows, as a stray cat hopped onto his dolly, Michael realized that he didn't want things to return to how they'd been before, but some version where he could have both Adela and the empty houses, Adela and the parties, Adela and Maxi, whom Michael had seen at the grocery store that morning sneaking a bottle of soda under his sweatshirt.

Udo came outside, a rucksack on his shoulder.

"Independence Day," Michael said.

"Benjamin Franklin," Udo answered.

Though they'd known him for six days, Udo felt part of the fabric of this place, along with Lena and her reckless friends. And the version of the German Lady that walked when most people were sleeping.

"Hold on," Udo said.

He opened his rucksack, stepped to Michael with the same directness Maxi had when he'd kissed him. Udo unwound the bandanna on Michael's wrist so slowly, Michael wondered if this were a seduction. Udo pulled a bandage from his bag, wrapped it around Michael's wrist.

"Ice three times a day," Udo said.

"I didn't realize you noticed," Michael answered, pummeled with sadness, though he couldn't say why.

"Good cousin," he said, and Udo nodded.

Michael pushed the dolly out of the driveway. His wrist was on fire.

⟡

After getting home one night to their windows lit up, Adela deliriously excited about the electricity Udo had gotten turned on for them, Michael went up to his room. And as he smoked a cigarette out of his bedroom window, watching cats go after one another with bitchy hisses, he saw the German Lady finishing up one of her late-night walks. She had on a dress she used to wear for holidays and parent-teacher conferences. An old man walked next to her. Mutti talked in such long stretches that her whole body rose when she stopped to breathe. Michael mimicked that breathing. This time, seeing his mother out didn't leave him sad or confused. Because as she talked, he saw recovery. In the words that flipped from her mouth, he pictured a life when their house would look like a place where people lived, when she'd have friends and a job, perhaps even a lover. The man nodded goodbye, and the German Lady slipped inside. Michael moved downstairs.

He found her in the kitchen, leaning under the faucet to douse her neck and face. Water dripped across her collarbone. When she noticed Michael, she held a hand to her chest, then smiled. Her dress was patterned in small flowers.

"You look nice," Michael said.

"Just needed some air," his mother answered.

Michael flipped on a light.

"That should have been my job, getting it turned on," she said, and looked like she might cry. Michael turned the light off, flipped it on again. Went to another switch and flipped that up and down, too, until their kitchen turned into a crude disco.

"Asshole electricity," he said, the light bright, then gone, then bright again.

"Michael," she said. The room went dark. "Michael." It turned garishly bright. In flashes, he saw her sadness gone, his mother trying to hold down a smile. And in that smile Michael understood that he was a part of her getting better. That in the things he brought home he was taking care. He stopped playing with the lights. Mutti touched his cheek with her damp hand. Michael wanted to lean into it, to tell her that he knew about the old man she walked with, that he didn't care. To ask what she thought of the wingbacks he'd recently found.

"Don't stay up all night," Mutti said.

She took the back stairs noiselessly, her head, then dress, then narrow, sandaled heels slinking into shadow.

"What was that?"

Adela stood at the kitchen door. Michael wondered how long she'd been there. She held a book in front of her chest, squinting in a way that made her seem old. He wanted to grab that book, to hump it as he'd humped Elie Wiesel. Any sense of her knowing things he did not vanished, and he felt a relief that he hadn't taken any furniture back, that he'd gone out with Lena that night and made her laugh so hard that she spit out her beer. Adela frowned, held the book tighter, and Michael understood that she was afraid, as he sometimes was. As the German Lady was, too, when she snuck out of the house, so regularly that maybe she was hoping for one of her children to catch her.

"Electricity," Michael said, and walked upstairs.

On the three-week anniversary of Michael's arrival in Germany, Lena pierced his ears in the bathroom of a kebab place.

"*Schwul*," he said, as she hoisted hoops into his skin.

"Kidney," Lena answered.

When they finished and Michael tried to order a kebab, Lena told him they were late for a party at her boyfriend's.

"Since when do you have a boyfriend?" Michael asked. His lobes stung.

Lena went on about a bonfire she'd taken Michael to where her boyfriend, Bastian, had been. Talked about the joke Michael and Bastian had had about someone named Linda. Michael remembered none of it. He wondered about the drugs he'd tried, the drinking that had suddenly become normal, whole pieces of memory leaving him like ice cracking off a berg.

Getting to the party, Bastian hugged Michael hard. He had a frog mouth and was shorter than Lena. Michael didn't recognize him.

A cat from outside slipped in behind them and Michael asked if it was a stray or . . . and he paused for the right German word, only to settle on: intentional.

"An intentional cat." Bastian smiled.

An American song played. A German tried to rap along. Smoke hovered above the crowd like cartoon thinking.

Bastian went to get them drinks. Lena and Michael moved into the living room. She told Michael that Bastian's parents were in Berlin for the weekend, though it was a Tuesday. Sitting at the far side of the smoke-drenched room, sharing a joint with another thin boy, was Maxi Pad.

"That's the Maxi who kissed me," Michael whispered.

"*That* one?" Lena answered. "But he believes in God."

Michael remembered Maxi's hand on his waist, the hiss of his breathing.

"Maybe you're confused," Lena went on. "You didn't even remember Bastian."

"But I remember *that*," Michael said.

"Maybe," she answered.

Bastian returned with drinks. He and Lena moved into the dining room, Bastian smacking Lena's ass to the beat of the song.

Michael smoked one cigarette after the next, trying to capture Maxi's attention while also acting as if Maxi were the last thing on his mind. After avoiding eye contact for minutes, Maxi glanced at Michael. His glances soon graduated to stares.

Maxi went upstairs. Michael followed.

"Jesus, America," Maxi said when Michael walked into the bathroom behind him.

"You like to pretend that you don't remember me," Michael answered.

The bathroom was small, with the same cheap cabinets Michael found in the houses he'd gone into. The shower door was opaque from soap. The room smelled of farts and toothpaste.

Maxi gave Michael a look that may have been mean or pleased. But he didn't ask him to leave. Michael closed the door. He bit the edges of his tongue as he undid Maxi's belt. Maxi a shower after many days of camping. A bird to let the Pilgrims know land was near.

"Take these off," Maxi said, pointing to Michael's pants.

"Stand here," Maxi added.

Michael stood in the bathroom's corner, each hand on a different wall. Maxi found lotion in the medicine cabinet. Michael pretended he didn't know what it was for until Maxi put it on his dick, then Michael's ass, and began.

Every part of Michael—from his ass to the back of his throat—burned. Then the pain ebbed, was replaced with strange changes in pressure, a sensation so good that Michael let out a choke at its discovery. He lifted a hand to touch Maxi. Maxi placed it back against the wall. He finished with a burst of grunting, ball-slapping thrusts. Imagining the look on Maxi's face, Michael came, too.

Maxi rinsed off in the sink. A constellation of acne circled his belly button.

As Michael began cleaning up, too, he found blood, felt a scraping ache. Only then did he consider the condom they hadn't bothered with, Maxi's scabbed face some symptom he'd chosen not to see.

"I'm not even fourteen," Michael said.

Fear grazed Maxi's face for a moment. Then he answered that he was sixteen, that they weren't all that different. Maxi's mention of them as similar was a gift for Michael to keep as he biked home, as he fell asleep on his floor.

But when he woke up the next morning, a complete, churning terror swept over him, Maxi one in a series of bad decisions Adela had tried to warn him against. Michael rushed to the toilet. Adela was in there. He knocked once, again. When she finally emerged, book under her arm, Michael felt too much relief to be mad at her. He ran inside and slammed the door.

5

When they started coming home alone together in third grade, Adela and Michael often found their apartment a mess. Dishes dirtying the counter. Dad's clothes everywhere. It left Adela feeling stuck. Michael seemed to sense this and made tidying up a game. "Look what the boys did," he'd say, and these mythical boys became their enemy, sneaking in to undo their apartment's invented order. Adela would turn the radio up as they scrubbed and complained, her brother in rubber gloves, dancing the vacuum from room to room.

In this house, though, nothing game-like between them remained. Adela felt more stuck than she'd ever been. Michael saw this, smiled, and continued on his way. "Look what the boys did," she said once after he and his dolly rolled down the driveway, Adela too unsettled to read or remember if she'd eaten that day. The certainty that had been her sixth sense had vanished. The more she tried to bury her new uncertainty, the more it leaked out. Sometimes it came with the same dread that walloped her as the plane had rattled down the runway. More often, it felt like being underwater. Everything but what was closest to her wobbled. Words she'd have been able to hear or say above the surface turned to swallowed vowels. And when her brother, then mother, snuck out at night, it felt as if they were swimming into something deep and dark she didn't have the breath to follow them into.

Two blocks from their house sat a phone booth, marred in graffiti. Particularly about Sigrid, an expert in all things mouth-related. Adela dropped in coins, listened to the phone's clicks and pauses. It rang. Her heart hurried. The booth was warm, the receiver cool against her ear.

"You've reached Kate and Paul," the machine's message began, aunt and father speaking in unison. "We're either out hiking in Stanislaus," Kate said, "or taste-testing margaritas," her father added. "But when we get back from wherever we are," Kate chimed in, "we'll call you back." As had happened the last few times she'd called, Adela breathed in to leave a message, but stopped. She had no number to give. And in the recording her father sounded like a moron.

She hung up, sat in the glowing booth, and counted her change. More terrible things about Sigrid were written on the floor.

Adela had started coming to this booth the first night she realized Michael and the German Lady had left her alone. Dad had written twice already, Adela the only one who'd bothered with his letters. When his second letter signaled his arrival at his sister's, when he sent along a picture of the house, small but neatly inhabited, and a phone number to boot, Adela started scouring their house for change so she could call. Each night she sat in the booth, waiting for her brother to pass. She wanted his surprise that she was out at night, too, though part of her worried that he'd look at her in the booth as if she were funny and sad and keep going.

Adela called again twenty minutes later, the machine interrupted by her aunt's breathless hello.

"It's Adela. Your brother's daughter."

"I know who you are," Kate answered.

"Hello," Adela said again, though she wasn't sure why.

Sigrid likes it on all fours. Or with her legs wrapped around Joachim's waist.

Her aunt talked about a concert she and Dad had gone to, seafood they'd eaten. As she moved to stories of his landscaping job and other ways he was thriving, Adela's feeling of missing him gathered steam.

"We just got electricity," Adela said.

"Progress," Kate answered.

The underwater feeling returned. An operator interrupted to tell her to add more change.

"Dad's working?" Adela asked.

"Saturday," Aunt Kate answered. Adela hadn't known what day it was. "But he's out. He's like the mayor."

Sigrid is ready for you.

Adela wanted to call Sigrid and warn her. Wanted her to become a friend who'd rely on Adela for her truthfulness and clear thinking.

"I heard you're living in a mansion," Kate said.

"It's awful here," Adela answered.

Aunt Kate lived in a house with a garden of succulents, the sky above it the blue of a warmer place. As Adela tried to picture that house, and Dad inside of it, she began to cry.

Her aunt made noise as if to speak but did not. Next came the sound of movement, as if Kate went from sitting to standing, outside to in.

"I imagine it's an adjustment," Kate said finally, followed by more quiet in California, where Dad was some sort of mayor.

"I'll tell him you called," Kate said. When she asked for a

number, Adela answered that they didn't have a phone. Kate sighed, as if she were being difficult.

Adela hung up and started crossing out Sigrid's number. In its place she scrawled, *Sigrid thinks you're full of shit.* Then, *Sigrid hates you.*

No one else had made it back to the house. Towels Michael had stolen filled a closet. Adela pulled one out, left it draped across the floor. "Look what the boys did," she said, thinking of how she'd been Michael's lodestar until something shinier had come along.

She stayed up reading. Michael eventually came home. He marched to the toilet with a speed and noise of midday. Adela waited outside. When he opened the door and saw her, he looked amused, and certainly stoned.

"All yours," he said, though he didn't move.

Adela's stomach cramped. For a moment she wondered if she was getting her period, but it had finished just a week before. And this ache had a different insistence.

"The middle of the night," she said.

"Thanks for the time check," Michael answered.

Adela stomped her foot, embarrassed to have let her feelings fly out. Stoned delight filled Michael's face.

Back in her room, Adela tried to read, but could only remember Michael's expression. Also Dad's popularity Aunt Kate kept talking about. She couldn't imagine their father with a slew of friends and wondered if, in leaving his family behind, he'd also left behind his version that scowled when Michael crossed his legs or told the German Lady she wouldn't need to smoke if she'd figured things out. "What things?" the German Lady had asked once. Dad's expression told her that that question was part of her problem.

Adela went back to the hall closet, took the rest of the towels Michael had stolen. She folded them under her sleeping bag until they formed a sort of mattress. Lying down, she was lulled to sleep by this new softness. And when she woke up the next morning, she was confused for a moment as to where she was, though she soon remembered and wished for the confusion again and picked up her plastic bag of coins. Adela returned to the telephone booth, where someone had commented on her graffiti with crude drawings and German slang she didn't know.

After weeks of wet coolness, the heat that arrived at the end of July seemed suspect. Adela and Udo lay on the beach, sun turning them sweaty. Adela pulled a book from her rucksack.

"I'm reading about the Bitch of Buchenwald," she said, using Ilse Koch's nickname.

"I've never been to Buchenwald," Udo answered.

The hair on his stomach was pale and feathery.

"We call her a witch, actually," he went on. "And not every story about her is true. Like she didn't make lampshades from Jewish skin."

"Right," Adela answered, though she'd read exactly that the night before and turned indignantly horrified.

As with every other book she read, Adela hoped this one would explain how people's meanness could metastasize. The sun was strong. Breath lifted Udo's chest. Turning the page, Adela found a slip of paper. Michael. *This is what I want*, he'd written. There was a joke from the States that this line connected to, but Adela couldn't call up its particulars.

Jellyfish washed up onto the sand, shining like lollipops. She couldn't see Kritzhagen's forgotten streets, only sand and birds and fast-moving clouds. *This is what I want*, Adela thought, listening to water that could have been water anywhere, the wind's universal itch.

"What about you?" Udo asked.

When it seemed he might not clarify, Adela asked, "What *about* me?" and smiled. A stick sat just beyond her. She picked it up, poked Udo's shoulder.

"You had slavery. Killed all the Indians," he said.

"That wasn't where I'm from exactly."

"You have all these books about here."

"I'm trying to learn," Adela answered.

"To be clear, I never met Goebbels."

"You're too young," Adela added, trying to hold on to the lightness from a moment before.

Udo moved to his knees and began to dig. She smelled his sweat, heard his digging fingers. A family arrived, planting their towels close to them, though the beach was mostly empty. Adela snapped the stick she'd been holding in two.

"You're digging," she said, but he didn't look up. Muscle moved across his shoulder.

Udo grabbed her book, threw it into the hole, and covered it in sand.

"That's mine," Adela said.

"You read the wrong books," Udo answered.

The night before, Adela had read how Koch liked the lampshades best when she could tell which part had come from someone's back, what skin once wound around a knee.

"I'll get you books," he said. "About things that actually happened."

Adela worried that he'd leave her behind as her brother had, Udo climbing onto the dolly, rolling away. Adela stood, wished she hadn't. Sweat stuck to her bathing suit.

The nearby family played paddleball. Their small, matted-looking dog barked at the surf. Adela thought of the German Lady and Michael sneaking out at night. The weight of each day without Udo to lighten it.

Udo grabbed Adela's toes until they cracked. She said that it tickled and he stopped, though it hadn't tickled but felt as if he were taking something from her.

The next morning, Adela biked back to the beach. She dug a hole, certain she'd picked the right spot, but found only damp earth. She dug a second, a third. No book appeared. Sand burned under her nails.

An old man, dressed as if for an office job, moved across the sand with a metal detector. He got close to her, sighed, and kept going.

At home there was a new table inside the front door. A letter from Dad on it. Adela opened it. She was reading about the promotion he'd gotten when Udo appeared at their front door. She'd pictured him gone for good, her books and misstatements leaving him tired or bored.

"Udo," she said, and felt lucky.

"Good cousin," he answered, "the library opens in fifteen minutes."

They arrived and found swaths of empty shelves. Watched a team of people stack new books onto them, the history the GDR had invented replaced with something closer to real. *This is what I want*, Adela thought. They walked down an aisle.

"Michael and I used to go to the library back home," she said. Her voice echoed in the high-ceilinged room.

"I've never," Udo answered, "imagined your brother as someone who likes to read."

"He went for other reasons," she said.

"Other library reasons," Udo answered.

As they examined books so new their spines cracked, Adela realized that Udo had only known Germany as East, so aligned with communism that he saw the Nazis as awful, too, also outside of him.

"This one," Udo answered, handing her a book on Koch's different history.

Part of Koch's story was familiar. The book took no pains to excuse her. Yet the details were less salacious, the adjectives fewer and plainer.

They sat by a window. Adela looked up from time to time to see Udo's eyebrows shift as he read. More books were added to a shelf that a minute before had held nothing.

"What's that?" Udo asked, and pointed to her legs.

Looking down at them, Adela realized there was still sand on them from that morning.

The next time Michael saw Maxi was at an intersection. Michael on his bike, Maxi in a car. He looked so skeletal that Michael turned more certain that he was sick, certainty something he began to see in degrees—*very certain, completely certain, more certain than the certain I'd felt before.* For a moment he imagined him and Maxi sick together and thought of an opera he'd watched on TV where people were in love and ill. Also the time he and Adela had visited their grandfather in a hospital, a place both orderly and full of people capable of helping.

"Hi," Michael said just as the light changed.

He got closer to the house, where the German Lady pretended sleeping all day was the best way to look for a job, where his sister's only concerns were books and Udo. Blood had blotted the tissues Michael used after he and Maxi were done. The red riddling Maxi's face screamed of infection. With Maxi right in front of him, sickness felt—like love or a small apartment—

shared. With distance, his alarm grew. Michael tried to swallow, but it stuck halfway down his throat. He dropped his bike in the yard, found Udo on their living room floor.

"Fuck a duck," Michael said.

"Your sister says that, too," Udo answered.

"Where *is* my sister?" Michael asked.

Udo told him she was in the shower and asked how Michael's wrist was healing.

Michael stammered out a sigh. Udo unwound his bandage, which again felt like seduction. Maxi hadn't seduced him, but blurted out instructions as if he were teaching Michael a game in gym class.

Udo moved Michael's wrist from side to side. The bruises were paler, the swelling a shrunken geography.

"It hurts?" Udo asked.

"Less," Michael answered, thinking of the men he'd never sleep with, the seduction he wouldn't experience. He closed his eyes to keep from crying.

"I'm guessing," Udo said, pausing so long that Michael wondered if he'd imagined those words, "that this is not about the wrist."

Michael lay on the floor next to Udo, his cousin so large he didn't seem like a person, but a landmark.

"I did something stupid," Michael said. Udo nodded for him to continue.

"Please don't call me disgusting or perverted," Michael added. His stomach shivered, his body no longer his to control.

"I wouldn't," Udo answered. "Unless you asked me to."

Udo had never joked with him before. Michael needed it then. He began his story. Occasionally, Udo asked a clarifying question. But nothing in his face changed when Michael said he was *schwul* or that he'd followed Maxi into a bathroom.

"You'll come with me tomorrow," Udo said. He touched the top of Michael's head, his hand so large it covered it like a hat. Michael wanted to be touched all the time, by himself or other people. "To take care of it."

"Adela's coming, too?" Michael asked.

"You only told me," Udo answered.

In the dim light of the house, Michael could only see the line of Udo's mouth, his nose as round as a heel. He teared up at the unexpected comfort of their sort-of cousin.

Adela arrived downstairs, told Udo she was ready. Michael turned on the black-and-white television he'd found. A news program showed Iraq invading Kuwait, the latter country one Michael hadn't known existed. For a moment he wished he'd told Adela instead. But his behavior would have been a confirmation of one of her long-held suspicions, while Udo told Michael he'd take him somewhere to deal with it. As the television showed men in a desert, hands high in surrender, Michael remembered the hospital where his grandfather had died, the quiet with which everyone talked, the clean brightness of its walls, and the nurses who showed up at each bedside with the click of a button.

6 Lübeck was Kritzhagen's well-married sibling. Its ornate buildings were brightly painted. Its stores loaded with towers of marzipan and tablecloths for four hundred marks. Udo and Michael passed young people smoking in cafés, but without Maxi or Lena's hard-shelled boredom. Michael understood then why they'd taken a train an hour west for his appointment, picturing Kritzhagen's windowless hospital, its Eastern protocols and equipment.

"Why doesn't everybody live here?" Michael asked.

"Everybody does," Udo answered.

Michael smoked a cigarette. Udo put out his hand for a drag.

On a cobblestone street that appeared polished, a cello from a nearby music school humming through an open window, they got to the clinic and stepped inside. Michael was lulled by its clean light, the fan of magazines on its table. Also the woman behind its desk who wore the benevolently wise expression of a television mother. But the waiting room was populated mostly by men. Sickness in their cheeks and eyes. Michael went to the bathroom, scrubbing his face to a riled-up pink. Kept the cold water running until his fingers ached in its stream. When he returned, Udo said, "They just called your name." Michael stopped as if he'd forgotten something, though he was considering what it would be like to walk out, to not know until his body one day fell apart or continued.

Udo touched Michael's back. Michael imagined, then dismissed, the idea of kissing him. Udo crammed into a chair that was too small for him.

The nurse who greeted Michael had a bland face and voice. He talked about how the test would proceed, the follow-up, all with a smile as benign as the rest of him. Michael wondered what the nurse looked like naked, if there was such a thing as a benign dick. It felt important then that he know this.

As the nurse asked about his sexual history, Michael began to harden, certain what was wrong with him was larger than the sex he'd had. When Michael said unprotected, the nurse handed him a pamphlet, a paper bag round with condoms and lube.

"It just happened," Michael said.

"But you mentioned earlier," the nurse answered, mild smile on his face as he referred to his notes, "alcohol and drugs."

Michael would have done it had he been sober, had it been behind a tree instead of in a bathroom that locked. He knew not to say this, though. Part of coming to a place like this meant it was his role to atone.

The nurse put on gloves and took blood. Amazed by its color, Michael asked if it was normal.

"The color of blood, yes," the nurse said. He kept his gloves on as he wrote Michael's name on a vial.

"Haas," Michael interrupted. The nurse's pen stilled.

"My parents are divorced. I've changed my last name along with my mother," Michael said, though the German Lady hadn't said anything about her name.

"Haas is certainly easier to pronounce," the nurse answered. He gave Michael a card with the date and time of his next appointment. "You're heading back to Kritzhagen alone?"

"My brother is with me," Michael said, and wished Udo were his brother, imagining a life with someone so substantial-looking in his lineage, the things he'd get away with, the kindness others would offer him because they were afraid.

On the train back, Michael asked Udo if he knew Maxi Pad. Orange-roofed towns slid by, Michael amazed at how easy it was to get to the West. When the German Lady had made this trip decades before, she'd barely made it past the border.

"When this is all done," Udo said, "I'll tell you how he got his nickname."

"This?" Michael said. Udo nodded, sure his cousin was fine, that Maxi hadn't given him anything other than some junior version of heartache. Michael pulled on a strand of his own hair until it ached. He listed things he saw through the window.

"You see what I see," Udo said.

Michael thought again of the bravery he could inhabit if Udo were his brother, though cousin was something, too.

"I'll tell your sister," Udo said, "that I was visiting a friend today."

"Where should I say I've been?" Michael asked. They passed a house with laundry on the line, a sign for a bank.

"Where you always are," Udo said.

He put a hand on Michael's arm, then took a nap, sleep a switch Udo could flip, a wish granted as soon as he thought of it.

Seeing her mother at the kitchen table, Adela grew queasy. Though she'd treated her mother's constant sleep as an annoyance, there was relief that she'd chosen to fall apart behind a closed door. Bringing it out in the open seemed like the next step in her collapse.

"Why are you up?" Adela asked.

"I can't be awake?" the German Lady answered. She wore a cardigan though it was warm out and asked Adela if they had a newspaper. It was seven in the morning.

"Why do you need the paper?" Adela asked.

"Help wanted," Mutti said.

Adela found one from the day before and handed it to her.

In their German weeks, her mother had grown thinner. As she flipped pages, Adela saw the bones in her hands, her wrists as small as a child's. The night before, Adela had been reading about Honecker when she heard the German Lady come back from wherever she was. Adela had looked at her watch, written the time in the book's margins: 1:18.

When the German Lady shook her head at each listing, when her performed smile appeared, annoyance became a light for Adela to follow.

"You didn't even look!" Adela said, as Mutti pushed the paper aside.

"Nothing to look at," the German Lady answered.

"A driver for a delivery van," Adela read.

"What do I know about truck driving?" her mother countered.

"It's only a van."

Adela read a listing for something called an assistant accountant. The German Lady picked at a stain on her sweater.

"Dad has a job already," Adela said.

Her mother made a toothache face. She exhumed an apple from the bowl, slid it into her pocket, and padded upstairs. Perhaps their mother had inherited enough to keep sleeping, to leave money for food and other necessities on the counter each morning. It was always there when they woke up. Michael said it made him feel as if they were spies, passing secrets.

"Feels more like a drug deal to me," Adela had answered.

She read other possible jobs to the empty room.

An old woman sat inside the phone booth. Had Michael been the Michael of a few months ago, he would have been with Adela, eyes on this lady as he whispered, *I wonder if that's Sigrid.*

The woman left and Adela slipped inside. The booth smelled of her oldness, her perfume.

Though it was early morning in the States, Adela got Dad and Kate's machine. But instead of hanging up, she tried to construct a normal-sounding message. New things about Sigrid filled the booth's walls. And for the first time since they'd found him on their lawn, Udo hadn't shown up that morning. The machine ran on. Adela wasn't sure if she should address both her aunt and father, didn't know if sounding chipper would get his attention better than desperation. Her dad and aunt might have been hiking or drinking, or on some other leg of their reunion tour. Adela finally blurted out, "This is a message for the mayor," turned horrified, and hung up. A woman passed, a kerchief over her hair. Adela wondered if this city had more women, or if she only imagined it did, these old ladies part of the men-less generation that had to find a way forward after the war.

As she sat there deciding whether or not to call again, Michael and Udo biked past. Michael smoked a cigarette, passed it to Udo. Breath caught in Adela's throat.

When she got home fifteen minutes later, she found Udo sitting in the yard.

"I was looking for you," he said.

"I didn't know if you were coming today," Adela answered. She thought to say more, but his arrival brought a relief she couldn't disturb.

"Was visiting a friend," Udo said.

A cricket hopped onto his leg. He flicked it away. Adela tried to convince herself that he and her brother had simply run into each other. She winced, then smiled, as the German Lady had when Adela told her to call about a job even if she didn't know what it was.

"Have you seen Michael?" Adela asked.

Udo's eyes stayed glued to the spot where the cricket had been.

"Michael?" Udo said. "I haven't seen him in days."

The peace between them in the States would sometimes break. Adela would announce a plan, and the part of Michael that usually craved her guidance revolted. Once, in history class, Adela had gotten into an argument with her nemesis Kevin Bartholomew after he'd posited that women's suffrage hadn't been that important because, as he said, "at least they weren't slaves."

"It's not crappiness by degrees," Adela had answered.

Two rows away, Michael scribbled on his notebook's cover. Mr. Hart asked her to refrain from using crappy.

After class, Michael left with a girl who wore a sleeve of plastic bracelets. As they walked down the hall, Adela heard him say, "My sister can be such a bitch sometimes." Adela turned incredulous, frightened by his easy mutiny. She waited until dinner that night—Dad who knows where, the German Lady pulling pickles from a jar and smoking out the window—and said, "At school today, Michael called me a bitch."

Michael jabbed food with his fork and answered, "Well, sometimes Adela *is* a bitch." Then he coughed.

"Michael," the German Lady said, shooing smoke out the window.

"Mutti," he answered, "you've honestly never thought Adela was mean?"

The German Lady could agree. The two of them might gang up, offer a list. The food Adela had been eager for a moment ago looked congealed.

"Everyone is everything at one point or another," the German Lady answered.

"So you agree," Michael said. Their mother's face folded, as if she'd stubbed her toe. The jar she'd been eating from sat balanced between her knees.

"Did I say I agreed?" she answered, and went into the other room, where she turned on the television. Adela didn't get up from the table, Michael either. They stayed as a new TV show began, as their food cooled and hardened. Stayed until Dad walked in, said, "What?" and Michael slipped into his room.

Each day, when Adela expected an apology, Michael stayed quiet, and she wondered if, in some elemental way, he was done with her. And even as she grew mad, she understood that this anger was a veneer, underneath it the surprise that he could hurt her.

A week after Udo had lied to her, Adela watched through her window as Michael left without his dolly. Morning turned to afternoon. Udo didn't appear. The German Lady slunk downstairs and ate a sleeve of crackers. She asked Adela what she was reading; Adela told her.

"All that's happened already," her mother said, scanning the book's cover.

"So I shouldn't read about it?" Adela countered.

Mutti brushed salt from a cracker. The sadness she'd tried to foist onto Adela a week before returned.

"I got into the *Gymnasium*," Adela said. Two weeks earlier, Udo had taken her for a placement test. And just the afternoon before, a letter arrived telling her she'd been accepted. Adela had only told Udo, who'd taken her out for an ice cream so large that it leaned each time she licked.

The German Lady put a hand on top of Adela's, removing it fast, as if she'd touched a too-hot thing.

"Child," Mutti said, "we should celebrate."

"Where do you go, when you go out at night?" Adela asked.

"I didn't know you noticed," she answered.

Adela's look told her to stop playing dumb. The German Lady nodded. Adela sometimes hated her mother, felt ashamed of this hatred, too. She wanted to tell her to snap out of it, that she was flailing as well. Adela understood Michael's impulse to vanish then.

Mutti mumbled.

"What's that?" Adela asked.

"I said I just walk. I can't sleep, so I walk."

"Maybe if you didn't sleep during the day," Adela answered.

The German Lady scraped more salt off her cracker, the sound a mouse making a home in their walls. "That's when I can sleep."

"That's stupid," Adela answered.

Her mother continued to nod. To agree instead of doing anything about it. Adela opened the paper to the jobs she'd circled, left it on the table, and walked upstairs, though she knew she'd be cited as difficult, as if her difficulty weren't an answer to one of the many questions the German Lady treated as impossible.

From her bedroom window, Adela watched a cat pull a mouse from some rubble. A carful of young men with Mohawks passed. Their hair scratched the ceiling.

Adela held her breath until it hurt. She tried it again, this time setting her watch so she would know how long she could hold it for.

Moving between looking outside and circling unfamiliar words in the newspaper, the sun low in the trees, Adela spied Udo and Michael biking side by side. Again, they shared a cigarette. When they got close to the house, Udo put a hand on Michael's shoulder and biked away. Everything in Adela that had wobbled underwater congealed into action. She slammed down the stairs and into the driveway. Michael pulled in and smiled. He wore Udo's rain jacket. When she said as much, he told her he'd found it in a house and then picked up mail from the stoop.

"From the California Father," Michael said, handing her a letter.

She pulled back the jacket's hood, saw the name Behm on its tag.

"You're a shit-fucker liar," Adela said.

"And also with you," he answered.

"Not everything is a joke."

Michael lifted his hands in amused surrender.

Leaning down, Adela pushed his dolly onto the street. She rolled it past their yard, through the intersection at the end of their block. Michael strolled behind her. The dolly ached against her palms.

"Dela," he called.

Udo's raincoat looked—on Michael—like a dress. He repeated her name, his voice high with jokey pleading.

"It's okay," he said. She didn't even know what the "it" was.

Getting to the river, she stopped. A minute later, Michael appeared.

"What is it you do?" Michael asked, his smile dopey and mean.

"I'm not playing," Adela answered.

"With Udo, I mean. When he picks you up, when you bike

here and there. Does he swim naked in the ocean? Get naked in front of you?"

"It's a sea," Adela corrected.

"Naked like a barbarian? Showing you his barbarian dick?"

"What is it *you* do?" Adela answered, angry and embarrassed, as if Michael had located something perverted and true about her. She muscled the dolly over the small stone wall separating sidewalk from river. The dolly flipped into the water, floating briefly before it gurgled under.

"Oh, sister," Michael said. "I don't think you're ready to know." There was so much pity and glee in his voice that Adela couldn't help but fling out the first insult that came to her, one their neighbor back in Glens Falls had loved: sissy faggot.

Michael's look of pity remained. Adela couldn't touch him.

He took off Udo's jacket. Slipped off his shirt, shoes, and shorts. There was more hair on his chest, his soft stomach replaced with muscle. Soon Michael was naked. In his undressing in front of her, it turned plain that he did not care. She might find him gross or an embarrassment and his day would continue, unbothered, like a smooth lake. Adela tried not to look, but disgust and curiosity battled. Hair darkened his thighs, his penis jiggled.

"Put on some fucki—"

"Let's see what the sissy faggot will do," Michael interrupted, and launched himself over the stone wall, landing in the water with the smallest splash.

He was under for ten seconds when Adela began to grow frightened; longer, and she looked for a car to flag down. She tried to calculate how long it would take her to run to Udo's, the only person in this place who might fix things.

"Long live the sissy faggot," Michael said as he emerged, dolly in hand before he lost it. Michael followed it back under.

She stared at the dimple he'd left in the water, part of her hoping the dolly would pull him to the river's muddy floor. *What is it you do?* Adela thought. She picked up Michael's clothes and walked away.

The woman who answered had a voice of indeterminate age.

"Is this Sigrid?" Adela asked.

The woman paused. Michael's clothes rested against the booth—a purple T-shirt he may have stolen. Jean shorts filled with holes.

"What do you want?" she said finally.

"There are things written about you."

The woman asked Adela who put her up to this.

"No one. I wanted you to know," Adela answered, though it was clear she did already. "I've been crossing them out."

In the quiet on the other end, she hoped Sigrid was deciding to trust her. And though it felt as foolish as the miracles Michael made up, Adela wished Sigrid would join her, the two of them erasing slurs while Adela told her how she'd been brought to this country, then abandoned. In the building across the street, the old woman from the pay phone sat in her window. Adela wondered if they'd ever have a phone, or furniture that belonged to them.

She spotted a new drawing of Sigrid in a foul, flexible position. And she understood that, even if Sigrid came, even if they drew over every word and drawing that depicted some sadist's version of penetration, more things would show up, the booth no more Adela's than it belonged to the people who wrote these things, or her father, who was never home to talk to her.

Sigrid breathed in. In that breath Adela could sense what was coming next, could have recited in tandem when the woman on the other end answered. "You have? Well, good for you."

Adela picked up Michael's clothes, returned to the river where she'd left him. But he was gone, her brother running naked through this city, people calling the police about a streaker darting down the middle of the street or hopping in and out of their gardens.

A few years before the move to Germany, Michael had woken in the middle of the night, desperate to pee. He'd moved down the dark hall to find the bathroom door closed, a blade of light underneath it.

"Mutti's in there."

His father appeared in the hall.

"Oh," Michael said. "I need to pee."

Dishes from dinner filled the kitchen. Something sat on the floor. As his eyes adjusted, Michael realized it was a potato.

In his lifetime, Michael had seen Dad throw a coffee mug, a stack of books, and dozens of shoes. Now he imagined his parents fighting after dinner and his father, seized by something only movement could subdue, taking a potato and hurling it to the floor.

"There's a potato on the floor," Michael said.

Dad didn't answer. Michael knocked on the bathroom door.

"I'm in here," Mutti said.

"I told you," his father answered. "She wants to be alone."

Michael wanted to be alone, too.

"But I need to," Michael said.

"I see that," Dad answered. "In the sink, then."

"What?"

"The kitchen sink."

"What?"

"Michael," his father rasped. "Do you really not understand what I'm saying?"

Dad moved aside pots and bowls. He pulled a chair to the sink. Michael creaked onto it. Out on Route 4, streetlamps rose in a zipper of light. Michael undid his fly. After fluttering in near-ready agony, he peed.

He finished and rinsed the sink, slid the chair under the table. Dad moved to the sink's basin.

"I cleaned it," Michael said.

Dad switched on the overhead light, wincing as he checked for yellow that wasn't there. *I cleaned it*, Michael wanted to say again, though he did not. There was always more food to throw.

As Dad stared at the sink, in a room that reeked of cooled food, Michael realized that the hard certainty their father held, something Adela carried, too, was a quality he hated. It was this certainty Dad had leaned on when he told Michael to stop talking with his hands, or when he'd forced him to play on a basketball team, then got angry when Michael—nine and in shorts too big for him—began to cry during practice. "Has anyone ever told you that there are times when you're meant to be embarrassed?" Dad had asked. They'd stood on the sideline. Michael afraid but also confused as to whether he or his father was meant to be embarrassed, if embarrassment was supposed to keep a person from doing something or was an afterthought. Dad's hands stayed on his arm; his underbite an opened drawer. But more than angry, Michael sensed that his father was ashamed. It was Dad's shame a student had located on what turned out to be his last day of teaching, their father exploding and pushing that young man into a bulletin board. Michael wanted a shirt that Dad said was for girls, and his father answered: "Don't you know?" A question he asked Michael as regularly as he said hello to him.

For a long time, Michael mistook his father's shame for his own. It became a habit, something he almost craved. But in

Kritzhagen, when he sought it out, other feelings appeared. And when Adela rolled his dolly into the river, Michael undressed in front of her, partly to see if this shame would come back for him.

Michael crouched between two parked cars, trying to figure out what he might do. Running the dozen blocks home felt impossible without clothes. There were no empty houses nearby. "Asshole Adela," he mumbled, though when he'd gotten out of the water and saw she'd left with his clothes, he'd found it almost funny. He rubbed his goose-pimpled legs that, in their German weeks, had thickened from biking and pushing his dolly up hills. A car passed. Michael's crouch deepened. But as he blew into his fists, he remembered a place from his notebook map that was only a block away. Michael moved his hands to his crotch and ran.

He and Udo had returned to Lübeck earlier that day, where the same nurse told him the tests came back fine. On the train home Michael had cried, not for sadness or relief, but because he'd had too much to hold. Udo placed a hand on his leg and said, "I told you you'd be okay," though he hadn't said that exactly, but with the steady quiet with which he listened, the careful way he'd wrapped his wrist, Michael had sensed as much. Sensed also that, had things gone the other way, Udo would have taken care of him.

Michael counted houses as he passed them, six left, then four, then one. He hid behind a shrub, trying to catch his breath. The dim house in front of him came into focus. In the months that followed, he would think back on Adela taking his dolly and his clothes, would watch his sister and Udo studying at their kitchen table, and hate her. For the clothes, but also the blankness she'd offer up when he made a joke or came home late or talked about a person from their American days. As fall fell into winter and Maxi would accept or reject Michael with mean indifference, it all would come to seem like Adela's doing. He'd start referring to her as the Asshole, mumbling that during a winter storm when Maxi turned him down, or on the night when Michael stared at her for minutes and she wouldn't look up at him. "*A* is for asshole," he'd said, the meanness he saw in her flattening everything else he'd once known and felt about her. If she hadn't thrown his dolly into the river, Michael would never have gotten naked to go in after it. If she hadn't ignored him when he told her that taking his clothes was a shit thing, he might have forgiven her.

But that night, what his sister had done felt like a gift. And as Michael moved closer to that house and saw Maxi's opened window, good feeling turned to helium.

Michael climbed through the window. His wrist barely ached anymore. Getting close to sleeping Maxi, he turned shy. He thought to grab clothes from the floor, to dress and leave the way he'd come in.

But Maxi stirred. Opening his eyes, he bolted to sitting.

"Oh," Maxi said, voice full of happy recognition. "You."

In that dim room, Michael could see Maxi's ribs in rows, his dick moving toward hard. Maxi patted his mattress. He gave Michael a sleepy smile.

"Here," Maxi said, sliding over to make room for him.

7

The house felt foreign without furniture. There were walls where Beate remembered windows, rooms she had no recollection of. And it was giant. Looking for the toilet, she found another bedroom. She stumbled on the pantry and whispered, "This place just keeps going." On their second night in Kritzhagen, jet lag putting her children to bed early, Beate was stuck awake. She started to clean, but it grew dark. So she walked. She passed the slurping bay, hoping it might speak to her. Skirted gulls gathered at trash cans and a waterside park in the midst of renaming. A sign for the People's Garden leaned against a wall, the new one unimaginatively titled WATER VIEW. Beate got to a puddle and wanted to step into it. She wanted to recognize something.

Walking again four nights later, Beate became convinced she was close to the sea. With each turn she felt certain she'd stumble onto sand, but found houses instead, then a long, lit-up building that looked like a prison. Two police officers smoked outside it. They nodded as she slowed. What was meant to be a fountain sat empty apart from a hedge of trash collecting there.

"What's this building?" Beate asked.

"Train station," an officer answered.

Beate remembered the station they'd left from decades before as large, with arching windows.

The officers lit more cigarettes. Beate wanted one. Even more, she wanted to be back in their tiny apartment in Glens Falls, the Hudson's cool scent slipping through the window as she smoked and waited for Paul to come home. As awful as Paul sometimes was, he'd made decisions. The roiling in her gut she'd felt when they'd first arrived at their house returned. The building in front of her was a single story, its doors girded in bars.

"Where is the *other* train station?" Beate asked, and tried to breathe in the cop's smoke, to remember some dumb thing her mother used to say about the earth being the earth no matter its particulars. A bus barreled past; its single passenger stared at nothing. She wanted to ask where everyone was. To tell the officers she had children she couldn't take care of.

"There's just one train station," the officer said.

He and his partner got into their car and rolled up its windows.

Beate had been relieved when Paul moved out. She'd warmed with mean triumph when she told him she and the children chose Germany and he looked as if his family moving thousands of miles away were a punishment he deserved. But a week before they were scheduled to leave, he showed up with Chinese. He spilled food on his lap, laughed as he dabbed his pants with a napkin. The children watched him with polite worry. Then he told them that he'd decided to move to his sister's in California. Beate ate quickly. She felt what she later that night recognized as rage. Rage that this man who'd ruined so much had a second chance. Livid that he saw their move and copied, as if leaning over her shoulder to steal test answers. That anger mixed with other thoughts—divorced friends of his sister's who'd only see Paul's handsome fitness, who'd listen to his story of the job he'd lost and nod fiercely as if he were the victim. Now Paul was in a place with electricity and neighbors when what Beate had thought would be a glorious return felt like squatting.

She was mumbling to herself about Paul—so lost in it that she couldn't have said if she were speaking German or English—when a car crawled up next to her. The driver rolled down his window and asked if he knew her. Like everything in this place, he was ugly and strange. A Freddy Quinn song played on his radio. Beate wanted to tell him that her husband had copied her, though she wasn't sure if husband was still her word to claim. She was in a city where she recognized nothing, without a job or a single friend. The reality of this left her dizzy.

"Hello?" the man said. "No German? Don't tell me you're one of those Turks."

His chuckles drowned out the car's wheels across the pavement. Fingers of heat climbed Beate's neck.

"No, thanks," she said.

"You don't even know me!" he answered.

"I thought you recognized me," Beate said.

His face relented as if she'd scored an impressive point.

On his radio, Quinn sang, "*Boy, never go to sea again, don't ever go again.*" She'd always hated Quinn. Girls in her seventh-grade class had teared up as he'd spouted out one trite line after another, reminding Beate that, despite her efforts against it, her parents had turned her into a snob.

Beate turned a corner; the car followed.

"Can I at least give you a ride?" the man said.

"I can't hear you," Beate answered.

He laughed with delight. Beate smacked the hood of his car.

"Hey, now!" he said, and she smacked it again.

They passed a pharmacy with a single bulb burning between

its aisles. Beate felt terrified, also angry with Paul, who'd led her to this place, this man, this street.

A sign for a basement bar glowed, and Beate slipped inside.

A handful of old men sat at the bar. The bartender cleaned a glass and had a graying pompadour. Beate ordered a schnapps, drank it in one swallow. The bartender poured her another. Beams ribbed the bar's ceiling.

"This place been around awhile?" Beate asked, an inkling rising in her that she'd been here or someplace similar with her father, the two of them slurping mussels from a black bowl.

The bartender nodded. One patron appeared to be on the verge of sleep. Another scribbled on some paper.

"It's usually this empty?" Beate asked.

"Off and on," the bartender answered, as the door opened, and the Quinn fan sauntered inside.

"I haven't been here in ages," he said, sitting next to Beate and ordering a beer.

She thought of her children at home, how she'd snuck out like some wily teen. *Just take them*, she could write to Paul, sure he'd write back that his sister only had one guest room, which he'd already laid claim to.

"You know her?" the bartender asked.

"No," Beate said.

"He's bothering you?"

"No," the man answered.

Two stools down, the scribbler smiled at Beate's unwanted company.

"Hans," he said, "tell your father it's been too long. That I'll call him soon."

"I'll tell him," Hans said.

"He's well?"

"Fine."

"Good," the old man said. "So you don't know this woman?"

"I don't," Hans answered. He took another sip, nodded, and left. Rain that had threatened all night tapped against the bar's window.

"What day is it?" Beate asked.

The bartender chuckled; the scribbler blew out his lips like a horse. It felt good to hear laughter, to be awake with others in a place she might have been to with her father, though she only remembered it'd been in a basement, that there might have been tablecloths.

"I've just moved back," she said in defense.

When the men asked from where and she answered, "USA," they laughed louder. The bartender poured her another drink.

"Are you from Hollywood?" one asked.

"Maybe a cowboy?" said another.

"That's her horse parked outside."

Rain rattled the window. The old men were dressed up but ragged.

"That will have to be my last drink," Beate said.

"You came alone? From the USA, I mean," another man asked.

"I lived here when I was young. I've come back for my parents' house. With my children."

The droopy-faced man appeared surprised at this. The scribbler answered that Kritzhagen wasn't Bosnia. The schnapps burned as it traveled down Beate's throat.

"No," Droopy answered. "It's nice that not everyone's leaving."

Finishing her drink and standing up, Beate realized she didn't have any money.

"Willy," she said, using the name she'd heard one of the patrons call him. "May I call you Willy?"

"That's my name," the bartender answered, his pompadour a piece of art. She said his name, hadn't said any names apart from her children's in weeks. No one had come, as she'd imagined, to see how she was settling in. No one there remembered her.

"Yes," she said. "I seem to have. I came in because of—"

"Hans Vogel," Droopy added.

"I wasn't thinking. I was walking. I know this sounds like some line—"

"Pay next time," Willy said.

Beate's drink was gone, but she didn't move. She hadn't had a drink since moving here and felt it loosen her shoulders. The droopy-faced man asked where she lived. Beate recited her address, feeling like a child.

"I don't live far from there," he answered. "We can walk together."

"You'll be great protection," another patron joked.

"That would be lovely," Beate said, and she and this old man, Rudi, left.

A car rumbled past. Streetlamps glowed against the puddles. Getting to her house, Rudi told her he knew it for some reason he couldn't now remember.

They said good night and Rudi walked in the direction they'd just come from. She was about to call out to him when he said, "I don't live far." He waved and she waved and it seemed neither of them wanted to stop waving first. And though this place stayed unfamiliar, she grew hopeful that if she kept walking, looking, something she passed a dozen times would catch, opening doors that looked like walls, trees rewinding to decades before when they were new and delicate, with leaves she could count on her fingers. She would get to a place and remember something she'd felt there—confusion, or a joy so strong it made her stomach ache. Beate stood in the driveway until Rudi disappeared. She walked across their lawn, hoping Michael soon found something to mow it with.

But as she stepped into the house, as she looked at her watch and saw that it was close to one in the morning, shame wiped those possibilities clean. Beate stared at the staircase. Michael might slide down it and ask where she'd been. Even worse, Adela. In her best moments, Beate appreciated her daughter's intelligence. In others, Adela carried Paul's sense of knowing better. She stood in the dark house, filled with furniture from god knows where. With each stair she took, she waited to be found out. Beate's heart raced and she wondered if it was normal to be afraid of one's children, to get to a new place and feel as young as she'd been when she'd left it. She got to the landing; it felt like a victory. She slipped into her sleeping bag and set her alarm, though when it sounded hours later, she smacked it off, stared at the ceiling, and decided that sleep was her best way to take care.

As Beate moved in and out of sleep, she heard doors close, louder sounds when Michael brought home what turned out to be two large chairs. When she got up and saw them, she was overcome by their stink. Beate considered cleaning the cushions' covers, but the washing machine the previous residents had left behind required electricity. She walked into the kitchen. Adela sat on its floor, reading. When Beate asked how she was, her daughter asked what she knew about one of the Wilhelms, looked unsurprised when her mother answered, "Not much, I'm afraid."

"I've never understood saying 'I'm afraid' like that," Adela answered.

Though it was a common expression, it felt like Beate's wrong to right.

"I don't know," Beate said.

"I'm afraid," Adela answered, and went upstairs.

There were eight men in the bar the next night, including a man Beate could only remember as the Scribbler.

"You're back," he said.

She sat next to him. On a napkin, he began a sketch of her face.

A painting on the bar's far wall showed a sailboat knifed by waves. She asked about it. Men answered with stories about a time when water meant escape. When swimming too far out meant the Volksmarine dragged you back in again.

Willy took Beate's glass and refilled it, though it was still half full. The men talked in shorthand about a place they'd known, jobs that vanished from one day to the next. Sometimes they told stories about their children who'd moved to Hamburg or Munich. Or they reminisced about a person who'd gone to the West as if they'd passed from living to dead, or maybe the other way around.

Though Beate did her best to ignore it, the knocking on her bedroom door continued. She lay on the floor and pulled her sleeping bag to her chin. "An emergency?" she asked, half hoping an emergency meant someone would find children left to their own devices, a mother who couldn't stop sleeping on the floor, and ask, *Where is the father?* She asked herself the same question when Michael and his dolly rumbled into the driveway. When her children whipped down the street on bikes she'd never seen before. In their weeks in this place, Beate had expected to wake up one morning and feel ready to be here, to walk into stores to buy things, chatting with salespeople about prices or the weather. But each night after the bar she lay staring at the ceiling. And each morning when she planned to wake up, sleep pulled her back under.

A final knock, and Beate's bedroom door opened. A woman stood in its frame. She was stout in a way men admired. Her short hair haloed in blond. Something in her posture seemed familiar, but Beate no longer trusted what she did and didn't recognize.

"Beate Sigrid," the woman said, smiling a familiar smile. It was her cousin. When Beate had left at age twelve, Liesl had been sixteen. The room felt large on top of her.

"Liesl Katarina," Beate answered. Tears raced down Liesl's face, which was pretty, despite its primer of makeup.

"Sleeping during the day," Liesl said.

Her voice had deepened since adolescence. She reeked of cigarettes. Beate added standing up to greet her cousin to the list of things she should've done.

Liesl moved to the floor and hugged Beate, which in their prone position felt both labored and intimate. Liesl's face was inches away. Her breasts pressed against Beate's shoulder.

"You're on the floor," Liesl said.

"I don't mind it," Beate answered.

"Your children don't mind it?"

Pieces of Liesl resurfaced—her easy indignation, commands in the guise of suggestion.

The letter to Paul that Beate had been working on lay under her pillow.

"I have an old boyfriend who can get you mattresses," Liesl said.

"You don't have to."

"The American husband knows you're sleeping on the floor?"

"I don't know what he knows," Beate answered.

In the letter, Beate wound around the idea that taking the children had been a mistake. She didn't have Paul's certainty, didn't come up with solutions that made sense to other people. When their son had been born and naming him felt like a test she hadn't studied for, he'd smiled and said, "Michael," as if it were the easiest thing. The letter crinkled under Beate's shoulder. *I am not feeling as I expected to feel here*, it began. *Little problems arise and it's like something is stuck in my throat.* As she lay there, Beate decided to replace that line with the more benign: *Here, it is difficult in ways I hadn't imagined.* Her cousin's chest crept up Beate's shoulder. The towel she used as a curtain flapped in the wind.

"I'm divorced, too," Liesl said. "I'm not saying you failed."

"I'm not divorced," Beate answered, hanging on to the technicality of the papers she hadn't sent back.

"But he's here?" Liesl asked.

Beate answered California. Liesl sat up and attempted some sort of hula.

"I'm just saying you're divorced," Liesl answered. "Like me. Cousins divorced together."

"You'll have to meet my children sometime," Beate said.

"Who do you think let me in?"

They'd opened the door, told Liesl that their mother was asleep, though morning was probably over. The way her children saw her crystallized, though Beate couldn't think how to otherwise proceed. Liesl's nails shone like a new car.

"So you've met them," Beate said.

"Yes. And their German," Liesl answered. Beate waited for a comment about how Michael butchered the umlaut. "They hardly have accents. Let's make coffee."

In the living room, Adela read one of her endless inventory

of books. Michael fiddled with curtains he may have found, or that may have been left by the people who'd lived there before.

"You've met my cousin," Beate said.

"Tante Liesl," Adela answered.

Liesl took a cigarette from her purse, pointing to it with raised eyebrows.

"You may smoke in here," Beate said.

"I was asking if you wanted one," Liesl answered.

Michael moved into their language of shifting eyebrows. Adela pulled a thread from her sweater.

"You do a lot with your face," Liesl said. Smoke from her cigarette snuck toward the window.

"Yes, I'll have one," Beate answered.

Liesl's son arrived with lunch. He was giant. When he spoke, Beate recognized his voice as something she'd heard most mornings through the floorboards.

They moved to the table Michael had procured, though Adela chose the floor. Liesl smoked while the rest of them ate. She talked about how the old folks' home where she worked was filling up now that they were Western and people wanted to use the bedroom they'd "stored Oma in for all the shoes they're going to buy."

"A lot of shoes," Michael said.

"I like your hair," Liesl answered.

He'd buzzed the sides. The top a sea of waves and reconsiderations.

"I'm trying something." He smiled.

"He's always trying something," Adela answered from the floor.

"If there's no struggle, no progress," Beate said.

"Yes," Michael answered. "That."

Beate wanted to be back in her sleeping bag. For day to fast-forward to evening.

"He found clippers on one of his searches," Adela added.

"Searches of what?" Liesl asked.

"He goes into some of the houses here."

"The empty ones," Michael interjected.

"How do you think we got this table?" Adela said. "These plates?"

"We can get you new plates," Liesl added.

"With what money?" Beate asked.

"Wasn't your parents' money returned to you? The money the GDR held after you—what was it—pretended to be someone else and snuck out?"

"There is some money, yes," Beate said.

Paul had recently sent a check, too. Beate thought of ripping it to pieces as she'd seen people do in movies. But each time she'd seen that performance of outrage she thought the same thing: *Take the money, stupid.* The thought of Paul's money left her feeling better, then worse, then tired.

"I thought my father talked to your mother," Beate said.

"My mother thought our phone was tapped," Liesl answered. "But these houses. You just walk in?"

"We need a lot of things," Michael said.

"No, we don't," Adela answered.

"You *are* sleeping on the floor." This came from Liesl.

Heat padded Beate's face. She sat on a chair Michael had found. Drank from a glass that had appeared in their cabinets. *There are no jobs*, her letter went on, though most days she was too disheartened to even look at the listings. The one time she'd called about a job the man who'd answered told her that if there was a job there he wanted to know about it, too, so he could apply.

Liesl thanked Beate for lunch, though Udo brought the food. Beate went to lie down. She wished it were eight hours later so she could wander to the bar, where Willy was always cleaning glasses, where Ernst Träger either answered her questions in detail or ignored her.

Two hours later, Liesl returned with a delivery van in tow. "I have a friend," she said, "who works in furniture."

Deliverymen slid a sofa into the living room. Michael commented on its beigeness. Mattresses came next; their white filled the doorframe like prairie snow.

"What do I owe you?" Beate asked.

"It's my welcome-home gift," Liesl answered. "Welcome home!" she ta-da'd. "Udo. It needs to be a little to the left."

Udo moved the sofa a little to the left. Adela sat on it and started reading.

Beate looked at the room for the first time in days. Over a broken windowpane, someone had taped a square of cardboard. A garish rug sat centered on the floor and a series of mousetraps lined its baseboards. Liesl moved to the door. Without her, they might have been sleeping on the floor forever.

"Why haven't you visited until now?" Beate asked.

Liesl appeared annoyed, appeared also to enjoy her annoyance.

"I only knew you'd returned because of a friend of a friend with a job at the housing department. She'd recognized your name on a folder."

After they'd defected, Beate's and Liesl's families had cut off contact, though she wasn't clear why. Part of Beate had forgotten about Liesl, though as her cousin stood in the living room, Beate couldn't understand how she'd gone on so long without her. Adela thanked Liesl for the furniture. Liesl touched her and Adela didn't even seem to mind. This bothered Beate the most—the easiness Adela suddenly projected. The sofa she curled up on after her residency on the floor.

Liesl announced that they had to go, and hooked arms with Udo. As she watched them walk down the driveway, Beate felt all the loveliness and difficulty of raising children alone. She wanted Liesl back. Wanted her to talk until the boredom of it lulled Beate to sleep, to remember the feel of boredom, its taste. Liesl and Udo climbed into her car. Beate slipped into her room, where a mattress now sat, along with a chair and lamp Michael had left there.

Beate hung out of her window. Michael and Adela talked to Liesl in the driveway.

"Come for dinner sometime," Beate called.

Both of her children found this invitation amusing. At least they were united in feeling for a change.

The next night Beate stayed in. Michael fell asleep before the sun set. Adela came into the kitchen, where Beate was eating toast, and said, "Toast isn't dinner." Later, both children asleep, she cleaned the cushions on the chairs Michael had gotten. As she scrubbed, images of Paul with some mystery woman taunted her. Paul's hand on her arm. His scruff scratching her neck. When the woman asked about his divorce, he'd tell stories about his nervous ex, downplaying his own anger which was toughest for Beate because she couldn't catch its rhythms. There were weeks when he smiled at everything and joked about his clumsy thoughtlessness. Then one morning she'd lean close and he'd say she'd woken him up "with the leaning." She'd be at work and he'd call, insisting she hadn't told him she had a shift. And though she remembered telling him, she apologized. Even when he was terrible, when she felt her own anger well up, her defense turned to a slippery path, Beate stumbling, Paul looking down at her. Perhaps she'd tricked him with pregnancy, as he sometimes suggested, though when she'd said she was open to abortion he'd answered no. Perhaps her shy fear, or the way she opened her eyes too wide when he told her difficult things, made it impossible for Paul to tell her the truth. Perhaps what she thought of as truth was another of her excuses.

A trap snapped, a mouse, newly dead, in its clutches. Beate scrubbed another cushion, sewed up a tear.

When she lay down, her sleeping bag on the mattress felt like a coffin. It began to rain, and Beate opened the window. She leaned forward until rain pummeled the back of her neck. She tiptoed down the stairs and paced the living room as she'd done when she'd tried to soothe her infant children. Michael had once come home terrified when he'd heard something at school about spontaneous combustion. Adela had rattled off reasons he wouldn't explode at the table, or in his room, or while sitting on the toilet. But as Beate paced, his worry felt right. She finally fell asleep when the sun began to rise. And Paul infested her dreams. She woke up not remembering anything in particular but knowing he'd been there.

As the Scribbler sketched Beate's hand on her beer, an old, amused-looking man turned to her and said: "I'm still a handsome one, yes?" and moved his stool closer.

The old man's eyebrows froze halfway up his forehead. Everyone else in the bar stayed quiet.

"You might fancy going to dinner with me," he added.

Beate thought of the car that had chased her there, its wheels on the pavement.

"You're too old for me," she answered. "And you need a haircut."

"Okay, then. Cut my hair."

Rudi laughed, cheeks round with beer. "Shut up, Rudi," the man said. His name was Nils. "Willy, hand me those scissors."

"I never said I'd cut your hair," Beate said.

"Listen to the lady," Willy added.

"I'm asking you," Nils said.

The men looked at her. If she seemed too eager, they might find her dubious. If she said no, they might decide she was too different from them. Beate wanted to keep coming there, to join in their collective remembering. The Scribbler held his beer in midair. The scissors sat on the bar. As Beate picked them up, Nils's grin spread to outlandish proportions.

"Beate," Rudi said. None of them had used her name before.

"Willy," she asked, "don't imagine you have a comb back there?"

He didn't, though an observer offered his. Nils wore a lascivious smirk.

"Remember I'm holding something sharp," Beate said.

"A tool and a weapon," another man added.

Beate started in back. The scissors caught as she worked to close them, and she worried she'd started something she couldn't finish. Beate pulled out a cord of curls. They clumped like damp grass and smelled unclean. On the radio, an old song played about getting love and losing love and the sea. She teased out pieces, sped up until she lopped one too short and chided herself to go slow, which reminded her of a poem she'd read in high school. "Slow," it had warned. "Slow!" it demanded.

Breath whistled in and out of Nils's nose. She didn't want to go to dinner with him, but as hair tickled her hands, the idea of being taken to dinner awakened in her a forgotten hopefulness. The back of his head turned tidy. She moved to the sides, checking for evenness as she'd seen hairdressers do. Nils's forehead was rutted with wrinkles.

"Close your eyes," she said, and moved to the front.

Beate combed hard, a reminder that a haircut didn't make him younger or her interested. He let out an *ooph* as the comb snagged. Dander dotted its tines. Hair once wily fell into place, and Beate warmed with competence. Bottles glowed in the scissors' blades.

"Now you look like the respectable drunk you are," she said.

Nils went to the bar's back mirror and smiled with surprise.

"Just so you know," Beate said, "I'm not cleaning this up."

Nils swept up his hair. Everyone else went back to not talking.

On her next visit, Lars Berger asked if she could cut his, too. Though she was relieved, Beate enacted reluctant surprise. She cut Lars's hair, and as she did, he told her about his daughter who'd moved to the West.

"I hardly hear from her now," he said.

"Too busy being Western," Beate answered. "Going to the cinema five times a day."

He asked about her parents; Beate told him they'd passed. She pressed a clump of hair off his neck with her thumb. "But they were old. When they had me."

"And you had your children young," he answered.

When Mutti had asked Beate why she was keeping the baby who turned out to be Michael, she didn't tell her mother that there was a greed she felt for Paul she'd rarely felt for anything, a greed that left her nodding when he'd said she should keep it, a greed that might have been her youth, mistaking what felt good for a place with sturdy walls and a basement.

"Maybe you and your daughter will be close again," Beate said.

Herr Berger's face told her she was sweet for saying what wasn't true. He bought her a drink. Beate was thinking of heading out when Max Kellner asked shyly if she might cut his as well. She agreed, cutting hair a communion she hadn't expected. Her hands turned wildness to order. She heard them breathing; her fingers lingered on their necks and collars. When she finished, Max slid fifteen marks into her hand.

"Is this my job now?" she joked.

"Aren't you looking for a job?" an old man asked, cranky, then smiling wide in crankiness's reprieve.

Max Kellner touched her shoulder with grandfatherly affection, and Beate felt, for the first time since they'd gotten to Kritzhagen, a relief in having returned. She hoped for more hair to cut but had to content herself with small currents of conversation until Rudi told her he was tired and the two of them walked home. He pointed out buildings, asked if she remembered them. "Maybe," Beate answered. She might remember one day. Might be in the midst of getting on a bus when the landscape in front of her unlocked and she remembered everything.

8

Within days there was a list on the chalkboard at the back of the bar. Its title: *Hair.*

"Look what you got yourself into," Willy said.

Most nights, Beate stayed until after the bar officially closed, cutting as Willy cleaned tables and flipped chairs on top of them. One night she finished with eighty marks and drank too many beers. She walked home alone. Streets she traveled down were a blur. A soreness spread across her neck that she knew would blossom into a headache. In the morning she crept into the kitchen. Michael sat at its table, Adela on a folding chair, reading.

"You're awake," Michael said.

"Is there aspirin?" she asked.

Adela read out loud about Kaiser Wilhelm's secret country getaway with a basement casino.

Beate's tongue was so dry that the aspirin crumbled across it, chalky and bitter and awful. She gulped down an entire glass of water. Michael looked at her with amused concern. He was perhaps growing a goatee.

"She's not awake," Adela said, as if Beate weren't in the room.

Beate walked upstairs, annoyed, though her daughter hadn't been wrong. Only when she got to her sleeping bag, when she lay down and felt the ache from the schnapps Herr Träger kept buying for her, did she count forward from their arrival date and realize that the day before had been Michael's birthday.

Liesl showed up one afternoon with groceries. Also with a woman named Dora who remembered Beate as a child. "Just the same," Dora kept repeating. Beate had no memory of her.

"Remember that poem you loved to recite?"

"Her mother *was* a poet," Liesl said.

"She studied poetry," Beate answered. Liesl's shrug suggested that meant the same thing.

Another morning she called and told Beate she was excited about dinner that night. Beate had been startled when the phone rang. She hadn't realized they'd gotten one and wanted to ask Liesl if she'd been the one who'd had it turned on.

"What dinner?" Beate asked, though she meant to ask what was exciting about this particular one. After Liesl's machine-gun cackle faded, she told Beate about the meal Adela and Udo had been planning for days.

"It was her idea," Liesl said.

"Adela's?"

"I always forget her name."

When Beate asked what the dinner was for, Liesl answered that it was a thank-you. "To me!" she added. "For the sofa and mattresses. When I told the girl I could get you a bigger table, she looked like she would weep."

"She's not really a weeper."

"Delilah," Liesl said.

"Adela," Beate corrected.

And that evening, Udo and Adela brought that new table into the backyard. In the kitchen, they chopped and stirred. "I got those pots," Michael said as he wandered past, as if pots were his singular invention. Beate put on a dress, told herself that this dinner would be exciting. *And now my cousin is here all the time. And her Viking son*, she added to the unfinished tome to her husband. She pictured Paul reading it to some woman. Part of Beate was ashamed, part of her wanted to warn the woman that his certainty would feel like a blessing until it didn't. Liesl arrived with wine. Forks clanked, and birds moved between branches.

"Udo tells me the divorce is official," Liesl said. Lipstick marked the rim of her glass.

"There are papers I have to return," Beate answered.

"I returned them," Adela said. "Was going to the post office anyway."

The papers had been in a folder Beate labeled *Germany*. Her daughter must have been snooping, or trying to find out how to get their phone turned on. Beate wanted to feel relief, to know that relief wouldn't give way to darker feelings of floating in the sea at night. *The earth is the earth is the earth*, her mother used to say. Beate had hated it. Now she nodded. Michael let out a noise that might have been a gag.

"You're choking?" Liesl asked.

"Close call," he answered.

Moths moved close to the candles; flames hissed against their wings. Beate wanted Liesl to stay, wanted to offer her and Udo their spare bedrooms. Her cousin's annoyance, her chuckling criticism preferable to her and Udo leaving in an hour.

Udo and Adela stood. When Liesl asked if they were getting dessert, Udo answered, "Didn't make dessert."

"Where are you going?" Liesl asked, and took a sip of wine.

"Party," Udo answered. "With people from *Gymnasium*."

"Michael should go, too."

"*Realschule*," Adela answered.

“The two of you are being snobs,” Liesl said.

After placement tests, Adela had been assigned to the competitive *Gymnasium*, Michael the lesser *Realschule*. He wore a tie that night she’d never seen. He’d been wearing ties for days.

“Michael, go with them,” Liesl said. “If you stay, you’ll be stuck cleaning up.”

“It’s the *Gymnasium*,” Adela repeated.

“Udo, I did not bring you up to be a snob,” Liesl said. “To say you have to be this way or that.” Liesl moved a knödel to one side of her plate, broccoli to the other. She shoved her knife between, as if it were a wall.

“Of course you should come,” Udo said. “I wasn’t trying to be . . .” and looked as if he were gnawing on a difficult piece of meat. Adela shifted from one foot to the other.

“Let me grab a sweater,” Michael said.

Adela sulked, though until their move she’d savored Michael’s role as her shadow. The children climbed onto their bikes and Beate worried they wouldn’t come back, that Liesl would leave her alone in this place she barely remembered.

“Don’t be out late,” Beate said.

Liesl handed Beate a cigarette. “It’s unbelievable, you being back,” she said.

“I know what you must think of me,” Beate answered. Light stayed bright, though nine had come and gone. She forgot how northern they were, how as a child the sun teased her from sleep. A nearby dog barked in slow succession.

“Because your son finds furniture?” Liesl asked.

“When Gregor left me,” she went on, “I watched television from when it came on until it signed off. While I was staring at the screen, Udo taught himself to cook. Well, to hard-boil eggs. For weeks we ate nothing but.” Liesl mimicked swallowing one egg, then the next. "So, no, I don't give a shit about the furniture."

Liesl used to babysit Beate when her parents went to concerts and lectures and, it turned out, meetings to secure their fake passports. The last time Beate had seen her, Liesl had come by to drop something off. A boy waited for her in a car, its engine complaining.

"But—" Liesl went on.

"I knew there was a but."

"You knew there was a but," Liesl repeated. "The but is that he might get in trouble."

"I know."

"So do something."

"Teach him how to boil eggs?"

Paul had said to Beate once, "You wouldn't need to smoke if you figured the rest of it out," though when she asked what "the rest of it" meant, he shook his head. Paul was a person of surprising gestures: Proposing a day after she told him she was pregnant. Lying in bed next to her and whispering so quietly it took Beate a minute to realize he was leaving her.

"Michael doesn't know how to hard-boil eggs?" Liesl said, and went inside, where she broke out a second bottle of wine. She talked about the one boyfriend she'd had who was surely Stasi, another whose handsomeness felt unbelievable until she realized he was awful in bed. One never talked. Another talked only about his mother. As Liesl poured more wine, Beate toggled between the fear of Liesl leaving and the relief when she did. Liesl moved on to her dad's move to Dresden.

"I mean, who moves to Dresden?" Liesl said.

"What's wrong with Dresden?" Beate asked.

Liesl cackled and filled her glass again, finally saying, "Cousin, you've gotten me drunk." She kissed Beate's cheek and left.

In three minutes Beate left herself. She turned right as she always did, walking until she met the river.

There were eight men in the bar that night, including one she'd never seen before. From the wildness of his hair, she knew what he wanted before he could say so.

Getting home that night, Beate put the money she'd made into an envelope and wrote Michael's name on it. Next to his name, she drew a heart. Inside it she wrote, *I know you've been fourteen for a while*, and slid it under his door.

When she got up in the morning, the envelope's corner still showed under Michael's door. Beate walked into his room. A collage of images culled from magazines sat centered on a wall he'd painted a deep green. The carpet in the middle was subtly patterned. The room had three lamps, each different, though equally ornate. On top of his bed, a headboard of colorful pillows. The room smelled of incense and nicotine. Beate stretched onto his bed, saw the room as he must each morning when he woke up. She turned the lamps on. The cool color on the walls switched to warm.

Next to his bed was an ashtray filled with butts. Beate took it, cleaned it, and put it back. She dropped the envelope onto his bed, which hadn't been slept in the night before. Downstairs, she sat on their new sofa, and watched *Das Erbe der Guldenburgs* as she waited for him to return.

Michael walked in with wet hair, his lashes so dark they looked mascaraed. The T-shirt he had on—celebrating a festival from the recent East—was flatteringly tight. He sat next to her, leaned his head against her shoulder. She wanted to tell him that his room was a wonder, that she'd remembered his birthday, but the cool musk of his hair left her teetering between happy and sad. She could've asked where he'd been, but he might ask her the same thing. And even if he answered, he wouldn't have really told her, just as she couldn't keep him from going into houses and taking things.

"I like to begin the day with a swim," he said, though his day was likely ending.

Beate wanted to thank him for the things he'd found, even more for his bedroom that made it clear he had no intention of leaving this place. There were times when Beate imagined it as temporary. She'd skim the phone book for a real estate office, remembering she wouldn't get much for this house, if anything. But with each chair Michael found, with the walls he decorated just so, he tied himself to this place, brought Beate back to it, too. He lifted his head from her shoulder, told her he had to shower, though when she passed his room five minutes later, Michael was asleep.

They were eating dinner when Adela told Beate that she'd called on her behalf about an opening for a department store clerk. August was winding down and her children had started school. Adela had a geometry textbook open on her knees. "I told them you speak English," she said. "They sounded impressed."

Adela had started to cut out job listings and tape them to the fridge. After one had been there a few days, she'd re-tape it in a higher location.

"You told them you were calling for your mother?" Beate asked.

Michael had cooked. The potatoes he'd overboiled crumbled when Beate's fork pressed against them. One of the children had bought new light bulbs, their dining room as garishly lit as a parking garage. Beate took a bite. Michael chugged his water. Adela pressed her napkin to her mouth before she spoke, a gesture Beate's mother once employed.

"I pretended I was you," Adela answered. "You have an interview in two days."

Michael made a noise. Adela glared at him.

"The faggot can't speak?" he asked.

"That's a terrible word," Adela answered.

Michael listed other terrible words. A fly landed on the potatoes and he shooed it away. "Terrible," Adela muttered.

"You know all about terrible," Michael answered. The fly landed again. Michael smacked it, killed it, reduced it to a smear.

"You, too," she said.

"A sissy and a faggot," he answered. "Though they sort of mean the same thing."

"Those words," Beate said.

"Tell him," Adela answered.

Her daughter stared at her. Beate looked down at the dead fly, at a living one that landed in its stead.

"I'll go," Beate said. "To the interview."

Adela nodded. Michael crossed his arms. Whatever had soured between her children grew more pungent each day.

Beate put on her nicest dress. She tucked combs in her hair, slipped the department store's address into her purse. As she walked, Beate felt the world of the living return to her. A woman leaned down to talk to another woman in her car. A man in painter's overalls sat in a café's window with a coffee cup pinched between his fingers. A mother told her child to stop it, though when the child mimicked her she tried and failed to hold in her amusement. Beate grew relieved at the interview Adela had gotten her, that it was in the afternoon. But as she got closer to the store, she imagined its lights as bright as those in their dining room, the chemical smells of new clothes and furniture. The cliques of coworkers, mornings she'd have to get up early to open the place.

She took a right instead of a left, ending up at the bar. No one but Willy was there, and as Beate moved down its stairs, as its basement coolness hit her bare legs, she realized it wasn't open.

"It's okay that I'm here?" she asked.

Willy's frown softened with recognition. He pulled a chair off a table.

"You basically work here," he answered.

She helped him with the rest of the chairs, checked the bathroom's supply of soap and toilet paper.

At home, Adela asked how the interview went.

"I don't think it's for me," Beate said.

"Confidence," her daughter added, then looked embarrassed. Adela probably said the same thing to herself, standing in the mirror, mouthing that word. Thinking it over and over as she'd walked to her first day at the *Gymnasium*, though perhaps she'd taken her bike. Beate had set an alarm to see them off to school, but it hadn't sounded, or had but she'd been so asleep that she turned it off with no thought other than the sleep she needed to get back to.

In the kitchen's far corner, Michael talked on the phone.

"Confidence," Beate repeated. Embarrassment colonized Adela's face.

"It's important," Beate added, but sounded insincere. She ended with a noncommittal, "We'll see," and climbed up to her bedroom. Her sleeping bag was replaced with sheets and a comforter, a small wall of pillows. Michael must have been here, making her bed partly out of kindness, partly because he'd grown nervous that she'd use that sleeping bag forever.

Beate came downstairs the next afternoon to find Liesl on the sofa. Liesl had made herself a coffee and had, according to the ashtray, smoked three cigarettes since she'd arrived.

"Cousin," Liesl said.

Beate sat next to her. She took a sip of the coffee. Liesl handed her a slip of paper, a name and number on it.

"A doctor," Liesl said.

Beate took another sip.

"It's a lady doctor," Liesl added. "As in a woman. Not a doctor for lady things. I talked to her after Gregor left. Did me some good."

Liesl's handwriting was the same as it had always been. She wore scrubs from her job, several gold necklaces. She noticed Beate looking and touched them.

"I didn't ask to talk to anyone," Beate answered.

A few days before, she'd imagined Liesl moving in. Now Liesl kept a finger on the paper. Beate wanted to be upstairs on her mattress, which had started to smell like the bar.

"Just so you have it," Liesl said. Her eyes stayed on the paper to see what Beate might do with it.

"Well, thank you for stopping by," Beate said. She kissed Liesl's forehead. Felt the crispness from whatever her cousin put in her hair. Liesl showed up every few days. She brought groceries or towels that her job was getting rid of. On the fridge, new job listings Adela had cut out. For one, she'd added an exclamation point. A series of arrows circled another. And the job Adela had set up an interview for, the one Beate had pretended to go to, sat there still. It was circled in marker. Next to its heading, a star. As if Adela knew that her mother hadn't gone to the interview at all.

⟡

After a night when she gave six haircuts, Beate came home to find the front and back doors locked. She stood in their yard and felt a sudden urge to pee. She stepped into the tallest patch of grass, lifted her skirt, and relieved herself, her face flushed from the drinks she'd had and the walk home and the things she'd let slide.

The walk to the bar each night was her one good thing. The looks the men gave her as she came in—happy, also trying to hide that feeling—felt like an answer to the question Adela often asked: Why are we here?

But as she jiggled the locked door, Beate understood that her children wanted to hurt her or show her how she'd hurt them, or remind her that the money she left for them each morning, the house she'd brought them to, were barely a beginning.

Beate tiptoed around their house's perimeter until she found an unlocked window. She hoisted herself onto its frame and ripped her dress on an errant nail, thinking about the letter to Paul she'd written, thrown away, and started again. *My only friends are old men*, the new draft had begun.

She stuttered through the pantry and into the dark kitchen, constructing that letter's end. *I am not ready to be the only parent.* She got to the dining room, negotiating its table and chairs. *I'll use the first checks you sent me to buy the children tickets to California. I'll stay here and become the woman in a large house children tell stories about.* That felt fine, the tall tales of her monstrosity, Beate back in Cologne when frightening the other children was a star on otherwise dim days. She'd planned to finish the letter, but as she walked up the stairs, the need to sleep walloped her.

With each step, Beate was sure she wouldn't make it up the next. She relished the idea of falling asleep here, her children finding her in the same spot the next morning. *There was a letter to your father I meant to finish*, Beate would say, her shoulders shaken awake.

Yes, Adela would answer, reading her mind. *We should stay with him for a while.*

But on her next late-night walk, Beate traveled on a path following the river and spotted a crew of young people in a park. As she got closer, she saw Michael among them. A frightening-looking girl leaned on his shoulder, a scowl on her face even when she laughed. In their faltering movements, Beate understood they were drunk. More people joined. Young women hugged Michael. One tweaked his nipple and he performed outrage, to the delight of his growing audience. Even in his altered state, Beate saw a large joy in Michael and in those who saw him. A young woman hugged Michael hard, lifting him off the ground. And Beate knew she couldn't send him to California. Michael moved into a shimmy. A few friends tried to copy him.

"Michael!" one of them shouted, the most important thing for that girl just then that he notice her.

⟡

Beate couldn't stop laughing. Herr Baum—a towel bibbed across his neck—told a story of a presentation he'd done years before with his shirt poking out of his fly. "People wouldn't look away," he said. "I thought they were in love with me."

The crew at the bar smiled without surprise.

The radio played a soccer match. This player had the ball. Cheers as midfielders moved it forward. The men listened with hands cupped behind their ears. Over a week had passed since the children had locked her out. Beate snipped around Herr Baum's ear. One side of his head was trim, the other wild. As Beate brushed hair from his shoulder, he lifted a hand to stop her.

"She's my mother," a voice said.

Adela stood in the middle of the bar, tall, meatless, face full of angry confusion. Beate started on Herr Baum's other side.

"You're cutting hair?" Adela said.

"How'd you know I was here?" Beate asked.

"Aunt Liesl."

"She's not your aunt."

The men watched Beate's dark-haired mirror. Beate kept cutting.

"Michael was picked up by the police," Adela said.

He and his friends had been drunk. They'd climbed the park's jungle gym and shouted nasty, amusing things. Beate pressed her hands into Herr Baum's shoulders.

"The houses?" she asked. Adela answered graffiti.

"He's in jail?"

"In Liesl's car."

"Where is Liesl's car?"

"Who do you think drove me here?"

Beate kept cutting until Herr Baum's hands stopped the scissors.

"You should go with her," he said.

"You're lopsided," Beate answered, and he looked embarrassed.

Beate moved to put the scissors on the bar, though at the last minute she held on to them. Herr Baum tried to give her ten marks, but she shook her head. Rudi shelled peanuts. Willy's pompadour looked as majestic as ever. She wished she'd told him it was extraordinary.

Outside, she found Liesl in her car. Udo and Michael sat in its backseat. Michael's shirt was missing.

"Where's your shirt?" Beate asked as she climbed into the passenger seat.

Michael shrugged.

"Please tell me you can answer such a simple question."

"I threw up on it," Michael answered. "They had me take it off."

"Who is they?"

"The police," Michael said and crossed his arms. "I was in the back of their car when I puked on my shirt. They made me leave it on the street."

"Graffiti," Liesl said. "What's happening to this family?"

"Nothing is happen—" Beate said.

"The boy almost arrested—" Liesl answered.

"He wasn't arrested."

"Because I know people," Liesl added. "And the place you've been hanging out."

Beate felt a door close, a train leave without her.

"I have a job there."

"Haircuts!" Liesl said.

Liesl used to sleep next to Beate when she babysat, her snoring filling the room. She made Beate perform prank calls and mocked her for what she didn't know.

"A bar like that," Liesl said.

They passed the train station Beate still didn't remember. In the backseat, Michael looked like he wanted to disappear.

"Leonie Felber told me you cut her grandfather's hair," Udo said. "Said it took years off."

They turned, and Liesl's blinker kept ticking.

"Cutting their hair," Liesl scoffed.

"Just old men," Beate answered.

"Why are you cutting hair?" Adela asked.

"A Stasi bar," Liesl went on. "The city's Stasi bar. Tell me you didn't know that."

The same men every night. Awake, as Beate was awake. The window was cool on her forehead. The blinker kept going. Beate couldn't believe Liesl didn't hear it.

"I didn't know that," Beate said.

In the backseat, Adela moved through a slideshow of Paul's sanctimonious expressions. Beate hadn't known. She wanted to say it again, but Adela wouldn't believe her. Or she'd see it as proof of Beate's indifference to anything beyond the perimeter of her own suffering.

Adela's knees pressed into Beate's seat. A small, shining stud glittered in her nose. Beate wondered if it was new, worried it wasn't, that she hadn't properly looked at her daughter in weeks. Adela's knees jabbed again.

"You want to call me an asshole?" Beate asked her.

"Would that make you feel better?" Adela said. Raindrops jeweled the windows.

"I want you to say what you want to say," Beate answered, though her daughter's blame would have at least been a distraction.

Liesl turned on the radio. Madonna went on about praying. Michael had gotten a tape of hers years before and sung at the top of his lungs about all the ways he was a virgin. "Of course you're a virgin," Paul had snapped, and Michael stayed in his room for the rest of the day. Now he'd been picked up by the police. Beate had left Herr Baum lopsided.

"I forgot that Michael's using your old last name," Liesl said.

"That's stupid," Adela answered.

"Better than your *new* last name," Michael said.

"What's that?" Udo asked. His arm hung out the window. Beate imagined his knuckles on the pavement.

"Goebbels."

Adela screamed. Liesl stopped the car. When it was clear Adela was through, Liesl started driving again. Beate asked why the police had called Liesl.

"I told them to," Adela answered. "They called our house first."

Liesl switched to the topic of new positions at the *Pflegeheim* where she worked. Told them about a supervisor she'd bring Beate to meet in the morning. "Working where I work," Liesl said.

"I thought jobs were unicorns here," Beate answered.

Liesl put a finger on her forehead, unicorn-style.

Their house seemed even larger spotlighted in Liesl's headlights. Michael slunk out, his back sheaved in muscle. He moved callously, his hallmarks of remorse and humiliation missing.

"Michael," Beate said. He kept walking.

"Stop," she said, and grabbed his wrist.

Michael pulled free, his expression so un-Michael-like, she grabbed for him again. He squinted in the headlights. He pulled away with so much force her nails left scratches on his hand.

"When I say stop," she said.

Michael held his chest high with a pride she'd always wanted him to feel. But the police had taken him. He'd thrown up in their car. She pictured him in the cruiser, cradling sick in his shirt as if it were a kitten.

"We'll talk in the morning," Beate said.

Adela, in her room, had turned on the stereo Udo had gotten

for her. The N-word bounded from under her door, though Beate had learned that this word was unspeakable, as Hitler had been when she was a child. Beate leaned up the stairs to tell Adela it was late. But on one side of their house was rubble, the other an old man without electricity, who didn't seem concerned about getting it back.

"Good night," Beate said to no one.

Liesl picked Beate up early. In the *Pflegeheim*'s parking lot, she scuffed out her cigarette, checked her makeup in a mirror.

"I don't deserve you," Beate said. Maybe Liesl had told the police that Michael had just moved here. That his mother was unwell. That there was a doctor she would call.

"Tra-la-la," Liesl answered.

Beate waited in a small office. A woman entered wearing an elaborately knotted scarf. She always wore scarves, according to Liesl, who said, "She can be a bitch, too."

"Beate Sullivan," the woman said.

"Haas," Beate answered, deciding at that moment to follow Michael's lead.

"I'm sorry?"

"*I'm* sorry," Beate answered.

"We're both sorry." They smiled.

"I'm recently divorced. I don't know how much Liesl told you."

"Your cousin is something," the woman answered. Beate gave her a circumspect smile. "So you're Beate Haas, then."

As Beate confirmed this, the woman's face changed. "Beate Haas who lived on Parkstraße?"

"I live there now," Beate said. "Again."

"It's Karin Brandt!" the woman said.

Her hug was strong. Beate leaned into it with a relief she hadn't expected. She closed her eyes to keep from crying at the messes she made and would keep making. Karin's shoulder was bony. She wore strong perfume. Beate had no idea who she was.

"You haven't changed!" Karin said, and told her how she'd come to school one morning and Beate wasn't there. She'd thought nothing of it until a few days later when all signs of her had been removed from the classroom. "We even went to your house. Me and Dagmar and Gerhild." Beate remembered none of those names. She thought of the American show *Candid Camera* that her mother had loved, this woman who taught political poetry laughing at sight gags and confounded expressions.

"And you're divorced," Karin said, and Beate watched her hastily borne marriage disintegrate, along with the youth she and Paul had leaned too heavily on. Paul supervised a team that mowed lawns, according to his one letter Beate read, with a truck to manage and mowers to load it with.

Karin told Beate that a former classmate was pregnant, that Stefan Kuhn, whom Beate was relieved to remember, had turned into a wild homosexual and gotten sick and died before his twenty-fifth birthday. Beate remembered Stefan and a handful of girls in fierce jump-rope competitions. Stefan bounced with glued-kneed precision; the girls jumped and held down their skirts at the same time.

"I can't believe you're back," Karin said, and clasped her hands.

Beate gave in to this reunion's excitement.

A few leaves on the tree outside had started to yellow. They'd only been in Kritzhagen a few months, though it felt endless. As Karin smiled and said that, barring anything unexpected, the job was hers, she walked Beate into the lobby, telling her that this building had once been a school. Beate pretended a job would fix things.

"We still find old textbooks as walls are torn down," Karin said.

"My daughter would love that."

"You have a daughter," Karin answered, with a smile that made it clear she didn't have one, or if she did, the girl was nothing like Adela. Karin touched Beate's arm. Beate decided to remember her, even if it wasn't true.

"I got a job," Beate said as she walked in the front door. Adela sat on the sofa, underlining fiercely. Michael was curled into a wingback. Both her children wore Walkmans. Beate thought to lie down, but made coffee instead. A few minutes later, Michael appeared in the kitchen, his headphones a necklace. Through them, a female singer oohed.

"Mutti," he said. "You know I'd be happy to have you cut my hair sometime."

Beate touched the side of his head, which he'd recently buzzed short. Tried moving her fingers through the top, which was long and pasted together with some sort of product.

"You do have a lot of hair," she answered.

"I do," Michael said. "And it might need cutting."

With almost no time passing, he'd forgiven her for going out each night. For the birthday she'd forgotten, the gift she'd been too embarrassed to give him in person. She was relieved that he'd returned to her; also wished he'd stayed angry until she made it her work to apologize. He was too easy, she thought. He moved with a new confidence that terrified her. "Confidence," Adela had said a week before, hoping that hearing the word would lead her to feel the feeling.

Beate poured herself a coffee, one for Michael, too. Cats on the garden wall hissed at one another. Michael and Beate looked outside where their apples were red and ready to pick. Once in in a while, one of them took a sip, or shifted in their seat, both of them knowing that her cutting his hair wasn't what either of them wanted.

1969

9 Though the heart attack was minor, Vati didn't seem relieved. He lay in a Cologne hospital and grumbled at the ceiling. When a doctor told him he was lucky, Vati answered that only idiots fell for luck and asked about the man's credentials. Outside, wet winter trees swayed. Beate buttoned up the cardigan she'd thrown on in the middle of the night when her father had come to her door and whispered, "I think I might be dying." In the cab to the hospital, he'd pointed to an upcoming block. "See that?" he asked. "I'll be dead by then."

But he'd lived.

Beate sat at his bedside, flipping through a magazine. A nurse walked in wearing squeaking shoes.

"Feeling better?" she asked.

"Better than what?" Vati answered, and bit his bottom lip.

Beate's blushing heated her ears.

"Your grandfather is lively," the nurse said later, as Vati took an openmouthed nap.

"My father."

"Oh," the nurse answered. "And where's your mother?"

"Room 272." The nurse pulled the blanket toward Vati's chin. In sleep, his face turned mean. "She had an operation three days before."

"So both of your parents?"

"Two parents in one hospital," Beate said. "Like a word problem." She had to dig a finger into her thigh to keep from laughing. She wore a dress she'd sewn, but hadn't had time for socks. Her feet stuck to the insides of her loafers.

Toward the end of their first year in Cologne, Mutti started to experience pain that left her leaning against park benches and sucking down handfuls of antacids. Finally—when Vati was at work, Beate at school—a neighbor found her lying on their building's stairs and took her to the hospital, where they discovered she needed a radical hysterectomy. "Radical," Beate had murmured until her father told her she was too old to talk to herself, though he did it all the time. Two nights later it was his turn. He woke Beate in the middle of the night: "My heart," he said, hair weedy and wild. "It's going crazy."

Beate spent half the day with her father. She switched to her mother in the afternoon. Later, a nurse showed her an empty room she could sleep in. Its window looked onto an air shaft. A pole to hold an intravenous drip sat next to the bed. Beate slept in bursts. She woke up sure it was morning, though the clock climbed toward midnight. The air shaft outside gave off a column of steam.

The next morning a different nurse woke her. "Why are you in street clothes?" she asked. "Where's your ID bracelet? How am I to know what's wrong with you?" She left a hospital gown, and Beate thought to play along, to pretend she had one of the sicknesses she'd learned about in biology—cystic fibrosis or color blindness. But she slipped down a back staircase instead, into an employee parking lot. She passed a clutch of cafeteria workers in hairnets. They smoked and drank coffees. It was six in the morning.

⟡

She forged a note from Vati explaining her absence: *My wife and I have been hospitalized for different reasons.*

"Differently sick?" the secretary at school asked.

"Heart problems and lady problems," Beate answered.

The woman's face tightened. She touched her nose with a pencil's eraser. When she asked whom Beate was staying with, she answered, "A friend in my building."

"What's your friend's name?"

"Dagmar von Grimmelshausen."

The secretary's eyebrows lifted.

"A friend but grown up," Beate said, and pictured the neighbor who'd brought Mutti to the hospital, a war widow whose adult son lived in England. Her apartment was a shrine to this boy, now man. His bedroom intact; his most recent correspondences patchworked her table.

The secretary asked her to bring the neighbor's phone number the next day, though Beate could sense that this woman wanted to abdicate responsibility. She went to class and even raised her hand in geometry, which she'd studied in the East already. "The first is scalene, the second congruent," she said. Beate grew excited to go home that night alone.

After visiting each parent in the hospital, both of them the color of boiled fish, Beate got to their apartment and closed the curtains. She stood in front of the bathroom mirror only in underpants. Her breasts, recent arrivals, were small. She put her hands over them and squeezed and thought about the substitute teacher they'd had when Frau Bern had been floored by the flu. At certain moments he'd been trembling and nervous. In others he seemed to see school as Beate did, as both stupid and necessary. He also had lovely forearms. She pinched. The pink of her nipples shifted to red. She stopped and moved through the house mostly naked, eating a hunk of cheese. When it was time to sleep and she was awake, Beate drank wine.

The next night she ate bread and watched television and drank more wine. The phone rang. Beate didn't answer. When it rang again, she picked up. It was Vati.

"Where were you?" he asked.

"The bathroom," she lied.

"I had a dream that I was in a basement," he said.

He breathed as if he'd climbed several flights of stairs.

"Was it frightening?" she asked.

"I don't know," he said. "I just woke up and remember being in a basement. Not what it felt like, or why I was there. If I could get out or had to stay in."

Beate imagined the basement's damp walls, her father a flailing bug on its floor. Vati so convinced it'd been real that he woke up and called her. Two nights before, he'd been convinced of his death. Each block he got to, he said, "Dead at the next one."

"I'm not sleepy," Beate said. "You can call whenever."

She moved to the bathroom mirror and pulled down her underwear. Through the neighboring wall, Frau Kammer talked to her dog, an animal always dressed up in different bibs and collars.

⟡

Two nights later, when Beate ran out of wine, she stopped a young man in the building who was sometimes pleasant to her. They stood in the stairwell. She asked him to buy her a bottle. He agreed without hesitation and she worried that he'd want to come in when he delivered it. But when he appeared, he showed no interest in coming inside and she turned disappointed, wondering if her worry had been a wish. He walked down the hall, his hair and turtleneck the same color.

On the fifth night she arrived home late. Mutti had kept her for longer than usual. She was filled with questions about the weather and the state of the apartment. *People keep talking of snow, but it stays raining. The apartment looks as you left it.* Machines beeped. Mutti's large breasts drooped under her hospital gown. "I'm doing well in math," Beate said, though there was no evidence that she was doing anything other than fine. Mutti touched her hand. Beate turned sad, though she couldn't think why. Each night she'd gotten naked and drunk wine and explored drawers. She'd found their fake passports under Mutti's stockings. Sitting next to her mother, whose chin and neck turned to a single entity, the freedom she'd relished for the last few nights suddenly seemed dangerous. As she let Mutti hold her hand, she imagined what might have happened had the young man wanted to come in, Beate so unsure of herself that she would have said yes without knowing if yes was what she meant. And if the young man had wanted to pinch her breasts as she had the night before, she couldn't imagine how she would have reacted. Knowing what she wanted turned as sinister as the freedom she had, the notes she'd forged, and the wine she'd drunk, Beate lying to everyone, and no one bothering to check if her stories were true. Her feet ached in her shoes. That ache moved to her stomach, where her heart also seemed to live. Everything in her came together as water wended toward a drain.

Beate's father returned home three days later and laid claim to the sofa. From across the room, it looked as if he had no eyelashes.

"Who was it you stayed with?" her father asked.

"A friend," Beate answered.

"I want to call her family," he went on. "To thank them."

Beate had at the ready the name of a girl from school who smelled of old bread. She'd bribe her with kindness. Or she'd give Vati the wrong number.

"I already did," Beate answered. He seemed satisfied, and she made him tea. He didn't bring up the fact that he'd called the apartment and she'd answered. Made no mention of the basement dream, the death he'd predicted as they passed the movie theater, then a stationery store. If he pressed her, she'd tell him the truth, that she'd wanted to stay in their apartment. Also that, after nights when it felt good, she turned frightened that she could forge notes and drink too much wine with no one telling her to stop. The kettle boiled. Her father turned on the radio and didn't bring up her friend again.

Mutti soon joined their apartment's infirmary. She walked slowly, spent each day in her bathrobe. Their illness disgusted Beate, though she knew this disgust was unkind. She wandered after school or napped in far corners of the library and dreaded the moment when she opened the door and her parents looked up from their spot on the sofa with expressions of curious fear.

⟡

When her parents had fallen asleep, Beate knocked on the young man's door. He answered fast. Something with drums spun on his record player.

"You're needing more wine?" he asked.

"Hello," she answered, unsure of why she'd come. Her parents had breathed loudly in their sleep, not snoring exactly, but one gasp followed by another.

"Because it feels strange to buy wine for children," he added.

"I'm fifteen," she said, though her thirteenth birthday was a month away.

One of his eyes drifted in a different direction. Patches of stubble spread across the man's jaw, though his cheeks were girlish. His fingers on the doorknob could move to her face, her belt's shining buckle. A rivet of crackling sounded between one song and another.

"I just wanted to thank you," Beate said. "I don't think I thanked you then. It was something I'd needed."

He nodded and said he was heading out.

"It's late," she said.

"I'm not a schoolboy," he answered.

Beate waited until his footsteps echoed on the stairs before following him. She kept her distance through their suburban neighborhood. They passed a restaurant closing up, a jewelry store with an obese cat in its window. The young man moved with stiff-shouldered purpose. His steps kept time, as if following the drums of a song.

They came to a park girls in school talked about. Homos supposedly met there, did this and that together behind trees. Her neighbor moved into the park. Beate followed. His loud shoes quieted. She slipped past trees, hoping to see him and some other man engaged in something she could only partly imagine. She sat on a dark bench but heard nothing but wind, the gossipy back-and-forth of branches. A different man moved through a streetlamp's puddle. He was handsome. His shirt's top buttons were open, though it was cold out. There was something magic in his exposed throat, his perfect sphere of hair. He moved into the dark and closer to the bench she sat on, slowing just in front of it. She could feel his lean, smell his cologne.

"Oh," he said, as Beate came into focus. "Oh," he repeated. "You shouldn't be here."

"I can be where I want," Beate answered, surprised by her audacity.

"Yes," he said. "But it's not safe."

She'd been by herself for days. Gotten up on time each morning and gotten herself wine. Now she sat in a park where men did things to one another, probably the safest place in the world for her. Her neighbor emerged from under a distant streetlamp, not handsome like the man in front of her. His mouth was the wrong shape, his eyes too close and small. She felt the same ache she'd had at the hospital when Mutti held her hand.

"Not safe," the man repeated.

"You're waiting for him," she answered, and eyed her neighbor.

"*Am* I?" the man asked.

"Him or me," Beate said. The handsome man stepped toward her neighbor, a repayment for the wine. Beate stayed sitting in the dark. She wished she could tell her neighbor that she'd followed him, that she'd gone into that park and hadn't felt afraid, that this beautiful man had only noticed him at her suggestion. Beate grew excited to see her neighbor in the hall again. She might ask about the record he always listened to. And he'd look at his hands—hands that had touched the handsome man's face and tight jeans—before he invited her inside to listen to it.

Beate slipped into the apartment. Vati lay awake on the sofa.

"Your heart?" she asked.

"I was going to the bathroom," he answered. "And needed a break."

"Breaks are good," Beate said. "I just needed to get some air."

"*Lufthunger*," Vati answered.

"I know it's late."

"Beate."

"I know you think it's a bad idea."

"Beate Sigrid," her father said.

She waited for him to list dangers she hadn't considered. Vati's pajama pants lifted to his albino knees.

"I need help standing up," her father answered.

Beate helped him, felt the bones in his hand against hers.

The next morning, Beate overslept. And as she rushed out of the apartment—brow sweaty, a stale roll in her mouth—Beate passed the neighbor in the hall. He had on the same outfit from the night before. Forgetting that she was late, Beate slowed down and smiled. She even tried to lift her eyebrows as she'd imagined her neighbor and the handsome man had, to show each other that they were interested. To her shifting eyebrows, Beate added a nod. Her neighbor walked past her without saying good morning.

1992

10

For a year and a half, Kritzhagen had been a place where riding bikes at night was nothing, school benign apart from its regular adolescent theatrics. Then Markus Bergmann shaved his head, and people looked at him with embarrassed fear. Michael—always on the lookout for new ways to malign his hair—noticed it. Beate, too. Coming back from late shifts, she saw neo-Nazis clustered on corners, streetlamps shining across their razor-burned scalps. Watched them skulk off the bus to shout out foul nonsense or unfurl steaming arcs of piss onto the sidewalk. Then one night they went for Beate.

She was on the bus, reading a magazine Frau Liebling had given her. Frau Liebling was one of Beate's favorite residents. She told her dirty jokes and flagged articles she thought Beate would like. This one profiled a fashion designer whose dresses looked like feed bags, a reminder of the things she'd sewn as a child. Beate was trying to remember what happened to those dresses when two skinheads slipped onto the bus and sat behind her. Passengers stared into their laps or out windows.

"You a nurse, nursie?" the closer of the two asked. He fingered a sleeve of her scrubs.

"I work at a nursing home," Beate answered.

"An ass-wiper, then," he said. His friend grinned. Beate imagined Michael at their mercy. The young man let go of her sleeve.

The bus turned toward the university and she saw them shifting, hoped they were leaving, and leaving her alone. They only rearranged themselves. Beate wanted to cry for the stupid hope she'd grabbed on to. The bus pulled to a fast stop, passengers swaying with the helpless unison of seaweed.

"You wipe any asses today, ass-wiper?" the first asked.

"Can you smell it on your fingers?" the other added.

Beate wanted to be home, to see that Michael was there, too.

At Lindenpark one person got off, three entered. It was nearing midnight. A man wore a uniform that implied something with cleaning. A woman in a flowered jacket sat at the front. She spoke to the driver, who nodded to her via the rearview mirror.

Just as Beate's fear reached a manageable level, one of the neos squeezed her knee. She tried to ignore it, but his hand lifted higher.

"Excuse me," Beate said.

Others on the bus looked back, then away. She felt shamed and angry, ready to yell at her fellow passengers until they did something. Instead she stood.

"This is my stop," Beate lied.

The neo's arm blocked her for a moment before he let her pass. As she walked toward the back door, they stood. She could smell their sour denim, the mints they sucked on. The doors exhaled open and Beate stepped outside. The neos followed her.

She looked for a rock she might hurl. Across the street was an apartment building. Dark windows checkered its façade, like the view from the place in Cologne where she'd once stayed.

Beate wondered if anyone had thought of Frau Eggers in years, wondered, too, if she'd have the luxury of turning these young men into a story. She touched the bus's brightly painted side, walked forward as the back door closed. There wasn't a rock in sight, only broken branches and some crows cawing at one another. Beate dumb and done for, thinking of the shame the other passengers would feel when they heard on the news what had happened to her. This led her, somehow, to Paul, who was about to get remarried, which allowed her to again blame him for everything. One of the young men coughed. She thought of his wet, red throat. They whispered, and Beate conjured their fusty breath. Twigs snapped under their boots; Beate's shoulders jerked toward her ears. The bus half-stepped back before lurching ahead and Beate banged on its front door. It opened and she climbed back on. Passengers looked out windows. She felt indignant until she realized she would have done the same thing.

Getting home, she found Udo reading at the kitchen table.

"What are you reading?" she asked.

"Greek myths," he answered.

Cleaned dishes dried on the counter. A barely opened window let in a breeze. Her daughter doted on Udo, though Beate didn't understand why.

"I have a favor to ask you," she said, and he nodded. "I need you to pick me up from work tomorrow night. It's late."

Udo nodded again.

"Do you know anything about Heracles?" he asked.

"I think he rearranged a river," Beate answered. "He was good, too, until he was really bad."

"What's really bad?"

"I think he killed his family."

The next night, Udo waited for Beate outside of the *Pflegeheim*. They rode the bus home together, which was empty.

⟡

The vacant lot, according to Udo, had once housed a fancy apartment building. But by the time he'd gotten to know it, its windows were boarded up. Whole shoulders of cornice fell off. A legend was that a hunk of it had dropped onto an old woman's head so that, when she came to, she remembered only children's songs and slang for bathroom activities.

"That place," Udo had told Adela. "Beautiful and scary all at once."

"There must be a German word for that," Adela answered, listing their favorite compound nouns—*Weltschmerz* and *Schattenparker. Kummerspeck.* Udo smiled. "Both beautiful and scary," he said, and came up with a new word for them to use.

When he was a child, Udo continued, the building burned down. People assumed the fire had been the government's doing, that they'd hated how Western it looked, or had thrown a dissident inside whom they were eager to see disappear. Crabgrass replaced rooms. Rubble was pushed to the sides or carted away.

The lot that remained was open on three sides. Until a few weeks before, boys had played soccer there. Standing in front of it now, Adela couldn't picture those boys, couldn't imagine how this half a block had once been a building that Udo said was "ten stories tall, or what felt like ten stories." All she could consider was the immigrants it suddenly housed, ones who'd poured into their city now that East was West and wedded to the West's rules. With Eastern Europe crumbling, refugees arrived in Kritzhagen. Also Adela's new friend Miri, with whom she could only communicate via gestures and lifted eyebrows.

Adela had been biking past the lot a week before when an immigrant somewhere close to her age was suddenly in front of her, large-toothed and Cleopatra-eyed. She wore blindingly white sneakers. "Knock, knock," the girl said, in English. Her voice was deep, and Adela wondered if she wasn't a teenager, but a small woman. She stared at Adela, who for a moment got stuck on things Liesl had said about the immigrants "stealing from anyone they could bamboozle." Shrugging off Liesl's voice, Adela pulled over.

"Who's there?" she asked.

"Knock, knock," the girl repeated, again until the *k* and *n* came apart. "Ka-nock," the girl said. "Ka-nock."

When Adela asked if she spoke English, the girl laughed. Her laugh was throaty and low, her teeth the motley yellow of a corncob.

Behind her, wind rippled across the dozens of tents fashioned from sheets and tarps. Smells of cooking and gasoline vied for attention.

"Are you hungry?" Adela asked.

"Hungry?" the girl mimicked. Her neck was thin, her jaw hard-carved. Adela fished in her bag for the apple she often kept there, but found nothing.

"Stay," Adela said, in German and English. The girl suddenly looked afraid. Adela smiled and the girl smiled back. "Stay," Adela singsonged.

Sweat splintered across her hairline as she biked the six blocks home. In the kitchen, she found bread and cheese and made a sandwich. That felt inadequate, so she slapped together more. Adela wrapped the sandwiches up, slid them into her rucksack, and biked back as fast as she'd traveled home. The girl sat on a corner of the sidewalk, retying her shoes.

"Knock, knock," Adela said, and felt stupid. She took a sandwich from her bag and handed it to the girl, who pulled its foil back with the prurient self-consciousness of a striptease. The girl, perhaps small woman, took a bite, then another, the last one still balled up on her tongue.

Adela had recently read about these immigrants in the paper. With communism's collapse in the Balkans, war and ethnic cleansing swept in. So people left, Germany or Austria their sudden promised land. They arrived in rust-ringed cars, roofs sagging with mattresses and other belongings. Kritzhagen's unwanted apartments turned stuffed. Some immigrants found empty houses, too, and Michael hummed a pop song about gypsies whenever Adela brought them up. Now they resorted to camping in this empty lot, using duct tape to repair holes in their makeshift tents.

Adela showed the girl her bag crowded with sandwiches. The girl clicked her tongue and put the rucksack onto her shoulders. When she moved into the maze of tents, Adela followed.

The path underfoot was a ribbon of mud. Small fires gave the place a cloudy feeling, though the sun was still out. Voices in tents rose in raspy exasperation. The girl stopped at a tent, took out two sandwiches, and handed them to the people inside. They stared. The girl smiled and talked. And though it was a foreign language, Adela understood that she was offering words of encouragement. The people accepted the sandwiches.

As they moved to the next tent, the girl took Adela's hand. In school, Adela grew uneasy when one girl sat on another's lap, or played with someone's hair. But this girl kept Adela's hand in her own and it felt natural and kind. They arrived at another tent, handing people sandwiches before they could say yes or no.

When there were no more left, the girl returned the rucksack and hugged Adela. She smelled of the harsh soap found in public restrooms. Adela leaned into the hug, felt the girl's nubby shoulder.

"I'll see you soon," Adela said.

The girl mimicked her. Then, pointing to herself, she said, "Miri."

"Miri," Adela repeated, hoping it was her name.

Adela introduced herself. "Dela," the girl echoed.

Adela rang the bell of her bike as she pedaled away.

At home, she found the mess she'd left in the kitchen. Michael walked into the room, glanced at it, and said, "Look what the boys did," then did a dance with his fingers.

Later that night, she and Udo studying, as they often did, Adela told him about Miri.

"You went into that camp?" he asked.

"Just some tents," Adela answered. She pointed to a function she'd completed for trigonometry. Udo nodded that she'd gotten it right.

"The thing is," Udo said, then stopped. He moved his mouth as if chewing. Looked for his pencil, which sat perched behind his ear.

"What's the thing?" Adela asked.

"You don't even know this girl."

It felt strange that Udo didn't understand her, when he often knew what Adela was thinking before she said it. She said she was tired. Udo clomped off to his room, which was now next to hers. Lying on her bed, smelling the cigarette he lit, Adela imagined the ground Miri slept on, the rain outside that probably dampened everything she owned.

Most mornings now, Adela stopped by the camp. She got up early to make sandwiches, carrying them on her bike along with her books and binders. She stood at the camp's edge until Miri appeared and said something in whatever her language was.

After the sandwiches were doled out, Adela got coffees that they drank sitting on the lip of the sidewalk. One morning as they sipped—Miri having communicated through a series of shrugs and grimaces that hers needed more sugar—a trio of skinheads passed by. Though Adela had seen them around the city before, with the arrival of the immigrants, their presence grew to an infestation. The three men leaned against a tree just across from them, as if by happenstance. One of them began to climb it and Adela realized that they were perhaps younger than her, though this didn't provide any comfort.

"You need something?" Adela asked, standing up.

"You're German?" one of them asked back, and made a sucking sound.

Adela battered them with American curses. The skinheads looked at one another with nervous surprise. One of them stepped closer, but Adela said, "Don't even talk to me with that shit-licking mouth." He tried talking even so. "I'm not fucking with you, douchebags," Adela interrupted, flinging out filth until they left.

"Sheet-licking," Miri said, mimicking things about fucks and scumbags. Then, looking Adela in the eye, as was her custom, Miri put a hand on Adela's forearm and said, in English both hesitant and clear, "You are the good." Adela felt close to crying, though she hated crying. Michael once told her she acted as if it were "puking with your eyes." Miri squeezed Adela's forearm, her smile wide and yellow.

"I'm late for school," Adela said, though she biked to the sea instead and later showed up halfway through physics, where her classmates were constructing pulleys and levers.

At home that afternoon, when Udo asked where she'd been that morning, Adela answered that she'd had to meet with a teacher.

"Nerd." Udo smiled, the guilt of that lie leaning on Adela's chest.

"At least I'm not a fucker," Adela answered, and his smile grew, winding back to the bike ride they'd gone on months before after Liesl announced the one-two punch of pregnancy and marriage. They'd biked out of Kritzhagen and onto tiny, pin-straight roads. After pedaling for close to an hour, they'd taken a break. In a nearby field, cows chewed winter grass, their tails as steady as metronomes. Adela asked if he was upset. "I don't know," Udo answered. Then he rested his head on her lap and grinned. Something in that grin—perhaps its rarity—was beautiful.

"I don't want to live with them," Udo had said. "Liesl and Heinz and the new brother or sister."

"You won't live with them, then," Adela answered. As she looked at his crooked, relieved expression, Udo moving in with her family became the logical next step.

Adela and Udo had private jokes about their teachers. A whole lexicon of expressions when Michael started in on a monologue about Tobias's witticisms or fashion sense. A few weeks after Liesl and Heinz had gotten engaged came Christmas. With Mutti working over on Christmas Eve, Michael out for the evening, Adela and Udo made a roast and exchanged presents and decorated the tree. Michael meandered in after midnight. He asked about their evening. Udo talked of watching a concert on TV, though they hadn't watched television. This trickery felt as decadent as the meal they'd shared, and Adela wondered if this was a precursor to love, doing the math about the distance of their actual relation.

"I'm exhausted," Michael said.

"You're drunk," Udo answered.

"Not mutually exclusive."

Michael ascended the stairs with balletic ease. He came home several nights a week with red eyes, but moved down the hall following the one, two, three of a waltz.

"We didn't watch television," Adela said. Udo turned the television on, smiled, and pulled on her toes.

Dad called for Christmas the next day and talked of a barbecue he was going to. "With Maria," he added. "A barbecue at her family's. Come this summer, they'll be my family, too. Though I'm telling only you right now."

Adela's stomach fell. She wore thick socks, though her feet stayed frozen. Dad had mentioned his friend Maria in a few letters. Once, as Adela read one aloud, Michael interrupted and said, "Bet you the two of them are fucking," then walked out of the room.

Later that Christmas day, Adela told Udo the news her father had broken to her that morning. "Getting married just a few weeks after Liesl," Adela said.

Udo slipped one of her ears between his fingers.

"That's my ear," she said.

"That's *my* ear," he answered. Next came his grin, carrying the sweetness of a child just up from a nap. An expression he'd kept to himself until she'd shown up, just as he told only her the things he was frightened of, what he hoped for. Downstairs, Mutti blasted Christmas music. Smells of cooking rose to the second floor. Adela felt Udo's fingers on her ear even after he'd let go.

The day after Adela cursed out those skinheads, her teacher—young and drunk for meaningful experiences—organized a debate about the refugees. Adela spoke first. She'd read tremendous amounts in preparation, citing the Spanish Civil War and the Fascist rise to power in an airtight appeal. As she talked, she thought of Miri and the sandwiches, Miri wearing three sweaters at once, Miri calling her "the good." Then Gerd Mögen chimed in. He stood, though that wasn't the procedure. "Fräulein Sullivan knows a good bit of history," he began, wild with eye contact. "Especially for an American." Classmates giggled. "But she neglected to talk about context." She tried to appear calm as Gerd talked about fleeing for safety versus "greedy relocation," which, in her unasked-for rebuttal, Adela argued made no sense. A later speaker devolved into complaints about the Poles who lived down the street from her, who "never seem to do anything."

Leaving school at the end of the day, Adela found Udo outside.

"I waited for you this morning," he said.

She thought to lie again, but didn't want to. "I was helping that girl," Adela answered. "Miri."

Udo stared at his bike's handlebars.

"Your new best friend," he said.

"I don't even know what she says to me."

It was Udo who was Adela's best friend, the person who listened to her angry worries about Michael and the German Lady, who stayed up with her to study for tests and left her in hysterics with his impression of their physical education teacher. But as she talked about Miri, he wore a look of barely concealed impatience. When she told him that people in the camp had begun to recognize her, he picked at a hangnail.

"Come," Adela said. She put a hand on his forearm, though it felt different than Miri's in both size and subtext. They hopped onto their bikes. Udo pedaled next to her without asking where she was taking him.

They arrived at the camp. Miri quickly appeared. She saw Udo and turned nervous. Adela smiled, took Udo's hand, and said, "My cousin."

Udo offered her a handshake. Miri high-fived him instead. She puffed up her chest. Moved her legs apart and plodded down the sidewalk, arms in front of her like Frankenstein's monster. Udo stared at the ground. Miri kept up with her impression of him.

"That's not nice," Adela said. "Miri."

"Dela!" the girl answered. She covered her mouth as she tried and failed to get ahold of herself.

Desperate to get out of there, to also pretend she'd had a reason to come in the first place, Adela pulled an apple from her bag, handed it to Miri, and climbed onto her bike. Miri stuck the apple into her mouth, roasted-pig-style, and kept up with her Udo walk and posture.

At home, Udo went into his room. He skipped dinner. When Adela passed his door, she heard music and smelled cigarettes and decided against knocking. It was late that night when he emerged. He asked her for help going over the Peloponnesian War. Relief left Adela ready to cry for the second time in as many days. She wondered what was wrong with her.

Adela quizzed him on the Peace of Nicias. Udo answered with information about alliances strained and shifting. He brought out a bag of caramels. From time to time, he handed her one.

Adela was in the middle of a question when Udo interrupted and said, "I didn't realize she was our age. The way you described her, I've always imagined a little girl."

⟡

Just after New Year's, Paul had called Beate to tell her he was getting married again. The night after that call, Michael and Adela watched her.

"There's a movie on television," Michael said.

"An article you might like," Adela added.

A winter rainstorm battered their windows.

It felt good to be watched, worried about. As Beate skimmed the article, as she watched the movie about a middle-aged lady, guileless with hope, Michael stared at his sister, who said, "Mutti, that article, yes?"

"Yes," Beate answered. The possibility of her unraveling had reunited her children. She was filled with a fierce love for them, though sometimes she didn't know what to talk to them about. "Quite an article," she said.

As she went back to the movie, keeping herself together became a bet Beate was bent on winning. She laughed at a silly scene. Squeezed her children's shoulders when she went up to bed. But the next day, as Beate painted Frau Garber's toenails, she felt woozy. She went to the bathroom to kneel in front of its toilet. Nothing came. After her shift, she waited for the bus. Liesl pulled up and rolled down her window.

"I thought you'd quit," Beate said.

A week before, Liesl had given notice at the *Pflegeheim*, citing her pregnancy, also her upcoming marriage to their city's most prosperous electrician.

"I'm here to give you a ride," Liesl answered.

"Udo told you?"

"He told me enough," Liesl said, and rested her hand on top of Beate's.

They drove home with all the windows down to keep Liesl's pregnant nausea at bay.

Getting to the house, Liesl invited herself inside. She watched as Beate drank two glasses of wine, as she rifled through Michael's jacket and smoked one of his cigarettes. Again, just as Beate should have fallen apart, the desire to win took over. She wanted to tell more people that her ex-husband was getting married just so she could shrug and feign being unfazed. To say something about marriage coming and going as if it were change falling into a gutter.

The doorbell rang and Beate remembered she had a third date that night with Josef Voigt, a man Liesl's boyfriend, now fiancé, had set her up with.

"I forgot about Josef," Beate said.

"He can wait," Liesl answered. "Go upstairs and change and wash your face." Her cousin saw face washing as the cure for many maladies.

Beate couldn't remember Josef's face. They'd gone to dinner; seen a movie. But after he dropped her off, she held on to nothing about him. There was a condition Adela had talked about once where people couldn't recognize faces. But at work, Beate never mistook one old woman for another. She knew the difference between the twins who lived down the street. But Josef remained a mystery.

At the end of their date that night, she invited him in and they fooled around. She took out his penis, felt its warm weight in her hand. The next day, Josef sent her flowers at work. Old people leaned toward them with trembling sniffs. Coworkers teased her or commented on the colors the florist had chosen. To Beate, the flowers felt like a branding. For the next week, her interest in him waned and returned and left her exhausted. Then they went out on a Saturday and he made her laugh hard. They went back to his house and had sex. And balding, hefty Josef was good at it. For an hour after, her interest in him turned complete. But as she got home, as she heard Michael slip up the back stairs, Beate realized that Josef was maybe just part of her game of getting better.

Spring brought final preparations for Liesl's wedding. "Just a little party," she kept saying, though her growing guest list and need for a band suggested otherwise. That Paul was getting married ten days after her was Michael's favorite thing. One morning, he and Beate drinking coffee in their backyard, he said, "Sometimes I like to pretend that Liesl and the California Father are getting married instead."

Two days before Liesl's wedding, Josef came to help set up. He and Heinz erected the tent and raked detritus from the lawn. When Heinz left to pick up plates, Beate told Josef that there was a better rake in the toolshed. He followed her inside. She kissed his neck and unbuttoned his shirt.

"You make me very happy," he said, and Beate was floored by certainty, though an hour before the grunts he let out while lifting things had bothered her.

Once Josef had gone home, the table a sea of blooms, Beate turned restless. Adela and Udo had fallen asleep. Michael's door was closed, though she stopped believing this meant anything. He woke up in time for school and did well enough to continue. And though Adela was organized and good in all the ways he was derelict, Beate saw Michael living in a way her daughter did not. Adela scoured the newspaper. She spewed out information about Bosnia and Sudan and women sold into sex slavery. Michael told stories about his art teacher who opened the windows in winter to remind them that suffering was part of art. "I know what suffering is really a part of," he said. "Suffering." When Adela alluded to him going out at night, what Beate saw in Michael was expansion. When he woke up red-eyed on a Sunday afternoon, she made him coffee. Michael mumbled something about the coffee's perfection, his voice an octave deeper than normal. There were nights, too, when she woke up and knew he wasn't home, and it hit her that she'd let him reach too far, too wildly. Her thoughts caught on the police, on young men felled by AIDS. The neos on the bus who'd stood when she did. It turned every sadness about Paul to nothing. She sometimes reminded Michael to "be safe." He'd kiss her forehead or ask a question about the *Pflegeheim*'s residents, whom he called "the olds."

That night, the house as prepped for the wedding as she could make it, Beate was stuck awake. She took a shower, only to feel more rattled. She passed Michael's door and heard nothing. *Safe*, she thought, and felt stupid. Beate stepped outside and started to walk. Nervously at first, imagining neos in alleys. She followed a route she could have traveled with her eyes closed.

She stopped outside the bar and watched Willy through its window, his hair still a marvel. The crowd looked less elderly, though as mouse-chewed as before. The chalkboard where men had saved haircut spots still hung on its back wall. It had been almost two years, yet it carried the quality of being both distant and right there, as Paul had when she'd heard his voice for the first time in months and he said, "I am to be married," and she felt hit by a gale, also grateful he'd said it so stupidly. Beate wanted to go into the bar, but she'd have fifty-eight people in her house in two days' time. And she wanted to see if Michael had come home.

On her walk back she saw a bus squeaking to a stop and climbed on. The bus passed a crew of neos sitting on the hood of a car. She worried that they'd flag it down, though they did not. At the next stop, a bicycle passed them: Michael. A cigarette glowed in his mouth. He pedaled past them and uphill. Beate willed the bus to move faster, but a man at the next stop spoke to the driver as he disembarked. The bus started up and passed Michael. At the next stop he returned the favor. Flashes of Michael emerged in a streetlamp's circle. Dark hair. Hunched shoulders. But as they got closer to the house, she didn't see him again. Neos sat on cars. Sickness ended boys just as they became men. Paul was marrying a woman named Maria, who Michael said sounded like she'd "sucked down a whole bucket of helium."

At home she found Michael in the kitchen, chugging a glass of water.

"Out cutting hair?" he asked.

"Don't be mean," she answered.

His eyes were red. His goatee impressive. She wanted to thank him for being home, though in doing so she'd have to admit that she'd been afraid. And she loved the version of her son ruled by interest instead of fear. She took a sip of his water.

"You weren't cutting hair, either, I imagine," she said. He smiled and kissed her cheek.

His goatee scratched. He must have loved the way that, at almost sixteen, he could turn his otherwise small self into a man. Michael had pedaled past the bus. The bus passed him back. Perhaps the driver—who drank coffee from a thermos and talked to everyone getting off and on—liked the game of Michael passing and falling behind. Perhaps he looked for Michael each night, happy when this boy-man grew large in his rearview mirror. Perhaps he watched out for her son, or at least noticed when he wasn't there.

⟡

Mutti folded programs. She wore scrubs from work, her hair in the braid she always kept it in now. The few times Adela had seen it out, she was startled by its blond expanse, Mutti transformed to a time when people read by candlelight and were accused of witchcraft. Michael said once that the braid made her look Mormon. "Amish," Adela corrected; he'd answered back with nonsense about churning butter.

The house smelled of vacuuming. Stacks of folding chairs leaned against a wall. Liesl, the soon-to-be bride, stood in the middle of the living room, palming her belly.

"Just in time," Liesl said.

"For what?" Adela asked.

"I have a list!" she answered. "I thought you or your brother could work on it. But you keep disappearing. Bea, your children like to disappear."

Mutti made another fold.

Adela moved into the kitchen. The counter she'd made sandwiches on was packed with plates. In the fridge, where her bread and cheese had lived, champagne bottles were crowded in steerage. Adela searched the kitchen for that bread. For the cheese so heavy she'd had to take breaks when carrying it home from the store. She called Liesl's name.

"No need to shout," Liesl said. Mutti stood behind her, holding a vase.

"Where are my things?" Adela asked.

"Dear," Liesl said. "So many things."

"Six loaves of bread. A block of cheese!" Adela opened the fridge, where a platter of cured meat was pinned down by plastic wrap.

"There's a wedding in two days," Liesl answered. Mutti said nothing.

As Adela imagined pulling her mother's braid, Liesl announced she'd moved the bread and cheese into the shed behind the orchard. "It's cool in there," Liesl said.

"That's why the mice like it," Adela answered.

"Tra-la-la."

Stepping outside, Adela found Udo sitting behind a tree. "I'm hiding from my mother," he said with a smile. Adela walked into the shed, found her loaves flattened, cheese softened to putty.

"Your mother," she said to Udo, who'd followed her.

He hefted the bread and cheese onto his back. They got on their bikes and rode through a part of the city where buildings were the color of tooth decay, to the apartment he and Liesl had lived in for years.

"We have this place for another month," Udo said, letting Adela inside.

He put her food in the fridge, came back with beer and two glasses. He poured carefully, keeping his largeness at bay.

"Let's sit," he said.

"Where?"

"The sofa."

Indents in the carpet showed where the sofa had been. They sat there. Adela placed her hand on an imagined armrest. The beer was cold and bitter.

"*Addo*," Adela said. She'd been helping him to study for the exams he needed to pass so that he could make his Abitur. They'd gone over Greek and Latin roots so many times she'd memorized the information.

"*Addo*," Udo said. "To add and join."

"*Fama*."

"Talk, report, rumor," Udo mumbled.

"*Paro*," Adela said.

Udo's eyelids fell to half-mast. "I didn't bring you here so we could study."

"You said you wanted to work on Latin today."

"I know what I said," Udo answered, lifting his glass to drain it.

Adela peeled an old newspaper off the floor. Bosnia and Jeffrey Dahmer vied for attention. As a breeze blew through the window, Udo stayed quiet on his side of the imagined sofa. He'd lugged her food on his back. Rested his head on her lap when he was sad or confused, or when he wanted her to see that he was smiling at something she'd done for him.

Udo pulled one of her toes. It cracked and he moved to another. She fought the urge to unfold her other foot, to offer also her fingers.

Perhaps this was romance, though parsing out one strong feeling from another felt like trying to separate ingredients from a finished recipe.

They studied on the bike ride home. Continued through dinner—omelets Udo made while Mutti was off with Josef and Michael was, as usual, missing. It turned late. They studied on Adela's bed, listening as the front door opened and Mutti and Josef came inside. Adela would have been meaner about Josef but understood the strangeness her mother must have felt with Liesl and Dad getting married within weeks of each other. Josef left twenty minutes later. He walked down the front path with his shirt hastily put on.

"Untucked," Adela said.

"I don't think I can do it," Udo answered.

"Why not?" Adela croaked. She imagined he was talking about kissing her. But he meant his exams, she realized, adding, "Of course you can."

"Heinz said I could work for him," Udo said.

"You don't want to be an electrician."

He lay down. His heat and largeness crowded her bed.

"Maybe I do," he said. "At university, I'll be alone."

"You wouldn't be alone."

"You'll be in my suitcase?" he asked, and his smile appeared. Adela imagined the two of them at university together, passing books back and forth, downing coffee to stay awake.

"In your suitcase," Adela said, but Udo had fallen asleep.

She woke up a few hours later, in the earliest lip of morning, Udo still asleep next to her. His stomach pushed her toward the wall. Adela moved against him. An erection filled his pants. Like the rest of him, it was considerable. And even as she stayed nervous, as it felt strange and good, Adela still couldn't figure out if this was what she hoped for. Udo breathed in subterranean hums. She pressed against him, her throat tight when she swallowed. Adela used the wall behind her for leverage.

"What are you doing?" Udo asked, and opened his eyes.

"We fell asleep," Adela answered, sliding toward the wall. Udo shifted so his hardness wasn't visible, then walked out of her room. Adela wanted to follow, wanted also to pretend nothing had happened.

A minute later, there was noise in the hall. Michael coming home. It was four in the morning.

"The middle of the night," she said, moving to her doorway.

"Hi," Michael answered. He wore a pair of checkered pants he'd found at a sale in a church basement and a tank top that showed off his swimming shoulders.

"You thought I was Udo?" he asked.

"I didn't think anything."

"It's always the quiet ones," Michael went on. "Like John Wilkes Booth and Jodie Foster."

"Hinckley."

"You're Jodie Foster," he answered, and went on about his sleepless nights after seeing *The Silence of the Lambs*. How the villain's skin dress reminded him of the experiments Adela used to read to him about where Mengele sewed twins together. She and Michael were no longer mistaken for twins. Michael stayed short while she'd grown tall. And every few days his face served as a gallery for a new kind of facial hair. As they stood in the hall, he went on about the genuine terror that movie had saddled him with, how slamming doors and dark windows turned him uneasy for days.

"Maybe instead of worrying about a movie, you shouldn't be out at all hours," she said. "All these skinheads."

"Good night," Michael answered.

The day before the wedding, Adela brought more sandwiches to the camp. Seeing Miri, she snapped out of her self-pity, though she couldn't shake Miri's impression of Udo, his retreat after. Also his comment about her age, which made Adela feel like a liar. Miri talked to people at each tent. Adela grew impatient, tried also to squelch that feeling. Tried also not to think about the fact that when she'd woken up that morning, Udo had been nowhere to be found.

Afterward, they went to their usual café. Miri walked in with her, though she'd waited outside before. At the counter, Miri held up two fingers, said, "Coffee," and pulled coins from her pocket. She spread them onto the counter. The clerk smiled and said, "That's not enough." Miri slid the coins closer. Adela took out money of her own, but Miri shook her head. She shoved her coins farther forward until the clerk relented. Adela thanked him. Miri took her coffee so quickly that some of it spilled down her hand. Walking out of the café, she mumbled to herself. When Adela tried to catch up, Miri walked faster.

"Miri," Adela said.

"Miri," Miri mimicked, and threw her mostly full coffee into a trash can.

Back at the camp, the skinheads from a few days before were outside again, with reinforcements. A half dozen of them stood there, wearing looks of feline meanness. They whispered, flicked cigarette butts in their direction. Miri slipped into a nearby tent, returning with two cast-iron pans. She smacked them together. The sound was deafening. The skinheads turned fast and looked afraid. Miri slammed the pans again. Another bang, and the skinheads shouted, the noise Miri made too loud for their words to register. Miri's arms began to shake. Adela took the pans from her, which were heavy. She admired her friend's strength, wondered if Miri had had a job back East that involved manual labor. Adela slammed the pans together, once, again. When her arms began to mutiny, Miri took them back. The skinheads winced. They shouted, but Miri smiled and kept clanking until the young men gave up and left. Miri's face bloomed with pleased relief.

"Heavy," Adela said.

Miri put her hand on Adela's forearm and Miri as Adela wanted her to be returned. Miri with her warmth. Miri repeating foreign words. The way she'd made fun of Udo turned small, entertainment mistaken for meanness.

Miri pointed to the pans. Adela named them. Miri took them back into the camp that in the last few days had grown even more crowded, tents crammed into spaces so narrow only a single person could sleep in them. A month before, this field had been full of weeds.

Adela biked home fast, until all she could hold on to was the burning in her lungs, the traffic she wove through.

Udo wasn't home. Michael was, though.

"There's a message for you on the machine. Maria from the County," he said.

In Dad's earliest mentions of Maria, he'd written that she worked for the county. For Michael, this detail became her moniker.

Adela played the message.

"That woman sounds like a cartoon," Michael said.

"Did you *hear* the message?" Adela asked.

Maria said hello to both of them. She asked about Michael's plans.

"I told her no already," Michael said.

He and Tobias had gotten jobs at a beach stand selling T-shirts and cheap sunglasses. Michael preferred that to Maria and Dad's promises of San Francisco and the cliffs of Big Sur. So when Dad, then Maria, asked if he was coming, Michael answered no.

"Maybe you need to tell her no again," Adela said, and asked if he'd seen Udo.

"Not home," Michael answered. He turned up the radio.

Glasses for the wedding gleamed on the table. Adela tried to imagine where Udo might have gone. She'd pressed against him the night before because it was something to try, because she hoped to understand what she felt for him, also if—when he pulled on her toes or clamped her earlobe between his fingers—he was trying to figure something out, too.

⟡

Tobias made the face Michael loved. It went from tired and bored to—with a shifting of his eyes—what Michael could only describe as sex. Tobias sipped, and more sex appeared. They lay in a park next to Tobias's grandparents' house—both of whom were infirm and loose with their prescriptions—which Michael had nicknamed the Pharmacy. A nearby playground clacked in the wind. Tobias had just turned seventeen. He acted as if the year between him and Michael were a shark-filled ocean.

"What are you hatching?" Michael asked.

"Who's hatching anything?" Tobias answered with fey confidence. He wore one of the many T-shirts he'd kept from childhood. Its logo, for a spring festival, stretched across his chest; its hoisted hem showed off his belly button. Michael could have written sonnets about that belly button—trailed with hair, moving from narrow to crooked as Tobias shifted. "But now that you mention it," Tobias said. He took Michael's hand to pull himself up, sat on Michael's bike while Michael pedaled. "Pronto," Tobias said. As they sped down one street then the next, Michael tried thinking about sex just enough to heat with pleasure, not so much that he turned hard. It felt like balancing on a fence's beam. They moved in an obvious direction, though Tobias, in his evasion, turned it into a game. "Look serious," Tobias said, as they stopped and strolled into the university library. Its façade was stacked. Its windows tall. Now that the wall was gone, Westerners had started flocking to Universität Kritzhagen. With that, according to Tobias, came a delicious variety of Western gays. His latest crush was named Emil. "He wants to be an architect," Tobias told Michael for the fifth time as they tackled the library's steps. "We have some lovely architecture, he says, here in our shit-ball city."

"Just to be clear," Michael answered. "You are not architecture."

"Flöhchen," Tobias said. "Come." Flöhchen—little flea—was his favorite nickname for Michael.

Once inside the library, they separated to search out his crush, though Tobias had only told Michael that Emil had sandy hair and always wore button-downs. Michael found two candidates. When he showed them to Tobias, he looked annoyed, then amused. A woman at a neighboring table shushed them.

Tobias's other university flings had moved fast toward sex. But Emil—his interest in ideas something Tobias found quaintly novel—barely looked at him the few times they'd spoken. He'd seemed startled when Tobias rested a hand on his arm. Tobias picked up a book on Dutch painting, then left it on a table. "Never fear, Flöhchen," he went on. They were shushed again. "Never fear," Tobias whispered. He told Michael of a party they'd go to that night, where Emil would surely be.

"How do you know?" Michael asked.

"It's in his building."

"How do you know where he—"

"Shh."

"Where he lives?" Michael whispered.

Tobias tapped his temple. Michael hopped on his bike and headed home. He passed a handful of skinheads. Their shaved scalps bunched like knuckles.

"Hey," one of them said. "Hey!"

Though none of them seemed to have bikes or a car, Michael made his way home on a series of backyard paths. People in houses watched television. A woman listlessly peeled potatoes. Getting closer to home, he thought of the party they'd go to. Tobias would make Michael go with him everywhere, searching Michael's pockets for cigarettes and whispering to him until Emil appeared and Michael would go home, the luck of the previous hour gone. But Tobias would find him a day or two later, so full of stories that he'd tell only Michael. And as Michael listened, as they laughed at some stupid thing, Tobias would lean on his shoulder.

"Ah, Flöhchen," he'd say, over and over.

Michael had met Tobias in his second month of *Realschule*. He'd been at a party at Lena's—her dad had recently moved out and gotten a girlfriend in Lübeck, leaving his place perpetually available—when Tobias walked up to him and said: "The rumor is that you're American."

Tobias's face was alight with lovely angles. His lips a red knot. A city of beer cans filled the coffee table behind him.

"I've heard that rumor, too," Michael said.

Lena sidled over. Tobias placed a hand on her breast as if touching a shoulder. Lena offered the same nonchalance. The two of them stared until Lena cackled and Tobias put his hands up in defeat. His shirt lifted, showing a sunrise of pubic hair.

"Tobias likes to make sure he's still *schwul*," Lena said.

"I even tried touching her *Muschi* once," Tobias answered.

"You did not."

Tobias started in on a story about a university boy he'd made out with in the bathroom of a pizza shop, how they'd groped one another against giant cans of tomato sauce. "He also chewed on my nipples," Tobias said. "Want to see?" Lena flicked his ear.

"The second and third rumor is that you're Udo Behm's cousin. Also *schwul*," Tobias said.

"When we were little boys," Tobias went on before Michael could answer, "Udo and I were best friends. I fell from a tree and he carried me three blocks until he found someone to drive us to the hospital." Tobias looked genuinely moved. "We even used to go skinny-dipping together," he said, sly smile returning.

The singer on the stereo moaned out lyrics.

"Good song," Tobias said.

"From my old country," Michael answered.

Tobias stared, and Michael was undone. At home that night he lay in bed thinking about Tobias's eyes in perpetual, almond amusement. Tobias's shirt lifting just so.

When Michael saw him at school a few days later, Tobias had no idea who he was until Michael started speaking English.

"Miss America!" Tobias said. He pushed peers out of the way for this important person. They gave Tobias put-off, unsurprised stares. After school, Tobias dragged him to the university. He pointed out one handsome man, then the next. "You like that one or that one?" he asked.

"I don't know," Michael said.

"If there was a fire and you had to have sex with one of them."

"Why a fire?"

"You'd leave the other to burn."

They lay on the university's lawn. A tree close to them was a wall of gold.

"I guess I'd take the first one," Michael said.

"Good boy," Tobias answered.

"You, too?" he asked, but Tobias shook his head.

Michael wanted to ask what they were doing there, but the afternoon felt like a giant soap bubble. *Pop*, he thought, but it kept going. He tried to watch drifting clouds, the light as it crept down buildings.

After that, Michael and Tobias were together all the time. When Tobias found a new uni boy, he disappeared for a while. But just when Michael was sure he'd never see him again, Tobias would resurface, heartbroken and gossipy, and Michael turned grateful. All the waiting for Tobias, Michael's mood moving between uneasy hope and gloom for several days, cemented something so that Tobias felt like his, though he wasn't his, only something Michael wanted.

The party was in an art student apartment. Posters stolen from the Berlin U-Bahn lined its walls, its hall a spine of smoke. They drank vodka cut with flat soda water. Someone brought a bottle of lime juice and was treated like the mayor until it ran out. Emil hadn't appeared.

"That one likes fisting," Tobias said, pointing to a man whose T-shirt was dark at the pits.

"What makes you say—"

"Watch how he dances."

With each drumbeat the man stuck his ass back. Tobias laughed into Michael's shoulder.

"That one likes blow jobs," Michael said, landing on a man with his mouth open.

"Ah, Flöhchen," Tobias answered. "You're so lovely and innocent."

"What?"

"Relax. It's our secret."

"No secret to tell," Michael said, remembering Maxi Pad and the bathroom corner, Maxi saying yes or no to him for months before Michael showed up one day and Maxi said, "Finished," and closed his window. Also the young Pole who'd come to Kritzhagen for family vacation the summer before, he and Michael jerking each other off underwater, or biking to a nature preserve where they'd fucked while bugs bit their asses.

Theatrical lights blinked red and purple in the living room. Music thrummed, and bodies clustered onto a makeshift dance floor. With his fingers woven between Michael's, Tobias moved them into the crowd. Shoulders pressed against them, bodies a hive of heat. The music shifted into a new song, its singer wailing, "Give it to me!" Tobias's hip hit Michael's. Another layer of drums arrived, the double Dutch of singing and rapping. Tobias's shirt was held closed by one shining button.

"Flöhchen!" Tobias howled, and held up a container of pills.

"From when Oma broke her hip," Tobias said. "Turns everything to Christmas."

He dropped a pill into Michael's palm. Elbows grazed his ribs. A young man moved behind, then against Tobias. Nothing changed in Tobias's expression, though he leaned in his direction. The young man wore a button-down. His hair could have been sandy. Michael let the song finish before he slunk off the dance floor. As he walked down the hall, a hand touched his arm. Udo.

"Cousin," Michael said. "Where's Adela?"

"We aren't married," Udo answered.

"You could get married, though. Join in on Saturday's ceremony. You and Adela and Liesl and Heinz."

Udo squeezed lime into his drink.

"Where did you find lime?"

Udo pulled a plastic bag of slices from his pocket. He handed Michael one.

"Not your first party," Michael said. "And I'm sorry. For the marriage joke."

"It just wasn't funny," Udo answered.

Tobias was suddenly in front of them, and Michael's throat clotted with hope. Tobias hooked a hand under Michael's arm, mumbling, "Not so fast," as if Michael had wanted to run away from him.

"Udo Behm! Just the two people I wanted to see. I wanted to tell you," Tobias said. "Or ask, rather. When I was young, you and I were best friends."

"When we were faggots together," Udo said.

"My sister hates that word," Michael answered.

"Bundle of sticks," Udo added.

Tobias chuckled, everything a delight.

"I used to be close with your mother, too," Tobias said.

"Loud Liesl?" Michael answered.

"You have nicknames for everyone," Tobias said. "But I wanted to ask. Yes, ask is the right word. I'd like to come. To the wedding."

"Like my date?" Michael asked.

"Like Michael's date?" Udo added.

"Flöhchen!" Tobias said.

In the hall behind them, the young man moved closer.

"That's Emil?" Michael asked.

He wanted to be mad, but Tobias had been right. The pills from Oma were magic.

"The more, the merrier," Udo said.

Tobias allowed himself to be pulled back into the crowd.

"There are other parties, you know," Udo said, and a new party felt like the best thing, along with Tobias at the wedding in his version of dressed up.

Michael and Udo walked to another party, splitting a cigarette and a can of beer. They passed the former Soviet barracks, which were fenced off, a crane towering above them. Michael looked to see if he could spot any kidney graffiti on its walls.

"They're knocking them down," Udo said.

"For what?" Michael asked.

"A hotel."

“Ha,” Michael answered.

They walked toward the beach. At some distant edge, a pinprick from a bonfire.

“It’s true,” Udo said. “Heinz just got the contract to do all the electricity.”

The last university boy had treated Tobias like a full, waiting refrigerator. He’d gorge on him for hours, telling Tobias to go down on him in bathroom stalls and empty classrooms. They’d had sex in the woods during a rainstorm. “The whole time he’d made me hold the umbrella,” Tobias had said. Michael wanted to tell him to stand up for himself, but knew that—had the situation morphed into him with Tobias—Michael would have happily held the umbrella, made it part of a story to share. When that last boy dispensed with him, Tobias found Michael and told him he couldn’t stay alone that night. They’d grabbed blankets and slept on the beach, shoulders touching. Michael moved to his stomach to hide his erection. He woke up in the middle of the night and realized Tobias was jerking off. When Tobias understood that Michael was awake, he said, “Please don’t look,” with a prudishness Michael found endearing until the truth of it became clear. After Tobias was asleep, Michael jerked off, too. He finished and fell asleep and woke up the next morning alone. And as he found Tobias’s splotch on the blanket and shoved it into his mouth, Michael told himself that soon he’d look older, soon more layers would fall away and Tobias would see him and realize that Michael was what he wanted. Now Tobias was coming to the wedding. In rooms full of candles and flowers, Tobias might see Michael the way he hoped to be seen. Maybe all that love would inspire something, even temporarily.

⟡

The caterer forced Adela to make her sandwiches in the dining room. Mutti came in with an armload of flowers, saw Adela, said, “Ah,” and kept walking. Michael showed up next, holding a cup of coffee. Sleep creased his face. He sipped and stared.

“What?” Adela asked.

“Just waking up,” he answered.

“So many places in this house to wake up.”

“Indeed,” he said, and found one of them.

Adela went to the camp with only half the sandwiches she’d intended to make, so preoccupied with Udo that she hardly smiled at Miri’s greeting. Miri turned concerned. She squeezed Adela’s forearm to ask if she was okay. Adela nodded. Miri’s expression lifted, and Adela wanted this to be enough. She got them coffees. They sat on the curb as they always did.

“Good,” Miri said, and Adela wondered if that was her only English word, Miri saying it about her as well as the coffee, also the sun coming out after a string of cloudy days.

Back at the house, Michael balanced on Udo’s shoulders. They hung a garland around the front door and passed a cigarette back and forth.

“A lot of flowers,” Adela said.

“A wedding,” Michael answered.

Udo stared at the flowers in his hands. Adela excused herself to take a shower.

She washed her hair, worrying that Miri calling her “the good” didn’t mean anything, embarrassed that she’d needed to matter to this girl who lived in a tent Adela had never seen. The hot water ran out. Shampoo slithered into Adela's eyes. "Fucking ass fuck," she hissed, as she blindly grabbed a towel, wondering why she hadn't invited Miri over to use her shower or take a nap. Adela needed to be better. She would get up the next morning and bring wedding leftovers to the camp. She'd go through her clothes and take anything she could spare. Adela flung the bathroom door open, stumbling onto Udo in the hall. Seeing her in a towel, he stopped. Adela's legs were goose-pimpled.

"Hi," he said, and looked at her knees.

"Hi," Adela answered. Water dripped onto her shoulders. Blushing blotched Udo's neck.

"Excuse me," he said, slipping past her and into his room.

Adela thought of a few nights before when they'd been going over the Romans—Udo tapping her knee when he needed a hint, the warmth coming off him as he slept next to her. Also his expression when he woke up to her pressed against him, shock or disgust or surprise that sex was something she thought about, that it might be something he'd want to give her.

11

Sixty people moved in and out of her house. They brought presents and took drinks and wore perfume. Beate greeted them all. She listened as people spoke of knowing her as a child, as strangers said she looked like a great-aunt she'd never heard of. When any conversation lasted too long, Josef was at her side, inventing a crisis in the kitchen. She kissed his cheek, his hand rested on her back, the doorbell kept ringing. When she and her children had gotten to this house two years before, Beate could no more have imagined this party than she could have pictured a boyfriend or a promotion, Paul remarrying and her life continuing rather than slipping off a cliff.

After the backyard ceremony, Josef signaled to the caterer that the show was about to begin. Josef had been there since six that morning. He'd secured the backyard tent and placed tables and chairs. When he'd gone to her room to shower and change, Beate had wrapped herself around him, his bald head blotched from the shower's heat, and allowed certainty to settle in. He moved his mouth down her throat and she told him that there wasn't time. She pressed her hands against his chest until they left marks.

Josef directed people to food and bathrooms. Michael and Udo moved through the crowd with drinks in hand and cigarettes behind their ears. Adela hovered on the staircase.

"Adela, come down," Beate said.

Her daughter wore the dress they'd gotten the week before. Her hair was up, showing off her long neck. The ring in her nose glinted, and she had on the cheap digital watch she'd owned since fifth grade.

"How long have you been hiding up there?"

Adela shrugged. A trio of women who worked at the *Pflegeheim* hugged Beate as if they hadn't seen her two days before. They exchanged pleasantries about weddings and Liesl, who looked lovely, her dress giving special weight to her pregnant cleavage.

"I know them from work," Beate said to Adela, as the women continued on. "I always thought one of them hated me."

"Which one?" Adela asked, taking two steps down.

"I was going to say the one with the terrible lipstick. But that's mean."

"Their lipstick *is* terrible," Adela said.

"Child, why are you hiding up there?"

The band started to play, and the crowd inside moved toward the door with a herd's stolid impatience. Adela's watchband was held together with electrical tape.

"I wasn't hiding," she said. "I just needed to use the bathroom."

Adela allowed Beate to hook an arm into hers as they walked into the backyard, where the band lurched into a song that might have been disco.

"Liesl *did* insist on a band," Beate said.

"And Liesl got one," Adela answered.

"Mother and daughter together," Josef said. "Don't move." He went to find his camera.

A woman Beate didn't recognize grabbed her hand. "It's Andrea Holst!" she said.

"Andrea!" Beate answered. She'd learned to feign recognition in the city, where each week more people claimed to remember a class they'd shared, a neighborhood game they'd once played.

"I haven't seen you in forever," Andrea went on. "Was it when Liesl was babysitting and I stopped by to visit?"

"Possibly!" Beate answered.

Josef scurried over.

"There might be dancing," he said, and the feeling of wanting him returned. She touched his tie. Tables in the backyard had been moved out of the way, and the band turned up its amps. Liesl and Heinz stepped onto the makeshift dance floor. As the crowd circled them, as Michael and Udo smoked behind a tree too small to hide what they were doing, Adela stayed next to Beate. Josef lifted his camera, told them to smile. A fast song ended, a slow one taking its place. Liesl and Heinz were in the center of it, dancing belly to belly.

⟡

Adela watched as the middle-aged tried to twist. Liesl's dress slid across her nascent baby belly. Josef held Mutti's hands, his forehead folded with effort. He seemed kind. The few times he'd been over for dinner, Adela walked a fine line between polite and dismissive. Now he couldn't stop smiling at the good fortune he saw in her mother. The singer reached for a high note and made it. Someone handed Adela a glass of champagne.

"I don't want this," Adela said, though the person had already moved on.

The music stopped. People filled tables. Heinz's brother began a toast.

"My brother," he said. "My brother, Heinz." On the yard's far side, Michael and Udo bit the insides of their cheeks. Adela hadn't studied with Udo in days. The brother, Karl, told a tedious story about the two of them swimming as boys, meanness masked as remembrance. As Karl waxed predictably about brothers, Michael whispered to Udo. "The little thing shrieked like a ninny as he got into the water," Karl said, and shifted into a drunken ramble about the women who hadn't wanted to marry Heinz. "There was the one who—Helga, Heidrun. Now, what was her name again, Heinz?" When Karl paused to ask to have his drink refreshed, Michael's head fell forward. Udo held his shoulder, as if keeping her brother from lifting off the ground. Karl wrapped up. Despite the lively applause, he looked ashamed. Adela was about to walk over and tell her brother and cousin they'd been rude when Karl moved back to the microphone.

"And now," he said, "we'll have a few words from the son. From Udo."

Udo moved his jaw as if chewing, which he did when angry or bored. Our Barbarian Cousin, Michael used to call him. Glasses clanged. In the windows, the sun's reflection was a melting lozenge. Udo moved to the microphone. Leaning down, he said hello. "Hello," he repeated. Some in the audience answered. "Liesl," he said. "Mother. You look beautiful." Liesl smiled. "And happy." His cheeks burned.

Udo's gentleness from their evenings studying together returned. Adela wanted to rescue him, though that would only acknowledge his faltering. And in the last days he'd barely talked to her. Michael sipped, he and Udo in some contest for greater drunkenness. Udo closed his eyes and Adela wondered if he'd even known he was meant to speak. The drummer's cymbal shushed in the wind. When Udo had stumbled on Adela in only a towel, he'd looked at it as if it were a blunt instrument she meant to hit him with.

"Congrats," Udo said, and walked back to Michael.

For a moment no one moved. Then someone laughed. Others

clapped to drown that laughter out. As Michael and Udo slid behind the trees, the music started again. Liesl spun on the dance floor, a cloud of cleavage and lace. Mutti and Josef danced, too. Josef held her close and Adela realized he was shorter than Mutti. The same was true with her father. Adela picked up the champagne she hadn't wanted.

As Adela moved toward them, she thought of jokes she and Udo had about Michael as Tobias's shadow, calling him goldfish shit and Tonto.

"Udo Behm!" Tobias cooed.

He followed close behind Adela, in a tie infected with dots. Next to him was a young man Michael quickly seemed to recognize.

"Thank you," Tobias said to Adela, "for helping me find Michael."

When she turned to leave, Tobias insisted that she stay.

"This is Emil," Tobias said.

Udo grabbed a branch and swung from it.

"Champagne?" the waiter interrupted. Udo nabbed two.

Michael settled on, "You're here," adding something about architecture.

The band switched to a Supremes song. "Look at them!" Tobias oohed, watching the guests dance. For a moment, Adela understood his appeal, how he tinged everything with playful amusement.

Someone congratulated Udo, who went back to swinging. "Thank you," Michael answered.

There was a stubbornness Udo used when he'd insisted on living with them. When his father had called after several absent years and Udo wouldn't talk to him. More people congratulated him. Udo acted as if he were alone. He and Michael passed a bottle of whiskey back and forth. "Disgusting," Michael said, after each sip.

"I'm excited to be here," Tobias said. "I used to be close with Liesl when Udo and I were friends."

Michael flipped from one uncertain expression to the next. He lifted his champagne but forgot to drink it. Liesl spotted Tobias and gave him a hug.

"The bride in white!" Tobias said.

"Shut up." Liesl smiled, she and Heinz off again in a flurry of matrimonial activity.

Tobias and Emil went to find something stronger to drink. Michael watched the path they left in the crowd.

"Did you know he was bringing a date?" Adela asked. She tried to soften her voice, though it sounded like she was talking to a slow person.

"It's a wedding," Michael said. She touched his shoulder, but he didn't respond. Mutti and Josef danced close to each other.

"Josef is a terrible dancer," Michael said.

"That's mean," Adela answered.

"Sissy faggot," he said, the two of them most similar in the slights they didn't let go of.

"You really aren't going to Dad's wedding?" Adela asked.

Maria had called a few times that week to tell them that airfare was getting pricey. When she asked if Michael was home, Adela said no, even when it wasn't true.

"I always found Dad scary," Michael answered.

"Maybe he isn't scary anymore," Adela said.

"You'll have to let me know."

"I never found him scary," Adela lied.

Tobias and Emil moved past a window. "I'm an asshole," Michael said. "Like how we used to use it to mean someone was dumb or late or wearing an awful sweater."

"We used it for everything," Adela answered.

She tried to catch his eye, to tell him with a look that Tobias was a fever that would pass. But he kept watching people as they tumbled out of the door, then a stray cat perched on their garden wall.

"I wasn't trying to be mean about Josef," he said. "Though I guess I sounded mean. Maybe the German Lady likes him."

Michael went to see what Tobias and his date were up to. The band's singer shook a tambourine. When Adela turned around, Udo was gone.

Michael kept close to Tobias and Emil. Whenever they whispered to each other for too long, he interrupted with some fact about the wedding. *There are more than three hundred tulips in the house. Liesl and Heinz are honeymooning in Spain, though neither of them speaks a word of Spanish. Maybe* taco. *So one word.*

After an endless bout of whispering, Tobias came up for air. He tapped Michael's sleeve.

"You look fancy, Flöhchen," Tobias said.

"Flöhchen," Emil echoed. "This is a nice house. Are you rich?"

"My mother is an ass-wiper."

"Funny," Emil said, in lieu of laughing.

As if she knew she was being talked about, Mutti sidled up to them.

"You aren't drinking too much, now?" she asked.

"Another sister?" Emil asked.

"The mother, Emil!"

Mutti blushed. Seeing her happy reminded Michael of the weeks when the closest thing to her being happy was a stretch of uninterrupted sleep.

Adela appeared to tell Mutti that she was needed.

"*This* is the sister," Tobias said.

"I let you in," Adela said. "Who are you again?"

"Emil," Tobias answered.

"Make sure Emil has a drink?" Mutti said as she left. Her dress gave her the illusion of floating. Udo stumbled toward them without taking in who they were.

"Blotto," Michael said.

"Blotto," Udo mumbled.

"I think you need to lie down," Adela added.

Udo took a slug of beer. Tobias beamed, as if watching a farce on television.

"I think *you* need to lie down," Udo said. "You and you and you," eyes on Michael, Tobias, and Emil. "Faggots together."

"That's a terrible word," Adela said.

"Michael thinks it's funny," Udo answered.

"My brother finds strange things funny."

"Your brother is right here," Michael said.

An older girl at school once told Michael about Udo's drunken eccentricities—at one party singing "We Are the World" to anyone who'd listen, at another sitting in a corner where he lined up empty beer bottles and ignored everyone.

Udo staggered up the stairs. Halfway up, he stopped.

"You gonna make it?" Michael asked.

"Are *you* gonna make it?" Udo answered. His left foot hung in the air, like those giant horses from beer commercials, their hooves bulky furniture.

"He's like a lumberjack," Emil said.

"Michael thinks he looks like a cow from a children's book," Adela answered.

"That's sweet," Emil said.

Michael wanted to stick his fingers hard and fast up Emil's nose.

Gum stuck to the bottom of Udo's shoe. Outside, the dancers moved in a routine that involved clapping on cue. A shimmy and a lean. A toe pointed forward.

Mutti announced that it was time for the cake. The crowd funneled into the living room, and Udo made it all the way up the stairs.

"I can't believe you're the mother," Emil said, and Mutti blushed again.

Sitting on the stairs, Emil and Tobias shared a piece of cake. Their fork went into one mouth, then the other.

"Give us a minute, Flöhchen?" Tobias asked.

"Little flea," Emil said, in a tone that made Michael's sweet nuisance plain.

"Please," Tobias said, he and Emil walking up the stairs before Michael answered. They got to Michael's room and closed the door.

Then Udo was back. In his five-minute reprieve, his stumbling was replaced with an impish lightness. He wrapped a giant arm around Michael's shoulder, held a bottle of whiskey above him as if it were a torch.

"You like that nickname they call you?" Udo asked.

"It's just Tobias, really."

"Blachh," Udo answered.

Liesl placed cake on Heinz's tongue. The room was warm and smelled of candles.

"Your mother is married," Michael said.

Udo answered with an exaggerated shrug.

"You happy?" Michael asked. He shrugged again.

"You want to get out of here?" Udo said.

"What about all this?" Michael answered, hand spanning the crowd like a game show hostess.

"All this, that, and the other," Udo said, and walked out the front door. Michael looked back to see if anyone noticed. But they were too busy eating or dancing or having sex in a bed Michael had never had sex in, taking what for a time had been his alone.

◇

When Heinz told Liesl it was time to go, she acted like he was spoiling the party rather than doing what she'd planned. Guests stood in the driveway, ready to wave goodbye as the couple climbed into a taxi.

"It's all gone too fast," Liesl said. She cried as she hugged Beate.

"You're crazy, cousin."

"We're crazy together," Liesl answered.

"I'll see you tomorrow!"

Liesl answered that tomorrow seemed far away. She made a joke that she was drunk, though she'd nursed the same glass of champagne all night. Two years ago it had been her and Udo in a tiny apartment. She had Heinz now, barraged with contracts, and a house they'd bought for nothing and gutted so the inside was like new. Liesl had come over one day with a catalog full of dishwashers and refrigerators. She'd seemed terrified of them, her greatest worry in marrying Heinz that the dishwasher would clean things too well. They hugged again and Beate saw the next day turn far away, too, the taxi taking her cousin to a different hemisphere. Liesl's chest pushed against Beate. Her breath hit Beate's ear. The wedding was over and her house would have to be put back together, the coming days brutally the same.

"Come now!" Heinz said. The guests laughed, sadness sold as comedy.

He and Liesl climbed into the taxi, and the band left. Someone found a boom box—one of Michael's endless spoils—and tuned it to a sixties station. Josef spun Beate awkwardly, gleefully, and she pulled him in close. Adela watched with crossed arms. A breeze shook the lights in the trees and a distant siren bleated.

"The toolshed," Josef said, his hand on Beate's back.

"It's just back there," she answered.

"I know."

"I mean, there are people here."

"Somewhere, please," Josef whispered. Beate took his hand and they moved up the back stairs.

"Two staircases," he said. "I didn't even know."

"This house," Beate answered, as if it had always felt like her greatest piece of luck.

In her room, Josef kissed Beate's shoulder. Just before he curled down her bra, he asked if it was all right. Beate nodded. His hand moved across the outside, then inside of her knee. Then came a knock, Adela saying, "Mutti?" Beate threw a pillow over her face. "Mutti, I'm sorry."

"I'll be down soon," she said.

Josef's fingers moved between her legs.

"Something's happening with the immigrants," Adela went on. "Refugees. Something bad."

"I'll be down," Beate answered. "Just a minute."

"The skinheads," Adela said. Beate remembered the young men who'd followed her off the bus and looked meanly amused when she'd hopped back on.

"They're outside the camp," Adela added.

Beate removed Josef's hand. She pulled down her dress and opened the door.

"I need to go there," Adela said.

"I don't know that that's a good idea," Beate answered.

Adela moved her lips, though no sound came out. In the

yard, a Rolling Stones song played. Beate's underwear was somewhere on the floor.

"I need you to go with me," Adela said.

Beate wanted to take her daughter's hand, but sensed it would be too much. She'd held Beate's arm that evening, sat next to her during dinner, and asked who this or that person was, if she was supposed to say hello to them.

The crowd of skinheads was larger than any Beate had seen before. A dozen first, then four times as many. Their pockets bulged with rocks, their laughs sharp and loud. Just before Adela and Beate got to the camp, a skinhead stepped in their way.

"You're dressed up," he said.

Adela and Beate were still in their wedding outfits, everyone else in jeans and leather. Skinheads stood in the street, ringing the camp. Observers filled the far sidewalk, lining its edge as if in preparation for a parade. More shaved heads moved into the street. Some held sticks. Some smoked. They ignored cars that tried to pass, standing directly in their headlights and flicking cigarette butts at their windshields. In the camp, a Roma popped up from behind a tent. Comments firecrackered about rodents in human clothes, new breeds of syphilis. As Adela tried to step forward, the neo stopped her. "You go there," he said, pointing to the sidewalk where the spectators stood. Adela wouldn't move.

Just over the skinhead's shoulder, Roma held boards as weapons. The place stank, like the Port Authority in July, where Beate and her children had once waited for a bus while a man in plastic-bag shoes mumbled things about Jesus and the mayor.

"Where are the police?" Beate whispered to Adela.

"They never do anything," Adela answered.

"You go there," the skinhead repeated. When they didn't move, he sniffed Beate's neck.

"Don't," Beate said.

His scalp shone like waxed fruit. It would have been easy to lift something, to smash it. Police sat in their cruisers a block away, waiting for something to happen.

"Adela," Beate said. "Why are we here?"

Her daughter's look told her to quit being stupid. In the camp just beyond them, flashlights blinked off and on in Morse code. A car tried to drive down the street, retreating when skinheads lifted their sticks toward the driver. Adela tried again to take a step forward. The skinhead blocked her.

Then a rock flew. Another. Beate pulled Adela back just before one landed where they'd stood. Skinheads pushed past them, closing in on the camp. Shouts grew to a wall. A Roma ran out, was hit with a sailing stone. Blood covered a neo's forehead. One of the camp's tents waved with flames.

Beate dragged her daughter back into the crowd of spectators, watching as shaved heads and winging shoulders made it to the tents. Beate tried to put an arm around her, but Adela resisted. Beate felt hurt, then chastened by the violence in front of them that her daughter had seen coming with the inevitable result of a recipe. Another tent caught fire; a sandstorm of smoke followed. Refugees ran, some stumbling as rocks reached them. A few spectators joined the skinheads. They wore street clothes, their hair short and long. A young immigrant moved between the remaining tents.

"Do you know him?" Beate asked.

"We have to do something," Adela shouted.

"The police are coming now."

Adela tried to step forward, but Beate grabbed her arm.

"Mutti," Adela hissed.

"No," Beate answered.

She held Adela in place with the other spectators, the neos turning the street in front of them into a battleground. Some threw rocks while others lobbed Molotov cocktails toward the tents, which burst into flames. The thickening smoke singed Beate's eyes. The neos shouted and threw. Adela pulled again, trying to free herself from her mother's hold.

"Fucking German Lady," Adela hissed. Beate held on to her more tightly.

Then Beate saw them. Among the hundred or so young men squeezing closer to the camp, some neo-Nazis, others having joined in for one foul reason or another, was Udo. Michael just behind him. A rock flew from Udo's hand. In the thickening haze, Beate couldn't see where it landed. He pulled another from his pocket, unfazed by the sirens or the spectators beginning to boo. Each time a rock landed near him, Michael covered his head. When he finally let go of the one he'd been holding, he dropped it at his feet. He looked mortified. Beate tried to figure out why he didn't leave. She shouted his name. Michael looked up with the confused fear of his younger version, afraid of dark halls and public bathrooms and the tree that used to tap his window. A neo next to him lunged at an immigrant who'd tried to make a break for it. A rock landed by Michael's feet. He covered his head in delayed response. Beate shouted his name again. He looked around, glancing at his wrist for a watch that wasn't there. Then he ran. In a few steps, the smoke had swallowed him. "Michael," Beate shouted, so distracted by his escape that she didn't see the rock Udo threw until it skimmed an immigrant's forehead. The man crouched down. Udo launched another one, which sailed into his target's abdomen. A third rock unfurled from his fingers. But before it reached the man, a young woman ran in its path, shielding herself with a frying pan. Adela yanked herself free from her mother's hold and ran toward Udo. The girl did the same. Udo was looking for something else to throw just as Adela drew close to him, just as the girl lifted her pan, swinging it with the same angry athleticism with which she'd stopped the rock, though this time it crashed into Udo's nose.

Adela pushed past skinheads being pressed to the pavement by police officers, crouching to protect herself from rocks hurtling through the air. She heard screams in foreign languages, covered her mouth with her hand to stave off the smoke's choking taste. Getting to Udo, she watched blood gush from his nose. And though Adela winced at the sight of it, there was a relief, too, that Miri had stopped him. Dazed and grimacing, Udo tried and failed to swat at the pan. A rock smacked his stomach, another hit his shoulder. Udo slipped onto his knees. When he waved a hand in the air, his palm was crimson. Miri lifted the pan again.

"Miri," Adela said, standing between her and injured Udo. Miri tried to step around her. A skinhead ran close to them, was yanked back by a police officer.

As Adela repeated her name and put a hand on the girl's forearm, Miri hit her with a withering look. *Of course you're protecting him*, it said. *You're the one who showed him where we were.* Miri's pan stayed in the air. Udo crouched, hissing with anger or pain. Miri moved the pan farther back, face red from flashing sirens. *You or him. You and him. The same to me.*

Udo stumbled to standing. *You or him*, Miri's eyebrows repeated. And as Udo reached for the pan, Adela stepped out of Miri's way.

Udo's arm took the brunt of the second blow and he hissed out terrible words: bitch and garbage picker and terrorist. Words Miri didn't understand. Words that might have been meant for both of them.

Two officers rushed toward them.

"She was only defending herself," Adela shouted, but the officers dove on top of Udo, who, as he lay on the pavement, turned his head to the side and threw up.

A third officer appeared and tried to pry the pan from Miri.

"She needs that," Adela said.

Adela felt Udo's eyes on her. She tried to stare at the burning camp, but the pull of his look won out, anything angry in him suddenly doused by fear. Adela didn't want his camaraderie or the blindness with which she'd moved when Udo had said the camp wasn't safe, when Michael told a story he'd surely invented about a gypsy leaving the grocery store with a loaf of bread in his pants. A puddle of sick sat next to Udo. His forehead was bloody. He stared at Adela with the scared regret of a scolded dog.

Then Miri started shouting. She pointed to Udo, barking out a stream of glottal words. Her voice grew so loud that one of the officers stepped between them.

The man Udo had hit, Miri's father, perhaps, said something. Miri turned, nodded, and walked to him. At the edge of the camp, the last of the refugees began to run. Miri and the man joined them, their shoulders rounded in preparation for whatever came next, their footfalls rain on a roof.

A fire truck arrived and began spraying down the camp. A man moved close to the tents to take pictures of its hissing remains.

As Udo stared at Adela, asking for help he didn't deserve, she realized, despite the last two years she'd treated him as a life jacket, that she hated him.

Udo repeated her name. When she ignored him, he followed it up with, "Good cousin." Adela shook her head. The police pulled Udo toward their car and his voice turned urgent. And as Udo began to pull against the officers' grip, Adela said, "No," not even sure what she was saying no to.

Adela didn't know then that she'd never see Udo again, that when she called Dad in the morning he'd stop her halfway through her story to say he'd change her ticket so that she'd come in a day rather than a week. Once in California, the awfulness of Kritzhagen turned obvious, became the story everyone told at Dad and Maria's wedding. A great-uncle told her she was brave. When he said that, Adela remembered Udo's bleeding face, how she moved out of the way so Miri could continue to injure him. She thought also of coming down for dinner the day after Liesl's wedding, greeted by Michael's scowl. "You were there with him," Adela had said. But Michael only shook his head as if she were an idiot, as if what Adela had just said to him were something she'd invented.

"You were," she'd repeated, and went upstairs to pack. When her suitcase turned full, Adela found boxes in the attic and filled them with the rest of the clothes, leaving nothing in her dresser or closet for her brother to find or bury. On the top of each box she wrote Dad's address, labeling the side of one *Fall*, another *Winter*, though she'd heard California didn't have proper seasons, that it never got cold there at all.

PART TWO

1971

12

Beate's father tried to look serious in photos, but in this one his mouth wasn't quite closed. Strings of hair were pasted to his head; his tie a shade crooked. Even more it was his eyes. They weren't looking at the camera, or at anything. Beate invented the article's alternative title—"Man with Dementia Found Wandering in Winona"—cruelty and truth twinning, as they often did. Mutti bought a cheap frame and slid the article inside. They'd been living in Minnesota just over a year. In his first semester Vati had taught philosophy, though the friend of a friend who'd gotten him the job had either lied or not known about her father's English, saying it was solid rather than rudimentary. His lectures were carefully written, though in translation Vati's ideas wended into murky waters. Even when he made sense, his accent was thick. And he switched to German without realizing, one bold, annoyed student making it her job to say: "You're doing it again. With the language." For the rest of the semester a translator was hired and the class addressed their questions to him. Now Vati taught beginning German. He balked at his students' incompetence, though he seemed resignedly pleased that they knew nothing while he knew everything.

A reporter from a Minneapolis paper heard of their defection and interviewed him just as the hysteria over communism was reignited by Vietnam. The article landed on the Sunday paper's front page. Beate hated the title—"The Brave Professor"—but most of all, the photo. At dinner, Beate sat so she didn't have to look at the copy hanging on the wall.

"What you said, about the soldiers who questioned us, how you felt for them though they were keeping us from what we wanted," Mutti said. "That was quite moving." Mutti had been with him during this interview, but spoke as if she'd just read it. They ate hard-boiled eggs for dinner. Someone walked back and forth in the apartment above them.

"They were frightening, I thought," Beate said.

Her father cut into his egg. Its sulfur smell rose.

"They were children," Mutti said.

"With guns," Beate answered.

"Beate," her father chided.

"What did I say?"

"It's how you said it."

"How I said it?"

"Are you repeating my words because you don't understand them? Or are you angry?"

She felt many things, like the dread of her second year of American high school, though there was also a relief in the return of classes. Moving through halls at school where people shouted to one another trumped the boredom of summer, when she slept late and got up only to lie on her bedroom floor, each free day a rocket ship she couldn't consider how to build.

"I think," Beate said—she crumbled the last of her egg onto her bread—"that they were frightening. That we can call them children now. But at the time . . ."

Beate waited for her father to ask her to finish the sentence. Instead, he looked at a book that sat open on his lap. Mutti started to clean up though they were still eating. The food on

Vati's fork wiggled, his tongue egg-yellow. Mutti looked at the picture on the wall she'd described as handsome, no one saying it wasn't handsomeness it gave off, but something infirm.

After two years in Cologne, Beate's father had announced that they were moving to Edinburgh.

"It will be better there," he said, adding, "Germany's too much of what it's always been."

Vati usually demanded precision in people's answers. When Beate said she didn't feel like doing something, he forced her to connect dots. *It's because I am tired, and I'm tired because I stayed up late last night listening to records, and I stayed up listening to records because other girls in my class talk of them as if they're religion, which many people think they need.* But telling her of their move, he spoke in speculation.

In Cologne, the strangeness Beate had first cultivated evolved into invisibility. She could sit through entire days of school, only speaking when she answered, "Here," during attendance. So when Vati mentioned Edinburgh, Beate thought to complain, then to ask what better meant, finally deciding that at least there would be new places for her to see.

And it had been better. People there found her foreignness winning, telling her she looked like an actress she'd never heard of, behaving as if she'd done something extraordinary when she used the past tense properly or realized without being told that she was in the wrong classroom. Within weeks she had a best friend (one of the many Marys in her class), even a boyfriend—Duncan—who was tall and kind and doted on her with an attention she sometimes loved, sometimes found smothering. Their romance had begun when he'd offered to help her with her English, continuing in forgotten library stacks where he unbuttoned her blouse and encouraged her to move her mouth across his penis. In the winter of that year, they'd graduated to sex. With her growing skills in and excitement about that activity, and the English she suddenly excelled in, Edinburgh felt to her like something of a miracle.

Then one evening in spring, Beate just back from the library, her father stood over her at their kitchen table, dropped an atlas in front of her, and told her to locate Minnesota. Her mouth was chapped from so much of Duncan's.

"That place sounds like that movie we watched on television," Beate said. "*Brigadoon.*" She thought of the men's kilts lifting as they danced, also Duncan pressed against her an hour before.

"Not like *Brigadoon* at all," Vati answered.

In the atlas, Beate found Minnesota, finger tracing the Mississippi's hard turns.

"We're moving there," Vati answered, then said he was late for a meeting.

Beate stayed at the kitchen table. Her stomach began to ache. She mumbled names of cities on the map in front of her, sure she'd mispronounced them. Mutti, who'd turned strange and quiet in Edinburgh—forgetting to make dinner and hanging laundry on any surface she could find—was taking a bath. Beate knocked on the bathroom door. Silence and a soapy water smell. She knocked again, said her mother's name. Not a splash to indicate a lifted arm, not anything. Beate opened the door to find Mutti lying in the tub, a washcloth over her eyes.

"You've come to see an old lady in the bath?" Mutti asked.

Her breasts were large. Beate wondered how she'd come from this woman. Mutti kept her hands on the washcloth, hands in Cologne that were always picking things up in the dead woman's apartment. Hands that, on the day before they'd left Kritzhagen, had gone into Beate's room to decide what she'd take and leave behind.

"We're moving to Minnesota," Beate said.

"There are thousands of lakes there," Mutti answered.

"I don't know that I want to go there," Beate said.

Mutti sat up. She pulled the washcloth from her eyes, glaring at Beate with what might have been contempt or fear. Beate refused to look away. Mutti pushed up her knees, then pulled her head under the water's surface. She was under for ten seconds, fifteen. Beate watched the water, part of her hoping Mutti wouldn't come up, part of her getting ready to reach in and exhume her mother. But then Mutti splashed to the surface, bringing with her a slosh of sound, water slapping over the edge of the tub and onto the floor, where it soaked Beate's feet. Mutti began washing her hair as if alone in the room. She lifted an arm to clean its underside. Scrubbed her neck and her breasts, eyes glued on the wall in front of her. Beate opened the door and left her mother alone.

For that first day of her second year of Minnesota high school, Beate wore a brown skirt she'd sewn and grown too tall for. It rose over her knees. The year before, girls had been removed from class for skirt length. No one noticed Beate's violation now. Part of her hoped to be called out, if only because she wanted her outfit to seem willful rather than the product of slender means. But as the principal passed her he probably remembered Beate in this skirt the year before, this girl the same except for the extension of her limbs. Getting to history, the teacher asked about her accent. When she answered, "Germany," he asked, "What part?" in clunky German.

"All over," Beate said.

The teacher was handsome in a stringy way. He slouched and had a pointed, regal nose. Chalk dust clouded the room.

"This is the part where you ask how I know German," the teacher answered, his delivery careful, construction correct.

"I figured you were native," she said; he laughed a little too loudly.

"It is nice to meet you, Beate," he said. "Mr. McDowell here."

Outside the window, the Mississippi flatly shone.

Mr. McDowell began with something about the Far East, sometimes stuttering with excitement. A hope that school might be different this year left her listening, leaning in, though a crush on a teacher was a distraction, not something she could build on.

"You're German?" a girl next to her asked.

Beate nodded.

"Cool," the girl said. "I'm Karen."

At lunch, Karen introduced Beate to her two best friends, who also found Beate's Germanness winning. The four of them smoked outside before afternoon classes. Beate told them her German story, lingering, as her father had in the article, on the defection, speaking truthfully about what had been scary, exaggerating the length of time they'd been questioned. These girls even found Beate's outfit cool, which felt like a trick, or plainness confused with sophistication. They asked her to meet them after school, where they told her about the art teacher who was queer and hilarious. One of the other girls—Samantha, who went by Sam—told a story about her uncle in New York City who was also a queer and didn't come home for holidays but sent great presents.

"Do other people know you defected?" Christine asked.

"Our history teacher," Beate answered, "knows that I am defective."

The girls laughed at the dumb joke Beate had held on to since Edinburgh, when she'd read that word in *A Tale of Two Cities* and had to ask Duncan what it meant. He'd smiled at her pronunciation and kissed her.

"He's also defective," Karen said, going into a mean, inaccurate impression of Mr. McDowell's stutter.

Two weeks later, Beate came home to a flurry of excitement. Mutti moved in and out of her and Vati's bedroom. She lifted ties into a patch of sunlight and squinted at them. Vati sat on their couch holding a folder.

"What's wrong with her?" Beate asked.

"Why would something be wrong?" he answered.

Mutti reappeared with shirts.

"She's taking out half your closet."

"Your mother is excited."

"Are you going to tell me? Why?"

"Yes," Vati said, snapping out of his geriatric daze. "The interview on Friday."

"What interview?"

"We talked about it at dinner."

Beate wanted to be in her room, to read her history book piled with too many facts. Her father went on about the Minneapolis television station that had seen the article and wanted to interview them, making it clear that she would be part of it. Classmates might see Beate on TV, towering over her old parents. *How are you so tall while they're so tiny?* she imagined the reporter asking. *My mother was tall*, Mutti would answer. *Why did you decide on Minnesota?* he might ask next. Vati could say, *I was tired of smelling the sea.* And the next day, students would pass her and make sniffing noises. *You smell that?* they'd whisper. *It's the sea.*

Beate turned up the radio and left her shoes in the middle of the room. She didn't want to be on the news. Didn't want her classmates to wonder if she lived with her grandparents. She peeled an apple, left its skin the floor.

"Please stop," her father said.

"What?"

"You're angry because you don't like it here."

"I don't want to be on the news," she blurted out.

"You're embarrassed of your accent?"

That was part of it. Even more, she felt like a prop. And people would see her parents—Eastern in everything but location—who until then had dutifully avoided school functions. Her foot traced the apple's peel. Vati creaked onto the couch.

"I'm trying to take care," he said.

Vati put a hand on her forehead, as if checking her temperature, though it was supposed to say things about affection and safekeeping. Beate nodded. She hoped he'd leave her alone. And he did, after eyeing the peel she'd left on the floor.

Mr. McDowell lingered over Beate's desk. It was the first cold day, and everyone showed off new sweaters. Beate wore the cardigan she always wore. Her legs ached from walking to school in the cold. Mr. McDowell wore a belt that was too long and knotted at its end. He dropped the failed quiz in front of her.

"You didn't study for this," he said. Karen and Sam and Christine looked up from the notes they were taking.

"I'd forgotten," she answered, in German.

"I announced it. You were to write it down."

Beate hadn't forgotten, but couldn't read the textbook without falling asleep. It was her go-to on nights when the stomper upstairs stomped late. Still, Mr. McDowell's kindness mattered. She came close to crying and lifted her hands in a dismissive flutter. Her friends looked to her, then their notes. After class, Christine called him an asshole.

"You failed, too?" Beate asked, and her friends eyed the cigarette they passed back and forth.

"He didn't need to announce it in front of the class," Christine said.

"Or he could have told me in his terrible German," Beate answered. She performed an impression of Mr. McDowell as a German robot until her friends were laughing and their cigarette was done and they went back in through the door they'd propped open.

Beate lay in bed that night unable to fall asleep. The robot voice had been mean. She wanted to blame this meanness on the defection, though the truth of it snagged on the fact that she was a coward. At two in the morning she smoked a cigarette out her window. Winona was a graveyard. Streetlamps turned parked cars an anemic yellow. She imagined Mr. McDowell on top of her, his hands on her waist, her breasts. Then she heard movement. One of her parents was up. Footsteps shushed across the carpet, stopping outside her room. "Coward," she whispered, in English, working to keep the *w* from veering into a *v*. She missed Edinburgh, with its miracle feeling that stuck to her each time she figured out a new word or sexual position. Apart from new friends in history class, people in Winona ignored her. Even her lab partner, with his shiny forehead and smell of boiled potatoes, saw only a girl who slowed him down. Perhaps it was the way her voice sounded. Or because she could rarely detect sarcasm in English, which made her seem dumb, or like a child. Perhaps Edinburgh had been the exception when she'd imagined it as a signal of something that had started and would continue.

Mutti moved the couch in front of the window and borrowed a neighbor's vacuum. The news reporter arrived with a two-person crew. Mutti stared at the footprints they left in the carpeting.

"We are thinking the sofa would be a nice place for talking," Mutti said, in her best English. The crew chose the kitchen. "Best for the light," the cameraman said, though Beate wondered if crowding the three of them in front of their cheap cabinets jazzed up their story. The camera was turned on and the interview began. Beate stood between her parents.

"Why did you decide to leave East Germany?" the reporter asked.

Beate remembered the young soldiers who'd interviewed them, Vati's voice thin as he'd answered their questions.

"We go from there. It was bad to be," her father began. "The DDR—or GDR, you say—was a difficult problem for academic life."

His wedding ring clinked against the counter. For the newspaper interview, Beate realized, his translator had been in tow.

"Okay?" the reporter went on. "During the war, were you a soldier?"

"Too old for the war. I am living there always."

"In the article you discussed"—the reporter flipped through his notes—"the punitive nature of the government, particularly as a professor."

"Yes," he answered. "I teach philosophy. And in that we have questions of things."

The reporter smiled without showing teeth. From where she stood, Beate could see Vati's unwell photo in its plastic frame.

"Tell me and I'll say," Beate whispered.

Her father winced out a smile.

"With the government controlling more and more, about thought in particular," he began in German, "it became a difficult place to think and express what one thinks. That, and the thought of our daughter having to grow up in such a place. It made it necessary for us to act."

Beate translated. Her father talked some more. When he spouted out the word intimidation, she fudged its English counterpart. Vati talked with confident animation. Mutti interjected and Beate translated for her, too.

"Why Minnesota?" the reporter asked. Her father smiled into the camera.

"We were invited. By the university. The generosity of people here," he said, and paused. "We have felt welcomed. After so many years where we only felt afraid."

Beate worked to get his pause right, his inflection. Worked to believe that this awful apartment and the flatness and weather there were things she savored. Finishing the interview, her father held her elbow, then went to lie down. Mutti returned the neighbor's vacuum.

At school the next day, Beate walked into history and Mr. McDowell lit up. "You were on the news," he said. "You'd make an excellent translator."

"I suppose."

"Would you?" he asked, switching to German. "Talk to the class about your experiences?"

Relieved to be back in his good graces, Beate agreed. The class settled, and Mr. McDowell began. "Who saw your classmate on the news last night?" A dozen hands lifted. These people had seen her bare-bones kitchen, her parents, storybook-old.

Walking to the front of the room, Beate was sure she'd faint. She wanted to make it quick. But Mr. McDowell gave her his twitchy smile and she thought of everything she could say about the soldiers, the skin puckering under Vati's eyes.

"We had fake passports," she began.

"Like spies?" someone asked.

"I guess. For a few hours I had a different name."

Mr. McDowell was rapt, the class, too. There was nothing like trauma survived to let others remember for a while that their boredom was a luxury. "We had to get off a train. We were sent to a room with soldiers."

"How many?"

"Four," she lied. "They asked us questions."

"What sort of questions?"

"They wanted to see if they could catch us in a lie."

"And did they?"

"I'm here, right?" she said. The class nodded.

But her friends in the back row appeared uninterested. She'd told them this story already. The three of them had held on to it as if it were singular and precious—like old coins or virginity. Now Beate turned it into anyone's for the taking. She stumbled, especially when Christine, who hoped to move to New York, wrote something in her notebook and showed it to Karen. Beate thought of the letters Duncan had sent even after she stopped writing back, also the months in Cologne when she'd been obsessed with Frau Eggers, until they moved to another apartment and Beate forgot her, too. Sam nodded to Christine, and Beate grew sure they'd discovered that she considered loyalty no more than what was happening in the southern hemisphere. But Mr. McDowell looked pleased. Beate focused on him. She understood then how her father couldn't pass up the way attention made him matter. Understood why he'd agreed to an interview in a language he'd been undone by.

⟡

Later that night, as her parents talked of the phone calls they'd gotten, the fruit basket the philosophy department sent, Beate pressed down pellets of rice with her fork. Her parents passed ineptitude off as its opposite. They ignored her until she was needed. She remembered Liesl telling her that she was an accident, marked by the trauma and scarring of a crash landing.

"I have a question," Beate asked.

Vati looked perturbed. Beate realized he'd been in the middle of a sentence. She stared at her plate as she continued.

"Why did we *really* leave?" she asked.

"You've already translated that for me," he said.

"Generally, I understand. But why not a year before? A week later? What specifically about then?"

"We'd been thinking of it for a while," he said.

"But the specific thing. Were you about to be arrested?"

"I don't know anything about arrest," Vati answered.

Part of her wanted to stop, though to continue carried the dangerous excitement of sledding down an icy hill.

"So there wasn't a particular reason?"

"There were many reasons," Vati answered. "You were one of the reasons."

"But what if I didn't want to leave?"

"You were a child," Vati said. "You're a child now." He pushed his napkin into a ball.

"Mutti, did you agree with the leaving?" Beate went on.

"Child," Mutti said.

"We're in the middle of nowhere, a place where we barely speak the language. I'm just trying to understand." In Kritzhagen she'd had a handful of friends who, like her, read all the time and drew pictures of houses and women in miniskirts. Friends who Beate would head off to the sea with on the first warm spring day, swimming until it was hard to feel their fingers. In Edinburgh Beate had had a sort of celebrity, also Duncan, always whispering about how he wanted to make love to her, which even in her remedial English sounded like a ridiculous combination of words.

"I'm only asking a question," Beate said.

"I think we should take this up another time," Mutti answered.

"Why?"

"Another time."

"Why not this time?"

Vati banged a fist on the table, once, then again, again. Spittle freckled his chin. He stood up and stuttered into his room and seemed like a child. Mutti went to check on him. There'd been no real reason. Vati had simply made declarations, his favorite kind of talking.

Beate had two years until college. And though Vati had said she could study in Winona for free, the next morning she found her friends and explained how much she'd hated telling her story to the class. "I was trying to save my grade," she said. "I need to get into college. And not in Minnesota."

Sam and Christine talked about schools they wanted to go to out East, places with tidy old buildings and cinnamon-smelling days. "Yes," Karen said. "We totally get it. We all want to get the fuck out of Dodge." Beate felt flooded with relief. She tried, too, to figure out, without asking, what that expression meant.

That night, Vati stayed late at the library, the night after, too. His idea of punishment, Beate assumed, realizing only later that he might have been afraid of her.

One morning, years before, in Kritzhagen and angry for something she couldn't remember, Beate blurted out: "Liesl said I was an accident."

Sun cut across their honey-colored kitchen.

"Did you ask Liesl why she said it?" her father asked.

"Because it's true, I imagine."

"Did you ask Liesl why she said it?" Beate shook her head.

A stack of essays filled his satchel, so many ideas for him to evaluate, so many ways to tell his students that they danced around an idea rather than stating it.

"Do you have questions for me?" he asked.

"About what Liesl said?"

"Yes," he answered. "Do you have questions for me about what Liesl said about you not being part of a plan?"

There was an answer he wanted. Beate wasn't sure what it was. Saying she didn't implied an easiness he seemed to enjoy in their child-parent relationship. Saying she did might show gumption. The answer was that she didn't know whether she wanted to ask or not, that saying yes or no would change something, though she couldn't say what, only that it would add to a pattern where she didn't ask difficult questions, or where she did. She was hungry, angry with Liesl, her father's questions a trick she'd wooed Beate into.

"I want to know why you always wear a sweater and a blazer over it. I want to know if you get hot, and what you do when that happens."

He looked at his bag, at the hallway.

"I am surprised that that is what you want to know," he answered.

And now, in their cheap Winona apartment, she was glad she

hadn't said anything real to this man who demanded truth and offered fiction in return. He came home a few nights after the interview's broadcast in a huff. "They've asked that I study English with one of the teachers," he said. He chewed his dinner at the front of his mouth, like a rodent. Beate ate fast and asked to be excused. She stayed in her room, what the realtor who'd shown them the apartment called a half bedroom. She could touch one wall with her hands, another with her feet. "I used to live in a large house," Beate mumbled. "Who fucking cares?" she added.

Beate began to speak English more. When her parents complained, she said that her teachers told her she had to pause on the German. "Speaking English only," she said, in English, "is the only way to learn." Her father adjusted his napkin, trying perhaps to remember the word for napkin in English, or maybe ungrateful.

Soon she started thinking about college. Despite her piecemeal education, she was ahead of most of her peers. And Vati had a colleague at a women's college in Massachusetts.

"The Pilgrims," Vati said.

"A different part of this state," Beate answered.

She'd done well in school because it had been easy, because there had been nothing else to do. Because the idea of doing nothing was a falling she was afraid of. Vati's friend would see her school report and talk of how impressive it was for someone who'd only recently learned the language, adding that, with the life she'd lived, she could practically go for free. Beate waited each day for a letter from the women's college, trying to remember Massachusetts' spelling. She sat in her small room. Held her breath until it ached across her chest, then her temples. Beate let it out just before she was certain something inside her would stop working.

1994

13

After Liesl's lawyer finagled Udo's sentence down to a fine and he spent a disaster of a summer living with his father, followed by fifteen months of conscription during which he drove an ambulance in a town near the Polish border, Udo returned home. He got a job working for Heinz, whose business boomed with the city's sudden influx of tourism. But he chose to live with Michael and Beate instead of his mother.

"After all I've done for you," Liesl said, as Udo unpacked his car. "All *we've* done."

He carried boxes into the house. Liesl kept talking. Her daughter, Annette, stayed strapped in the backseat of Liesl's car, gnawing on a coloring book.

"Heinz has even given you a job," she said.

"If Heinz doesn't want to," Udo answered.

"There's no talk of not wanting," Liesl said. "But I have the apartment over the garage set up. I won't even care if you have girls over. Or boys. Maybe you're like your little cousin. I read that it runs in the family."

Michael had just gotten home from his job as a busboy; his skin and clothes smelled medium rare. He folded himself into a wingback in hopes that they wouldn't notice him.

"Good cousin," Udo said, and dropped a stack of boxes.

Liesl clomped in behind him. She was tan from a recent trip to Majorca. She wore a gold ankle bracelet and bracingly high heels.

"Michael, tell your cousin he's being ridiculous," Liesl said.

It did seem ridiculous. Even though Mutti had agreed that Udo could stay with them, she'd admitted to Michael that she didn't understand why he wanted to. But Udo walked in and looked worn out in a way Michael hadn't seen in him before. As he moved back into the driveway, hauling duffels on each shoulder, he slouched with defeat, though Liesl later insisted this slouch came from weight gain. Each blink appeared effortful, as it had for Michael when Tobias and his boyfriend moved to Düsseldorf. But Liesl refused to believe that sadness was real, mistaking it for laziness or something unmanly. As Udo unloaded a crate of CDs, Michael understood that living with them was something he needed.

"It seems like what he wants," Michael said.

"Tra-la-la," Liesl answered. She lit a cigarette and told the room that she had things to do, as if it'd been holding her against her will.

That night, as Michael and Mutti made dinner, they heard Udo heading out the door.

"Where are you off to?" Mutti asked.

"Don't know," Udo answered. The weight he'd added in the last year erased anything mean in his face. His shirt was carefully ironed.

"You look like you have plans," Michael said. Udo shook his head.

"We have enough food," Mutti added, and—with the same heavy slowness with which he'd unpacked his car—Udo sat down.

As Beate and Michael joined him at the table, Udo gave

them a smile that was both sweet and revealed the work it was to stay afloat.

"I didn't know," Udo said, which may have been about the food, or him living with them, or Adela citing him as a primary reason that she'd stayed in America.

For months, Udo toggled between tentative and overeager. In happier moments, he turned too helpful and too social. He cooked elaborate dinners. He asked Mutti questions about this or that old person. Asked Michael if Tobias had finally fallen for him. "Tobias is gone," Michael answered, and slid his headphones on.

One night, Michael arrived home late to find Udo and Mutti waiting. "I made dinner," Udo said. Michael wanted to say that he'd eaten already, but he was stoned and starving, so he sat down.

"In America, people eat in front of the television," Michael said as he slid an ice cube across the roof of his mouth.

"How *is* your sister?" Udo asked.

"I don't really talk to her," Michael said.

"Sure you do," Mutti answered.

She would have said more, but Josef arrived. When Mutti and Josef excused themselves, smiling like teenagers, Michael and Udo cleaned up.

"You like Josef?" Udo asked.

"Josef is a tree," Michael said, and lit a cigarette, soggy fingers staining the filter.

"A tree is just there," Michael continued, and thanked Udo for dinner and took off on his bike. He rode past his new literature teacher's building. He'd decided this teacher was *schwul* as fuck and planned to read for class in hopes of being called on. As Michael biked, he dreamed up intriguing things to say. *In consideration*, he might start. *Vis-à-vis*, he would add, all the while twirling a pencil between his fingers.

A month later, Michael made plans to take a weekend off to head to Berlin for Christopher Street Day. Lena wasn't interested. His friend Jacob said he had plans, which meant it scared him. He decided to go alone. Michael and Udo watched the latest episode of *Wetten, daß . . ?* Then came a news brief that showed Helmut Kohl in Berlin.

"I'll be there soon," Michael said.

"Moving to Berlin?" Udo asked.

"A weekend. To be gay and alone."

"My roommate when I drove the ambulance was gay and never alone," Udo added. He pulled on a beer. His shifting feet shook the coffee table. He talked of his plain roommate coming home with men, most of them very handsome. "Like you're handsome."

"Cousin," Michael answered. "Are you saying you want to kiss me?"

Udo's lips were the pink of uncooked chicken.

"No kissing, no, thank you," Udo said. "But you shouldn't be alone."

"And gay," Michael added.

Udo nodded. "I'm not afraid of gay people. I know you think I hate and hate."

"I don't think anything!" Michael answered.

A car honked on the street outside. Someone yelled with impatience.

"But it's a parade of gays," Michael went on. "Men kissing and grinding in the streets."

Television light bounced off Udo's face. A synthesized theme song played. As the show veered into more sexist jokes than Michael cared for, quiet Udo emerged.

"You worry they might try to kiss me?" Udo asked finally.

"They will try to kiss *me*," Michael said.

Udo turned off the television.

"If you don't want company," Udo answered.

Michael had nowhere to stay that weekend, no plan other than how he'd get there. There might be a night when he, tired and unwanted, would sleep in a park and get mugged. The mugging would at least be a story to tell, though it would be a story of failure.

"Company is nice," Michael said.

Udo showed off his sad smile, sweet and effortful in the same swallow.

In Berlin, instead of the rainbowed welcome Michael had expected, they found tree-lined streets and outdoor restaurants, entire quiet blocks. Michael had written the addresses of gay bars on the inside of his palm. They walked dozens of streets until they found one. There was a crowd, though the otherworldly electricity Michael had expected was missing. They swilled beers. Udo left to use the bathroom and came back with a party they were invited to.

"How did you get us invited to a party?"

"At the urinals," Udo said.

"You must have a gigantic dick," Michael answered.

They walked in and out of neighborhoods in search of the party, certain they'd never remember where they'd parked the car.

The party was in a warehouse full of men, shirtless and sweating. He and Udo took pills that made everything glitter, though it may have been the lighting. The building was once a factory that made belts and bags. Bolts of leather filled corners, and the whole place smelled musky. A beautiful man—shirtless, wearing rope as suspenders—stood close to them. Udo nudged Michael toward him. Michael planted his feet in weak protest.

"There's a café on Oderberger Straße," Udo barked over the music. "I'll see you there in the morning."

"Which café?"

"If I'm not there, it's the wrong one."

Udo turned toward the exit. Michael wanted someone to find his gigantic cousin beautiful. He wanted him to stay.

"What if Ropy doesn't want me?" Michael croaked.

Men coiled their fingers into each other's belt loops. They laughed loudly and wanted to be noticed. Michael wanted to be noticed, too, but couldn't imagine what came next. Someone could say hello and Michael would repeat, *Hello, hello, hello, hello.* He also needed to pee. The closest thing to a bathroom was a large back window. Men stuck their dicks out and pissed into an alley. The pill Michael had taken felt useless, then willfully defiant. He dreamed of getting into Udo's car and driving home. People in Kritzhagen asking how it was, Udo and Michael answering, *Fun*, and looking anywhere but at each other.

"Why are you saying fun like that?" Udo asked.

"I'm not saying anything," Michael answered.

"You'll be fine, cousin. If the handsome one doesn't take you home, someone else will. But go for the handsome one." Udo moved through the door. Michael sloshed beer around his mouth and spit it on the floor. He felt young, frightened in a way he knew should bring him shame, and wondered if anyone there would help him if he started to weep. A man with roller skates over his shoulder asked for a cigarette. Michael lit it and the man stayed. Though Michael wasn't interested, he kept spinning the skates' wheels, relieved by the man's chatty attention. A few times in their conversation, Michael worried he'd throw up. He excused himself to pee, going to the roof instead, where the man in the ropes had gone. The roof was packed and dark apart from the streetlamps that leaned over its edges. The *Fernsehturm* blinked. Ropy stood near the roof's edge. He and Michael paused next to each other as if by happenstance.

"I like that you're small," Ropy said.

Michael lifted one of his suspenders. The skin underneath roiled. By early the next morning, the two of them in a flat in Mitte—Ropy's real name Kurt—Michael had grown bored with the way Kurt winced each time he got near the rope burns, his constant remonstration: "Gentle." Michael left at four in the morning. He went to a bar that was technically closed, though there was life inside. He knocked for a minute before somebody came to the door.

"We're not open," the man said.

Inside, everything seemed to be happening. A breeze tickled Michael's neck.

"And I'm not really here," Michael answered, and smiled so wide his face hurt.

Ten minutes later Michael found the bar's back room with its lights off, feet entwined as if dancing. As he walked through it, someone pulled Michael next to him.

At seven he stumbled into the sun. He asked a man in a park for directions to the street Udo had mentioned. "I'll tell you for five marks," the man said. Michael smiled and kept going. "Two," the man shouted. "A cigarette!"

In the café, he found Udo reading the paper.

"Yay or nay?" Udo asked.

"Yay *and* nay," Michael answered. He downed a coffee. A newspaper article showed balloons, men in lipstick.

"I might need to sleep for an hour or two," Michael said.

They walked to a hotel Udo had found the night before. Michael took a shower and slept until noon. They wandered down Joachimsthaler Straße. Men in drag, along with dykes of every consideration, funneled together like streams into a river. The sun was hot and Michael took off his shirt. Udo followed suit. The pills they'd taken before leaving the hotel had Michael leaning close to strangers, feeling their shoulders against his even after he'd passed them. Though there were men that Michael might have kissed or groped or gone to the park with, which he'd heard had an entire forest dedicated to fucking, he stayed close to Udo. Music played. Everyone around them moved together like one large limb. As the crowds thickened, Michael climbed onto his cousin's shoulders.

A man walked next to them. He waved at Udo. When Udo waved back, the man put his arm around Udo's waist. "He's mine, actually," Michael said, calves resting against Udo's sweaty chest.

The man kept walking next to them, kept smiling at Udo, who smiled back with polite resignation. When the man tried to take Udo's hand, Michael returned to the ground to protect his cousin. A song blared. Michael and Udo danced. Udo found an abandoned boa and wrapped it around Michael like a leash. They pantomimed animal and keeper. In certain flashes, Michael went wide-eyed with wildness. In others, he showed the religious calm of the tamed.

Though he didn't yet have a license, Michael drove them home the next morning. At a highway rest stop, they downed coffees. Every once in a while, Udo laughed at the memory of men sucking each other off, or the sadness on his stalker's face when he watched Udo and Michael dance together. "For a minute, I was going to let him suck my dick," Udo said.

"Like you give change to a homeless person," Michael added.

"It was probably the pills talking," Udo answered, and took a sip.

Though they joked about other things the pills had almost tricked Udo into, Michael knew it was his cousin's goodness talking. The further they moved from the immigrants, from Adela's exit, the more relief Michael felt in having defended his cousin, which he'd done first because Adela's need to punish Udo had terrified him. Udo was good, Michael realized as years stacked on top of one another, as he watched Udo make Mutti dinner in the week Josef left her. Michael and Udo moved into their twenties, renting apartments two blocks apart from one other. When Michael was heartbroken, it was Udo who came over, once picking Michael up and putting him to bed, telling him that he'd never feel better if he kept sleeping on the sofa.

When Udo brought up the immigrants, Adela was his focus. He told Michael how he'd written her, though she'd never written back. How he thought of that night as a line he'd crossed and couldn't cross back. "I'm shit on a shoe," Udo said, often when he was drunk, his head so close to the bar that it looked as if he were asleep. "You did a shit thing. You do other things that are the opposite of shit," Michael said.

"What's the opposite of shit?" Udo asked, and never seemed convinced by Michael's answers.

2009

14

After working for a decade at one bar or another, Michael piled together his savings, along with loans from Mutti and Udo, and branched off on his own. He gave his place an English name: Secret Police. He installed lamps that were metal and military, painted the walls a Soviet red. Vintage GDR posters lined the walls. One over the bar said: SOCIALISM IS THE FUTURE. Another celebrated the kerchiefed women of their former republic. Michael spent weeks shaping the drink menu, which included creations like "Don't Drink the Kool-Aid" and "The Party Line." Some nights before the bar's opening he'd forgo sleep. As the sun rose, he would realize he'd spent an entire night unpacking glasses or rearranging furniture. Udo called him a vampire.

"Vampire," Michael would answer back when his cousin stopped by the not-yet-opened bar at sunrise.

"Vampires together," Udo would say, when Michael asked why he was up, too.

As sun burned through the bar's small windows, Udo pulled pastries from his pocket and said to Michael, "I'd like a cousin coffee."

"I think you mean a coffee, cousin," Michael answered.

"No. I mean a cousin coffee. A coffee made by you," Udo answered, and laughed.

Sometimes Michael asked if he'd been out all night. Sometimes they'd fall asleep with their faces on the bar. They'd wander back to their apartments, two blocks apart, calling each other a few hours later to make sure they'd made it to work.

Friends made jokes about the two of them being married. "Married people have to want to have sex with each other," Michael would answer, his friend Jana answering back that he'd clearly never been married before. But Michael and Udo loved those jokes, also the nicknames a coworker of Udo's gave them one afternoon when Michael showed up at a store they were installing dimmers in to bring Udo a sandwich: Little Husband and Big Husband.

Then Udo met Angela, a mousy bank teller, and jumped into a period of blissful infatuation. In a month he'd moved in with her. By the third, he'd proposed.

"A surprise," Udo told Michael one afternoon. They got in his car. They shared a cigarette and Udo tried and failed to sing along to a popular song on the radio.

They got to Mutti's, stopped just before her driveway. In the last year, the lot of rubble next door had turned into a pair of new houses. Dirt for lawns. Saplings shivering in front of them.

"Fuck a duck," Michael said when Udo unlocked the door of the house closest to Mutti's. Mutti's windows lined up with Udo's. A suitcase of Angela's clothes sat in the empty living room.

"Not kidding," Udo answered. "Angela and I live here now."

He mentioned a job he'd done for the man who ran one of the new hotels, how he was sure this man and Michael would make a perfect match.

"Set it up," Michael said.

"I have no idea how to do that." Udo laughed. "I was just

going to give you his name and let you do your thing." His hands folded in porno sign language.

"So you're telling me to rape him," Michael said.

Udo, giddy about everything, rested a hand on Michael's shoulder.

A month later, Udo and Angela were married. They got drunk at their wedding, stumbling across the dance floor and tripping on things that weren't there. They danced with Angela's nose smushed against Udo's torso and left without her shoes.

Angela and Udo moved into the house, so lovestruck they couldn't pick out a single piece of furniture. They had a sofa that Liesl had given them. A mattress was angled on the floor of the largest bedroom. Everything else stayed bare. When Michael texted Udo, he often got no reply. When Udo did respond, his answers were full of jokes Michael wasn't in on. One night, Michael just back from his bar with a young man in tow, his phone rang. He ignored it. As he showed the man his apartment in a recently refurbished building, with windows that showed views of the river, the ringing started again. "Let me just turn this off," Michael said, but saw it was Mutti calling, so he answered.

"I need you to come over," she said. "It's important."

Since Mutti never made requests of this sort, he told the young man there was an emergency. The man looked at him doubtfully until Michael showed him the four missed calls from *Mutti's Cell.*

Michael showed up to find his mother in her yard. Next door, at Angela and Udo's, a fight raged. Angela ripped down the sheet Udo had hung over their bedroom window. She dragged it from room to room, shouting things Michael couldn't catch, turning on all the lights. Udo followed and turned them off again. Angela shouted again and Udo stepped fast toward her, holding her against a wall in a gesture that seemed almost tender until Michael saw the red grimace on Udo's face, Angela's hands pinned under his. Michael ran to the window and knocked. Startled, Udo stepped back from Angela, who took that moment to run outside and get into her car. Udo followed, standing behind her car. She tried to back up, but he held his ground. The car's bumper pressed against his shins and Udo growled, "Do it!" Finally Angela barreled across their lawn and down the street. Udo ran after her in only a pair of shorts, though outside it was freezing. A car coming from the other direction honked at him.

A week later Heinz called Michael and asked if he'd seen Udo, who hadn't shown up to work in days. Michael got to the house and found Udo jumping rope in the empty living room. He stank of sweat, his face the red of a cardiac episode.

The rope clicked across the floor. Udo tried to smile, but looked injured. Michael grabbed for the rope and caught it the second time. It burned against his palm.

"I'm single again," Udo wheezed. "Ladies don't like fatsos."

A mostly eaten chicken lay on the counter. Michael pressed Udo on what had happened, but his cousin only said that she'd left. He asked what was going on when Udo had Angela against the wall, and his cousin said, "I was holding her hands so she'd stop hitting me." Michael thought back but couldn't remember Angela's hands on him.

Udo turned on the television. He dozed, woke up again.

"I emailed her," Udo said, eyes mostly closed.

"Angela?"

"Your sister," Udo answered.

He slouched so low that his ass hung off the sofa. They watched a movie about a man who loved to sleep with married women. One scene had him hiding naked in a closet; the woman's husband had just come home. Each time the husband walked past, his shadow knifed under the door. For some reason, Udo found this funny.

"What did she say?" Michael asked. "My sister."

The main character was found out. He ran naked out of an apartment, the angry husband close behind.

"When does she write anything?" Udo answered.

Michael stopped by the next day while Udo was at work. He picked clothes off the floor and washed them. When he'd visit each night there was a new mess, more food on the counter that Udo picked at. One night he ate only apples. Another was fish sticks straight from the pan.

Texts from Udo started to arrive at strange hours. *I think Angela realized that there's something wrong with me*, Udo wrote at five one morning. Michael squinted at the screen. A young man he'd met at a party snored next to him. *I had a dream that I had three children but they refused to leave the house*, showed up a few nights later. The day after, Michael's phone lit up during the bar's busiest hour: *Do you think Adela will think I'm a monster forever?* Followed by: *Am I a monster?* Then: *Don't answer that.* When things slowed down at the bar, Michael drove past Udo's; his car wasn't there. He checked other bars, then Angela's parents' house, though she'd filed a complaint and Udo had to keep a distance of fifty meters.

A week after came a call at one in the morning. Michael patted his nightstand and spilled a glass of water. He found the phone under his pillow. His bed was warm, the room cold around him. Outside, soupy fog.

"Cousin," Michael answered.

"How did you know?" Udo asked.

A crowd roared in his receiver. Udo said something Michael couldn't understand.

"What?" Michael asked.

"Geography."

While useless in literature and history, Michael had taken to geography's memorizing with a zealot's fervor. "Abuja, Accra, Addis Ababa," he used to mumble as he biked to and from school. "Beirut, Bishkek, Colombo," he'd murmured at parties as he worked up the courage to talk to a beautiful man.

"I need to know the capital," Udo shouted.

"Where are you?"

A cacophony of dropping and retrieval. A woman called out Gibraltar.

"Sorry," Udo said. "I thought you'd know."

"Where are you?"

"Trivia!" Udo shouted, as if he'd been saying it all along.

"But where?"

"You don't remember."

Udo was shouting. Michael shouted back. Outside, people passed on bicycles.

"Are you fucking someone?" Udo asked.

"Ha!" Michael said. "Sleeping. Where are you?"

"Trivia. So you don't know?

"What?"

"The capital of . . . Hold on." Rumbling rose, as if the phone were held into wind. Michael turned his bedside lamp on. "Kazakhstan."

"Oh," Michael said. "Let me think. But where are you?"

"Trivia."

"In Kritzhagen?"

Michael wanted a cigarette, though he was in the midst of a quitting episode. He chewed on the skin edging his nail, looked for clothes in case Udo was stranded as he'd been the week before when he'd called from a bar in Bad Doberan, a town so small Michael was impressed that there was a bar there at all.

"I don't think so," Udo said.

"Jesus."

"What?"

"You don't even know where you are."

"No," Udo said quietly. "I mean, what's the answer?"

"I'm thinking."

"You're talking," Udo grumbled. "Talk, talk, talk."

"Thinking."

"Talking."

"Hanging up."

"No!" Udo howled.

"Find out where you are, please, Big Husband. While I'm thinking."

Michael opened his refrigerator. He gnawed through the dried outer layer of a chocolate bar. From his window he could make out slices of the river.

"Astana," Michael said, and there was more noise. "Hello?"

"Astana!" Udo called out.

Clatter, then quiet. "Fuck," Michael exhaled. He dialed Udo's phone. It rang and rang. He dialed again and ate the chocolate bar. He dialed and put on clothes. As he grabbed his keys, Michael realized he had no idea where Udo might be. He lay down and woke up hours later, the sun padding his face like a hungry pet. He called Udo again. His voice mail picked up, Angela's voice in the background of his greeting.

But as fast as he'd fallen apart, Udo got better. Michael came out of his apartment one morning to find Udo waiting for him.

"I'm going for a swim," Michael said.

"Here to swim with you," Udo answered.

They went to the hotel pool Michael swam in during colder months. Udo tried to race him, though four laps in he gasped and held on to the wall. He met Michael the next day, too, in a jacket over his swimsuit so it looked like he had no pants on. Udo slid into the water. Goggles sank into the fat that filled out his face. He completed ten slow laps before he retreated to the wall.

A few weeks after that Udo bought a tiny sailboat for almost nothing. Though it was winter, he took it out every day. Michael drove to the harbor to meet him. Udo came in from a sail, the boat so low Michael could only see his cousin hovering above the waves.

One morning in March in the throes of a warm spell, Udo invited Michael and Mutti out on the boat. Mutti's braid lifted like a kite's tail. When Udo sailed them into larger waves, she clutched her collar, then laughed, then put her hand on Udo's shoulder.

"I told you I can sail, Tante Mutti," he said.

They floated over waves, and the sun warmed their faces.

"Did you see?" Udo said, and had them lean over the side of the boat. Just before its bow, he'd painted its name—*The Lady Michael.* Mutti beamed; the sail turned pompous with wind. A couple biking down the beachside path appeared to be racing them.

"A dare," Udo said. "That you take a dip."

He and Michael spoke in dares: ask that one on a date; eat the blubbery fat off a rib eye; don't jerk off for eight days. Though it was March, summer light burnished the water.

"Just because it's warm outside," Michael answered.

"Why it's a dare," Udo said. His sunglasses were mirrors. His gut rested on his knees. Udo hadn't gotten drunk in months. Though he was heavy still, muscle began to reemerge, like grass pushing through snow. Michael stripped to his underwear and stood on the boat's bow. Trees at the shore were quilted in green. Michael stared at the water as if it were a wall he might crash into.

Then he was in and breathless. Michael loved actions that wiped thinking clean—sex, certain drugs, this moment in the frigid water. With a few quick adjustments, Udo turned the sail full and pulled away, toward Denmark, a place they talked about as if it were a pretentious friend.

"Fucker," Michael howled, and pushed into a front crawl.

"Muzah fucka," Udo answered.

The boat slowed. As Michael got closer, Udo pulled away again. Water stung the backs of Michael's knees. His fingers began to go numb just as Udo lifted him into the boat. Once in a while, water shrugged over the bow.

"I think I'm ready to go home," Michael said.

They moved into the city's grid of docks, Udo's the smallest vessel there. He dropped Michael and Mutti off and said it was too nice to be inside.

"Don't you have, like, a job?" Michael asked.

"Heinz is on another vacation," Udo said, as if that explained, and turned the boat back toward the sea. They watched the sail pull him away, saw him wave just before he moved behind a bend in the shore.

As sun fuzzed the sky and gulls croaked, Michael wondered if Adela had ever written him back. His sister lived in South Africa and had a son. Michael hadn't seen her in a decade.

"That boat," Mutti said.

"I think he's in love with it," Michael answered.

Michael liked to pretend that this was the last time he would see his cousin, instead of Udo's call a few nights after. The dirt and the dog. Michael insisting that they undo what Udo had done, his cousin as red-faced as he'd been after Angela had left him and he'd jumped rope until it turned hard for him to breathe.

Michael was at the bar eight days later when Mutti called. He said hello and was answered with shrieking. For a moment he thought she was being attacked, that she'd dialed him in a last-ditch effort.

"Where are you?" he shouted, so loud that his nonplussed bartender, Justine, appeared startled. Both he and Justine had been slicing limes. Michael's sticky hands gripped the phone.

"Who is hurting you?" he asked, and imagined her gone, that loss large, one he wasn't ready for.

"I'm not being hurt," Mutti said. "I'm trying to tell you something." Her voice was calm, also deep, as if she'd smoked a pack of cigarettes in one sitting. "But Liesl keeps screaming."

⟡

As Dirk stood at the door—box in his arms filled with plates and forks, in a tank top patterned in the neons of a victory flag—Michael realized that he hated him. Dirk hadn't talked shit about him or lied or given him crabs. But he deployed control in the guise of kindness. Used reliability as a service he expected payment for. So when Dirk showed up at the house Michael had inherited from Udo only weeks dead, a house Michael hadn't invited him to; as Michael pulled himself away from a home improvement show where sisters got to remake each other's houses—one certainly hating the other for the paint colors she'd chosen; as he moved to the door when the knocks wouldn't quit and peeked through the window, confirming his suspicion that it wasn't one of the errant flower deliveries that still showed up, Michael's hate swelled. He imagined punching Dirk. Michael had never hit anyone.

"Housewarming presents," Dirk said, bags on either side of him.

"I'm not having a housewarming," Michael answered. Dirk kissed him.

Michael had been in the hotel pool a few months back when he'd realized that the man in the next lane was racing him. Even before he'd seen the face that turned out to be Dirk's, he'd fallen for his legs, the shifting heft in his Speedo. Now his cousin and best friend was dead, Michael having thrown a fit when he'd found out Liesl had had Udo cremated before he'd been able to see the body.

Dirk invited himself inside.

"Jesus," Dirk said.

"Is dead," Michael answered.

Dirk's handsomeness—which Justine called unsurprising—suddenly made Michael cringe. He wanted chipped teeth, crowds of tattoos. An ass that had never seen the sun.

The main floor was empty except for the sofa and television. Apart from the guest room where Michael now kept everything he owned, he hadn't changed a thing. Plastic cups filled the sink. Milk in the fridge hardened to curd. Unimportant notes Udo had written cluttered the counter, and a calendar stayed on the wrong month. Taking out the trash had been Michael's one concession.

"Oh, Michael," Dirk said at each turned corner.

"Yes?" Michael asked, and Dirk looked at the walls, the cabinets' handles.

After Udo died, Dirk had made sure Michael ate and brushed his teeth. Forced him to watch silly movies, some of which Michael wept through. Dirk watching him cry felt like more debt, his tally blocks long. They stopped in a hall. Dirk shone with the tamped-down joy of reimbursement.

"I have hooks," Dirk said. *To hang yourself*, Michael thought.

Hating Dirk filled Michael with so much energy that, for a moment, he was able to see beyond mourning. He wanted Dirk to say more stupid things. To crumple the notes Udo had written, which were useless to hold on to, though Michael would anyway.

"And candles for the smell," Dirk went on.

"What smell?" Michael asked.

Dirk's look—of constipated pity, of rescue to bill Michael for later—was the last straw.

"I'm sorry, Dirk," Michael said. Anger's energy shifted to something bulky and dull.

"We'll just clean it up and do some home improve—"

"I don't want home improvements," Michael said.

Dirk's smile tightened. On television, one of the sisters painted a wall.

Seven minutes later, Dirk said: "My friends were right."

"That I'm a dick," Michael guessed.

"Exactly," Dirk said, and moved toward the door.

Perhaps Dirk wasn't as calculating as he'd imagined, but liked Michael too much. But being called a dick livened him again. Michael knew Dirk would call his friends to commiserate. *Dick*, they'd say as they sat at one of the city's lesser bars. Clinking glasses, wishing him shit.

"I'm a dick," Michael said, though it no longer seemed to mean anything.

One night years before, Michael had been in Berlin. Early spring rain chewed through the snow. He'd gone home with a man who lived in an old flat in Prenzlberg. Graffiti lined the stairwell. A shower sandwiched in the kitchen. He and the man fucked fast and napped briefly. When the man went to refill the apartment's coal oven, he left its door open for a moment so that its light projected giant versions of them across the wall. And, in a routine he'd probably done before, he pushed his pelvis up, the shadow of his cock a risen person. "So big," Michael said. "I don't know how I'm supposed to put that anywhere." Though it had been cold, Michael opened the window. Rain shocked the crook of his elbow. And he felt lucky, for this city with men whose beds he might lie in, the maze of crooked streets, bars with men who'd glance at him and keep looking.

After Michael ended things with Dirk, he fell back on sex's purpose. He checked in at the bar and continued on to Hamburg. As that city's skyline glowed, the Autobahn whirred through his opened windows. A few hours later he was in the apartment of a couple that laughed at everything until Michael stuck his tongue down the throat of one of them to turn things serious. He drove home early the next morning via a coastal road, though it took twice as long. In Kühlungsborn he stopped and swam and lay on the sand afterward. By the time he got to the house, he wanted only to plant himself on the sofa and watch television. He pulled into the driveway just as Mutti was leaving her house next door. In the decade since her brief marriage to Josef ended, she'd turned stout, her blondeness overtaken by gray. Mutti wore a dress like a sack. She tapped on his window.

"Did you send your friend away?" she asked.

"You like to spy on me," he answered.

"I just look out of my window and see," Mutti said. "You didn't like that one, though."

"I didn't," he said, and pictured Dirk at a store, getting Michael curtains and a broom. Pictured Udo on the water, so taken with sailing he didn't notice darkness claiming the day.

Mutti fiddled with her necklace. Michael's cheeks itched from the couple's stubble. He wanted sleep, to hear Udo's gruff timbre. Mutti kissed his forehead and drove away.

Michael used the spare key and went into Mutti's house. He made himself a coffee, lay on her couch, and skimmed through magazines. Cindy, Mutti's ancient cat, slithered out of the carrying crate she spent most of her time in. Her smell followed with a minion's devotion. Cindy opened her mouth, let out something between a hiss and a meow. One of her fangs had fallen out. Her fur was thin, the skin underneath it the color of boiled chicken. "You hated Dirk, too, yes?" Michael asked, and her arthritic tail shivered. Cindy probably hated Dirk. But Cindy hated everyone.

Michael started swimming twice a day. He swam down the coast past towns he'd never been to, continued until his shoulders started to rebel. He texted the teacher he'd slept with in the past—a man who always talked about poetry and sentences—and wrote, *I'm coming over. No talking.* When they were done, sheets ropy around their ankles, the teacher asked, "What was the no-talking thing?" Michael kissed him and left. He drove to the bar. Moving inside its locked door, he jerked off. His free hand rested on the counter, which was sticky and collaged in stains.

Michael went back to Hamburg that night and met a man with a boyfriend at home who didn't approve of sex outside the relationship. When it got late, they snuck onto the roof of the man's building. Gravel gouged their knees. The man kept shushing him, telling Michael that his boyfriend had perfect hearing.

Afterward, Michael wanted Udo to talk to. He'd have laughed at Michael's threesome story. Would have asked why he and the man on the roof didn't put clothes between their knees and the gravel. Michael sat on Udo's sofa. Coins were wedged between its cushions. Leaving the coins and notes and the sheets on Udo's bed did nothing, but still Michael did it. Sometimes he sent texts to Udo's disconnected number. *Three men in one night*, he wrote. *I still have a crush on the shawarma guy. You have five euros and 42 cents in your sofa.*

Michael found a man online in a nearby suburb. He was handsome, at least according to his pictures. His house neighbored a potato field.

"You're a potato farmer," Michael said as he walked into the house, which was tidy and small. They were half undressed before they made it to the sofa. The man had a dog, which clacked across the floor. It was knee-high and wiry, with a wet, wide snout. It circled them, until the man gave it a look and it settled. The man moved on top of Michael. He kissed him hard, with skill. *He was a great kisser*, he could have told Udo. *Has a thing for armpits*, he would have added. Michael sank into the sofa's too-soft cushions. The man's tongue explored Michael's throat. "Maybe the floor's better," Michael said. They moved, the dog again activated. The man's mouth meandered across Michael's stomach. The dog's tail whipped his head. The man had a thing for eye contact. *He was lovely or crazy*, he would have written Udo, who'd have answered that Michael was lovely or crazy, or would have offered up the closest thing he gave to advice: *Be not stupid*. The man invited Michael to stay over. They moved to an attic bedroom. A round window, as if from a ship, crowned the bed. The man slid under the duvet. As Michael hesitated, the dog moved in, in his stead.

"You're really a potato farmer?" Michael asked, hoping to be a dick again, for this man to shake his head and let the dog stay.

"You like potatoes," the man answered.

Michael excused himself, went to the bathroom, and turned

the tap on. He jerked off in the mirror. At certain moments he looked handsome, at others he was an exaggeration of hollow cheeks and large chin. Water whirred from the faucet. Michael came. He cleaned up and climbed into bed with the man, whose name he'd forgotten.

The man fell asleep with his arm across Michael's chest. In five minutes his leg joined in, sturdy from something that was probably not farming. Michael distracted himself with thoughts of this man in a field, hands the color of earth. The dog farted, and Michael tried to remember the man's name. He couldn't come up with a letter or number of consonants. Dog and man breathed in syncopation. Michael's stomach and heart flipped as if one organ. With the first light, he got up. The dog's tail thumped as Michael searched for his shoes.

Michael blamed the boat. The tiny, stupid boat Udo had gotten after his divorce from Angela. Once a few months had passed, Michael was able to say that the warm spell had tricked Udo as it tricked everyone. But when it first happened he was hit with a choking hopelessness. Michael blamed Udo, felt struck down by his own meanness, then turned so sad he would lie on the floor or cry behind the bar until Justine called him a cab. Mutti turned hands-on. She called Michael's doctor, accompanied him to the appointment, where the doctor started by giving Michael a pamphlet on antidepressants, he and his mother arguing later as to when the best time to give a pamphlet was, landing on either never or the middle of the appointment. He remembered the clinic Udo had taken him to, the tests he'd known would turn out fine.

In those first days after he'd died, Michael found out surprising things about his cousin. Udo had a large amount in savings. He also had a will. Sitting in a lawyer's office, Michael learned that Udo's money was to be split between Udo's half sister and Liesl and Mutti. His car given to Heinz. The lawyer looked down at her papers. "And the final thing," she said. Her blouse was shiny. Her eyebrows and hair were different colors. "The house."

Sadness caught in Michael's throat, also a widower's recognition. The lawyer shuffled papers. On her desk, tea steeped in a mug. "The house is given to Michael Haas," she said. "And Adela Sullivan."

It was Phone Tap Friday at the bar. Anyone willing would write down a secret they'd once shared over the phone, the thing they would have been most ashamed for the Stasi to have heard. It brought bigger crowds each week, and each week the risk of renting and transforming the bar fell further away. At ten, entries closed and Michael stood on the bar to read the confessions aloud. Once finished, he and Justine would choose a Shamed Citizen of the Week, who, in turn for their confession, drank free. The first winner admitted to fucking her boyfriend's younger brother in a high school art room. Entries turned more sordid from there.

Michael and Justine mixed and muddled and poured. The iPod shuffled to a Kraftwerk song. "*Stop the radioactivity*," the singer droned. "*It's in the air for you and me.*" A customer ordered three Brainwash shots.

"So many people here." Michael looked up to see his mother. Customers on either side of her held fans of money.

"A thing we do," he said.

Justine saw Mutti and waved. As subversive as she cast herself, she still grew shy around elders. She called Mutti Frau Haas, though his mother had told her a half dozen times that her name was Beate. No one offered Mutti a seat; Michael found an extra stool and slid it behind the bar. Mutti sat and said she didn't want to stay, though when he offered her a beer, she accepted.

"I have something to tell you," Mutti said.

"Bad?" Michael asked.

As Mutti shook her head, she gave off a whiff of perfume. She'd told him once that she wore perfume to keep the smell of old people from getting into her clothes.

A large man leaned in to order, and the loss of Udo appeared in a sudden gust. Something in this man's jaw, in how he slid his arms onto the bar, seemed stolen.

Customers worked to catch Mutti's eye as if she worked there. She shook her head, smiled. It was her younger self Michael still conjured when he thought of her, hair bright blond, so nervous at the looks from customers that she would have started making drinks though she didn't know what was in them.

"Hold on," Michael said to his mother, and climbed onto the bar.

"Hello, citizens," he said into the microphone. He kept his face stony, voice clipped. Justine turned off the music. "We are here for the protection and betterment of our great society to share the shameful goings-on in our city. Let's begin." A few people giggled, likely those who'd written confessions down. "*I once watched my brother drown a cat*," Michael read. "Short and to the point. That's entry number one, comrades. Though that feels more like a public service." Laughing and booing. Michael gestured to the booing person that he was watching her. Had Michael been in the audience, he would have seen this shtick as artless camp. "Number two," he said. "Oh! *I slept with my chemistry teacher in eleventh grade. For several months. I also started spying on his wife, who was a cow*." Candles lit customers' faces.

The next few entries focused on sex in strange locales. Michael's own tales of public sex would have blown these out of the water. He finished reading and climbed down. Mutti looked at her drink. Justine looked mortified.

"Found it disturbing?" Michael asked.

Mutti shook her head. Her face had loosened in middle age. No matter how many times he saw her, this softer, graying version left him disappointed and relieved. Her shirt was the green of a cartoon frog.

"But what I had to tell you," Mutti said.

Perhaps she and her on-again, off-again dentist friend had decided to move in together, though Michael had seen no evidence of him at Mutti's house as of late. Their sort-of relationship had started when Mutti went in for a cleaning and he'd remarked on the quality of her teeth. "As if you were a horse for purchase," Michael had said, her look telling him that he was terrible, also not wrong.

"It's a bit busy," Michael said to Mutti. "It's urgent?"

He took two orders. He and Justine hadn't decided on the Shamed Citizen yet. Part of him wanted to declare that there would be no winner until people had something real to confess. No one cared about fucking, about what your brother drowned. The man who looked vaguely like Udo moved toward the bathroom. Michael wanted to follow him.

"I'll come tomorrow," he said. "We can talk then."

Mutti left, sliding past the bank of people leaning in to the bar. Michael winced down a whiskey. Customers waiting to be served watched him.

Unable to sleep, Michael went for a swim at first light, going for so long that halfway back he dragged himself from the water to lie in the sand. Just after, he found himself at the bar. The cleaning crew, Albanian sisters with square torsos, saw him and smiled. "So clean," they kept saying. The place burned with bleach. They stood on a ladder to dust poster frames. With each reach he imagined one of them losing her footing. Michael thanked them and left. He drove to a coffee shop below Dirk's apartment. He hoped Dirk might stop there before work and see him and scowl. *A dick and a fucker*, Michael wanted him to say. *You and that cousin deserved each other.* Had Dirk said that, Michael might have wanted him again. He waited for Dirk to pass so Michael could tap on the glass, Dirk's smile dropping as his middle finger rose. That would have been the best thing. Dirk did have lovely hands.

⟡

The government lawyer. The furniture dealer in the basement of his shop. The hairdresser who stank of cheap shampoo. Anton and his boyfriend the journalist. The journalist without Anton. Hand job from the one in the ski cap. Blow job from the one with dry lips. Markus, who was between jobs. Linus, who'd just come back from Thailand. After each one, Michael found a bathroom or a backseat or a copse of trees and jerked off though he'd just come, sex turning a fly into a hornet.

He and Wilmar moved into the woods off a hiking trail. Branches scratched their arms. Wilmar opened his mouth as though to swallow Michael whole and left as soon as they finished. Birds bounded through trees. Michael got himself hard again. His dick throbbed, but he kept on. When he emerged from the woods he came upon a woman walking a dog. Her look told him she knew what he'd been doing. He picked dirt off the bottom of his shoes and saw texts from the Potato Farmer, also from Mutti, saying she needed to talk to him: "Not a bad talk, just a talk." He texted the Potato Farmer back to say he'd come over that night. He walked past two women who smiled at him. Michael smiled back. He wanted to apologize, to tell them it had been something he'd needed.

Grief lived in Michael's body. It knotted his stomach and ached behind his eyes. Left his mouth dry and strange-smelling. Sex became its antidote, a vigorous tug-of-war between giving up and thrashing forward. And he was good at it. He loved its tastes and smells, the nonsensical things called out in the height of it, the stroke-struck faces. Even as his body began to rebel, coming taking almost an hour, the collar of his foreskin holiday-red, he pushed forward. Just as he swam twice the length he had the summer before. Just as he either abstained from smoking or lit the next cigarette before the last had been smashed into an ashtray.

⟡

Standing on the Potato Farmer's stoop (why couldn't Michael remember his name?), he saw more texts from his mother: *I just need to tell you something . . . You hate surprises . . . Fine, Michael.* Her anger felt good, a victory. He rang the bell. (The farmer had mentioned his real job, but all Michael could come up with was the dumb joke he was so fond of.) The dog barked, was quieted with a nasal command. Feet flapped across the floor. The farmer offered Michael a glass of water. Michael declined and kissed him and things began. Again they started on the too-soft sofa. The dog vied for attention and was thwarted. As they undressed, the farmer stopped. The soreness in Michael's crotch had turned second nature. But the farmer stared at Michael's inflamed foreskin.

"It's been busy, is all," Michael said.

"And maybe all that busyness . . . ?" The farmer added.

Michael flicked his dick. It bounced to attention. It also hurt. "It's just busy."

"This is more than busy," the farmer said. "Come to my office tomorrow."

"What office?"

"I'm a nurse," he said, his face making it clear Michael should have known this.

He handed Michael his boss's card. Frau Doktor Dora Birnbaum. The farmer slid his underwear on, and the dog sniffed his knee.

"I'm tired," the farmer said.

"Let's sleep, then," Michael answered. But the farmer shook his head. *Nurse*, Michael thought. *A nurse with a dog. A nurse who isn't inviting me to sleep over.*

"I'll put you on the schedule for tomorrow," he said.

Michael wanted to ask the nurse what his name was.

After Michael found a middle-aged couple online, too jazzed about a threesome with him to say anything about his dick, after he kissed and touched each of them with a surprising hunger and fell asleep with one wedged on either side of him, Michael returned home. The sun lifted as he drove through Kritzhagen, dreaming of the spare room at Udo's he'd claimed as his. It had stayed untouched when Udo lived there. In it, Michael felt a creative license he did not in the rest of the house. He drove and thought of spinning the blinds closed, the soft hold of his duvet. But as he pulled into the driveway, he saw a boy sitting in Mutti's yard. The boy waved; Michael waved back. His injured dick burned. The boy crossed into Michael's driveway.

"I know you," he said, in English, and Michael realized who he was, along with the surprise Mutti had tried to tell him.

He looked less Asian than Michael imagined he would, with a face that would inspire people to ask where he was from. The child was kindergarten-sized, though Michael knew he was somewhere closer to seven. He held a drawing pad at his hip on which he'd sketched a house. Its chimney leaned. Trees like broccolis sat on either side.

"It's that house," the boy said. "My grandmother's."

The child's eyes were dark and wide. Only his hair—corkscrewed with frizz—betrayed the fact that they were related.

"You're the uncle," the child said.

"'Michael' is fine."

"Michael is fine," the child repeated.

"Peter," a voice, his sister's, called from inside.

"You have any nicknames?" Michael asked.

"Peter is my name," the boy said, as if Michael had tried to tell him a truth he wasn't ready to hear.

Then Adela was outside, too. Her face had taken on a hard quality, her brow lined though she was only thirty. Her neck was thinner and carried a constellation of moles that Michael didn't remember from before. The card from the doctor sat in his pocket.

"You're back," Adela said.

"You said you didn't want it," Michael answered, pointing to Udo's house.

"I'm just here."

Paper from Peter's pad fought with the wind. Adela hugged Michael. Her smell was the same and flattened the years they were apart. Made him realize that he would never smell Udo in this way again. Michael wanted to lie down.

"You're just here?" Michael said.

"Visiting for a while," Adela answered.

"I need to take a shower," Michael said. Fabric shushed against his foreskin. He couldn't remember when it had started to look injured. "I'll come over in a little bit."

The last time Michael had seen Adela was a decade earlier, just after she'd graduated from college. Mutti was all set for the two of them to fly to California for the graduation when Adela wrote that she wasn't going to the ceremony, that she had no interest in pomp and circumstance. Michael, bartending at one of the hotels then, made up a drink called Pomp and Circumstance, which failed, mostly because people couldn't pronounce it.

But after the German Lady insisted they do something to celebrate, Adela wrote back to say that she'd never been to Boston. So they met in Boston, Adela a skinny vegetarian who made lists of museums for them to explore, restaurants where there would be more options for her than a bowl of pasta. She was exceedingly polite, as if her mother and brother were strangers, which left Michael annoyed and prone to acting out. One night, each of them in their respective hotel rooms, he went out and met a man at a gay bar who was fascinated by Michael's English, which sounded native at one turn, foreign at another. "Like you went to some Swiss boarding school," the man said. "Let's go with that," Michael answered, and spent a day and a half with him, leaving a message for his mother and sister that he'd run into a friend. When he came back, Mutti looked distressed. Michael asked what had happened. She answered that nothing had happened, only that when she'd tried to ask Adela how she'd been, or if she ever felt like she might come back to Germany, his sister told her about other places she wanted to visit. Continents where not everyone looked as they did, with food and smells and weather she had trouble imagining.

"Where is she now?" Michael asked.

"Went back to the same museum we were at two days ago.

Said it was hard to go to places with other people and really look the way she wanted to look."

"She's an asshole," Michael said.

Mutti looked like she might cry. Michael decided he'd head to the same gay bar that night, hopefully to find someone new to pass the time with.

Mutti's look seemed to sense this, and she shook her head.

"She's not an asshole," she said, "just because she does things one way and you do them another."

After his shower, rather than go to Mutti's to see his sister, Michael got back into his car and drove to the doctor's office where the Potato Farmer worked. He sat in an exam room and stared at posters on healthy eating. When the doctor came in, Michael tried to turn himself into a joke. "Your nurse wouldn't even sleep with me," he said. He expected her to wince at his injury, or chide him for not being safe. Wanted her to ask him what he'd been thinking. Michael would answer that not thinking was what had gotten him into all of this, though it was thinking too much that left him miserable knowing that he'd never have a break from himself.

"Let's take a look," the doctor said.

Michael slid his underwear down to his ankles. The doctor leaned closer. She looked at his injury as if she'd seen the same thing hundreds of times before.

1974

15

Lying in their beds after they'd shut the lights out, Beate said to her roommate, "My parents pretend that Thanksgiving isn't a thing." She told Kate how they got mad when the grocery store was closed, the buildings at the college locked. Water turned on and off in the bathroom next door.

"Your parents sound like characters," Kate said.

It was the Monday before Thanksgiving.

Kate asked again if Beate wanted to go home with her for the holiday. Unable to think of an excuse that didn't sound rude, the fear of days alone in their dorm swelling in her, Beate agreed.

"Pilgrims," Beate said.

"Indeed," Kate answered. Indeed was one of her favorite words.

On the bus ride there, Beate began to run out of things to talk to Kate about. After several quiet minutes, Kate turned to Beate, explaining her father's worry when she decided to go to Mount Holyoke. "Thinks I'll become a lezzie."

"Laura Hanft on our floor is," Beate said.

"Half of our floor is," Kate answered, her barking laugh too loud for the bus they were on. They were headed to Kate's small upstate New York town, a place she made jokes about. "We're such hicks, we don't even know how to say it. Green-witch."

"How are you meant to say it?"

"You're hilarious, B."

Beate wished she'd stayed at school. She would have kept her door locked, fear her entertainment. She might have befriended an international student stuck there, too. The bus stopped in Albany before continuing.

"My mother is dead. I think I told you," Kate said. "Cancer. Roller-coaster fast."

"I'm sorry."

"Indeed," Kate answered.

Gray trees reached toward the sky. They moved past houses just off the highway. Beate imagined living next to it might feel bothersome at first, but that the traffic eventually turned to background noise, the rushing of a river. They passed a mall. Cars clustered in front of it as if huddling for protection.

Kate's father had a walrus mustache. When he saw his daughter, he hugged her for a long time. Beate was moved and embarrassed, then embarrassed that she was embarrassed, certain she'd inherited Mutti's easy public shame. She smiled as if she were comfortable, even as the clock's second hand wound through most of a rotation.

They drove through flat, grand Saratoga, then out of it and uphill. Greenwich was small, battalioned with farms. The house they pulled up to was one story, its garage as large as the house. "Here we are, B," Kate said.

"Yes, B," her dad added. "Home, sweet home."

Kate's dad—Mr. Sullivan—ordered pizza. Somewhere in the back of the house, a door clicked closed.

"I told you I have a brother," Kate said.

"You told me a story about how he was always naked. As a child."

"Indeed," Kate said, and turned on the television.

Beate was relieved for its distraction. Her parents were likely on their sofa, Vati reading, Mutti listening to the radio. Mutti listened to it for hours. Sometimes her mother got up to make tea or eat half a sleeve of crackers. Sometimes she wrote lists of English words, checking the dictionary to see if she'd spelled them correctly. Beate thought next of her dorm, quiet except for the lights' hum, each shift of wind throttling her. Fear felt preferable to this strange house or to the quiet of Winona, and she remembered her excitement in heading east for college, switching buses in Chicago, knowing she could get out there and no one would know.

"What's that?" Beate asked, after Kate said something she didn't catch.

"I know," Kate answered.

Kate's dad returned with the pizza. They ate at the dining room table, which was crowded with mail. The overhead light glared, and grease dripped onto plates. Kate's brother walked in wearing shorts and a T-shirt.

"My son runs all the time," Mr. Sullivan said. "And I ask him what he's running from." A smile shifted his mustache. The son stared blankly, then said hello to his sister and Beate. He was small, with olive skin and dark hair. His leg tapped under the table.

"You liking America, Beate?" the father asked, pronouncing her name as if it were a root vegetable.

"Beate," the brother corrected. He scowled, his annoyance on her behalf funny. Beate looked down at a pile of catalogs but couldn't keep her laughter in. The father looked ashamed. This quieted Beate. "I wasn't laughing at that," she said. "Sometimes I remember things."

Crumbs clung to the father's mustache. The brother darted back to his room.

Beate was given the couch in the den. She brushed her teeth and changed into her nightgown, which Kate called prairie garb. She had no idea how she would sleep on this tiny couch, remembering the one in Cologne with buttons that woke her whenever she shifted. The brother stopped at the door.

"You know it's a pullout," he said, walking in and removing the cushions. The sofa morphed into a bed with a bread slice of a mattress. He slid a sheet across it. His legs brimmed with hair.

"You really defected?" he asked.

She nodded. "I didn't know."

"Kate didn't tell you, I can see," he said, and slid pillows into cases.

"I mean about defecting."

Something about this young man erasing her stupidity made her feel the need to repay him with the story of the soldiers and the train, the dead woman's apartment. "She had all this jewelry that I thought was worth a fortune. I planned to steal a piece in hopes that we could buy a small house somewhere," Beate said, though she'd never thought the jewelry was real. The brother grinned at her invented detail. In his smile, something softened. He smelled of soap. They piled blankets on the bed.

"My parents wanted to keep going after Minnesota, but got tired," she said.

"Otherwise you'd be in Borneo now."

"Or west of that."

"You want to watch something?" he asked.

He turned on the television. They watched late-night talk shows, laughing as Steve Martin played the banjo with an arrow through his head.

"I don't know why this is funny," she said. His shoulder was warm next to hers. He was dressed for summer, though the house was cool. A few times his hand touched her leg, staying there until she looked at it. Beate worked to stare instead at the television, or the bookshelf with gardening tomes and paperback mysteries with cracked spines.

The next morning, Kate prepared Thanksgiving dinner, moving through the kitchen like an expert. She wore her mother's apron and followed recipes written by the dead woman's hand. At dinner, Kate's father toasted his wife. By the toast's end, Paul—the brother—was crying.

As Beate and Kate cleaned up, coffee gurgling in the machine, Kate apologized.

"For what?" Beate asked.

"My brother likes to show the world how sensitive he is."

"He wasn't sad?"

"We're all sad."

A roaring in the next room from a game on television.

When Beate asked if she liked her brother, Kate answered, "You're an only child, right?"

Beate pushed into the pot and scrubbed. Her parents were probably in bed already.

"I am," she said.

"No one likes their siblings," Kate answered. "At least not normal people."

Beate wondered if her parents had finally stopped treating Thanksgiving as a surprise, if Vati still showed up to his closed office building. If Mutti listened to the radio because she couldn't think of what else to do in an apartment with carpet that bunched like old skin and neighbors who played loud music though her parents had written notes asking them to turn it down, calling Beate first to see if they'd used proper sentence structure.

Paul came into the den again the next night. On television, they watched a comedian who tried too hard to be funny, then Stevie Wonder. His head traced figure eights. Toward the program's end, she put her hand on Paul's leg. It was warm. Stevie Wonder—his hat floppy and bright—pounded piano keys, and backup singers shook tambourines. He put his hand on top of hers and voices rose. Beate's tongue traced the inside of her mouth. She wondered why she didn't always notice her tongue and teeth negotiating one another. Then Paul kissed her.

The last night, they took off each other's clothes. Paul had chest hair, like a man. It tickled as he pressed against her. She wanted to laugh but bit her lip, then his, and Paul flicked his underwear off with his feet. When they finished, Paul told her about Kate taking care of their dying mother. "She slept in the room with her when it got too sad for our father." He loved his sister with a largeness that was perhaps smothering.

"She thinks I'm an asshole sometimes," Paul said. "When my dad made that toast. When I cried. I think she's angry because she's even sadder but pretends she's not."

He kissed Beate's mouth and throat, moved his fingers across her breasts. Beate's appetite for him was so blazing that when he went back to his room, she missed him and felt ashamed. She wanted to lie on top of him again, mistook each sound for his feet on the floor, thinking of how she'd once asked her boyfriend in Edinburgh to move into her and stay for a while. *He is inside of me*, she'd thought, and it felt like they were breaking an impossible barrier. She wanted to ask Paul the same thing.

The sun showed up. Beate turned the bed back into a couch and tried to read Germaine Greer. Dogs outside barked in a call-and-response. She heard a door open and watched her own door, as if staring hard enough would bring her what she wanted. Paul was still in high school. He was an inch shorter than her. The front door clicked open and she saw him outside, beginning his run. "He wants to get a running scholarship," Kate had sneered when they were washing dishes. "Because there's a future in running." Beate thought of Paul's feet on the pavement, of her hand on his chest as he breathed in his sleep.

On the bus ride back to school, Beate tried to work up the courage to tell Kate what had happened. But each time she thought to speak, Kate pointed to something out the window. Or she was so buried in her copy of *Middlemarch* that Beate let her be. Once in a while, Kate read her sentences. "Blameless people are often the most exasperating," she quoted. "Indeed. B. Not doing any work?"

"I get sick reading on buses."

"There was a girl at my high school who was like that but pretended she wasn't. We took a trip to Albany, to see the state senate in action or some such nonsense, and she read for half of the trip and then suddenly, like she'd caught fire or something, she jumps up, right? Opens a window and pukes like mad."

Beate asked if the girl went back to reading, the relief of benign conversation moving everything hard far away.

The bus moved into Massachusetts, where lit-up windows brightened dingy houses. Some people already had Christmas trees. Mutti considered Christmas trees in November obscene, though Beate understood it was these people's greed Mutti objected to. On the last night, Paul had stayed on the pullout until four in the morning. They'd slept naked and Beate had woken up shocked and thrilled at his company. Each time she settled back into sleep—his hip pressed into her, his penis warm on her skin—she wanted more of him. She'd known him for three days. Already he felt essential. Beate memorized his smell, how his tongue moved in his mouth when he watched television. She wanted more. She seesawed between wanting something so certainly and the terror that he'd already turned important. Had she stayed in the dorms, befriending an international student, she wouldn't have met him. Beate lusted after not knowing him. She and the international student, maybe one from South Korea, could have taken the bus to Northampton to see *Alice Doesn't Live Here Anymore*, which Kate had recently come back devastated from. They might eat at a diner and talk about something from home that made this life seem strange, the student asking Beate about Germany, Beate answering as if she still lived there.

The woman on the cover of Kate's book wore black and arranged flowers.

"Is that like *Jane Eyre*?" Beate asked. "Wandering around the moors, serious and . . . I can't think of the other word."

"I don't remember *Jane Eyre*," Kate answered.

Beate had fallen in love with that book, Jane's sincere obsession both ridiculous and right. Wandering the rainy moors after leaving Mr. Rochester was unreasonable, and a few times Beate had muttered to herself that Jane just needed to have brought an umbrella. But she lusted after Jane's fear, too, the wanting that came with it. As the bus pulled out of Pittsfield, an itch to move hit Beate and she excused herself.

"That bathroom is the most disgusting one on planet earth," Kate said. "It's less than an hour, if you can hold it."

"I don't think I can," Beate answered.

Even the bathroom's stench and suspect stains couldn't distract her from picturing Paul asleep with a hand on her hip bone, thoughts that hadn't existed in her three days before when she'd been on this bus or one just like it, certain staying alone in the dorms would have been better. Pretending she was an international student because that was easier than other answers.

There are tests, Mutti had written. Her mother only communicated through the mail, which made her feel farther away. So, when Beate's mother wrote of her father's possible illness, it carried the distance of history, like the novels Beate read where people said everything and nothing via letters. *We are hopeful, and the doctors are kind*, Mutti added, writing in simple sentences, as if Beate had forgotten German. Beate read that letter and felt nauseous. She checked her mailbox again to see if she hadn't missed something from Paul, even as she understood that the tests weren't a precaution but a confirmation of her father spluttering toward some sad finish.

It was a Saturday. In the dorm, a line of young women waited for the pay phone to dutifully call parents in Cleveland and Washington, D.C. Beate spent it in the library. She used Mutti's letter as a bookmark. Coming back to her room, she asked Kate if she had any news from home. Her roommate talked about a problem with her dad's roof, a high school friend who was pregnant, but said nothing about Paul.

A week and a half later there was a second letter. *The tests were right*, Mutti wrote. She wanted to cry, though crying didn't come, Beate preoccupied instead that she'd heard from Paul just once. *Your father will be sleeping a great deal when you're home for Christmas. By then he might have no hair*, Mutti added. Beate thought of the hair on Paul's chest, thought again that she should cry. She finally found tears by imagining Paul joking to some friend about the German girl he'd had his way with who didn't even know what a foldout couch was. *Because of communism?* the imagined friend asked. *Because she's not all that bright*, Paul answered, and they laughed in the mean way young men sometimes did, and her tears thickened. Beate wrote Vati in the margins of her notebook, as though to transfer feeling.

As Beate walked toward her dorm after the last day of finals, a young man got out of a car who looked like Paul. Perhaps it wasn't him. Perhaps she'd remembered him wrong, or wanted him so badly that a near-miss would do. He waved and she waved, and a smile shattered the scowl of his face.

"Kate told me she wasn't getting picked up until tomorrow," Beate said.

It was a cold, brown-grass December, though each morning she woke up to a smell she imagined was incoming snow. Young women passed. Clouds of breath trailed them. The clock tower rang, and branches ticked in the wind.

"Come with me," Paul answered. Beate didn't move. She was opening herself to joy, also the weightless falling she'd lived with since Thanksgiving. She knew little about him, yet he'd uncovered something that, in its best moments, turned her giddy, in others left her talking to herself without realizing. He wore a ski cap and a shadow of scruff. She would go with him. The falling felt good then, some spoil of war. They got in his car. Radio commercials wound one into the next.

"The heat in this thing is shit," he said, and banged a vent with the heel of his hand.

They drove through town, where people moved in and out of glimmering stores. A group of young women passed through a crosswalk. "That sounds like Meredith," one of them said, and Beate wanted to know what sounded like Meredith, if it was some idiocy or a way Meredith was a thoughtful friend. At each stoplight Beate thought, *I could get out here.* She could go to her dorm and tell Kate that her brother had come early. Could sit in the library's stacks and skim tomes about one war or another while Paul drove through campus to look for her. In Mutti's letter, she'd complained about the cost of the taxi to and from Vati's treatment and informed her that they wouldn't get a tree this year. Beate didn't want to leave the car. But there was something terrifying in being in it with him, in having wanted him badly without understanding why, the two of them unwound by the same sickness. The car traced the Connecticut River. In the late afternoon light, its ice was gas-stove blue.

Passing Hadley's strip malls, they fell into stop-and-go traffic. The driver in front of them kept pressing on his brakes. "C'mon," Paul said. "I think they're looking for something," Beate answered. Their brakes brightened; his scowl returned. Paul got close enough to the car in front of them that Beate could read the word Massachusetts on its license plate, a word that had taken her a week to learn to spell. He leaned on the horn.

"What's that?" Paul asked. Beate hadn't realized that she was talking to herself.

"Oh. That's just the way to say the name of your town. In German."

Annoyance tightened Paul's face. Kate had talked of him as moody, difficult. How he'd thrown tantrums as a child about the wrong sandwich, a perceived slight. The brakes in front of them stuttered off and on. "Jesus Christ," Paul said. *I could get out right here*, Beate thought again. She touched his arm, and his face loosened. Beate felt powerful, relieved when the car in front of them turned into a place that sold stereo equipment.

When Paul pulled up to a motel, it made perfect sense. When he took a bottle of wine from the trunk, it felt right in a way Beate didn't trust, because she didn't know him, though she pretended she did. She lay in bed after he'd fallen asleep, after sex left her not worn out but wired, and felt happy, lucky, afraid to think those thoughts, her feelings a soap bubble—beautiful, bulbous, wobbling toward its end. She avoided thinking about anything beyond this room or the heat coming from Paul. Avoided thinking about a week later, when Beate would be beside her father's hospital bed. She hadn't gotten Mutti's letter that told her he'd been admitted there, a place he'd end up staying. "My letter must have passed you as you came to us," Mutti said, and leaned against Beate's shoulder. It felt strange. Vati wheezed and woke from a nap with confused fear. Beate felt him trying to hand her that fear, and thought about Paul, the plan they'd made to meet halfway for New Year's in Toledo, Ohio.

Vati cleared his throat. His eyes watered.

"Do you remember our house?" he asked.

"In Cologne?" Beate asked back.

"That was an apartment," he answered. He was asking about Kritzhagen. With her finger, Beate traced Paul's name on her jeans.

"I remember it first thing in the morning," Beate said.

"What it looked like?" he asked.

"I remember the trees in rows. How vines crawled up the back of it."

Beate traced the *P*, the *A*.

"The house itself?" Vati asked.

The *U* and *L*. The *P* again.

"Sure," she said.

A few days later, Beate took a bus to Toledo. She tried to distract herself with signs she saw but kept wondering if Paul had cut his hair as he'd threatened to. When thoughts of Vati took over, she opened a novel and read until nausea wiped thinking away. The novel's narrator had moved from a warm island to England, where she was always cold. She was some sort of dancer, though dancing brought her no joy. Thoughts of Vati swatted at her; she reread paragraphs until she had them memorized. And as the bus moved close to Toledo—her parents with no idea or interest as to where she was—Beate realized that Vati had been asking about their house in Kritzhagen because he didn't remember what it looked like and was hoping she could tell him.

But in that motel in Hadley, Beate didn't know about Toledo or the house her father no longer remembered.

A clock ticked on the motel room's wall. Paul breathed out and in and Beate pretended that this was the only place, felt terrified at the thought of the next day, Paul going one way, her another. Paul woke up. He smiled so sweetly that her worry felt dumb. "You're here," he said, tracing her hip bone with a finger.

Paul slid on top of her. She kissed him hard when he suggested they stay at the motel an extra night. Smiling into his neck, Beate thought, then forgot, to call her parents and let them know she'd be delayed in her return to Winona, where Vati was asleep in its hospital more and more each day until, six weeks later, Beate back at school after winter break, she walked into her room to find Kate standing just inside the door.

"There was a call for you," Kate said. And before her roommate said anything else, Beate understood that Vati was gone.

2009

16

Ines slipped her head onto Beate's desk. Her scalp—like her face and arms—screamed with sunburn. Ines had worked at the *Pflegeheim* for a few months, her basic competence making her largely forgettable. But the week before, she'd called in sick for four days and gone to Majorca with her boyfriend, trying to cover her sunburn with makeup, but somehow forgetting about her arms and hands. Now Ines sat with her forehead on the desk. Beate had just fired her.

Beate hated firing. She disliked its meanness, hated even more the stunts people thought they'd get away with. She looked out onto Linzer Straße's refurbished buildings, hoping to visit Ingo's office and dissuade him from adding a fourth kind of ornamental grass to his garden. But Ines kept her head on the desk. Beate touched Ines's shoulder.

"Ow," Ines said, without urgency.

"You're burned there, too?" Beate asked.

Ines sat up. She picked up the picture Beate had on her desk, one of Adela and Michael as children at an Adirondack lake. They squinted toward the camera, their shoulders pressed against each other.

"Grandchildren?" Ines asked.

"My children, but long ago," Beate answered.

Ines showed no signs of leaving, and all the obligation of being in charge rushed in. Beate wanted to put her hands up, to abdicate. Anything to distract her from Adela's return, which left Michael petulant and both him and Beate up in the middle of the night. She passed through her living room at two in the morning and saw him through the alley of space between their houses. This led her to Udo. Beate had always found him strange. Though he made good money, he'd lived with her until he was twenty-four. When Josef moved out, he'd taken care of her as if she were infirm. But as strange as Udo was, she'd found comfort in the way he took up half her sofa when they watched a movie, bringing his own popcorn and beer. A month after he died, she and the dentist split. Beate kept the breakup a secret. Then one afternoon Michael mentioned that he'd seen the dentist out to dinner with an overly tanned woman and she felt angry, mostly with her son. She avoided him for days, seeing him only through the windows of Udo's former house, including one evening when he had a young man over. Each time she passed a window, more of their clothing had found its way to the floor.

"Ines," Beate said, and stood up, hoping movement might provoke her former employee's exit. "There is a week's severance. I know it isn't large."

Ines lifted her head, her eyes as red as her face. The coffee smell grew stronger, probably from Frau Sonntag's office, the woman in charge of admissions who, on most days, wore yellow. Beate regretted standing's illusion of certainty. But her standing seemed to startle Ines, who gathered her purse, wincing as she placed it on her shoulder.

Children's clothes hung everywhere. Shirts lined the banister like prayer flags. In eight days, the house Beate carefully curated had gone to shit. "Shit, Cindy," she said as she walked into the living room, peering into the carrying crate where her cat spent most of its time. Beate pulled a sneaker out from under her. "Shitty, shit, shit."

Beate had adopted Cindy a year before. She'd gone to the shelter and said she'd wanted a small dog, but the clerk walked her through a room of cats instead and Beate wondered if she'd said cat, if this was the beginning of the aphasia that left so many people at the home talking to pictures on walls. Some of the cats were fluffy, some wild. Then came Cindy. She was old, "Probably dying," the clerk said. Cindy looked sad and angry, and in that moment—a hundred animals mewling under harsh lighting—Beate felt sad and angry, too. She took Cindy; the clerk appeared relieved. And Cindy kept living. Her fur fell off in swaths. Teeth tumbled out as easily as eyelashes. She ate and slept in her crate, or on a shelf in Beate's closet, swatting at her once when she tried to grab a turtleneck. Beate knelt in front of the carrier, the cat's smell stronger than she'd remembered. Perhaps the death the woman at the shelter had predicted was now upon her. The thought of Cindy—mean and hermetic—dying crept up Beate's throat.

The door opened; Adela and Peter gusted in. Her daughter dropped shopping bags on the floor. Her grandson stared at Beate with a librarian's impunity.

"Oma," Peter said.

"What's all this?" Beate asked.

"Things," Peter said in German. In one week, he'd picked up words and phrases with unsurprised ease. From the shopping bag he pulled out a tiny bathing suit, pint-sized shirts. Adela had gotten herself a sweater. She was always freezing.

"Why are you on the floor, Oma?"

"Visiting Cindy."

"Cindy!" Peter squawked. The cat attempted a hiss.

"I can't believe everything here now," Adela said. "Almost like America."

"It hasn't changed that much," Beate answered, though hotels replaced the barracks and forgotten houses were occupied. The oldest people living there had died; the young recovered enough from the surveilled socialism of their early decades. Boarded-up boulevards became restaurants and a furniture store where Beate bought the dresser for the guest room that Peter was the first person to use.

"You have to remember, we've been living in South Africa," Adela went on, a dash of Paul's condescension let off its leash.

"I was born there," Peter said, and asked how to say born in German.

He pulled out his drawing pad, on which he'd scrawled something that may have been the sky or the sea.

Adela had followed Taro from one diplomatic post to the next, getting a nursing degree, working at rural clinics. Every conversation Beate had had with her seemed to boil down to this: millions of people are dying and no one cares. A year before, Taro's diplomatic climb moved him to Ghana, and Adela didn't go with him. She'd cited work, the life Peter had, speaking Afrikaans and Sesotho, the neighborhood friends he called cousins. Also an end she and Taro had been moving toward. When Beate asked about this end, Adela told her about families who'd lost breadwinners with the speed of a changing season. When she asked about Taro, Adela spouted out a trite phrase about people changing and switched the subject. When she asked if Adela and Peter were going back to Pretoria, she answered that the clinic had a new, terrible director.

Peter wore flip-flops, the price tag still on. Sliding one off the boy's foot, Beate tried to remove it. The tag was tough; she broke it off with her teeth. "My feet were there!" Peter said, with soprano delight. "*Meine Füße!*" Then he announced he was hungry.

"We just ate," Adela said.

Twigs and blades of grass, Beate thought. "Growing boy," she answered.

She worried that Peter's smallness wasn't a reflection of his father, but a stunting. Beate got rolls from the kitchen. Peter ate two. A confetti of crumbs crowded the floor around him. Adela opened the package of socks and put a pair on. She left the rest on the floor. *Turning to shit*, Beate thought again. She wished to be back at her office, where she turned any chaos on her desk to order at the end of each day. Peter flicked Cindy's crate; Adela said nothing. Cindy bounded out of it and up the stairs. For something possibly on the verge of death, she could run like the wind.

After Josef had moved out, Beate found herself living alone for the first time in her life. One night she walked into the smallest guest room, climbed under the bed's duvet, and fell asleep. When she woke up, the alarm in her actual bedroom sounded mayday. Though late for work, Beate washed her dishes and fluffed the pillows until the house carried the just-tidied quality of a hotel. The next night Beate slept in the guest room again, felt ashamed until she realized that there was no one there to witness it. She turned her alarm to its highest volume and padded down the hall.

When the house's comfort turned to a muzzle, she'd sometimes call Liesl, though she and her cousin had less to talk about now that Heinz's business had mushroomed and Liesl played tennis and went to lectures she called boring, though she liked the rooms they were in and the cucumber in the water. Beate also had friends from work, Ingo in particular, who came over on short notice. They'd sip brandy in the yard while Ingo named all the flowers and weeds. Ingo's one significant lover had defected in the GDR days, was felled by AIDS shortly after. Ingo spoke of his departure as if he'd just gone to the store. Beate found that to be the most common Eastern trait, time not near or far but carrying the flatness of a single page. After a few drinks, Ingo would say good night with a pat on the back, as if he were humoring her.

But on other days solitude became something she lusted after. Beate ate alone on the good china. She went into rooms she hadn't been in for a while—Michael's former one, which she'd converted into an office. Udo's, where a soccer poster still hung on the wall. She'd explore closets and read old report cards or magazine clippings she'd kept without remembering why. And Beate would leave for work each morning reluctantly, as one might leave a new lover, walking through the kitchen and living room, the dining room she sometimes ate in by herself.

Beate heard Peter's voice before she saw him. "*Du bist aber eine böse Katze*," he said. Peter spoke to Cindy, his German spreading each day like an unattended rash. Beate was about to say hello when she saw Liesl and Adela in the kitchen. Like Michael, Liesl had avoided visiting since Adela's return. The last time she'd seen Beate's daughter was fifteen years before, after the debacle with the immigrants, Adela spouting things about justice that were both difficult and true.

"Heinz and I went to Japan once," Liesl said loudly now. "We took mineral baths in these wooden tubs. Heinz was convinced he'd get splinters in his ass!"

Adela answered that she'd never been to Japan. Beate hoped

her daughter had offered condolences to Liesl, who'd slept in Udo's room for weeks after he'd died.

"Oma," Peter said.

"One minute," Beate answered.

"There she is!" Liesl said. "I need to talk to you about Ines."

Adela wore baggy jeans that made her thinness more conspicuous. A connect-the-dots of cherry pits sat on the table in front of her.

"Ines?"

"Fired three hours ago and already forgotten?" Liesl answered.

Though Liesl hadn't worked at the *Pflegeheim* for over a decade, she knew of everything that happened there, sometimes before Beate. Liesl's wedding ring was sandwiched between other gold bands.

"You didn't have to fire her," Liesl said.

"I had no choice," Beate answered. "Ines called you?"

"Ines didn't need to call," Liesl said. "And it seems like you did have a choice. Yes or no. Stay or leave."

Liesl spouted speculation as if fact, treated doubt like a fly to swat at. Being in charge often left Beate uneasy, especially when she over- or underreacted and staff members looked at the floor when they passed her. She'd briefly seen a counselor after she and Josef had split. One day, the woman said to her, "You're not a joke, you know that, right?" Beate answered that it was like telling the sky it was a different color. In their last visit, the counselor asked Beate why she'd never cried there. Beate saw that as another failing, and thought of the last, awful week before Josef moved out, when one morning he'd put down his coffee and said: "It's amazing how you've fooled people." But tears wouldn't come. She paid the counselor and waited until midnight to leave a message to say she wouldn't be coming back.

"Is there a phone chain?" Beate asked. "What else do people report to you about me?"

"You had a choice," Liesl answered.

"The complaint was reported to my boss."

Adela sipped a glass of water. The swallow slid down her beanpole neck. Liesl touched Beate's arm, and it felt good to be touched. The night after Udo's body floated onto the shore, Liesl had slept in Beate's bed with her. Beate had woken to Liesl where Josef had once slept, her face bruised with mascara.

Beate sometimes felt a failure for not finding a confidante other than Liesl. But every time she thought to ask for her spare keys back, Beate couldn't think of anyone else she'd want to discover her body if she died in her sleep. Liesl poured each of them a whiskey. She held the bottle up to Adela, who declined.

"That's my girl," Liesl said as Beate held the glass to her lips.

"I'm not a girl," Beate answered, as she always did.

"You've become a grown woman," Liesl said to Adela.

Adela startled and examined her hands. Beate wanted her to eat something. Wanted to understand why she'd come back.

"Your boy," Liesl went on. "He looks like the father."

"*Vater* is father," Peter said as he moved into the kitchen.

"You've never seen Taro," Adela answered.

"In pictures," Liesl said. "Fahzuh."

Cindy flew into the room. Peter waved, and the cat—surprised or annoyed, or because she could—clawed him and bounded up the stairs.

Adela ran to Peter and wrapped his injured hand in her T-shirt, showing off her stomach with the same hard angles as her face. Liesl's eyebrows rose. Blood besmirched Adela's shirt.

"Cats have AIDS," Liesl said, as if it were as universal as their tails and their disinterest.

"The cat has no AIDS," Beate answered. "She's just old."

Liesl shot Beate a look: *This girl has always been too much, in a different way than I am too much. A nurse in the slums. AIDS and prostitutes and orphans.* Both cousins downed what was left in their glasses.

"Cindy," Peter said, as if the rest of them had forgotten the animal's name.

"Do you have anything to clean his scratches?" Adela asked.

In the bathroom, Beate found bandages right away, but relished the room's clean quiet. She'd decorated it with photos Michael had taken years before. One showed the sea and sky in symmetrical bands. The other, a close-up of a shoulder. As she stared at the opened medicine cabinet, Beate imagined coming out to find her company gone. The quiet might be a relief; it might haunt her, like the ringing in her ears after seeing a band at Mount Holyoke.

The pictures Michael had taken filled the mirror's reflection.

A few people slouched at the bar of Secret Police. Tables sat empty, apart from one filled with university students. The beauty of being young crowded their faces, even those heavier or more lopsided than they wanted to be. Michael stood behind the bar. He leaned toward a man on its other side. Part of Beate wanted to slip out in the same way she'd come in. Michael and the man leaned closer; the crowd of students was pummeled with laughter. A hand touched Beate's shoulder.

"Frau Haas," Justine said.

Justine was tall, pretty, and frightening-looking at different turns. She wore a sleeveless T-shirt with a cartoon of Lenin on it drinking a Coca-Cola.

"Everything okay?" Justine asked.

"Sometimes I can't sleep."

"Not being able to sleep is how I got into this business. What can I get you to drink?"

Beate hesitated. Michael laughed into the young man's shoulder.

"He can flirt on his own time," Justine said.

"You can call me Beate."

As Justine interrupted Michael's conversation, Beate sat at the bar. Justine was a head taller than her son, with bleached hair and long, lithe arms. Michael once told his mother that one man then the next let her down. Beate felt a flare of love for this young woman. She wanted to protect her, though couldn't think how she might do that. The beer arrived. Michael kissed Beate's cheek.

The man he'd been talking to was handsome. Michael never had a shortage of handsome men. In the few months he'd lived next door she saw plenty of them arrive and depart, including the now-former boyfriend who looked like he belonged on a billboard, shining and clean and made of paper.

"You're up late," Michael said.

"Sometimes I don't sleep," she answered, though he already knew this. "I don't mean to keep you," she said. "But actually, I do. When's your next night off?"

The table of students engaged in giggling disagreement. Michael looked at the man, his expression both flirtation and the recognition that he'd been caught. Her lovely, slippery son. A loud song started to play.

"What if I have plans?" he asked.

"I need you to make yourself free," she answered. "Dinner with Adela and Peter and me."

"I'll come because we're family?" Michael asked.

"Or to be nice to your old mother."

"You're not old," he answered.

Finally he agreed, and she finished her beer. And though she knew she shouldn't have, at home Beate sat in her darkened window until Michael and the man from the bar came home. They kissed as soon as they got inside. The man pressed Michael to the wall. Beate wasn't meant to see her son in these moments, but couldn't stop looking. She was proud that he took what he wanted, wished she could tell him that. She watched and hoped that this man, that all his men, felt as good as she imagined they did, that Michael met each one and felt a flood of fortune.

The man knelt in front of her son, Michael's face in something like prayer.

⟡

Adela read labels on everything. When Peter picked cheese off Beate's plate, she took it from him, and a scowl fireworked across the boy's face. She and Peter were both thin, though Adela needed nothing, while he wanted everything. Peter smeared sunscreen on his face so thick it left a film. He ate so fast that he coughed to clear up a choke and kept going. He had the same hunger for German. He asked translations for everything he picked up, every action he completed. He also loved Cindy. This only grew after the animal scratched him. "Cindy," he called when he didn't know where she was. "Cindy!" he squealed when she scurried out of a room. Beate waited for Adela to remind him that the cat wasn't friendly. But her daughter read a magazine or put on a sweater or asked about a painting on the wall.

One afternoon Beate left work early to take Peter to the beach. They stepped close to the water. Then a wave crashed and he flew back to their blanket. "It's only water," Beate said. He looked at her dubiously and stabbed a stick into the sand. When he finally agreed to go in, he clung to Beate. The Baltic's foam wrapped around their ankles. He let out squeals of delight or terror or both. He held her neck as they went in deeper.

"Oma, Oma, Oma," he kept saying.

His breath droned in her ear. He spoke in a language she didn't understand.

"What are you saying to me?" she asked.

"My face needs to stay above," he whispered.

His fingers cinched her shoulder. Nearby children jockeyed for a raft.

"You can't swim?" Beate asked.

Perhaps he'd never seen the sea before. The quiet order of Kritzhagen's streets, its wet and windy days, all of it strange to him. He held on harder as a wave came. "Oma, Oma, Oma," he said again.

As they left the beach, weaving between chairs she'd only ever seen in Kritzhagen—with sides and a roof to protect from wind and whipping sand—Beate bought them ice cream. But as they strolled home, Beate remembered that Peter wasn't meant to eat ice cream. When she told him as much, he held his cone closer.

"I guess we don't need to tell your mother everything we did," Beate said.

"How will she know?" he answered, delighted at his grandmother's worry. He licked again and wrapped his sticky fingers around hers.

But when they got home, Adela took one look at his chocolate-stained palms and figured it out. In her annoyance, she looked older than her thirty years.

"Please don't ask him to lie," Adela said.

"She didn't ask anything," Peter answered.

"You didn't tell me he couldn't swim," Beate said.

"Something happened?"

"Oma was with me the whole time," Peter answered, with such bravado that it seemed he was covering for something else. He went outside and lay under an apple tree, pulled out clumps of grass and threw them in the air. The hopeless ineptitude Beate sometimes felt rallied, as it had in their first German weeks when she saw temporary as permanent and lay down in its traffic. Her house, with Cindy and a fridge filled with forbidden meats and cheeses, was a carousel of mistakes. For a moment she wished that her daughter was gone, then felt buried by unkindness. She remembered this same swoop of feeling after Adela's move to California, when days, then weeks, would pass and everything seemed easier without her.

"I'd forgotten," Beate said.

Adela eyed her mother skeptically, then went upstairs. Beate picked up the clothes her daughter and grandson had left strewn across the floor.

Peter packed his mouth with bread. He swallowed in gasps. The vegetable casserole Beate made sagged in the middle of the table.

"You have a bar," Adela said.

Michael put down his knife and fork. "You know the name?"

"Secret Police," she said.

"*Polizei*," Peter added.

Michael tapped a stub of bread into his plate. Peter breathed and chewed.

"You imagine I'm offended by it?" Adela said.

"It doesn't seem to you like I'm poking fun?"

"What's wrong with fun?"

Michael seemed unsure, though he'd learned to mask it with the flirtation he turned on when talking to old ladies or barking dogs. He touched his cheek, as if thinking deeply. Watching him was like seeing a heron swoop to a landing, a spider spin a corner into silver. He lifted his glass in the air.

"Cheers to that," Michael said. He and his sister clinked glasses. Peter moved onto his knees, insisting everyone clink with him, too.

"It does seem, though," Adela went on, "like a bit of an easy target."

Michael laughed with performed delight.

"Easy Target should be the name of my next bar," he answered.

Their last time at this table had been mostly silence, Michael taking too long to pass something, Adela frowning when he chewed with noise. Now they smiled into their plates. The terrible casserole Beate made—no meat or cheese—anchored the table.

"Fish in a Barrel," Adela added.

"Sitting Duck," Michael said.

"Easy Duck?"

"Easy as Duck!"

In a nearby yard, a mower wound into action.

"Why do you live next door?" Peter asked Michael.

"Your adult dream isn't to live next to your mother?"

Peter's testy confusion was treated as a delight. Adela bit into the casserole. She saw food only as fuel, the joy of ice cream nothing next to its animal costs. Beate's daughter, like a Russian novel, was both admirable and difficult to hold. Michael poured more wine. Every once in a while, a question was asked and answered.

As dinner proceeded, her children slipped back into the rhythm of their early years, though Michael—with his comments about the Stasi or his expensive watch—tried to resist. "A friend of mine just bought a five-hundred-euro sweater," he said. His hand touched his shirt, which also looked expensive. "I hope it's warm," Adela answered. When he mentioned that

Gerd Mögen, whom they'd both known—Adela as a classmate, Michael as someone who tried to kiss him when he drank too much—was now the leader of the province's conservative party, Adela answered that Gerd had always had an interest in politics. "To politics," Michael toasted. "Even the wrong kind," Adela added.

They made jokes about Cindy that had the smoothness of practice. Michael morphed into a crackling-voiced imitation of the cat. Adela picked it up without pause. They turned Cindy into a chain smoker, born during the GDR, a fan of the autocratic order of her kitten days.

"So quiet on the streets then," Michael mewled.

"Quiet because everyone was terrified," Adela said.

"Terror," Michael answered, "keeps the riffraff out of my roses."

When Peter went for another roll, Adela stopped him. "There is other food in the world," she said, and put salad on his plate. Beate wanted to feed the boy, who stared at mayonnaise and meatballs with prurient, angry wonder.

Michael and Adela talked about a former Glens Falls neighbor.

"I was in love with him and he was awful," Michael said.

"He *was* awful," Adela answered.

"How awful?" Peter asked.

"Eat your salad," Adela said.

"I asked for a roll," Peter answered, and pushed his seat farther from the table.

"We didn't believe in waste in the GDR," Michael said, Cindy's creaky voice returning.

Her children kept talking, about their shared and separate pasts. Michael told a story Beate had never heard about a friend who'd gotten sick and died young. Adela touched his hand, the sun spotlighting their faces.

As Michael made more jokes about Cindy, Peter asked, "Why is he talking like that?"

"He's imagining what Cindy's voice would sound like," Beate answered.

"I know. Why?"

Michael spoke of inheritance. Peter asked for the word's translation, though he didn't know it in any of his languages. As they talked of AIDS orphans and bar patrons, Beate ate salad off Peter's plate. Peter asked for more translations, and Beate told him. Michael refilled Adela's glass again.

While her children cleaned the kitchen, Beate and Peter watched a nature show about deep-sea creatures. "*Spinnenkrabbe?*" Peter asked, and she answered, "Spider crab." Water turned off and on. Beate toggled between wanting to be alone and wanting them together, herself part of it rather than on the side. She felt angry, embarrassed at her anger, and remembered Kate when they'd been friends telling Beate she took things too seriously because she was an only child.

Above the clatter of cleaning, Beate heard her children say "the German Lady."

"Just a lady, since we're in Germany," she mumbled.

"What?" Peter asked.

The screen showed a deepwater shark with twice the normal number of gills. "It stays on the seafloor during the day," the narrator explained. At night, it moved to the surface to feed. Peter's body was warm. The shark's gills flapped as it ate its dinner.

"Trying to remember a word in English," Beate said.

Adela checked on them from time to time. Perhaps she didn't trust Beate with her son. Maybe she still imagined her mother out at bars, cutting ex-Stasi hair. Annoyance warmed Beate's cheeks, and she wanted to understand why Adela was back, why Michael—after ten avoidant days—suddenly acted as if her visit were just what he'd wanted. Soon Peter was asleep, his tiny feet on Beate's lap. The television cameras moved through ink-dark water, and Peter took a breath. More clatter in the kitchen. Beate wrapped her fingers around one of Peter's feet, so small it disappeared when she held it in her hand.

⟡

Beate spent the morning meeting with an orderly who'd upset three residents in as many days. The woman told one man he wasn't allowed to leave, as if they were running a prison. She informed Arnie Böttcher that his radio was too loud though no one had complained, and tried to create a sign-up sheet for a common-room television. Getting back, Beate slid into Ingo's office. He handed her a coffee, joking that he'd spiked it.

"Still dealing with invaders?" he asked, and Beate realized she'd talked of Adela and Peter's visit only in terms of the dishes they left in the sink, their clothes everywhere.

Ingo's mustache was remarkably even. He showed her new pictures of his dogs, which looked the same as the last ones. A summer shower peppered the window before the sun prodded it out of the way.

"Frau Garrin told Sabine yesterday that she was going to hurt herself," Beate said. "Now Frau Garrin is only allowed plastic utensils."

The two of them took sips at the same time.

The receptionist buzzed. "Is Frau Haas there?"

"Why would Frau Haas be here?" Ingo answered.

"Let her know that an Englishman keeps calling for her. Can I transfer him to you?"

"The Englishman?"

"Frau Selig told me that Frau Haas is with you."

"In that case, then," Ingo answered.

"Beate Haas," she said, picking up the phone.

"I forget you're using your old name," the caller answered.

It was Paul. She hadn't heard his voice in years.

"Just my name," she said.

Ingo moved out of his office, though she gestured that he should stay.

"Well," Paul said. "I don't want to worry you."

"When you say that—"

"Yes," he answered.

"I get—"

"Yes," Paul answered. "It's about our daughter."

When Beate left that morning, Adela's bathing suit drooped over a chair. The core of an apple she'd eaten browned on the counter. Peter had been up. He'd stared at Beate as she'd eaten a yogurt.

"What *about* Adela?"

"It seems," he said, "that she's missing."

"Missing from where?"

"She was living in Pretoria," he said. "Which is in South Africa."

"Yes, with Amahle the babysitter and best friend."

Paul paused, to take in information or register surprise.

"Her phone's no longer connected," Paul went on. "I called the clinic where she works and they said her last day was weeks before."

Beate rested her head on the desk as Ines had, her laughter startling even her. Frau Selig across the hall looked up.

"B," Paul said.

Ingo came back in and appeared startled, too. Everything turned funny—the plastic forks Frau Garrin had to use. The orderly expecting the old to acquiesce as if they hadn't once made hundreds of decisions for themselves and others.

"She's not missing," Beate said, and more things took on a comic gleam, even the moment from decades before, in bed in their tiny apartment, when Paul told her he was leaving.

The next night, the family had dinner at the beach. Michael found out that the *pommes frites* were vegan and met them at their blanket with an entire tray full.

"Don't you have to be at the bar?" Beate asked. He answered that it was dead this early.

Peter and Michael walked to the sea's edge. High clouds slid across the sky. Without pause, they moved into the water. A few days before, it had taken Beate minutes of coaxing just for Peter to dip his foot in. Part of her admired the progress; another part wanted this progress to be made with her. Michael lifted Peter, whose face widened with what Beate assumed was fear.

"Do you see that?" Beate asked.

"Who knew," Adela said, "that Michael would be good with children?"

Instead of walking home with Beate, Adela and Peter climbed onto Michael's bike. He'd added a seat in the back for Peter, whose inability to ride a bike at nearly seven was something Michael waxed catastrophic about.

"For a minute I thought you'd found a bike for your sister," Beate said. "Like Udo did when we got here."

Adela strapped Peter in. Michael looked at his watch. Bringing up Udo left Beate feeling foolish, also like a child. The only other family left on the beach played Frisbee. Nearby hotels twinkled with light and sound.

"See you at home, Oma," Peter said.

"Not if I see you first," Beate answered. Peter fell into his regular expression of perturbed confusion.

Adela thanked Michael for the bike and he hopped into his car. He didn't offer Beate a ride, though she didn't exactly want one. Adela thanked Beate, too; for what, Beate wasn't sure. She said, "You're welcome," and felt small, as she often did when left orbiting outside her children. She'd been alone for so long that she didn't know how to be something else. When she tried, she felt worse or foolish, or retreated instead, though Beate once told Kate that she didn't feel like she was retreating, but being herself.

"Exactly," Kate had answered, and Beate felt that she couldn't win.

Four nights later, Beate came home to an empty house, adding her shoes to the detritus her daughter and grandson had scattered across the floor. Michael might have taken a night off, he and Adela and Peter on some adventure. He'd recently purchased a booster seat so Peter could travel in his car. Mornings, he took the boy swimming—Peter's flip-flopped feet thwacking against the path, Michael asking if he was ready. A towel snaked across the rug. A message from Liesl crowded the answering machine. She went on about how busy she was, offered unwanted updates on Ines's job search. "Oh," Liesl's message went on, "Heinz says hello and wants to know if you want our television. We're getting a bigger one."

Beate turned on her smaller television. Obama was on the news, then an explosion in some desert city. She tried to focus on the world's larger calamities but imagined her children and

Peter at a restaurant that Beate would like to have gone to, on a friend's boat as it bobbed across the sunset-studded sea.

They didn't return until after ten. Peter—who usually walked in first and loudly—was carried by Michael. Her children looked tired and pleased, as if they'd hiked up a mountain together and were rewarded with vistas. Peter's hand was fattened with bandages.

"What happened?"

"Bad Cindy," Peter mumbled.

"Painkillers," Michael added.

"When you were at work," Adela said, "Cindy bit him."

The carrying crate was empty. When she'd explained Adela's story to Paul a few days before, he'd been annoyed that she hadn't let him know. He'd also talked about a mudslide in another part of Africa as if it were Adela's duty to pull people from the wet, whirling earth. Thoughts of being buried alive—sludge in her throat and ears—crowded Beate's thinking.

"You didn't think to call?" she asked.

"Michael was with me," Adela answered. "Could be my translator."

"*Allergien*," Peter said. "*Versicherung. Fieber* is fever."

"Where's Cindy?" Beate asked.

"Sleeping somewhere, I imagine," Michael said. He sniffed; Adela held down a smile.

"Yes, the cat smells," Beate answered.

"Mutti," Michael said.

The German Lady, she thought. Peter's eyes fought to stay awake.

"What was he doing?" Beate asked.

As Beate's question came out in defense of her pet, her kids must have been reminded of her badly ordered priorities. Beate at that bar. The days she slept while Michael brought home bread and pillows.

"I used to do that, too," Beate said. "Take you to the emergency room with every fever. There was a time," she went on, wanting to hold up a mirror to their sameness, "when, Adela, you were two or three. Michael, we'd moved and you'd been given your own room and were so angry that you and Adela were no longer sharing one."

Peter shifted on Michael's shoulder. The bandage on his hand was thick and round and gauzy.

"So you'd sneak into her room each night," Beate went on. "Your father even put a hook on the outside of your door, but you found a way out. With a coat hanger, I think. You snuck into your sister's room and somehow, when you were getting into bed next to her, she fell off and hit her head on the corner of something. It wouldn't have been a desk, since you were young. Anyhow. Your father was at work, so we had to take a cab. Michael, you were the upset one. You cried and cried and, when you looked at your sister, cried harder. The cabdriver kept saying how much over the speed limit he was going, in hopes of calming you down. And when we got to the ER, Michael, you were so upset that I had to carry you in, while the driver carried your bleeding sister."

Adela and Michael yawned in tandem. Beate wondered where Cindy was.

"It was my fault, then," Michael said.

"I don't think. I was just remembering," Beate answered. "Let me make us some food."

Michael answered that they'd eaten already.

"We've been thinking, too," Adela said, and looked at Michael. "About what makes sense, because of Cindy." She and

Peter would stay at Michael's, Adela went on, Cindy and Peter an untenable pair. When Adela had hit her head, she'd gotten four stitches. They'd had to wait for hours until Paul picked them up. Beate felt relieved that her children hadn't returned Cindy to the shelter, though it might have felt the same to her cat as the crate where she spent most of her days. They picked up Peter and said good night. Their clothes were everywhere. Beate wanted them to stay, was also glad they were going. Wanted some version of things she wasn't able to consider.

Beate found Cindy in Udo's former room. She went to sleep in the guest room that had been Peter's hours before, when he did or didn't do something and the cat reacted with her teeth, her children rushing him to the hospital where a nurse asked if they were the parents. They might have smiled at that question, each waiting for the other to answer it.

17

Peter turned avoiding the linden's shadow that spread across the living room floor into a game. He and Michael had just come back from the beach. Their hair dried in salty curls. As Adela cooked something with cumin for lunch, Michael told stories about the trio of young drunks who always showed up at the bar. "The week before, one of them passed out in the bathroom," Michael said. "Another cried after being dumped, though he couldn't seem to remember his girlfriend's name." He left out stories of the fight they'd started a few months before, in part because it didn't fit with his other anecdotes, also because Udo had been there to stop it.

"There was a man at the beach," Peter said, in German.

Adela chopped. Parsley's piquant scent filled the room.

"A friend of Uncle's," Peter added.

"'Michael' is fine," Michael answered.

"He was running and saw Michael and stopped to wave."

"Did Uncle wave back?" Adela asked.

"He was swimming," Peter answered.

"I was coming out of the water by then," Michael interjected, imagining his sister's chopping intensifying as she announced that Peter shouldn't swim with him anymore. Adela's surprise return had brought Michael a surprise excitement, also the worry of toes stepped on and jokes she wouldn't find funny. Her chopping stayed measured. Her eyebrows lifted into an expression he remembered: *There is certainly a larger story.*

"He laughed," Peter said.

"And Peter threw sand at him," Michael answered.

"It fell out of the shovel."

It had pelted Markus's—the runner's—legs. Had Peter not been there, they might have gone to one of Markus's preferred places, an empty road or *Einkaufszentrum* bathroom. When Michael asked Peter why he'd thrown sand, he said, "I didn't know him."

Adela appeared amused. Returning to Germany, she thought nothing of leaving Peter alone in the front yard. One afternoon, Michael had stopped by the house to find Adela napping while Peter turned lights off and on and left the refrigerator open.

"A friend," Adela said.

"I have friends," Michael answered.

"That I don't doubt."

"You make me sound . . ." he said, switching to German when he didn't know the English for sordid. She didn't know its German equivalent, and for a minute he tried to explain. "Wrong or filled with feelings."

"Filled with feelings," Adela answered, her smile a rodent creeping behind a wall.

In the kitchen, what she'd been cooking began to burn.

"Fuck a duck!" Adela called.

"A child in the room."

"*Sie hat einen schlechten Mund*," Peter answered.

He jumped into a new sheaf of sun. What had smelled sweetly of garlic turned acrid.

"Fucking fuck," Adela whispered.

"We could always go to the bakery," Michael said.

"Everything in this country is bread."

"Asshole bread," Michael said.

"Asshole yeast," she added.

"Asshole yeast infection."

Peter covered his ears. He hopped into a triangle of sunlight. Adela's quiet cursing continued as she tasted the concoction, its char sticking to her teeth.

Michael tried it, too—chickpeas and onions burned to bitter—then spit it into the sink. Adela scooped up another spoonful.

"You don't need to eat that."

"I wasn't paying attention," Adela said.

Her lips glistened, and a bug batted the windowpane. Michael slid the food into the garbage, tied its bag, and brought it outside. After dropping off the trash, he knocked on the German Lady's door and went in, hoping to find something they might eat in her kitchen. Her house was quiet. Mutti was likely at work. As he walked through the house, he saw that all signs of Adela and Peter's hurricane had been wiped clean. Michael saw their mother each day in her kitchen as she washed dishes, or sipped tea when she should have been asleep. She must have watched, too, as Adela left socks and clothes everywhere, as Michael moved up and down the stairs.

Through Mutti's window, he watched Adela move through Udo's house, pulling an apple from the fridge, taking a bite, then leaving it on the counter. Michael thought of the emails Udo had sent her that she'd never answered. Michael had gone through his cousin's email after he'd died. In one, Udo had written, *I don't expect to be forgiven, but want you to know that I've taken responsibility*. Another: *Please just let me know that you've gotten my messages*. Next door, Adela turned on the television. She lifted her legs on the couch's cushions, though, even through two sets of windows, Michael could see the dirt darkening the bottoms of her feet.

Finding nothing in her house that Adela and Peter were allowed to eat, he walked outside and got into his car. Michael drove and texted the teacher, who was on summer vacation and often available. Then the concierge who could sometimes find them an empty room. No one answered. Michael got to work and moved behind the bar. He pulled down his pants and jerked off. A few minutes after he'd finished, the cleaning ladies arrived, using buckets as purses.

"Always working, Mr. Michael," one said.

"Work is good for you," Michael answered, though he didn't know why he'd just said that.

Mops swatted the floor. Michael rinsed his mess from the prep sink, though one of the sisters—he always forgot who was Fortana, who was Dazana—urged him away with a, "We clean."

Michael took an unmopped corridor to the office. Part of him wanted to jerk off again, even with Fortana and Dazana one room away.

In the bar's main room, the sisters called out: "Not open." Then came a knock at the door. "It's your sister." *So many sisters*, Michael thought. Fifteen minutes ago he'd been alone. His belt buckle had clacked as he thought about the shawarma guy, whose beard extended down his neck. In the bar, Adela examined posters. She spoke to one of the cleaning sisters, whose German was better than she'd let on.

"Six years, we've been here," the woman said.

"I've been to Tirana once. Though you're probably not from Tirana."

"Not far!" one of the sisters said. He really did need to learn who was who.

When the sister asked why, Adela answered: "I was working."

Michael thought of Adela with her backpack of sandwiches. He had no idea she'd been in Europe a decade before.

"It's better here when it's open," Michael said.

Adela's expression tightened; the anger he'd felt watching her through the window must have come through. But that anger lost its footing, replaced with a nervous excitement at her return. He wanted to tell her that the bar—with patrons and music and lighting—had a magic it lacked in its bleachy, daytime state.

"If you're staying for a while," Michael said—he didn't know what Adela's plan was or why she'd returned—"if you don't feel like it's beneath you or something, I could always use someone else here. Weekends are a bit of a mob scene."

"Peter," she said.

"The German Lady could watch him."

"What about Cindy?"

"Can't she watch him in your house?" Michael said in the Cindy voice they fell into more and more, though it annoyed Peter.

Adela examined the SOLIDARITÄT poster, the Katarina Witt photo on the ladies' room door.

"I'll think about it," she said.

"Wait," Michael answered. "Where's Peter?"

"I told him not to touch anything while I was gone."

"That's okay?"

"I'm kidding," Adela said. "The German Lady took him to the movies."

"She's working."

"It's Saturday."

The bar shone from cleaning.

"You could start tonight," Michael said. "Just to see if you like it." It felt strange to lay himself so bare.

"Let me think about it," Adela answered.

"We had posters like this at home, too," one of the sisters—Dazana, Michael was fairly sure—said. She seemed eager to talk again to Adela.

The first time they'd seen this bar, the sisters must have sucked in confused disgust. Must have been friendly to Michael because they thought he was terrible or dumb. They might see a dead cat on the side of the road and joke that they should pick it up for him so he could stuff it and act like it was his pet, an animal mowed over as amusing as year-long prison sentences for nothing.

"Want to hear something funny?" Adela asked, and told him how Peter kept confusing the German word for night with the similarly pronounced naked. She rested her hand on Michael's forearm. And though he was glad she was here, touching his arm, he also remembered another email Udo had sent her a year before, in which he'd written several times in a row, *Now I am better.*

⟡

Two days later, Beate walked in from work to find her children sitting in her living room.

"We have a proposal," Michael said.

There was something officious in their presence. Adela's shoes sat in the middle of the floor.

As Beate slumped into one of the wingbacks she'd recently had reupholstered, Michael explained how Adela would help in the bar on weekends if Beate would watch Peter.

"I have the killer cat," Beate said.

"Could watch him at our place," Michael answered.

Adela played with the tassels on a throw pillow. Beate did the same thing when she was bored or watched television. She and Adela were similar in many ways, but something stayed blocked between them. "I have to head back to the bar," Michael said. "But the two of you can suss out the details." Beate hadn't said yes.

Outside, Peter spun with a stick in his hand. Beate hadn't been invited next door since Adela and Peter's migration.

"I won't watch him over there," Beate said. "A house without furniture."

Her children looked at the floor, their mother as unhelpful as history had proven her to be. But they'd ambushed her, then turned contemptuously amused. Outside, Peter howled, Beate impressed by his volume.

"But what I can do is lock Cindy in her crate. Can leave the crate in my room. Cindy is capable, but she can't open doors."

"Like I said," Michael answered, "the two of you can iron out the details."

"This means you're staying?" Beate asked Adela, after Michael left.

In their occasional phone calls over the years, Adela had always discussed her work, then Peter. Talked of women getting antiretrovirals but only taking them when they felt symptoms, or splitting one dose with other infected friends. When Beate said it sounded hard, Adela answered: "There are so many more sick people." Now Beate would watch Peter, who toggled between grumpy and tender, who sought her out each morning. The day before, he'd greeted her by reciting the German alphabet, forward then back.

"Child," Beate said, "it's good that you're staying. I was just asking."

Adela moved the pillow to her stomach. Her brow was thick,

like that Mexican painter who loved wild colors and monkeys and painting her dreams.

"I know," Adela said. For a moment Beate forgot what question her daughter had just answered.

After a few days of deliberation, Adela agreed to start working for Michael. On her first day at the bar, Beate locked Cindy away and Adela and Peter walked in. He took a roll from the kitchen and bit into it.

"You can't just take things," Adela said. She wore jeans and a pair of boots Beate hadn't seen before. "You have to remember that you're a guest."

She kissed Peter's forehead and went on her way.

"You're not a guest," Beate said.

Later that evening, she and Peter sat outside. He was drawing pictures of Cindy when her cell phone rang. It was Paul. He opened with a short monologue on California's collection of bone-dry days.

"You're calling with a weather report?" Beate smiled.

"I'm calling with a question," he answered. She'd forgotten about the deepness of his voice, his precise consonants. She'd seen his name on her phone and turned excited, then embarrassed. Peter's crayon scratched against his paper. "I'm wondering what Adela's plans are."

"You'd have to ask Adela," she answered.

"She hasn't responded to my emails."

"I take it that that is unusual."

"B," he said.

"I'm sorry," she answered, though she wasn't sure what she was sorry for.

"She's a bartender?" he asked.

"Along with our son."

Michael had declined the invitation to Paul's wedding, didn't answer Paul's email after his half-sister Leticia was born a decade before. A certain respect, perhaps, left Michael outside Paul's domain. Or giving up felt easier. As Paul talked, Beate felt dumb for the hope she had no cause to feel. She wished people would tell others to give up instead of spouting adages about following dreams as if they were as necessary as brushed teeth, as easy as catching as a cold.

Paul sighed, and she thought of his chest rising. Beate had recently found a picture of him online. His hair had turned white. Perhaps his chest hair had whitened, too. She used to put her hand on that chest, feeling its muscles rearrange. Used to slide her fingers into that hair until they were partly hidden. *Give up*, Beate thought, though that idea was met with other feelings she tried but failed to squelch.

"Asking our children questions is harder than you'd think," Beate said.

"When she was two years into Berkeley," Paul answered, "I asked what she might major in, and Adela told me a story about a street fair."

"When I ask Michael if he has a new boyfriend, he shows me shoes he wants to buy."

"Shoes," Paul repeated.

Beate wondered if he was sitting or standing, what people passing him might see. Dumb, she thought, though dumbness felt good, easy, and she pulled more things she remembered about Paul out of the ether.

Sometimes Peter ate dinner with Adela and Michael. More often with Beate. As he watched her cook, he asked how to say slice or bake or leftovers. Occasionally, Adela or Michael came over after work to claim him. But mostly he stayed with her. In the morning, he and Beate sat in the dewy yard working on vocabulary or the dative case. When he mastered a new verb, she'd kiss the top of his head and he'd create sentences featuring her. *Oma waits. Oma and Peter will wait. Oma and Peter have waited.* Windows thrummed open. Laundry on lines floated and fell.

If neither Michael nor Adela were up by the time Beate left for work, she'd bring Peter to their house and leave him in front of the television. Sometimes she made them coffee. "You should tell them you made it," she said to Peter, who looked confused, then clear. He spouted out more German words: coffee and making and lazy. His face fell as he realized Beate was leaving him. "I'll tell them also," he said, trying to delay her exit, his German growing every day, "that I am my own babysitter."

⟡

Michael worried that the bar would bother Adela. That she'd hear orders for one too many Communist-themed drinks and a curdled taste would stay with her. On her first Phone Tap Friday, she bused tables and lugged buckets of ice, all of it done happily. After Michael stood on the bar and read entries, she said, "You're good," and went to deal with a spill. Later, Adela poured beers. Someone at the bar looked at its largest poster and asked: "Solidarity with whom?"

"Against the West," Adela answered. "The GDR supported Communists everywhere."

When customers commented on drinks, Adela explained a name's origins. A young man scoffed at a cocktail named after decomposition. She told him that Zersetzung had also been a Stasi strategy, sharing stories of resistance groups the Stasi infiltrated, operatives convincing each of the group's leaders that the other was a spy.

During her third shift someone asked if she was the historian, and the things she'd read to Michael decades before became part of the bar's subversive charm. Adela talked to the university students who filled the place about the uprisings of 1953 and the Republikflucht. Told them how her grandparents paid a thousand marks for fake passports. Justine reminded her that there were glasses in need of cleaning.

On her third Phone Tap Friday, Adela asked if she could announce the entries. The poster behind her showed a couple ecstatically marching, ghosts of Marx and Lenin in the background.

"Sure," Michael said.

"Sure," Justine added.

Ten o'clock came, and Adela climbed onto the bar. The microphone's cord whipped around her feet. She looked at the mic, then at her brother. Adela appeared terrified. Also tall. She shuffled entries, and the crowd quieted. The trio of drunk regulars began to hoot. Michael was getting ready to hoist himself next to his sister when she said hello. A few patrons answered.

"I'm sorry, citizens," Adela said. "That's not what I expect when I say hello to you."

"Hello!" more people shouted. Adela's face hardened. "Hello!" the crowd wailed.

"Let's begin," Adela said.

She glanced at the first confession. One of the three young drunks called out: "Lady on the bar!" They were red-faced and loud and took up more space than they needed.

"First entry: *I used to jerk off to catalogs for nursing supplies*," Adela read. The drunks whooped and were shushed. The next entry was about a hand job given to a large Asian man, whom the person called a sumo. "An actual sumo wrestler?" Adela asked the crowd. "If not, I believe that's racist. At the very least, mean."

Stepping off the bar, she said: "I liked the one about the grandmother." In that, the confessor admitted to taking small sums from a grandmother's purse—one mark, then ten, even after Oma noticed and felt like she was losing her mind. "The rest were bragging."

The winner, a young woman, walked sheepishly toward the bar to claim her prize.

During quiet moments, Adela asked about the posters and the people, about Michael's list of suitors he could message day and night. And as she asked questions, as she tried on his sunglasses and muddled sugar and mint, it became clear that she'd missed him. In his version of her California years, then her job in a township hospital, Michael assumed he'd been forgotten. But even as she'd treated young women who went from healthy to breathlessly sick in a week, his life had been a story she'd constructed.

The drunk trio made a loud exit. One of them barked, "Sumo!" A man at the far end of the bar kept smiling at Adela. He had a full mouth Michael pictured putting to use.

"One of my people, yes?" Michael asked.

"I don't think so," Adela answered.

"She's right," Justine said. "That's Gert. He manages a bike shop." Justine told them how Gert grunted in lieu of using words, reminding Michael of Udo saying nothing for an entire dinner. Michael excused himself and went to the office, not jerking off because the probability of getting caught was too high.

When he came back out, Adela and Gert were talking. She leaned and made faces large and coy, and Michael realized she was doing an impression of him. Gert made a joke. She rested a hand on her cheek. Gert asked a question and she whispered her answer.

"We're short on glasses," Michael said, though a press of them sat behind her.

"Fuck a duck," Adela answered, as she and Michael walked away. "What was that?"

"A rescue."

"If I need rescue, I'll do it myself. You're just upset because you thought he was cute, too," Adela added.

"You thought he was cute?" Michael asked.

"Not from your side of the river."

The bar closed. Gert stayed. As they put up stools, Gert told Adela he'd wait for her outside.

"Outside?" Michael asked.

"As in, not inside," Adela answered.

"Outside and inside and outside and inside," Michael said, faster, more salacious each time. "Outside." His hand smacked the bar. "Inside." His hand again.

Adela passed him with a tower of cocktail shakers. "What am I doing?" she whispered.

"Outside and inside," he whispered back, and she covered her mouth. His sister had probably never gone home with a man she'd met at a bar.

She came home the next morning with stories of Gert draped across her, Gert who'd mumbled in his sleep that someone needed to open the store. When she woke up in the middle of the night, she found him awake, too. "And ready. It's like he's eighteen," she said.

"The best, when they're like that," Michael said. "Insatiable."

They lay on Michael's bed. It was six-thirty in the morning. She wore a T-shirt of Gert's, and her hair spilled across Michael's pillows. When she went quiet, he asked if she was asleep.

"Just thinking," she said.

"About?"

Adela pulled a pillow to her face.

"You should see him again," Michael said.

"So I can tell you more stories?"

"So you can have more fun."

Peter walked in without knocking. His bathing suit on, hair lopsided from sleep.

"We'll swim soon," Michael said.

"You slept in here last night?" Peter asked Adela.

"We were talking."

"I'll be right down," Michael said.

Peter's bathing suit sat high up his waist.

Biking to the beach later, Peter tapped his shoulder.

"We'll be there soon," Michael said.

"Breakfast?" Peter asked.

They stopped at a bakery, where Peter stuffed sweet rolls into his mouth. His sticky fingers held Michael's shoulders as they joined the other beachgoers who funneled toward the shore. Michael was ready to swim. Even more, he hoped Adela would see Gert again, that there'd be more stories, Gert something he and his sister orchestrated together.

That afternoon Michael met up with the concierge. They went to his place, their shirts off before they'd closed the door. Each time Michael kissed a part of his body, the concierge named it: "My foot," he said. "My stomach."

"Out having fun?" Adela asked, when he got home.

"Am I that obvious?"

She pointed to his shirt's mismatched buttons.

"It's never scary?" Adela asked. "So many of them?"

"When I first started doing it, I was sometimes afraid," he said. Afraid that it would hurt, that he'd come before anything good happened. AIDS and his feelings for young men had exploded together, like dependent variables. He felt afraid sometimes, he told her, but continued.

"Sometimes when I was at work," Adela said, "I worried about you."

"I'm careful," Michael said. "And with Gert?"

"Shut up."

"You still never told me," Michael said. "If it's straight or curved. Fat or skinny."

Adela had started making complicated drinks at the bar. People came in to ask if it was true that they had a historian working there. One young woman, drinking an Eastern Bloc, barked that this was the best museum she'd ever been to. Adela reddened and leaned onto Michael's shoulder. She was always leaning on him, picking lint off his shirts or fussing with his hair. Adela had come back. She had no job other than the one Michael had given her, no mailing address apart from the house they again shared. And though she changed the subject when he asked about her plans, Michael toggled between hope and the feeling that hope turned him stupid, and couldn't help but wonder if she might stay.

"Details?" Michael asked.

"Gert," Adela answered, blushing into her brother's shoulder again.

⟡

It was late at night that Adela talked. About Berkeley and Pretoria. Dad in California, who, for the years she lived there, treated her with an insulting politeness. She told stories of Aunt Kate, who smoked a mammoth amount of weed, their half-sister Leti, who was too sweet to be interesting. One night, the two of them sat on the deck. They passed a sorbet container back and forth.

"Do you talk to Taro anymore?" he asked.

"Do you still talk to Tobias?" she asked back.

Adela asked if the noise she heard was the Baltic.

"Just wind," he said. "But you just left?"

"Pretoria?" she asked, and he nodded.

"I needed something else," Adela said. Her feet rested on the railing.

"There was a night," she went on, "when I got home late. Peter kept repeating the time that I'd been expected. He followed me into the kitchen, where I tried to make dinner. As I chopped veggies, he stood right behind me, trying to figure out the math of how late I was."

"Peter," Michael said. Adela ate another spoonful.

"He kept saying, 'How many hours?' though he should have calculated minutes. 'How many? How many?' I took the bowl of vegetables and threw them against the wall."

The spoon scraped against her teeth. Their father had loved to throw shoes.

"He laughed like a maniac. So loud that I went into my room and locked the door. And I passed out. Didn't wake up for hours. When I went to check on Peter, he'd locked his door, too. And the food had been cleaned up."

In the German Lady's place next door, a light turned on.

"I ate all this," Adela answered, and dropped the container onto the deck.

"Any decisions on your plans?" Michael asked.

"I'll stay for a bit," Adela said.

When he asked if a bit might be longer, she answered maybe.

Adela fell asleep with her head on his shoulder. Michael's phone buzzed. It was the Potato Farmer, who wrote: *I guess you were right. You'd just been busy.* Though Michael was pleased to hear from him, to think of his perfect legs, his sister kept sleeping on his shoulder. Michael stayed, even as his shoulder began to hurt, his ass numb from sitting so long.

The drunk trio ordered straight vodka. Michael poured them beers instead. They groused and slammed their glasses on the bar. "Assholes," Justine mumbled when they left. Ten o'clock came. Again, Adela asked if she could announce the confessions. Michael said sure. Justine looked at the rag in her hand. Again, Adela stared at the mic for too long. She shifted and kicked over a glass, then held the mic so feedback invaded the room. But she righted it and started, her voice loud and serious, and the worry Michael felt a moment before untangled. In the first confession, someone stole from a store and pinned it on a hated bully. The story felt too neat to be true. The next involved showing a boob to a cousin so he wouldn't rat out her cigarette smoking. "Cigarettes?" Adela said. "That feels more like a crack-smoking sacrifice." The way she stood, her feigned seriousness, was another impression of him. Michael wasn't sure whether or not to be flattered. Adela unfolded the next entry.

"*In my teens I was briefly a neo-Nazi*," it began. "*I was a mess and angry*," she continued, moving the mic to her opposite hand. "*And there was a time when our city was inundated with refugees. I did some bad things and regret them. That's my confession.*" Michael surveyed the crowd. There was a man in his late twenties who might have been old enough. Another with short-cropped hair. People looked at their drinks or phones, or up at Adela, a cloud of risen smoke at her shoulders. Adela seemed scared of the microphone again. She finished and hopped off the bar. Justine was barricaded in glasses.

"That's a Lie Detector," Justine said. "The two on ice are martinis."

Michael filled a shaker. The cash register rang, and customers shouldered up to the bar. Gert lifted his glass for another beer.

"We need to pick a winner," Justine said.

"The neo, clearly," Adela answered.

"Ha," Justine said. Her hammer-and-sickle earrings caught the light.

Michael hadn't known where he and Udo were going until they'd moved toward the stockade of skinheads and his cousin had picked up a rock. The skinheads had grinned, handed him more. Handed Michael one, too, which he held, hoping to turn into part of the background.

"I'm not kidding," Adela went on. "Like the Stasi really cared about overhearing people talk about their sex lives."

"Adela," Michael said.

"If we want real confessions."

"We want people coming here to confess murder?" Justine asked.

"Is this murder, Michael?"

Adela's teenage version emerged, eager to confront this confession's author. To remind Michael that he'd stood behind Udo, that they'd all pretended her anger had been the real problem. Michael wanted to go back to the office. To grab his phone and find someone to sleep with. The crowd of customers was three people deep.

"It could have been murder," Michael said. Adela's face stayed hard and he knew he'd let her have this one. "But it wasn't."

Justine shook her head. A customer ordered a Party Line. Michael looked at his sister and said, "Up to you," deferring to her as he had when they were young and he looked to her for everything.

Adela jumped back onto the bar. "The winner," she said. The crowd kept talking. "Ladies and gentlemen. We need silence." Twice before, Michael and Justine had made bets as to who the winner was. Justine had gotten it right once. Michael never. "The winner," Adela repeated. The crowd hushed. Justine rattled a shaker. Adela read the neo's entry verbatim.

Conversation blasted the room. Each time someone moved—to go to the bathroom or order a beer—people stared. Patrons waved to Michael for drinks, but he watched his sister standing on the sticky bar. Euros scattered at her heels. "Going once!" She looked pleased.

"Going twice," Adela said, and fanned herself with the entry.

When no one came forward, she jumped back behind the bar.

Gert stayed as they closed up. He and Adela leaned in close conversation. "Think they're talking about bikes?" Michael asked Justine. She asked if she could head out.

Adela and Gert left on his bike. Seeing Michael in the bar's door, Gert said: "My car broke down." Gert seemed young, though he and Adela were the same age, his sister who saw the world's forgotten and, with everything she did, let them know she remembered them. The bike moved with buoyant grace. Adela had smiled as she'd announced the winner. And as she'd stood there, flushed with pleased anger, Michael remembered how she'd held Udo's arm outside of the camp as the girl with the frying pan hit him.

◇

As August tilted toward its end, Adela and Gert decided to go to Juist. The morning of the trip, Peter followed Adela from room to room. He sat outside the bathroom as she showered and got in her way as she packed. But when she left, he was all sunshine. He and Beate sat on her sofa, conjugating the verb to see. And he pummeled her with questions: What are German schools like? Why were his mother and Gert going to a beach when they lived next to one already? Where were all of Germany's black people?

Rain's white noise washed the windows, and low clouds brimmed the trees. They watched movies and played card games—easy ones first, then harder. Peter grew obsessed with each game until he mastered it, the cards large in his hands. When he figured out a strategy, he looked like he would burst, and Beate turned smitten, letting him play long after he should've been in bed. On the second day, wind joined the rain. The fruit trees leaned. Squirrels darted with peevish fear. Juist was an island, Beate told Peter. It allowed no cars. That's what made it different. He answered that he was hungry, and she scrambled him an egg. Peter ate it with an apostle's careful devotion.

Despite the rain, he and Michael went swimming. Peter came back and asked, "How do you say ice cube in German?"

He and Beate took a tourist cruise up and down the coast. Peter insisted that they stay on the deck, though it rained and the boat bounced. Their hands gripped the railing. Water hit their faces in juicy pops. Peter howled and told her to howl, too. Beate did, half-heartedly. "Again. And better," Peter said. Beate closed her eyes. Planting her feet, she howled. Peter joined. The ship rose and fell beneath them.

Back in the ship's cabin they drank hot chocolate, and Peter asked more questions: Does the boat scare fish? Does it ever snow here? Why does Michael kiss men?

"The fish know better," she said. "It snows a few times a year. Michael kisses men because he loves them."

"How do you know?"

"He loves them the way your mother and father loved each other."

"About what fish know."

She made a fish face, and Peter wiped fog off the window. He grew tired and napped with his head on Beate's knees. When he woke, he asked for the translation of drowning.

While she was at work, Peter stayed with Michael. Beate got home to him in the yard, waiting for her. The rain stopped, though clouds and wind remained. He held small stones behind his back, her task to guess the number.

"Twenty-three," she began.

"Oma," he chided.

"Six," she tried. He revealed two.

The next round she guessed two. He'd gathered six. For the third, she wagered five, but his hands were empty. A few minutes later, she heard a knock at the front door and shushed Peter, perhaps because she felt giddy from the way he employed strategy, how he couldn't keep his delight down when her guess was only one off.

"Why *shh*?" he asked in his terrible whisper.

She slipped her hand over his mouth. He stuck his tongue against her fingers. Though Peter found this hilarious, he somehow stayed quiet. "Someone's knocking," Beate whispered, wanting more games with her grandson, who howled and savored everything she fed him.

"And we're hiding from them," Peter said. They slid behind a shrub.

At the door stood Liesl. She wore a short skirt. When

knocking produced no results, she rang the bell once, again. Perhaps she knew Adela and Gert had gone out of town.

"Your cousin," Peter whispered. He looked from his grandmother to Liesl, not knowing this woman's son had pushed his mother away from this place. Beate's phone rang. Liesl looked toward its sound, saw them, and scowled. Her cleavage shone as if lotioned.

"Good morning," Beate said as she answered the phone. It was Paul.

"Afternoon where you are," he answered.

To Peter, Beate said: "Tell Tante Liesl I'll be right there."

"Is that Peter?" Paul asked.

"We were hiding from her," Peter answered.

"A joke," Beate said.

"Can I talk to him?" Paul asked.

"Your grandfather wants to talk to you."

"Sofu?"

"The other one."

She handed Peter the phone. He stared at it, then said hello.

"You never responded to my invitation," Liesl said.

"I don't know that I got it."

Liesl walked inside, Beate following. A pile of unopened mail filled the front table.

"Some of these are from your bank," Liesl said as paper whispered between her fingers. She stopped at a large envelope, the address written in her hand.

"A dinner party I'm having tonight," Liesl said.

Liesl's dinner parties were a thing of legend. For Chinese New Year she'd purchased a twenty-foot paper dragon that bobbed with the heat from the table's candles. For May Day, she wound her largest tree with fabric and made flower crowns for the women to wear. Christmas meant three trees, boughs over every doorframe.

"It starts in two hours and you hadn't called me back."

Beate didn't remember a call from Liesl, then did, vaguely, as if grabbing at pieces of a dream. Her life was the *Pflegeheim* and Peter's growing tenancy. Paul's calls every other day turned friends and obligations into a past era, something to remember rather than act upon.

Peter answered his grandfather's questions with clipped noes and yeses. One time he nodded, then smiled. "I was nodding a yes. But you can't see me."

"He wants to talk to you," Peter interrupted.

"Tell him I'll be right there."

"International is expensive," Liesl added.

"It's not 1975."

Peter held the phone at his hip.

"I don't have anyone to watch him," Beate said.

Liesl smiled as if she'd caught her cousin in a lie, took out her own phone, and dialed. The person on the other end of the line listened as Liesl explained and gave directions.

"Ines will be here at seven," Liesl said.

"The one I fired?"

"She's looking for work," Liesl answered. "And I've heard she's a great babysitter."

Liesl left, and Peter passed Beate her phone. She told Paul she'd been talking to her cousin.

"The one with the boobs?" Paul asked. "Adela used to call her that."

When she asked if Adela had other nicknames for Liesl, he said he didn't remember. Paul's voice brought to life the shape of his eyes when he was considering. She felt nervous and dumb and wanted to be alone so she could see her face in a mirror as she talked to him.

"Who's Gert?" Paul asked.

"He might get Peter a bike," Beate answered.

"Why is Adela away with him?"

The little Beate had heard about Taro made Gert seem like a strange successor. Taro finished college in two years and won an award from a senator. *Taro got a job at the consulate in Johannesburg,* Adela had written to Beate several years before to explain her move to a third continent. Gert worked with his hands. His voice never rose above a whisper. Perhaps Taro had let Adela down too much. Maybe she relished the way Gert was easy.

"They're dating, it seems," Beate said. "Michael calls him her boy toy."

"And he rides bikes?"

Paul's voice didn't carry the impatience she'd remembered, but appealed for direction.

"Maybe it's a phase," Beate said.

"Like Michael being gay?" Paul answered, a smile in his voice. The cleft in his chin probably appeared, stubble there he could never adequately shave.

"A phase for two decades."

"A hobby, then," Paul ceded.

Peter stood at the end of the driveway. A boy biked past. Peter waved, and the boy stuck up his middle finger. Peter stuck up his as well. The boy lifted a second one and almost fell from his bike. Peter looked amused. A neighbor across the street shaped shrubs with a clipper.

"Oh," Paul said. "I remember another nickname for her: Saint Teresa."

"Wasn't she excommunicated?" Beate asked.

From six thousand miles away, she felt Paul's laugh across

the back of her neck, like a hand. Beate tried to tell herself she was being stupid, but that voice barely registered.

When she got off the phone, Peter asked more questions about Juist. “I’ve told you all I know,” Beate said. “I’ve never actually been there.”

⟡

Liesl’s house was modern and large, with shrubs Michael said were sculpted to look like poodles. Unlike her other parties, where Liesl hired a staff of caterers, tonight she answered her own door.

Music played that sounded Brazilian. Guests filled the living room. As Liesl handed Beate a glass of wine and her daughter skulked through the room, Beate saw Josef and his new wife, Stefanie, in the crowd.

“You didn’t tell me,” Beate said.

Stefanie was short and younger than Beate. Hair dyed. Lipstick bright. Beate’s dress was gray. When she’d worn it a week before, Adela told her she looked like a professor.

Liesl waved a canapé in dismissal. “Because you wouldn’t have come.”

“Exactly,” Beate said.

“Not every man you were once married to is your enemy,” Liesl answered, and Beate thought of Paul’s laugh, the tick of the *t* when he said her name. “Go say hello.”

Beate found a colleague to talk to. When Heinz came around with wine, Beate lifted her glass for more. Josef moved in her direction and Beate slid into the kitchen, where Liesl’s friend Anke placed salad on plates. Anke worked at the *Pflegeheim*, too. Beate once had to chide her for giving a resident a cigarette.

“Let me help,” Beate said, and Anke nodded.

“Liesl roped you in?” Beate asked.

Anke answered that she was thinking of starting a catering business. The room smelled of roasting meat.

"You'd leave the *Pflegeheim*?"

Anke stared at her cutting board. When Beate had had to discipline her, she'd stared at the floor.

"This is not—" Beate went on. "I'm not asking as someone who—" She hated the word boss, the imitations of niceness others summoned because of it. Anke examined each of the sixteen plates for a similar number of tomatoes. "In any official capacity," Beate finished. "My ex-husband is here. Liesl hadn't told me. It didn't end well."

"In divorce," Anke said. She handed Beate a bowl of tomatoes and pointed to plates in need of more. "I've always wondered if it would feel—not nice—but evidence of a life lived, to say, 'my ex-husband.' Just hearing that someone has an ex-husband, I think: *There must be a story*."

Liesl's friend Frieda sat next to Beate and complained about a recent meal she'd had in Cologne. "With the candles and the prices," Frieda balked.

Across the table, Josef's bald head shone in the candlelight. Stefanie tapped his knuckles with her nails. As she started her salad, Liesl made a noise whose closest animal equivalent was a purr.

"Beate," Josef said.

"Josef, Stefanie. Hello."

Stefanie wore a large necklace. She was very tan.

"Josef's company put a new roof on my garage," Frieda said.

"Josef and I were once married," Beate answered. No other conversations were happening at the time, spotlighting theirs. People took sips of wine and water.

"You're well?" Josef asked.

"Fine," Beate answered.

"Her daughter and grandson are here from Africa," Liesl said.

"Your daughter is African?" a guest she didn't know asked.

Liesl answered that she'd lived there. "Working with AIDS," she went on, as if the disease were Adela's colleague.

"Adela's son?" Josef said, and looked hurt that he didn't know.

"Adela is my daughter," Beate said to Stefanie.

"I know," Stefanie answered, and ate a tomato.

From another guest Beate didn't recognize: "Is it right that your son owns that bar where people have to admit to working for the Stasi or some such thing?"

"No one admits to being in the Stasi, do they, Beate?" Liesl answered.

"But this is the one," Frieda added, "with the memorabilia. The GDR the butt of a joke. I had a cousin in jail for seven months for nothing."

"Humor is one way," Josef said, "to deal with the past."

The sweetness of his effort returned. Josef had transformed her house for Liesl's wedding. He'd helped Michael with geometry. When Beate had been sad, he'd asked if she was okay. "And what if I said no?" she'd answered once. When he'd tried to hug her, she'd shaken her head and he'd moved away, as if he'd been scolded.

"We should make concentration camp jokes next?" This came from a woman Liesl knew from tennis. She had slender, muscled arms.

"It's not my bar," Beate said.

"But you've talked to him?"

"I stopped telling my son what to do a long time ago."

A moment of polite laughter before questions continued: *What is the Stasi game? Do the waiters wear Stasi uniforms? What made your son think this was funny?*

Heinz tried changing the subject to a football match he'd seen.

"But your son's young. Where did he get the money to buy a bar?"

"He's frugal," she said, wanting to add that he was German, after all. Adela—who used to read books about the Stasi, Goebbels, and Koch, too—would have had a perfect defense of his place, zooming in on these people's discomfort. Beate looked up from her salad. The rest of the guests seemed to be waiting for more of an answer. "He saved," Beate said, not adding that she and Udo had loaned him money.

"This is a friendly dinner," Liesl said.

"And this is a friendly conversation," the tennis woman answered.

"If people are interested, we can head to the bar after dinner," Beate said. "Talk about it there rather than ruining the lovely evening Liesl and Anke have worked hard to prepare."

Anke came in to find the salads mostly uneaten. Beate took a large bite. It was good. She would have told Anke, but her mouth was full.

"What did you say to him when he told you about the bar?" Frieda asked. "As someone who'd lived here."

Anke cleared salads. Beate stood to help but was rebuffed. She wished she and Peter had hidden better, that she'd had her phone on silent.

"I don't remember," Beate said.

"Not word for word," the tennis friend replied.

"Just a general sense," Tennis's husband added.

"I don't remember."

"You don't remember at all?"

Liesl banged her fist on the table.

"I didn't have this party for fighting about bars and history and other nonsense."

Five months before, Beate had gone with her to identify Udo's body. She'd stood behind her cousin as the sheet was pulled from his face. "That's him," Liesl had said. "It really is."

Liesl's face now was beautifully made up, also tired. Grief a race without a finish, without the adrenaline of the possible. Liesl had planned a dinner in hopes of cresting the surface for a bit. Beate hadn't read the invitation.

"And you two were married?" A guest at the end of the table—perhaps Edith from golf—asked. Liesl had talked about Edith with annoyed envy for a purse she had, her lower par.

"I've been married twice," Beate said.

"Once to me," Josef added.

More polite laughter.

"Now he's married to Stefanie," Beate said. "Who owns one of Kritzhagen's best salons."

"She cuts your hair?" someone asked.

Beate shook her head. She couldn't look at her cousin, whose sadness felt contagious. Beate dug her fingernails into her leg. She'd worn a dress she could have gotten away with at a funeral. Thoughts of dead Udo, a sheet pulled to his shoulders, swatted at Beate. Her fingers dug harder. "It really is," Liesl had repeated, in a room that smelled of chemicals, fluorescent light on Udo's face and shoulders. *He doesn't see that light*, Beate had thought. *Doesn't feel the table against his back.* He wasn't elsewhere but gone. Perhaps Liesl had had a party too soon. Her daughter Petra moved out of the kitchen.

"Beate cut hair briefly, Stefanie," Liesl said. "I don't know if you know."

"When?" Stefanie asked.

"I'd just come back," Beate said.

"From Africa?" the tennis friend asked.

Shrimp tails wreathed people's plates. Liesl shook her head. Perhaps she wanted these people gone, this party not lifting her, but reminding Liesl of the distance between her and the living world.

"Her daughter isn't African," Liesl said, and twisted pasta into her spoon.

Anke was serving fruit tart when the doorbell rang. Heinz was trying out a bit about Merkel and Obama, funnier because Heinz never did things like that, rather than because of its execution. Anke came back and whispered to Beate: "It's Ines, who used to work with us."

Ines stood on the front steps, in a T-shirt featuring a cartoon animal.

"Peter said he needed you," she said.

"I'll be home soon."

"He said he had a question," Ines continued.

"Did you ask him what it was?"

Ines pulled on the sleeves of her shirt. Inside the dining room, she heard Liesl say: "Adela's boy."

"The African," someone joked.

Forks scraped plates. The tart was delicious, but Beate was full. She went into the dining room, picked up her plate, and walked outside.

"Where is he?" Beate asked; Ines eyed her car.

Peter sat in the back seat. Beate handed him her slice. She should have been annoyed by his interruption, but felt relief. Her new best friend was about to enter the second grade.

"You had a question?" Beate asked.

"Somebody's already eaten this," Peter said.

"*I* have eaten it," she answered. "You had a question."

Peter kicked the seat in front of him. He put the tart down and mumbled something Beate couldn't make out. She brought him inside. Made Peter say hello to Liesl, introduced him to Josef.

"I used to be married to your grandmother," Josef said.

"You're the grandfather?" Peter asked, and Josef laughed. Her grandson's face soured.

"I'm not the grandfather," Josef corrected.

"Peter wanted to say good night," Beate said, though she'd brought him in. She wanted these people to see her and her grandson together. They said good night and walked outside.

When they got back to Beate's house, Peter said: "I remember my question, Oma."

"Okay."

"Do you think she's coming back?"

She was about to say who, then felt like an idiot. Peter sat on the bottom step, eyes glued on her. A dollop of tart stuck to his chin.

"Tomorrow, *mein Kleiner*," she said. "Let's get you upstairs."

"You call me that because I'm small?"

"A term of endearment," she answered. Peter's scowl asked: *How am I supposed to know that word?*

"It means that I like you."

"Okay," Peter said, and plodded to the guest room. Beate sat at the foot of his bed. He asked about the dinner party, telling her to answer in German. He asked who Josef was, if not the grandfather.

"I was married to him after the grandfather. Sometimes when people—"

"I know what divorce is," he said. "I just don't know how to say it in German."

In the middle of the night, she called Paul. She asked how old his youngest daughter was.

"Twelve," he said.

"Ooph."

"She's good, though. Like her mother."

"Not like our people?" Beate said, once a single entity with him. "Peter calls you the grandfather, as if you're the only one in the world."

"When you first moved to Germany," Paul said, "Adela told me Michael nicknamed me the California Father."

Mowers sounded in the background. She thought of the tan Paul got in the summer, the thrill she used to feel in seeing him naked, his tan line marking what was hers alone, what now was someone else's, what was really only his. In one of the recent pictures she'd seen online he'd worn an ugly baseball cap and a neoprene band around his sunglasses. Beate didn't care.

"I didn't mean to bother you," she said, though she'd wanted just that, then felt silly for turning hopeful each time she heard from him.

"Why are we calling each other?" Beate asked.

"I was checking on Adela," Paul said.

"You've checked on her," Beate answered. She wanted him to tell her she was being how she'd always been, Beate straining to figure out what he'd just thrown. Wanted him to say, *Really?* with the same ire he had when, once, after a fight, Beate had taken off her clothes and kissed his neck. A ticking in California may have been a sprinkler.

"You called me, B," Paul said.

Beate put her head on the kitchen table.

⟡

Peter stepped into the bar. He climbed a stool as if it were a ladder, his storm of hair barely cresting the counter.

"Supposed to be in the office," Michael said.

"The office is boring," Peter answered.

"That was the agreement."

Peter's brow fell, a reminder to Michael that his nephew hadn't agreed to anything.

It was Ingo's birthday. He'd planned a last-minute dinner party and invited Mutti.

"But Peter isn't invited," Mutti had said that morning, she and Michael and Peter eating breakfast in her kitchen. She stood up and wiped down the already-clean counter.

"I can take him," Michael said.

"To the bar?" she answered, her eyes blown wide.

"He can watch movies in the office. A sofa there, just like there's a sofa here."

Mutti stared at her coffee. "It's more than just having a sofa," she said.

But Peter, who'd heard so much about the bar, wanted to see it in person.

After Mutti said, "I don't know," for the third time, Peter scowled and she nodded and he hugged her knees. Delight crowded her face. Michael worried what might happen to Mutti if Peter and Adela left them.

Peter stood on his stool, leaned his elbows onto the bar. Patrons looked at him with sweet amusement, and as Michael pushed hair from the child's eyes, he realized that they mistook his nephew for his son. A table of women seemed wooed. One of them, coming up for another drink, said, "The two of you have the same hair." Peter answered with a doubtful squint.

"You can be out here for three minutes, then back into the office," Michael said.

"How do you say jail in German?" Peter asked.

"How do you say," Michael said, then reminded himself that Peter had turned seven three months before. He made a tray of Don't Drink the Kool-Aids for a crew of college women from somewhere in the West. Days of rain kept customers away, gave everything a wet dog smell.

"This place has, like, saved us," one of the women told Michael. "The rest of this city is so boring."

"Not boring if you know where to look," Michael said.

"It's all terrible beach hotels," the woman went on.

"Well, I'm the mayor of the not-boring part of the city."

"Mr. Mayor." The young woman smiled.

"What?" Peter asked when he got back behind the bar.

"What, what?" Michael asked back.

"What did you say to those ladies?"

"A joke about being the mayor."

"You're not a mayor," Peter answered.

On a napkin, the boy tried to draw a bicycle.

Rain hit the windows. Candles bobbed as people moved out and in. Michael filled his tray with empty glasses and full ashtrays. The night Udo had vanished it had rained. Michael wondered if his cousin had checked the weather before heading out on his namesake. He hoped Udo had been killed quickly, a wave burying the boat, but as he dumped detritus into the trash can he felt the ache in knowing that he'd never know exactly what had happened. A text tickled his pocket. Adela. *Gert and I are extend-*

ing the trip one more night. He wanted to ask if she'd ever emailed Udo back, or send her a picture of Peter at the bar with a caption that read: *Guess he takes after the German Lady.* But part of Michael was still afraid of her. He settled on: *Enjoy the fucking.*

"This shit place!" one of the three drunks who haunted the bar said, the other two stumbling in behind him. They had round faces and juvenile beards. As they careened closer, Michael realized that their drunkenness had reached new heights.

"Drinks!" one of them barked.

"Drinks!" another garbled.

Theirs was a particular maleness Michael hated. They grinned, and it felt mean. They looked him in the eye, and it was belligerence they offered.

"Peter," Michael said.

"Not three minutes," his nephew answered.

"I'm breaking my promise."

"Baby at the bar!" one of the drunks said. He tried and failed to pick up a menu.

"I wonder what's the baby's favorite drink," one of them slurred.

"The Party Line!" another guessed.

"Peter," Michael repeated.

His nephew watched these young men with fear, also interest. Despite his size, signals of his someday self emerged in the directness of Peter's gaze, the sarcasm he could detect in two languages.

The trio's leader leaned next to Peter. "Maybe the baby has a recommendation," he said.

"Maybe the baby," a friend repeated.

Michael picked up his nephew and carried him back to the office. Peter went limp with resistance. As Michael put him on the couch, Peter bit his uncle's shoulder.

"I'm not fucking around," Michael said.

"Fuck fucking fuck fuck," Peter answered.

"Those are not good people."

"I know," Peter said. He tried to stand on the sofa, but its cushions did him in. Michael left and locked the door. Peter kicked it. Michael heard him scream fuck, in English then German, then something about tits for breakfast. Michael was impressed. He also hoped his nephew hadn't gotten that from him. His shoulder ached where Peter's teeth had sunk into it.

The three men slurred drink orders across the room. Justine stacked glasses, and Michael moved behind the bar.

"You have any Nazi cocktails?" the leader asked. He pulled a lime from the caddy and sucked on it. Michael flipped its lid down. The young man lifted his hands in false apology. He looked to his friends, lime lining his teeth.

"Kristallnacht Sour," one minion said.

"Hitler and Tonic," another stuttered.

"Enough, please," Michael said. More droopy-eyed amusement from the three, who repeated, "Enough," over and over. One stumbled, was saved by a stranger's shoulder. A quiet kick sounded as Peter failed to overwhelm the door.

Udo often sat at the bar's corner. Even drunk, he would have asked these men to leave, and they would have listened. Michael missed him terribly.

The drunks gripped the bar and spoke in stage whispers.

"We'll settle for beers," the leader said.

Michael looked at the tap, part of him ready to give in. Justine stepped forward.

"We're not serving you," she said.

The cowardly relief of being rescued warmed Michael's ears.

"You're not?" the leader said.

Michael moved next to her and said, "Gentlemen."

"We *are* gentlemen!" a drunk answered.

"A Nazi bar," a different one repeated. They lit cigarettes. Every once in a while they called out: "Gentlemen," or "Enough, please." Michael felt young, made useless by fear, more terrified as he remembered he was meant to be in charge. Justine and a customer shot each other looks. One of the men lurched toward the table of the Western women and asked them to buy beers in their stead. Michael wanted Adela there, wanted Udo. Wanted the spinning in his gut to stop long enough so he could think of something. A drunk swatted a low-hanging fixture. The lamp's beam spun over shoulders. Customers whispered, and a man at a back table dialed his phone. Michael skimmed through things he might do, but held on to nothing. Peter kicked again. A drunk knocked over a stool.

Michael switched on the overhead lights and turned off the music. The bar transformed into a parking garage.

"Closing early," he said. "Finish your drinks and leave, please."

"Closing early!" one of the men mimicked, his impression of Michael hysterical, feminine. The men turned giddy.

Patrons filed outside, where the rain had left behind shining puddles. "Gentlemen," one of the drunks said. "Enough, please," his friend answered. They waited for the rest of the customers to leave before weaving outside. They eyed the Western women climbing into a taxi. As it puttered down the street, the men called after it with dumb, obscene words. To be a woman, Michael thought, to have men call them ladies, then bitches, then talk about the body parts they hoped to see and feel. The men stumbled in the taxi's direction.

"What did we do when this happened before?" Justine asked.

Michael answered, "Udo." He wished his cousin had thought of him as he landed in the water, then hoped he thought of nothing, the ache of him gone a hand on his throat.

"Guess I'll have to bulk up," Michael said.

Justine stacked stools. Michael opened the office to find Peter on the sofa, turning the volume up and down on the computer. He watched a video on New Guinea. Men with barely covered cocks next to a muddy river. Michael's phone buzzed. It was the teacher, awake, interested.

Just need to drop something off, Michael wrote back.

He hoped Ingo's dinner was over, but knew he could get Mutti to call it a night even if it wasn't. She'd be happy to see Peter. She'd likely missed him. If Michael told her that Peter had bitten him, her expression would suggest he was exaggerating, would ask how Michael deserved it. Peter pouted. Michael wanted to tell him he was acting like an asshole, that he had somewhere better to be, but said, "We're leaving." Peter ignored him. He asked his nephew if he wanted to climb onto the bar to blow out candles. "Not my job," the boy answered, and turned up the volume again.

Michael slid money into the safe and flicked out the lights.

"You sleeping here?" Michael asked.

Peter came out, a glint of fear in his eyes. Michael locked the front door and thought about the teacher's chest. The teacher might see Michael's reddened shoulder and ask what happened. *Kids can be assholes*, Michael could say. Or he'd tell the teacher that he could bite him if he wanted to.

Peter swished into the booster seat and buckled himself in. Michael's phone pinged. First came a message from Mutti, saying, yes, she'd meet him at home. Next was a picture of the teacher in the smallest slip of underwear. Michael walked toward the driver's-side door when he heard noise and felt the hit across his back, the window stinging his forehead. The next hit landed on his neck. The third burned across his cheek. "Faggot," one of the drunks said. Another kicked Michael's knees.

Michael put up his hands, hoping they'd accept a truce, only to have his arms yanked behind him. He felt his shoulders tear. That pain turned to nothing as his face was flung against the car's side-view mirror.

Inside the car, Peter didn't move. Michael knocked on the window, realizing his mistake right after. A drunk lifted his head as if he'd been rudely awoken. He squinted at the car. But as he moved toward its doors, Michael heard the car's locks catch, saw Peter's hand move away from the locks and cover his ears. One of the men banged the window, another threw Michael to the ground. Michael's mouth turned wet and salty. As a foot stamped down on his fingers, as he let out a hiss of pain and spat blood onto the front of his shirt, Michael suddenly heard the wail of his car's horn. He wished he could see Peter pressing on it. Another kick, and Michael turned short of breath. He squinted through the swelling on his face. His mouth and ribs burned and the horn kept sounding. As Michael hacked more blood onto the pavement, he realized that a car was coming toward them. Peter must have seen, too. Another kick, this time to his face, and Michael closed his eyes. The horn's blaring continued. And as the car got closer and slowed, as its driver shouted and another car slowed behind it, Michael thanked god that Peter had his mother's brain.

18

When Taro grew keen on an idea, he'd point, an ink-blotched finger rising, his eyes lifting beyond those he was talking to. Adela noticed this first. Then his forearms. When she reached his face, she realized he was beautiful. She tried to stare at her notes or a scuff on the wall. But her need to look at him won—childlike in its insistence, adult in its attention to detail. Taro was a TA in her American foreign policy seminar. He spoke with an earnest smartness that left others in the class following at a far distance. He made complicated points about economic violence and Adela felt the same restless excitement that captured her years before when she'd taken off from Frankfurt by herself. When he poked holes in a person's points, Adela spent the rest of the afternoon thinking about a phrase he'd pulled from the air, how what had seemed certain a moment before was revealed as rickety.

Adela read everything off the syllabus, found syllabi for graduate classes and read that material, too. She listened to him so carefully that she had to take deep breaths not to get stuck on a word, or his finger jabbing the air. Adela jotted down his phrases word for word. She read them late at night and thought of the quiet deepness of his voice. Taro wore the same button-down each day. Adela found out a month later that he had three identical shirts, three pairs of the same pants; an apartment with only a bed, table, and chair. "People usually ask," Taro said on one of their first nights together, "why I don't have anything."

"You have enough," Adela answered, and he told her she was the most beautiful.

"I find that hard to believe," she answered.

"Don't do that," Taro said. Adela turned ashamed. Of his directness, or because being called beautiful felt like a sham.

Sex with him carried the same quiet confidence with which he spoke. Halfway through, that night, she'd come unexpectedly. Adela grabbed his forearms, kissed Taro's shoulder, and whispered for him to keep going.

Taro dropped out of his Ph.D. program just as Adela finished her senior year. The two of them stayed in a rented room in Oakland so small that it only fit a twin bed. They slept pressed against each other, planted tomatoes on their fire escape that they pulled off the vine, biting into them as if they were apples. Adela found work at a nonprofit. Taro got a job selling Christmas trees. He came home with a reject tree that filled the little space left in their room. They had no ornaments, so Adela decorated it with old postcards, and Taro's smile grew wide. He had a beautiful, wide face, a mouth that always wanted to kiss Adela's neck and stomach. He spoke about her breasts as if they were a best-loved poem. Taro never slipped into slang. He told her about the childhood summers he'd spent reading the dictionary, about the day he'd tried to memorize the *X* section. "Xanthate is a salt or ester," he said as he fiddled with the tree's branches. "Xeric: requiring a small amount of moisture." His head rested on her rib cage. He defined xiphoid and xylose, told her he'd never had a Christmas tree before. At work the next morning, Adela found sap stuck in her hair.

Then he came home one day with news of a diplomatic job

he'd been offered in South Africa. Adela hadn't known he'd applied for it. She tried to gird herself for what she was sure came next: news that he was leaving her. When he said instead that he wanted her to go with him, Adela's face flushed, and she remembered Udo's dream of the two of them together at university, how she'd felt something for him until it abruptly ended. But Udo felt far away, in distance, also importance. It shocked her how long she hadn't thought of him, after years in Modesto where she sometimes talked to his imagined version, sometimes pictured him pressed against her. She and Taro lay in their bed. "I hadn't said anything about the job," he said—traffic outside rose and fell—"because I didn't imagine I'd get it." He went on that he wanted it, wanted her more. "So you would go or stay based on my answer," Adela said, half in jest. Taro nodded. A voice on the street called out the name Ricky. Taro's look of need floored her, then lifted her. Adela said yes.

Arriving in Johannesburg, Adela saw sick people everywhere. Some lived in shantytowns. But they also cleaned public restrooms and worked the front desk at the apartment complex where the embassy staff lived. Watching a woman who sold newspapers go from young to old to gone in one summer, Adela remembered Miri, thought of the world's indifference she'd witnessed even at Berkeley. When classmates had talked about a problem, they'd spoken of the past or a theory. Or they sloughed off a difficult discussion for a cigarette or a story of a roommate they hated more than they had a right to.

Outside a tourist shop, a woman asked for money. Adela saw sickness in her face and gave it to her. When she watched an ambulance pull slowly away from a building, her heart sped up. Some days, Taro came home and she couldn't talk to him. Or she asked him why he chose this part of the world, then felt ashamed at her selfishness. After a day when she cried as she hadn't in years, holding on to the collar of Taro's T-shirt with a bully's fervor, she found a clinic and began to volunteer there. She took patients' information. Kept children occupied as mothers went in for appointments. Sat with young women reeling from test results. One from an affluent family had come to the clinic because of its anonymity. "I'm going to die," she kept saying. She wore the uniform from her private school. Her hair was plaited in a way that made her look younger than seventeen.

"There are options now," Adela said.

"But I won't get better," the young woman answered.

Afterward, Adela went behind the clinic. A nurse gave her a cigarette. She smoked half of it, threw up, and said she felt better.

Patients at the clinic started to recognize her. An older man—whom she later found out had infected his wife and girlfriend—called her Yoyo. A mother of three called her Sefate, which meant tree. Others called her Gorra Ou, which she learned was slang for asshole white person. "Look at Gorra Ou playing doctor," a woman said when she found out Adela had no medical training. "Gorra Ou must feel really good about herself," a man answered when she told him that his appointment wasn't until the next day. She tried to explain herself; the man walked away.

But there were other patients who sought her out, young women in particular, whom she talked to after their appointments were done, about the boyfriends who'd gotten them sick but claimed they hadn't, jobs they'd lost, or problems with their insurance. And each time a patient looked for her, Adela felt the distance between them and her shortening, and worked past her shift or offered patients rides home. Some asked about Adela, grew incredulous when she told them of her life in Germany and California. Some of them even learned German phrases, wishing her "*Guten Tag*," or calling her Fräulein. "The Fräulein is here," one woman said each time she came in. Another patient told her of his love of *The Sound of Music*. When a patient died, she went to the funeral—often the only white person there. And if she got to talk to a family member, they often knew who she was. One time, a relative said, "Yes, you're the German Lady."

Then one night Taro talked about a promotion in Pretoria and Adela became terrified. She thought of the patients expecting her at their next visit, how on days the clinic was closed she burrowed into medical textbooks to understand how antiretrovirals worked, and why.

"Since when do you care about a promotion?" Adela asked. Taro wore a tie. The clothes he once taught in were now reserved for weekends.

"You're not the only one trying to do good," he said, and went on about the community health services he'd found funding for, his finger jabbing at the sky. Adela said no.

"You said you wouldn't go without me," she answered.

"But you're not making money," Taro said. "And," he added, pausing again before he went on, "there are plenty of sick people in Pretoria, too."

Adela didn't have enough of her own money to stay. She walked through Braamfontein and chided herself for the pretend-certainty she'd watered and weeded. Felt a hate for Taro as fierce as the love that had struck her when he'd been her TA. She stayed at the clinic until the cleaning staff told her she was in their way. Slept on the sofa of a doctor friend. After three days of this, Taro showed up at the clinic. He wouldn't leave until she talked to him. When she finally came out to the waiting room, he told her he'd go wherever.

"Cleveland?" she asked.

"What's in Cleveland?" he asked back.

Adela answered, "Nothing."

They went to their apartment, and the sex they had wound back to their first months in Berkeley, when it was hard for her not to look at him.

"I've applied to nursing school," Adela said. "In Pretoria."

They lay naked on their bed. Taro moved his fingers through her pubic hair.

"Where I've been offered a job?" he asked.

"Unless there's another Pretoria," she answered, and lay on top of him. They had sex again, though her heart hadn't slowed from their previous round.

For years Adela had focused on ideas with the steadfastness of a bird sitting on an egg. Now she wanted action. Not debates or theories but needles in veins so sick people could sleep. As she went through nursing school and started her first job, she thought of Mutti's stories of the *Pflegeheim* residents. A year into her job, Adela found herself pregnant, which made her happy in a way she didn't understand. Taro became euphoric, too. She worried about working in the clinic as her pregnancy grew conspicuous, but patients touched her stomach and told her stories of their children, of their mothers living hundreds of miles away. Taro kissed her stomach each morning. He thrummed her belly button when it started to stick out. Adela worked until Peter left her too breathless to get up a set of stairs.

"I don't think it's good for Peter," Taro said one night when Adela came home late. He sat on the sofa, their child asleep next to them. Peter was a month from five.

"I was talking about you working all the time," Taro added when she didn't answer.

"And *you* working all the time?"

"Both of us, then," Taro relented. But his tone, the points he seemed ready to make but didn't, made it clear that he saw her job as the lesser. Taro asked if she was hungry. She said yes but went to lie down. She remembered him years before reminding her that he made all the money. Both of them kept working.

One night, though, things felt different, easy. They had a lovely dinner. Peter told them stories about a boy in his class who always talked about Jesus. "And I asked him why he never brought Jesus to the playground," Peter said. They laughed. Peter looked relieved. In bed that night, Adela slipped out of her T-shirt and underwear. Taro did the same.

When they finished, Taro said: "That felt strange." She answered that he was an asshole.

"I don't think I'm an asshole," he said. Naked, he went to sleep on the couch. Adela spent the night mumbling at the ceiling. Each time she got close to sleep, she sensed she was falling off the bed, grabbed the headboard or moved her fingers to the floor and pressed against it.

The next morning, she found Taro asleep on the couch still. His ass glowed in the sun. Peter walked into the room, looking from one parent to the other as if his father weren't sleeping but injured. When his regular look of annoyance surfaced, her son summoned up a "What's wrong with him?" before shaking Taro awake.

A month later Taro told her of a director position he'd been offered in Ghana. Adela had a stethoscope around her neck. She kept taking it off and on.

"I'm guessing you're not coming," he said.

"What a way to ask," Adela answered, though he wasn't asking. At work that day a man who'd been a model patient looked exhausted. After his blood work came back, she saw a drop in T-cells so large that she had to go to the bathroom and wash her face. As she did, Adela left the water running, though it was expensive. And a year after that, the job in Pretoria having worn her down to a frayed nerve, Taro called and told her that he'd finally gotten the position in Washington he'd been waiting for. Taro of their Berkeley days had spoken of the government as a dour foster parent. Now he went on about working from within the system. Being a single mother had flattened Adela. Peter wanted her close just so he could ignore her. When she was tired, he was awake. When work was its busiest, Peter claimed that he was sick, that she needed to be the nurse for him. So, when Taro emailed about a friend's clinic in D.C. that was a perfect fit, she said nothing for a week, then yes. *I'm going to visit my family first*, she wrote. Because it was on the way. Because Udo's death left Germany suddenly open to her, as Kritzhagen must have been for Mutti after the wall switched to past tense. *California?* Taro had written. *The other ones*, Adela answered.

The rain didn't let up. Gert lay next to Adela, unobtrusive even in sleep. As she slid downstairs to check her email, she saw another message from Dad. Emails from Taro that told her he'd registered Peter for school. *Figuring out flights*, Adela wrote him back, though she was figuring out whether to go or stay. The plan had been a visit. But within weeks of arriving in Kritzhagen, the version of Michael as selfish and disinterested molted into the younger one that used to wake Adela up to tell her when he'd had a terrible or fantastic dream. Each time she'd thought to tell him what her plan had been, what the new plan could be, she switched subjects. Because being back was easy. Adela rarely saw things as easy. And she worried that, on telling Michael they were staying, he'd lose interest in her. So, when she'd start to talk about D.C., she said something about the clinic instead. When she thought to admit that she'd fallen for Kritzhagen, Adela asked Michael about a man he slept with.

Dunes behind the house genuflected. The day before, she and Gert had biked to the end of the island. The wind pushed so hard it felt as if they'd been pedaling in place. When she'd called Kritzhagen, Peter told her he'd learned to play spades and asked when she was coming back. "I just left," she'd answered.

Gert came downstairs—tall and shirtless, thin apart from the smallest spread of stomach. He moved his tongue into her mouth though neither of them had brushed their teeth. Adela pressed her hips against his.

Twenty minutes later, Gert said: "What if we stay an extra day?" Adela didn't have to be at the bar until Friday. Taro had written back immediately: *How long does arranging flights take?* Thirty seconds after: *I mean, I can arrange them, if that's what's holding up the show.* Taro from a decade before would never have used a phrase like *holding up the show,* would have pointed at nothing if he'd heard those words, deconstructing the problems with that metaphor.

"An extra day," Adela said, and curled against Gert's shoulder, a shoulder that might turn into more than an interlude. She decided not to answer Taro's email, to think only about the hours they had to fill, the ride into town to get dinner.

⟡

She stood outside the house that had been Udo's, technically now half hers. Adela had read the emails he'd sent over the years, which unfolded on her screen as one endless apology. More than angry or annoyed, Adela had felt pity for him. Udo was stuck, as she'd felt when they'd first moved here.

Inside, Peter and some young woman played cards.

"You were supposed to come back yesterday," Peter said.

"I left a message," Adela answered.

"Did you get Oma's messages?" Peter asked.

Adela held up her dead phone. Peter scowled, then put down a card.

"This is Ines," Peter said.

"The babysitter," the young woman added.

"Supposed to come back yesterday," Peter repeated.

"It was just a day."

Peter slapped down another card.

"I think he—" Ines said.

"Michael's okay," Peter interrupted.

"Was worried," Ines finished.

Peter stood and began walking upstairs. Adela imagined him forcing Mutti to call over and over, her phone going right to voice mail, Adela so busy being on vacation that it wasn't until they were on the ferry back that she realized her phone was dead at the bottom of her bag.

"You thought I wasn't coming back?" Adela said.

"Michael's okay," Peter answered, from the stairs' landing.

"What are you talking about?" Adela asked.

"About what happened to him."

"What happened?" she asked.

"The assholes from the bar," he answered.

"Peter!" she said, thinking of those three belligerent men, her stomach dropping as it had while the ferry from Juist pushed through wind and waves. "Where is Michael?"

"It was in the paper," Ines said. "I guess they beat the crap out of him."

"I think you can go," Adela answered.

The young woman's eyes opened wide, though she didn't

move. She was waiting to be paid, Adela realized. Adela looked through her wallet, found nothing.

"I'll get the money from Frau Haas," Ines said, and left.

Adela plugged her phone in, though it was too dead to start up. She looked around the room for the newspaper so she could read the story. She had to pee, but held it.

"Michael wouldn't serve them," Peter said, his voice so loud it echoed. "They waited until he was outside. One of them was named Michael, too."

Peter moved into their bedroom; Adela followed. Clothes crowded the floor.

As she stood in the bedroom they treated as their own, Adela realized that if someone asked where they'd be in a week, she wouldn't know how to answer.

"Where is Michael?" Adela asked.

"Shut up," Peter said. He kicked clothes covering the floor. When she'd left, their things had been folded in their suitcase.

"Shut up," he said again.

"I didn't say anything," she answered.

Adela picked up her clothes and dropped them into the suitcase. Peter walked to the suitcase and threw them back across the room.

"Stop it," Adela said. She grabbed his arms but he yanked himself free.

The drunks from the bar had assaulted her brother. Peter had imagined her gone. When she asked about Michael again, Peter answered, "Hospital," and tossed a pair of jeans across the room.

"They were so drunk they could barely walk," Peter went on. "One of them almost fell over after he hit Michael. But he got up again, and he—how do you say kick in this language?"

"How do you know all this?" Adela asked. Peter tossed a sweater, its arms spread as if cheering.

"I was there," he answered.

A man spoke to Michael, whose bruised face stayed stuck in a wince. He held a cup of ice chips and could barely open his left eye. Machines beeped in rhythm.

"That's the Potato Farmer," Peter said, followed by, "He's not really a potato farmer." Her son hugged the man's knees. Adela felt like she'd been away for longer than a week.

"How was Juist?" Michael asked.

"Give the two of us some time," Adela answered.

Peter and the Potato Farmer left. It was raining in Kritzhagen, as it had been in Juist. Every once in a while, it clapped across the window.

Michael looked a mess. The drunks had come at him hard, with fists and feet. Peter had watched it happen.

"I've been thinking," Michael said. "I'm on some drugs, you know."

Someone wearing a ring of keys walked past. Michael's hands were bandaged.

"Why was he there with you?" Adela asked.

"I keep thinking about Udo," Michael answered. "In the water and—I don't know. How it happened. If he wanted it." One of Michael's eyes had been beaten closed, his jaw a ridge of distended purple. His swollen lip or the meds he was on, or both, garbled certain consonants.

"I think he was always waiting," Michael said.

"Why was Peter at your bar?" Adela repeated.

"You're supposed to ask what Udo was waiting for."

"Peter was with you. At the bar, Michael," Adela said, though she'd been the one who wouldn't answer her son's questions about school, Peter's interest in German a raft for him to hold. As she listened to a nurse squeak down the hall, as Michael touched his nose with a gauze-softened fist, Adela couldn't believe she'd let them float for so long.

"I think he was waiting for you to forgive him," Michael said.

"Peter's seven."

"Udo always talked about you," Michael answered.

"He told me what he saw."

Michael's bruises glistened with ointment. The drunks had hit him, Peter in the car that rattled each time his uncle fell against it. Michael talked in a stream about the community center where Udo had volunteered. How he'd convinced Heinz to hire some of the immigrants he'd trained there, these men so loyal that they'd shown up to his funeral.

"Michael," she said, gripping the bed frame.

"Are you going to hit me, too?" he joked.

She winced at the thought of it, at jokes he made even now.

Michael gave her a boneheaded smile. He'd always treated terrible things as amusing. For a time Adela had, too. She couldn't imagine how she'd explain the delay to Taro, her bartending job, a sort-of boyfriend who changed bike tires, her brother all the while acting as if it were wonderful.

"I don't care about Udo," she said.

Rain soft-shoed down the window. Her brother's blanket slipped, his legs bruised and bandaged, too.

"If I'd called you," he said, "or texted while you and Gert were in the middle of your fuckfest, and I told you Peter was in the bar's office watching TV, you would have said no?"

His unharmed eye stared at her. The bandage on his forehead fought the force of his lifting brow.

"You would have said no?" Michael asked again. "Would have predicted what would happen, like it was something you read in an asshole book?"

Adela touched his arm, but he shooed it away. She wouldn't have cared. Each time Peter tried to show her something true, she went to the bar or took a nap or stayed away with Gert for an extra day. One of Michael's toenails was missing.

"But you didn't," Adela said. "Ask me."

His heart-rate monitor sped up. She waited for a nurse to come in and check on him.

Michael's look told her to stop pretending; for a moment she was worried that she didn't know how to do that. She wanted to blame her brother, to hand him everything she hadn't done or seen. But he hadn't forced her to work at the bar, hadn't insisted they stay with him. He'd only woken up each day, pleased or confused or relieved that she was still there. Like Peter, he'd asked her questions. Adela hadn't answered them.

Michael's heart flew. A hundred and thirty bpm, Adela guessed.

"You're always happiest when you have someone to blame," he said.

Adela remembered when she used to worry that he could read her mind.

"I don't think," she said—he breathed, fast and with sound—"that I'd call it happy."

In the window behind him, Adela saw a hotel, the wet beach.

"And now you left Peter with someone you don't even know," he said.

"I know you," she answered, realizing he meant the man with the nickname.

Michael shifted and his gown inched upward, showing off

his wounded shins. Adela wouldn't go back to the bar. Wouldn't stand on it and rank people's raunchy fiascoes. Her face heated at the fun she'd bled from that place, her dream that someone would claim the neo confession. The look of shame she'd wanted from Michael, who'd been with Udo at the camp decades before, standing behind Udo rather than trying to stop him.

Adela needed to find Peter. To tell him that school would be in Washington, where his father was. That she'd get a job as a nurse again and be awake in the morning when he got up.

She walked to the nurses' station. She asked the woman there if she'd seen a small boy.

"What's his name?" the nurse asked.

"Michael," she said.

"My name's Peter," Peter answered.

He stood in the hall, the Potato Farmer next to him.

Adela walked toward her son and leaned down. She tried to see in his face how these last weeks might have changed him. He looked the same. It was only his hair that had grown. The first thing they'd do in D.C. was get it cut. She took his hand. He looked confused.

"What have we been doing?" she asked.

Peter's look answered: *You weren't even here.*

But then he smiled. He put his hand on her knee and she hoped to remember this as a moment when their course began its correction.

"I was telling him," Peter said, pointing to the man who surely had a real name, "what Oma and I did while you were gone."

She thanked the Potato Farmer, told Peter they had to go. He walked toward Michael's room, though the elevator was in the opposite direction. Adela didn't want to see Michael's mauled face again, worried she'd forget everything she'd just realized, or pretend to forget it as Michael and Peter did a comedy routine about the drunks who'd broken three of his ribs, sprained his wrist, and left him with a concussion. *One of them had your same name!* she imagined her son saying, as if it were the most hilarious coincidence.

But when they got in there, they found the German Lady sitting on the edge of his bed. She'd brought Michael magazines, also pudding. Her hand touched the one space on his arm where there was no bruise. She opened one of the pudding packets, spooned it into his mouth. She wiped his lip, and Michael gave her the closest thing to a smile he could muster. Mutti fed him another spoonful. The overhead light shone across his bandages, on Mutti's gray hair. Michael's heartbeat was slow again. Peter stood in the doorway rather than walk inside.

"It's okay?" Peter finally asked.

Mutti looked up, as if brought back from a daydream. Adela saw something young in her face. Mutti when they'd lived in Glens Falls. Mutti at Liesl's wedding.

"I think your uncle is tired," Mutti said.

Adela had wanted to blame her, blame Michael, which made nothing feel fixed or better.

"Get some sleep, Michael," Peter said.

He raised a gauzy fist.

"Imagine that's a thumbs-up," Michael mumbled.

Peter lifted a fist, told Michael to imagine, too.

"We'll see you tomorrow?" Mutti asked Adela. Each morning she, like Michael, must have woken up unsure if Adela and Peter would still be here.

"Tomorrow," Adela answered, knowing it wasn't true.

Outside, rain was light and cool. Before they got into Michael's car, Adela stopped, pulled her phone from her pocket, and told Peter she needed a minute.

When Taro answered, she said, "I don't know what I've been doing."

He stayed quiet on the other end.

"You there?" she asked.

He answered that he was.

Peter climbed into the car he'd been in two days before when those awful young men had attacked Michael. She tried not to think of what would have happened had the men come after him a minute earlier, Peter on the street with Michael, her son panicking instead of making perfect choices. The car's driver's-side mirror was smashed. Adela imagined Michael thrown against it, the bandage on his forehead covering dozens of cuts and bruises.

"*You* there?" Taro asked.

"We're both here," she answered.

Taro gave a sniff that she hoped was a laugh. Peter rolled down the window, shrugging to ask what was keeping her. Taro asked Adela if she was ready.

"I left something at Oma's," Peter said that night, after they'd finished packing.

An annoyed sigh leaked from Adela before she said, "Fine."

But when they got to Mutti's house, Peter wandered from room to room. He picked up objects from shelves. Opened the kitchen's junk drawer. Adela was relieved that her mother wasn't here.

"What are you looking for?" Adela asked. She felt ready to sleep for days, though in a handful of hours a taxi would come to take them to the train station, train to a plane to a city neither of them had been to.

"I don't know," Peter said, and moved into the dining room.

Adela lay down on the couch. Closing her eyes, she worried that she'd sleep so hard that they'd miss the cab and have to explain to Mutti in person where they were going, what the plan had been. She and Michael used to make fun of the way their mother turned the *w* in coward into a *v*. "Covard," she said, and fought to keep her eyes open.

As she lay there, Adela wondered what would happen if the German Lady appeared just then, Peter rushing in and telling his grandmother that they were leaving. Perhaps Mutti would get angry. Maybe she'd retreat as she had when Adela had decided to move to California. As Adela's eyes grew heavy, as Peter kept opening and closing drawers, she imagined the German Lady in front of her, telling her that leaving was a mistake. *Okay, then*, Adela might have answered, Mutti crossing and uncrossing her arms. *Convince me.*

⟡

When Michael and Adela were in fifth grade, she'd come down with the flu. Classmates asked where she was, and Michael answered—without thinking—that she'd died. The more he was cajoled, the more serious he got. He stood on the asphalt behind the cafeteria, a basketball bouncing nearby.

"A freak virus," he said.

"Why are you here, then?" someone asked, breath bright with chewing gum.

"Too much sadness at home."

Most classmates saw through his lie. But a few paused, and the what-ifs in their expressions felt powerful. The next day he wore black and wouldn't talk to anyone. When people called him a liar, Michael closed his eyes. His heart raced at the certainty of getting caught.

When Adela returned to school, she heard of his stories and confronted him.

"What a bunch of liars," Michael said. They stood in the hallway between the two fifth-grade classrooms. Her nose red, her narrowed eyes a hand grabbing his collar.

"You said I was dead," she answered.

Michael told her it was a joke.

"What kind of joke?" she asked; he couldn't answer. Part of him had enjoyed the attention of it. Part of him wanted to try on life without her. But mostly he didn't know what kind of joke it was. Even as he'd gone into detail about the virus squeezing one lung, then the other—he couldn't believe what he was saying.

For days he tried to atone. He stole her favorite Life Savers from the Cumberland Farms and handed her a pencil when hers broke. She wouldn't talk to him. Michael felt his insides tighten. He had to go to the bathroom constantly, and when he went for the third time in one morning, he overheard Susan Doin—who rarely said anything clever—mumble that maybe Michael had gotten the virus, too.

A week later, taking the shortcut to school, Adela told him he had toothpaste on his chin.

"Maybe I want it there," Michael answered.

"Maybe you look like an asshole."

"Maybe I am an asshole," he said, and she nodded. Leaves crunched underfoot. A crow cawed across the sky. Michael saw the sky after a week where everything was in his head, where he bumped into familiar furniture and crossed a room, forgetting why. But as his sister returned to him, a piece of her stayed hidden, and he knew something had been chipped, recovery and injury uneasy twins.

"Uneasy twins," he said to Mutti when she came to the hospital and told him that Adela and Peter were gone. Adela had sent her a long text from the airport. Peter had left a drawing for her titled, *Oma, Oma, Oma*, as if she were three people in one.

"I brought more pudding," Mutti said, and looked like she would cry.

She pulled the pudding from her purse. Michael told her it was his favorite.

After Adela left, Michael returned to the memory of his cousin and friend who'd thrown rocks at people who had nothing, who stayed when others left. Michael kept a smattering of Udo's ashes in a small ceramic box his cousin had given to him.

Back in Udo's house, a place that he'd briefly pretended was Adela's and his, Michael wound back to the last time he'd seen Udo. Udo had shown up at his apartment at three in the morning. His hands and knees dirty, his face red.

"Something happened," Udo said, and sat on Michael's kitchen floor. Dirt streaked his hair. In the small kitchen, he looked enormous.

"What happened?"

"It was an accident," Udo answered.

"What was?"

Udo covered his eyes. Michael imagined a terrible thing done to Angela or some stranger. He felt afraid for his cousin, afraid of him. Udo explained that he was driving and a dog appeared out of nowhere, that he couldn't stop in time. He breathed hard. His feet ticked back and forth and smelled awful.

"Did you find out whose dog?" Michael asked.

Udo sucked in a breath as if about to slip underwater.

"I didn't know what to do," Udo said. "I buried it."

"You have to unbury it," Michael said. "Unbury it and find its owners."

"What if it doesn't have owners?" Udo asked, peevishly loud.

"What if it does?"

Udo nodded, so quickly it looked as if it hurt. Michael

touched him and Udo stilled. He slipped on clothes and went with him.

Udo found the spot right away. He took a shovel from his trunk and got to work. The shovel chugged. Udo grunted. When a fragment of fur appeared, he used his hands and looked like a dog himself. Every once in a while, nearby headlights brightened trees. The dog was medium-sized and shaggy. Udo picked up the animal, dirt shivering from its fur. In the glaring headlights, dog at his chest, Udo seemed monstrous. Michael saw something disgusting in Udo then, who buried the dog out of rattled guilt, who needed someone to tell him what he should have known. Michael rarely felt fed up with Udo, but in that moment he wanted to call him an asshole, to tell him Adela's unreturned messages weren't as crazy as he thought.

"Check for tags. Then put it in the backseat," Michael said.

When they finally located the owners, it was morning. They parked in front of the house. The dog in the backseat had begun to stiffen. Just when it appeared Udo would sit there indefinitely, he got out, picked up the dog, and walked to the door. Though Michael stayed in the car, through the opened window he heard Udo knock, a woman's voice as she answered. The woman leaned close to the animal. "An accident," Udo kept saying. "Why is she dirty?" the woman asked.

They drove away, and Udo became a different person. He turned up the radio, asked Michael if he was hungry. Michael answered that all he needed was sleep. But he wanted to ask Udo what was wrong with him. He closed his eyes for the ride back to his apartment. He got out and didn't look back at Udo, who in his relief turned vulgarly happy. Didn't remember what he said to his cousin, if he said anything. And though that night he'd thought to tell Justine about the dog, he felt like an accomplice. Udo texted an effusive message of thanks. Michael answered with a *Sure.*

Now his ashes sat in a box Udo had given him. Michael thought to spread them at the beach, but the sea had enough of him already. Considered the yard behind the house, but that house had brought him mostly misery. He could sprinkle them in front of the Adult Learning Center where the Roma camp had been. Udo had volunteered there, teaching basic wiring to immigrants, part of him forever trying to atone, atonement not a single act but a perpetual emotional fitness.

The box sat next to the sofa. Udo was gone. Michael's greed for what was left of him remained. Already Adela felt like an ill-conceived affair. Already the anger of her going carried the hazy frame of memory.

A few days later, Michael was up at six in the morning. His ribs ached less than the day before. Sun moved across the wall. Then Mutti's back door opened and she walked into her yard. Dead Cindy drooped in her hands. Michael moved to the door with careful steps. Seeing her son, Mutti's face contorted.

"Morning," she said, and tried to smile, which made her look worse. She seemed to sense this and looked down at Cindy, who was probably still warm.

"First Udo, now Cindy," Mutti said. "Jesus, that's a ridiculous thing to say."

Dew cooled their feet. The trees behind Mutti were hit with light and as still as a painting.

"Every day you look better," she said.

He thought to hug her, but she held the cat like an offering. And hugging hurt his ribs.

"Can you keep me company?" Mutti asked. "I need to dig a hole."

After Mutti finished burying Cindy, they drank coffee in her kitchen. Dirt browned her fingernails. The radio reported on the Middle East's endless combustion, also the story of a local politician embroiled in scandal.

"I know I shouldn't care about a cat," Mutti said.

"You should," Michael answered. He wished he'd been kinder to Cindy, whom Mutti had just buried between two cherry trees.

When Michael's doorbell rang, he joked to himself that it was the shawarma guy.

"You're looking better than a week ago," the Potato Farmer said, standing outside.

"How did you find my address?"

"Don't I work for your doctor?"

"Isn't that a doctor-patient violation?" Michael asked.

"You'd like me to leave?"

Four questions, Michael thought. He invited him in.

The Potato Farmer said nothing about the empty rooms, the piles of dishes.

"You're less busy now, I take it," the farmer said.

"My ribs are beginning to heal."

The Potato Farmer wore shorts and a button-down. Every time Michael saw him, he remembered that he was handsome. Michael asked if he hated the nickname. The farmer asked if it was Michael's mother he'd seen pulling out of the driveway next door. "We're neighbors," Michael answered. "Which is an accident, or a story." When Michael asked after his dog, the Potato Farmer said, "I imagine you'll see him soon," and blushed. Michael wanted to kiss him but had a stitch in his lip. And leaning forward gave him trouble.

"I just wanted to see you," the Potato Farmer said.

"Nice to be seen," Michael answered.

"I'm going to take a nap," Michael added. The Potato Farmer stood. "You don't need to go. But it won't be that kind of nap. Everything hurts a bit too much." They went upstairs and lay on Michael's bed. It felt nice to feel a shoulder against his own, to listen to another person's breath. Had Udo been around, the Potato Farmer would have been a character for them to invent—his house lined in tubers, back permanently curved. Udo wasn't here, he tried to remind himself. He was gone, or here but in a box. Ash and slivers of bone that Michael sometimes looked at, that he sometimes rubbed between his fingers.

When the farmer said he had to get going, Michael hobbled to the door. He said goodbye using his actual name.

Mutti's car was gone. She must have been at work, relieved for its activity. Cindy's carrying crate sat next to the garbage. Michael crossed to her driveway. The clematis that grew over her garden shed shivered in the wind. Michael picked up the empty carrier and brought it into his house. Mutti might want it again someday.

Back inside, Michael took the container of ash and went into the bathroom. He stood in front of the mirror and dipped a finger inside. He started with an eyelid, smearing until it turned gray. Dust slid into his eye and he closed it. He tried his cheeks next. It didn't stick as makeup did, some streaking, some floating away.

"A faggot monster," Michael said.

He walked through the house with the ash on his face. He stood on his deck and hoped someone would notice his exceptional ugliness. His phone sounded. From a number he didn't recognize came a text: *I heard about Cindy.* Another message arrived a moment later: *Peter spent the first few days of school pretending he spoke only German.* Adela had been in this house a week before. He wanted to ignore her message, or write: *He left half of this house to you*. Michael missed Adela, was glad she was gone. Ash slipped down his face. Michael touched his cheek and stared at the gray on his palm. The phone rang this time. And as he stood on the deck, hands streaked with what was left of his cousin, he let it ring a second, a third time, and decided whether or not to answer.

2016

Wolfi asked if Peter was joking. They lay on the beach, the *frites* between them collecting sand. In the ten months since Peter had last seen him, Wolfi had become a man. His voice deep, shoulders yoked. Time turned fast and sneaky.

"She told me as we drove home from the airport," Peter said.

"And what did you say?" Wolfi asked.

"I didn't ask if she was joking," Peter answered. Wolfi let out an amused grunt.

Peter didn't tell Wolfi that, when Oma announced that she'd sold the house along with the furniture she wasn't taking, he'd cried. That when he and Oma got to the house he hadn't gone inside, but snapped branches off her trees.

"You're hurting the trees," Oma had said.

"They're hurting me," he'd answered, and pulled down another one.

When Oma started in on something else, he answered: "Don't tell me I'm being ridiculous. My mother's favorite thing to say to me. Like when Malcolm cries all night and I tell her it kept me up. Or when I asked if I could go to school here for a year."

The scratches lining his hands stung from the salt water.

"So she's selling it," Wolfi said, and moved onto his back.

The hair on his toes, his thick neck, all spoke of seriousness, when their last three summers together had been effortlessly silly.

"Sold," Peter said.

"Shit," Wolfi answered.

"Total shit," Peter agreed.

A girl passed and waved. When Wolfi waved back, she turned to her phone.

"Oma tried to make it better by saying she could visit us in America more."

"I've never been to America," Wolfi answered.

It was Oma and this place Peter had fallen for. The sea they could bike to, Wolfi down the block who picked up the previous summer's thread the moment they saw each other.

"Who was that girl?" Peter asked.

"Friend."

"With benefits?" he said, in English.

"That's someone else," Wolfi answered, and purred out the name Julia. Peter's face turned warm; he excused himself and trotted back into the water. "My best friend lives in Germany," he sometimes told people at school, and they'd look at him as if he'd made Wolfi up. "Fuckers," Peter would mumble, and walk out of the cafeteria.

He swam out far, avoiding jellyfish and a shoulder of driftwood. A lifeguard whistled and waved. Peter waved back, but the whistles continued. Peter was the only person between Germany and Denmark. Water beneath him wound dark and cold.

"Want to go somewhere?" Wolfi asked when Peter returned, and they traveled farther down the beach where Wolfi's girlfriend and her friends lay on a blanket. They wore bikinis and expressions of sweaty boredom. Peter found them terrifying. But each of them knew who he was. The girlfriend, Julia—who was pretty and, like Wolfi, looked like an adult—hugged Peter.

They talked about the American family who'd turned famous from a sex tape. Peter pretended to find it interesting. Wolfi watched him and Julia together as if this moment had been a dream and a worry. *Because I'm difficult*, Peter understood, and for the rest of the afternoon projected difficulty's opposite.

⟡

Peter's annual summer trips to Kritzhagen had started when he was ten. Oma and Michael had flown over for his mother's wedding to Bob, who was as boring as his name suggested, and he returned with them. Oma's house came back to him immediately. When he and Michael biked to the beach, Peter led the way. German came back with equal ease, so much so that he articulated a complicated idea on his second night there and felt like he was speaking in tongues. He'd met Wolfi that summer, too. Within days, he and Peter were inseparable. He told Wolfi about D.C., also Pretoria. Wolfi told him about his older sister's boyfriend whom his parents hated.

"Hate why?" Peter had asked.

"Because he's Turkish," Wolfi said. "Not that they'd ever admit that that's the reason."

Each summer Peter returned, staying for six weeks, sometimes longer. Comforted by his grandmother's quiet warmth and the freedom she gave him, her stories of growing up in one country, then the next. He learned nuanced German and fell for this city's cold beaches. Even more for Oma, who looked like a grandmother from a storybook but swore in English. Then there was his uncle. Peter stopped by Michael's bars before they opened. "Your new best friend is here," a bartender would say as Peter parked his bike by the jukebox.

"Hello, new best friend," Michael greeted him.

"Hello, old best friend," Peter answered. "And I mean old like *old*."

"Right. Because I'm an old person."

Getting back to D.C., Peter compared his tan with Angie Sanchez's next door. He'd tell her stories about the house that seemed haunted but was not, the German movie theaters with assigned seats and carts that sold ice cream and beer. Spent the next ten months cursing Washington's joyless people and swamp-yard weather. Also his mother, so busy with her policy job and with Bob, who taught biology. In Kritzhagen Peter had a kind of celebrity. In D.C., he was seen as mean and strange. He emailed Oma regularly. She sent back pictures of a new thing she'd planted, a sign he'd find funny. He texted his uncle who hated being called uncle. *How is my uncle?* Peter would write. *Does uncle's new friend have tattoos? Dear bastard nephew*, Michael would reply. *I wouldn't call him a friend*. Peter wrote their exchanges in a notebook and read them at his father's when Dad's girlfriend talked over the television.

He returned to Kritzhagen each summer to a slightly older grandmother, an uncle with another bar added to his empire. Peter wandered into the attic to read letters his grandfather had sent decades before, a man Oma spoke of fondly now, she and him talking on the phone from time to time or sending each other articles. On other trips to the attic he searched out pictures where Oma looked so young it made him laugh. Or examined a notebook his uncle had used to map out this city when they'd first moved here. And Oma told him stories of Mom as a child. Stories of relatives who'd lived in this house a hundred years before, like the great-several-times-over-grandfather who built this house when the city's edge was miles away.

But this summer, there were boxes where a bureau had been. Art had been taken from walls, extra beds sold.

“Where will I stay next time?” Peter asked on his second night. He and Wolfi had played Ping-Pong in his basement. They’d smoked weed, Peter not admitting that he’d never smoked it before. Then Julia had shown up and he went back to Oma’s. His mouth felt like paste. TV news showed city blocks in Nice cordoned off with police tape.

“I can’t imagine you’ll want to come much longer,” Oma answered.

Peter’s foot tapped the bare floor, its rug sold or given away.

“I can,” he said, surprised by how little she expected from him. Her combination of warmth and sadness felt just right. When she was down, he’d turn ridiculous until she laughed or smiled with sad appreciation.

“When you’re twenty, you’ll still come in the summers?” Oma asked.

“When I’m older I can come when I want.”

“Your uncle has space, too.”

“Then I’d be stuck with him and Frank, and have to deal with all that.”

“All what?”

Michael and Frank had been together for a few years. They lived in Frank’s place close to the coast. Frank did something with the government. He was handsome and his shirts were always tucked in. Peter had no idea what he and Michael talked about.

“All that love.”

Oma mussed his hair.

“But it’s been done,” Oma said. “The new family comes at August’s end.”

“Crazy,” a woman interviewed on TV said via a translator. Peter could become a translator, could live in Hamburg or Berlin, which people talked about with the irritated envy of a more adventurous sibling. He left the room. He wrote terrible words on his bedroom wall, then tried to erase them, angry with Oma and with himself and with his eraser for giving up so easily.

⟡

Coming back from visiting a friend in Viersen the winter before, Beate found the second floor inundated with leaks, so many that she had to borrow buckets. "This place is falling apart," Liesl said as she showed up with her contribution. Her daughter Petra played a game on her phone. "It's big here," Annette said. Liesl smiled as if her daughter had said something extraordinary, though Beate forgave Liesl's doting on this girl, thinking of the long slog of grief that would always weigh her down. Liesl left and Beate moved through her extra bedrooms. She couldn't remember when she'd last been in them.

The next day she hired a roofer; another man to take away the furniture that had been destroyed. "You can take that, too." She pointed to a desk she never used. "There's nothing wrong with it," the man answered. Soon after, on a whim, she looked at an apartment with a view of the sea. She remembered their apartment in Cologne, the story of each day told in a neighbor's barking dog, the man who'd bought her wine leaving at the same time every morning. Letting go of the house turned to a relief. When she told Michael, he looked serious for a moment. Then he grinned. "Adela and I text about that sometimes," he said. "Betting as to how long you'll hold on to this thing."

"I thought you loved it," Beate said.

"There are a lot of things I've loved," he added, and she answered that he didn't have to make everything dirty, though she adored how he joked with her so crassly. Selling the house quickly turned real. A real estate broker came. "It just keeps going," she said, and cited a price so good that Beate reddened at what she'd been sitting on without realizing. She could stop working sooner than she'd planned. Could wake up each morning to a view of the sea. And it felt crazy, then, that she'd stayed in the house for so long, that she hadn't thought to picture anything different.

⟡

After a morning at the beach where Wolfi waited for Julia like a nervous dog, Peter biked to his uncle's new restaurant. Its floor-to-ceiling windows overlooked the sea. They were open, and breezes tunneled between tables. Peter pictured it lit up at night, the water dark beyond it. A woman working there pointed to an office where Michael should have been, but wasn't. Through a back door he heard his uncle's voice, a person laughing with him. Michael must have said something stupid or funny or mean. Peter peeked his head out. Michael stood next to a younger man, probably a waiter. They shared a cigarette; the man rested his hand on Michael's hip. Then Michael kissed him. Their mouths moved as if eating. The man stopped and said he had to get ready. Seeing Peter in the doorway, Michael guffawed.

"That wasn't Frank," Peter said.

Frank was handsome, like Wolfi, who wouldn't leave their spot on the beach that morning in case Julia showed up. Peter had swum out on his own. He passed a girl who'd told him he didn't look German and he'd answered, "I'm from ISIS," before diving into a wave.

"Frank doesn't care," Michael said. "Probably does it, too. What's that thing you say about faggots in your army?"

"That isn't a thing anymore," Peter answered. "And faggots is a terrible word."

"You sound like your mother," Michael said.

When he got home, Oma understood something was wrong. Peter found he couldn't keep it to himself. They sat on the sofa. Oma held a glass of wine. Her bracelets looked like rolls of masking tape.

"There are parts of my son I don't understand," she said.

"Frank probably does it, too," Peter mimicked.

"Maybe he does," Oma said. "Can you imagine, though? Seeing someone and saying you're cute and just—" She made a kissing noise. "But you probably don't want to talk about kissing. With an old lady."

"Can I have a sip of your wine?" Peter asked.

"A sip."

Oma didn't treat his distress as a joke. Didn't call him ridiculous, perhaps because she understood that what looked ridiculous to others was difficult and real.

The room echoed without a rug.

"My mother told me once that you lived here with only sleeping bags," Peter said.

"Briefly," Oma answered. She slid books into a box. A reporter on television discussed a street fair that had been canceled. "Officials cite security challenges," the woman said.

"But then we got beds."

"From Liesl," Peter added.

"Your mother likes to tell that story."

"What about the goat story?" he asked.

She'd told him the story of her great-grandfather several times; Peter always wanted to hear it again. Even though Oma hadn't been there, she talked of the goat her great-grandfather had doted on. How her great-grandmother was making dinner when the goat pushed at her with its horns.

"A friend of mine eats goat all the time," Peter said.

"In Pretoria?" she asked.

"Adams Morgan," Peter answered, and picked up a box. Though he hated this move, he wanted to help her. His paternal grandmother lived in Seattle and was always in her garden. When she'd told him to pick a melon on his last visit there, she'd asked how the one he'd chosen could have seemed ripe to him, as if ripeness were a subject he'd studied in school. He told Oma this story. She laughed and touched the back of his head. He leaned into her hand, as a cat might. He wanted to ask her how Cindy died, but didn't want to alter the feeling in the room.

Sneaking another sip of wine, Peter thought about telling Frank what he'd seen. But Frank would respond in some buttoned-up way, or say, *You know your uncle.* Peter thought about the ways he was like his uncle, also how he was different.

The table overlooked the sea. Oma went on about the place from decades before. "All the terrible carpet is gone!" she said. "What you've done with this place, Michael."

Michael and Frank sat across from them.

"I just noticed that you're going gray," Peter told his uncle.

"Makes me look distinguished," Michael answered.

"Or something," Peter answered back. Michael looked delighted. Frank and Mutti talked about an offshore wind farm that Frank had gotten to see.

"But you, Uncle, did not?" Peter asked.

"I'm a lowly burgher."

"So lowly," Peter answered, unable to resist their banter. Michael and Frank probably had an understanding. Perhaps Michael told him what Peter had stumbled upon. When his mom and Bob had gotten together, Peter's dad was a mess. "The idea of her with him," he'd kept saying, and even at nine, Peter understood that his father meant sex. But Michael kissed one person, then another. The thought of so many mouths was terrifying.

Their salads came. Peter worked to eat slowly, but the food was good. And he was always hungry in Kritzhagen. "The sea air," Frank said. "The beach," Oma added. "Whatever debauchery he's involved in," Michael said.

"Learned from the best," Peter answered.

"Wind beneath your wings," Michael answered back. Sometimes in D.C. Peter thought he heard his uncle's voice and turned around to look for him.

The waiter from the alley moved past them with a tray of drinks. He smiled wide and easily. As he moved toward the back door, Peter excused himself.

"Don't just go to the bathroom to throw it all up, now," Michael said.

"It's not the food that makes me want to throw up," Peter answered, meaning to be mean, though Michael appeared charmed. Love for these people heated Peter's cheeks. He moved between tables.

Peter found the waiter in the same alley, smoking a cigarette. He paused at the door, audacity and fear pulling him in different directions. The waiter noticed Peter watching.

"I'd like a cigarette," Peter said.

"How old are you?" the waiter answered.

"How old are *you*?" Peter asked. His throat was dry. His tongue tasted of salad. "You know Michael is like forty. And he's my uncle."

"You're not from here, right?" the waiter said. "Your German is perfect."

"America. Thank you."

"I was in New York once."

"New York is big," Peter answered, and the waiter inhaled. "I'd still like a cigarette."

The waiter had stocky fingers and nicks on his throat from shaving. Noise sounded in the kitchen.

"You can't say where you got it," the waiter said. "And don't smoke it now."

"I wouldn't," Peter said, though that had been his plan. He wanted to ask the waiter if he and Michael kissed all the time. If this was what it meant to have feelings for other men, kissing and sex as simple as a shared sandwich. Peter's fourteen-year-old body was his to rub and clean. Sharing it with so many others was as unthinkable as taking his dick and balls out on the Metro.

"Promise?" the waiter said with a singsong that made him seem stupid.

Back at the table, the fish Peter had ordered was waiting for him.

"Isn't that the best thing?" Frank said. "Coming back to your food being there?"

Peter and Michael shared looks announcing that the list of things trumping this was long and wide. Something in the kitchen clattered. A woman one table over held a hand to her chest.

"People drop things," the man with her answered.

"It's just," she said, "I wasn't expecting it."

At night Peter and Oma packed. Sometimes they watched news programs showing Syria or France, or the investigation of a Baghdad wedding that had recently been bombed to oblivion. Oma held a pillow over her stomach. Peter wondered where Wolfi was. He'd gone to Wolfi's house that night, but no one was home. He wondered if the sister still had the Turkish boyfriend. If Wolfi's parents still pretended not to have a problem with him.

The next day, though, Wolfi found Peter at the beach. In the two and a half days since he'd last seen him, Wolfi looked like he had aged another year. He whispered about a party at Julia's house that night. His breath smelled of soda.

"Her parents are in Majorca," Wolfi went on. "So a party. So you'll come with me."

"Tonight?"

"Late," Wolfi said. "So you'll have to . . ." He pantomimed sneaking out. What was cockeyed between them righted. They went into the water and Wolfi raced him, though later he said he hadn't been racing at all. And though he had a foot on Peter, and adult muscles, Peter almost beat him.

⬥

Julia's house, with its shrubs and echoes, reminded Peter of Liesl's. People gathered in a sunroom. Some swam in a lit-up pool and tracked chlorine smells into the house. When a girl asked where he was from, Peter said he was a Syrian refugee. Wolfi and Julia vanished. Peter stayed. He drank more than he ever had before. He was dared to kiss a girl and did, though it didn't feel as he'd hoped and as he kissed her he thought about his uncle's mouth on the waiter's, and how, when he'd gone to the beach with Michael and Frank, he'd opened his eyes underwater to look at Frank's legs.

He biked home very late, the city so still he could hear the sea from blocks away.

Oma snoozed on the couch. Asleep, she looked older. Someday she'd be gone. Someday it would be Peter without all of them. The great-several-times-over-grandfather had built this place for the spot's isolation. Now there were houses everywhere. Peter didn't even know what this man had looked like.

When Oma told stories about him, she'd say: "I'm not sure if all of this is true." Peter would turn equally obtuse. A hundred years would drive forward and wipe him from living memory. The new family buying this house knew nothing about the goat or the orchard Oma's father had planted. They might chop down those trees to bring in more light, might find the hoof marks a nuisance and redo the floor. Oma took a breath. She was here, as the great-several-times-over grandfather had once been. Also Oma's parents, whom she talked about sometimes and got sad, though she said she was happy remembering them. Perhaps one day he would think of her in the same way. Perhaps he'd have someone who'd want to hear stories of Oma in this house and in Cologne and Minnesota. Of Michael kissing a waiter in an alley, Oma watching the news with a pillow over her stomach. His mother in Pretoria fighting a disease that might become as antiquated as polio. *Everyone was afraid then*, Peter might say, fear in the past tense. A breeze blew through the window. Everything seemed to be leaving. Peter's summer here, with four weeks left, already over. There were more boxes in the corner than had been there that morning.

"You're being ridiculous," Peter mumbled, and tried to conjure Frank's legs kicking in the water the afternoon before. To think of what might be in the kitchen for him to eat.

Oma's eyes opened so wide that all the confusion and fear of the elderly seemed hers.

"You're just coming home?" she said, and looked at her watch. "Three in the morning."

"I didn't know you knew. That I went out."

Her look told him not to be stupid. He felt dumb, angry at her expression.

"I'm supposed to take care of you," Oma said.

"Nothing happened."

"Out at all hours."

"You don't have to worry about me. It was a party. At a house. Probably the safest place in the world." He'd heard Oma tell Liesl about the new security guard they'd hired at the *Pflegeheim* who used to be in the army. How she'd hired an orderly who wore a headscarf and some residents didn't want her near their things. "I have no problem with them," Liesl had said. "But why can't she just take the thing off at work? She probably has beautiful hair." Oma twisted a ring on her finger.

She'd stayed up imagining scenarios that a few years ago she'd never had to consider. At Dulles, Peter's mom had stood outside the security line until he'd made it through. She told him to call after he got off the plane, and again from Oma's car. His father texted him: *Don't get too much sun!* and tried and failed with emoticons. Part of Peter wanted to write to his mother: *Made it out of the airport. No bomb.* To his Dad: *I'm telling people here that my name is Al-Qaeda.* But Oma looked afraid now, also tired, and Peter knew he'd sparked those feelings.

"I'm sorry you were frightened," he said, thinking of the awful scenarios she'd imagined as he dangled his feet into a pool and had another beer and kissed a girl because he'd been dared to.

"I should have told you about the house before you got here," Oma answered.

"My mother told me about a time you'd moved to a new apartment and left a note taped to a wall."

"I don't remember that," Oma said.

"My mother doesn't tell me things, either. She wore giant sweaters for a month before she told me she was pregnant. I thought she was getting fat."

Oma smiled. "Your mother fat," she said. "She eats berries and twigs."

"Moss and lichen," Peter answered.

"You'll not stay out until all hours," Oma said.

"You going to tell my mother?" Peter asked.

"When you were young and we got ice cream," Oma said.

"I hate when people don't answer questions."

"I'm getting to it."

She told a story of getting him ice cream, though she wasn't supposed to—he remembered those years when dairy was forbidden with anger still—and his mother had figured it out. Then Oma said: "This is between you and me. You are not a child. Not a grown-up, either. This can't become a habit." She lifted a hand and he held it. Peter wanted to cry, for the feeling of things falling away he couldn't shrug off.

"I'm sorry," Peter said.

Oma made a gesture as if wiping crumbs from her fingers. Peter wanted to sleep, to pretend the room upstairs would always be his, that a man who did something with banks wasn't moving in with his family a month later.

Michael arrived one afternoon to help pack. They wrapped plates in newspaper. Peter sometimes stopped to read articles and asked the meanings of words. "That article is old news," Michael answered. When Peter asked about the waiter, Michael checked to make sure a cabinet was empty. Gray ringed his head. It did make him look distinguished, especially with his tan. One flight up, Oma moved through rooms. Peter wanted to know about the waiter and other men. He remembered men from years before, he and Mom sleeping in a dead cousin's bed, Michael down the hall with a new one every few days. Peter asked again. He'd watched his mother push in the same way when she wanted to know. Knowing felt like the only thing, also what Michael wouldn't give him.

"Feel free to tell me that you hate hearing this," Michael said.

“I hate hearing this,” Peter answered. Michael looked amused, also unsurprised. Peter tried to think of more original answers.

“Frank and I are good. I know you think you saw something.”

“I don’t *think* anything.”

“Think it meant something,” Michael said, and finished the box he’d been packing.

On the last night in the house, packing finished, Oma asked if they should order food or go to Michael’s restaurant. “Restaurant,” Peter said. Again, they ate by the window. The waiter his uncle probably did plenty with slid between tables and it felt like a dance. There were candles and good food. His uncle let him have a glass of wine. Frank arrived, looking handsome, and this place felt good, safe, though it was as safe or unsafe as any other place. Michael joked about Peter’s tan.

“You’re so dark, people might wonder.”

“I told one girl I was from ISIS, as if that were a place. Told another one I was a Syrian refugee. She believed me for a minute. Even when she heard Wolfi call me Peter.”

Michael beamed. Oma toggled between amused and horrified. She left a handful of potatoes on her plate. Peter picked one up. When he went in for another, she smacked his hand away and he pretended it hurt, while she pretended she was angry.

“Wolfi went along with it,” Peter went on. “Said his family sponsored mine. That we were living above his garage.”

“Didn’t think he had it in him,” Michael said.

Wolfi had become a man. When Peter had gone back to D.C. last September, Wolfi messaged him almost every day, the habit of the other like a fresh wound, and he’d felt like Peter’s, felt like someone else’s now. He’d invited Wolfi to stop by the house one more time that afternoon, but he hadn't shown up and Peter hadn't been surprised.

"I didn't, either," Peter said.

As they ate dessert, the street lit up with noise. Michael moved to the front door. Peter followed. One car had crashed into another. A stop sign had been run, a turn made without looking. People spilled out of the restaurant, relieved at the quotidian disaster outside. The offending driver got out of his car fast. The woman who'd been hit stared at her steering wheel. For a moment, Peter worried that she was dead. But he saw her shift. As he got closer, she rolled her window down.

"Don't move," Peter said. Oma called for an ambulance.

"I'm fine," the woman answered.

The restaurant behind them glowed and was beautiful. Peter couldn't see the water, but heard it and smelled it, felt its mist against his skin. The woman went through her purse. Peter again advised her not to move. Michael went from table to table. He paused at Frank, who said something before Michael continued.

The woman looked up at the dozen diners and waitstaff on the sidewalk. Peter repeated his instructions to stay still.

"Where did you all come from?" she asked.

Peter lay in bed and wondered what the woman had been thinking right before she'd been hit. He heard the quiet hum of the radio and went downstairs. Oma sat at the kitchen table. The clock showed that it was just after four.

"Thinking about the house?" Peter asked.

"You scared me," Oma answered. "About the accident."

"They'll both be fine," Peter said.

The clock's ticks were loud. The table they sat at was one Michael had gotten decades before. Stolen, according to Peter's mother, who'd told him that when Michael had taken things from abandoned houses she'd been afraid for him.

"I wonder if it was easier," Oma said. "How I left this place before."

She'd been expecting a weekend, over as soon as it began.

Peter thought of other easier things. Apartments with fewer rooms to tend. Dying in your sleep. Oma looked older than he'd remembered, their time together a shallow breath. He sat in the kitchen with her where she'd fed him and taught him blackjack, a place that felt more his than either apartment in D.C. Oma had once lived in Cologne. In Minnesota. In some town called Glens Falls that his mom threatened to take him to from time to time. *We're still here*, he thought as the sky began to lighten. The house echoed, as it must have when they'd lived here with only some sleeping bags.

"You were my biggest worry," Oma said. "When I decided to sell this place. I tried to tell myself that you're a teenager now, that it's your job to be a teenager and not keep me company."

The kettle whistled, and Peter turned it off. His stomach tightened.

"But I sold it anyway," she said. "Maybe it was a test to see if it was true."

"Oma, that's stupid," he said, though it wasn't stupid, though it frightened him, also comforted him that she said things that were real, unlike his mother's sunshine statements about hard work leading to purpose, though it just seemed to make her tired. Peter would keep coming back. When he was older he might stay longer, or live in Berlin and visit on weekends, his German so good that people would hear that he was born in Africa and think it was a joke. He'd return to the States and speak English with an accent, the way Michael did. *I will think in German*, Peter decided.

"I'll keep coming back," Peter said.

"You don't need to say that," Oma answered.

"I'm just saying what's true."

Oma put her hand on his. Her eyes watered. He wanted to say that he felt lucky to be here to watch the movers take this table, these chairs, to go through the room that had once been his mother's, a box of books in it that Oma was shipping back to her in the States labeled: *Library*.

As the sun started to rise, Michael showed up.

"Been out all night?" Peter asked.

"Nice to see you, too," Michael said. He brought rolls. They took jam and cheese from the fridge and began to eat.

Beate boiled water for coffee, glad that Michael had come early, that there was food and the sun was up when the rest of the world stayed sleeping. Michael said funny, ridiculous things, Peter answered in kind. The rolls were still warm. Beate was hungry in a way she hadn't been in days. Michael mentioned that the accident had made the paper.

"But no one was hurt," Peter said.

"Nothing happens in this place," Michael answered, which felt untrue.

One of them spoke from time to time. Birds outside turned frantic at the day's unfolding. The coffee was hot and sun warmed their faces.

"My boys," Beate said. "Tell me something."

Sun climbed the trunks of trees, the rolls disappeared; Michael's hand tapped his knee. Beate thought of other moments she'd wanted to slow. When Adela had walked arm in arm with her at Liesl's wedding; when she'd realized that she'd wanted Josef as her own. When Michael told her what she already knew about his interest in men. The two of them had walked down a street on an autumn evening. Beate told him that it didn't matter. As he'd leaned his head on her shoulder, she'd tried to memorize its heat and weight and shape.

She thought of Paul in the motel outside Hadley, Beate forlorn when they had to check out. About getting to Lübeck and realizing she and her parents had gotten to the West, though she'd hardly had the chance to notice the East as they left it.

Michael yawned, and Peter—perhaps unconsciously—mimicked him. Everything perfect, also too fast. Beate closed her eyes.

"Your grandmother is tired," Michael said.

"Your mother is just thinking," Peter answered.

Perhaps she was remembering something about the house, or grew sad at the thought of her final meal here. Perhaps she was both happy and sad, which Peter often felt in Kritzhagen. This mix of feelings left him afraid, also ready, though for what, he couldn't say. Oma opened her eyes. Thoughts of her gone were replaced with her here just now, happy and sad, too. Peter was sure he got that play of feelings from her. That he understood her in a way his mother did not, not Michael, either, who loved her but acted as if she were strange and amusing. *Ready*, Peter thought again. Oma touched his hand, Michael poured the three of them coffees, and the day she would leave this house began.

ACKNOWLEDGMENTS

First, I want to thank my friends who took the time to read and offer feedback on this book's early, messy drafts and help me shape it into a coherent story. A huge thank-you to Amelia Kahaney, Anne Ray, David Ellis, Elizabeth Harris, Marie-Helene Bertino, and Melanie Martinez. This book would not have existed without you.

Thank you to the dear friends who supported and encouraged me as I wrote this book: Alexis Wheeler, Amy Fox, Colin Dickerman, Ellen Porter, Elliott Holt, Flannery Denny, Helen Phillips, Laura Swindler, Lesley Finn, Lois Gelernt, Maiya Jackson, Mia Barker, Nassim Zerriffi, Todd Seidman, and Ed and Nancy Lynch. I feel incredibly lucky to have you in my corner.

To Cathrin Wirtz: thank you for being such a champion of this book.

I want to thank my agent, Jody Kahn, and my editor, Jackson Howard, for taking a chance on me and this project. Their dedication, encouragement, and insight made this a far better book. For that, I will always be grateful. Thanks, too, to the entire team at MCD and Farrar, Straus and Giroux, especially Sean McDonald, Mitzi Angel, Jonathan Galassi, Debra Helfand, Abby Kagan, Nina Frieman, Brianna Panzica, Elizabeth Schraft, Justine Gardner, Dave Cole, Brian Gittis, Claire Tobin, and

Sheila O'Shea. Thank you to Alex Merto for the beautiful cover. Thanks also to Matthias Lohre for completing such a thorough German fact-check of the book.

I'm lucky to have worked at an incredibly supportive and dynamic school for many years. Thanks to everyone at MCS, particularly my colleagues and my weird, wonderful students.

I'm indebted to the teachers who encouraged me, particularly Clorinda Valenti and Rachel Stein in my younger years. And to the extraordinary teachers at the Brooklyn College MFA program, especially Stacey D'Erasmo, Josh Henkin, Mary Morris, and Michael Cunningham: thank you.

A huge thanks to my family, particularly my mother, Christine Demmer Grattan, my sister, Anna, and my brother, Christian; also thanks to my brother-in-law and my amazing nieces and nephews. I also want to thank my relatives, both past and present, in Germany, who were a huge inspiration for writing this novel, particularly the memory of my grandmother, Käthe Demmer.

I lost several people over the course of writing this book. Their absence has left a huge imprint on me and changed me and the story I was telling. I want to thank and send love to my aunt Luzzi Ihling and my uncle Georg Demmer. Also—and especially—my father, William Grattan. I miss you every day.

Finally, thank you to my partner, David, for your patience, humor, and endless support during this process.

A Note About the Author

Thomas Grattan's short fiction has appeared in several publications, including *One Story*, *SLICE*, and *Colorado Review*, and has been short-listed for the Pushcart Prize. He has an MFA in fiction writing from Brooklyn College and has taught middle school English for more than a decade. He lives in New York City.